GROWING UP IN THE SOUTH

—

AN ANTHOLOGY OF MODERN SOUTHERN LITERATURE

—

Edited and with an Introduction by
Suzanne W. Jones

D1308120

C
A SIGNET CLASSIC

For my family and the friends
I grew up with in Surry, Virginia

Acknowledgments

I am indebted to the Virginia Center for the Humanities for a fellowship that gave me the time and a place to read and select these stories and memoirs about growing up in the South. In preparing the manuscript, the always prompt help of four people proved indispensable: my editor, Tracy Bernstein; English Department administrative assistant Wendy Levy; reference librarian Marcia Whitehead; and graduate student research assistant Annie Pruett. I owe a very special thanks to a number of readers whose opinions have helped to shape this collection: Virginia public school teachers Susan Hawkes, Susan Hull, and Alan Seaman; students in my southern fiction classes at the University of Richmond; graduate student research assistants Bruce Smith and Kate Cooke; and most especially my husband, Frank Papovich, who teaches southern and western literature at the University of Virginia, and my stepdaughter, Sasha, who grew up in a South very different from the one in which I grew up.

Contents

III. Negotiating Southern Communities

IV. Challenging Southern Traditions

Introduction

When I think of my high school English classes in rural Surry, Virginia, in the 1960s, my most vivid memory is of reading William Faulkner's *Go Down, Moses* in my American literature class. I had always loved reading, but the experience I had with Faulkner touched me more deeply than any other. I was moved by his provocative prose, by his sense of the past, by his passion for place, and by his intense dramas of southern race relations. Faulkner spoke to me in a way that other writers I had liked that year—Hawthorne, Dickinson, Fitzgerald—did not. In reading Faulkner's work, I found myself, my family, and my community as well as the rich, complex social history of my region. That much Faulkner was not in the standard-issue literature book for eleventh grade. I was lucky to have a teacher who believed in supplemental reading and who cared about keeping us attentive on those long, hot days right before summer vacation. Her strategy worked for me.

I would like for more young people to have the opportunity to experience the challenges and rewards of the full range of southern literature, which is why I collected these stories and memoirs about growing up in the South. Certainly writers like William Faulkner, Ernest Gaines, Peter Taylor, and Eudora Welty rank among the very best American authors of the twentieth century. Literature by such writers can help relate art to life, as it did for me thirty-five years ago, and it can also make us more sensitive to each other as we become more aware of different viewpoints. In her autobiography *I Know Why the Caged Bird Sings,* Maya Angelou reflects on the importance of place:

> What sets one southern town apart from another, or from a northern town or hamlet, or city high-rise? The answer must be the experience shared between the unknowing majority (it) and the knowing minority (you). All of childhood's unanswered questions must finally be passed back to the town and answered there. Heroes and bogey men, values and dislikes, are first encountered and labeled in that early environment. In later years they change faces, places and maybe races, tactics, intensities and goals, but beneath those impenetrable masks they wear forever the stocking-capped faces of childhood.

In the past the South has been defined and the South has defined itself in contrast to the rest of the United States—variously by its history, its geographic boundaries marked by the Civil War, its conservative ideology, its economic system supported once by slavery and now by nonunion labor, and by its culture. As time has eroded some of these distinctions, those who study the region debate whether a distinctive South still exists. Southern novelist Walker Percy once claimed that the mass media was homogenizing the regions of the United States, and he bemoaned the resulting loss of personal identity. More recently, cultural geographers have echoed this concern. However, not everyone agrees about the degree to which American regions have completely lost their identities. As I lecture on southern literature across the South, converse with English teachers in Virginia's public schools, and teach southern fiction at the University of Richmond, I have noticed that young and old, native and nonnative to the South, still perceive some distinct regional differences. Older people sense difference in a southern preoccupation with history, both familial and regional; younger people see difference in customs and values—ways of being in the world. Some who study the South wonder if all things "southern" are simply pale copies of idealized notions, replicated by a mass culture that commodifies myth. Others sense the South gradually reimagining itself in light of the civil rights movement and recent economic and demographic changes while retaining some of its cultural distinctiveness. In her memoir *Landscapes of the Heart,* Elizabeth Spencer apprehends the South's complicated sense of itself in remembered feelings that she experienced each time she left her small Mississippi town to vacation on the Gulf Coast:

> Out there, I thought, astonished, is Mexico, the Caribbean, South America. We are leaning outward to them. Everybody back on land, all along the coast, feels this presence, whether they consciously know it or not. . . . Here at the Mississippian's southernmost point of native soil, one had to recall what inland Mississippi was like, how people in its small towns (or even in larger towns like Meridian and Jackson and Columbus) related inward, to family life, kinfolks, old friendships and hatreds. How hospitably newcomers were welcomed, but how slowly accepted.

While the civil rights movement has legally changed race relations, southern communities—just like many communities across the United States—still have much work to do if they are to be fully integrated. Complicating the task is the increasing ethnic diversity of the South, created by the influx of Cuban-Americans in Florida, Vietnamese-Americans on the Gulf and Atlantic coasts, and Mexican-Americans throughout the region. These new southerners have only just begun to tell their stories.

The memoirs and stories in this collection focus on

the experiences of childhood and adolescence and young adulthood. They treat concerns of growing up common to all regions: loss of innocence, sexual awakening, family relationships, social adjustment, schools and teachers, religion and values, initiation and identity, emotional development and growing responsibility. Some of the interests and techniques of southern writers emanate from what was once a predominantly rural way of life: the support and suffocation occasioned by a close-knit community and an extended family. Others come from concerns specific to the South because of its history of slavery and segregation. Several of these threads run through the historical and imaginative fabric of other sections of the United States, but the particular weave in the South continues to make for a distinctive literature.

The memoirs and stories in Part I recall the sights and sounds of many places and voices. Elizabeth Spencer reminisces about summers on the Gulf Coast spent at a wonderful old hotel between Gulfport and Biloxi, but her memoir is more meditation on southern identity than nostalgia for a lost past. In striking contrast, Harry Crews captures the scenes and cadences of his impoverished childhood among sharecroppers in rural Bacon County, Georgia. Yet both writers share feelings of being securely anchored by their memories of childhood places, even if those places exist "nowhere but in memory," as Crews writes. Although Crews and Spencer suggest that we do not fully know a place until we have experienced it with all of our senses and then nourished it in memory, Bobbie Ann Mason's narrator in "State Champions" wonders if we can know a place at all before we have put time and distance between ourselves and our hometowns. Her narrator's memories of junior high school coalesce around the gym in Cuba, Kentucky, home of the phenomenal Cuba Cubs basketball team, but the narrator realizes how differently she sees that time and place twenty years later and many miles away. Gustavo Pérez Firmat, born in Cuba but raised in Miami, says in the preface to his memoir, *Next Year in Cuba,* that he is "someone who has sought out a new relation between person and place, someone who's found, or founded, another home." He writes, "Although it may seem that in order to move past exile one has to renounce one country for another, I prefer to think that moving past exile means staking out a place that spans more than one country, more than one culture, more than one language." The Miami of his teen years is "a place that is two places at once."

Unlike Bobbie Ann Mason and Gustavo Pérez Firmat, Eudora Welty lived her entire life in her family home. In her memoir *One Writer's Beginnings* she recreates the Jackson, Mississippi, of her childhood with such sure strokes that readers see it through her writer's eye—as a small town full of stories, spread by women gossiping on the telephone, by seamstresses going from house to house, and evangelists from town to town. Welty speculates that listening "for" these stories, not just "to" them, may have predestined her own stories to assume "the form of a monologue that takes possession of the speaker." The works of younger southerners like Randall Kenan provide evidence that Welty's practice of creating a conversational narrative voice continues among this latest generation of southern storytellers. In an excerpt from *Walking on Water: Black American Lives at the Turn of the Twenty-First Century,* Randall Kenan speculates on how a sense of place affects identity but also on how misguided notions of racial authenticity affect an individual's sense of self. The subtitle of his chapter, "Cyberspace, North Carolina," provides ample evidence that southern places have changed from Miss Welty's childhood. Once predominantly rural economies have become less so, southern towns have grown into cities, and technology now leaps old boundaries with the click of a mouse.

The stories in Part II evoke the power of the family

to impose roles, to provide support, to cause pain, and
to celebrate life. Alice Walker's "Everyday Use" plays
the themes of sibling rivalry and parental preference
against the question of racial identity, when a worldly
daughter returns to her provincial family for a visit.
Another family reunion is the backdrop for William
Hoffman's amusing story "Amazing Grace." Here
country and city cousins clash, and the grandmother
refuses to bake bread until her grown son, who has
moved to the city, is properly baptized in the river
back home. For Lee Smith, family relationships become the locus for exploring the paradox of southern
manners, the way polite and decorous behavior can
disguise truth and extinguish vitality. In "Artists," she
examines how the revelation of family secrets can
change our perception, not only of our families but of
ourselves. Shirley Ann Grau's "Homecoming" centers
upon generational conflicts over proper behavior and
over the expected thoughts and feelings about death
and war. Grau juxtaposes a teenage girl's reaction to a
casual boyfriend's death in Vietnam with her mother's
memories of her husband's death in the Korean War.
Focusing on new patterns of family behavior rather
than old, Ellen Gilchrist evokes the contemporary
urban South in "The President of the Louisiana Live
Oak Society," a story of streetwise boys from New
Orleans who find themselves doing drugs and lying to
their parents, even as their parents lie to them and
find their own means of escape. Mary Hood ap-
proaches family dynamics from another perspective—
exploring the strong yet fragile bonds between family
members and illuminating the illusion of independence that occurs when people have family to depend
on. In "How Far She Went," the tension mounts as a
grandmother does battle with two tough motorcyclists
for her teenage granddaughter's loyalty. The stories in
this section are sometimes humorous but always poignant accounts of how we take our closest relatives

for granted and how family love can be fostered or destroyed more easily than we ever know.

The stories in Part III illustrate the power of a community for good and ill, and the tensions created within southern communities by race and class differences, indeed by difference of any kind. Richard Wright's story is set before the civil rights movement, when segregation was legal and racial discrimination was a way of life. In "The Man Who Was Almost a Man," race and gender stereotypes create a no-win situation for Dave, who tries to increase his stature with a gun. Wright examines the dilemma of a black youth growing up in a region where the white power structure did not allow black men the dignity and respect of adulthood, but diminished them and undermined their self-worth by calling them "boy" and treating them accordingly. In "Everything That Rises Must Converge," Flannery O'Connor reveals the de facto segregation that continued in the South even after the U.S. Supreme Court outlawed segregation.

Turning his attention to class divisions, Peter Taylor, in "The Old Forest," explores an upper-class white man's struggle for identity. Taylor's young protagonist finds himself torn between his desire for the companionship of a bright woman of questionable family background and his need to remain firmly ensconced in his own country club set by marrying into a prominent Memphis family. Gail Godwin paints a portrait of a similar dilemma, but from the perspective of a middle-class white female. In "The Angry Year," a college junior finds herself attracted by the mystique of wealthy fraternity men and sorority women, but repelled by their superficiality and conformity. She expresses her ambivalence in her satiric weekly newspaper column as well as through the two men she dates—the handsome, rich president of the Dekes and the intellectual coal miner's son whose ticket to law school is the GI Bill. Both Taylor's and Godwin's protagonists discover that the security of conformity is often stronger than individual desires. The limited range of behavior allowed by traditional southern gender roles concerns Michael Malone in "Fast Love" and Jill McCorkle in "Carnival Lights." Malone's protagonist, whose favorite pastimes are chess, debating, and bicycling, knows that his father and his childhood friends would have preferred him to be less intellectual and more interested in contact sports and cars. Jill McCorkle's protagonist, Lori, finds it difficult to control the way her community narrates her life. "Carnival Lights" begins, "I never slept with Donnie Wilkins like everybody says I did." A high school guidance counselor's refusal to guide Lori toward a career in engineering or architecture because she is a girl leads Lori to hope that "women's lib" will soon come to her hometown.

In her autobiography *Proud Shoes,* Pauli Murray writes of the old southern difficulty of dealing with difference: "Always the same tune, played like a broken record, robbing one of personal identity. . . . Folks were never just folks. They were white folks! Black folks! Poor white crackers! No-count niggers! Rednecks! Darkies! Peckerwoods! Coons!" The characters in the stories in Part IV wrestle with these labels as they try to move beyond them. Both William Faulkner and Ernest Gaines show their fascination with how individuals can break long-established southern traditions. They focus on male roles and the southern code of honor, which historian Bertram Wyatt-Brown argues made nineteenth-century white southerners put reputation in the community above conscience. In Faulkner's "An Odor of Verbena," Bayard Sartoris is pressured by his community to avenge his father's death. This incident serves as a test of his character since he must choose between his personal code of right and wrong and his community's code of honor. In Gaines's *A Gathering of Old Men,* set a century later, Cajun Gil Boutan is similarly put in a position of feeling forced to uphold family honor. His brother has been killed by a black man, and Gil's family expects him to join the vigilante group they are forming. Having become close friends with a black teammate on his college football team, Gil is embarrassed by his family's reputation for harassing blacks, and he would like to leave justice to the authorities. In each story, the protagonist's masculinity is called into question because he refuses to fight. In the excerpt from her autobiography *Mary,* Mary Mebane recounts her parallel struggle against the low expectations her family had for black women. Luckily for Mary, books and music opened her up to a larger world than the rural segregated South, and her aunt Jo, with her "strange, big-city ways," put some "unsuitable notions" in her head.

Several of the selections in Part IV are set during the 1960s civil rights movement, a tumultuous time in the South. These stories and memoirs show the power whites have wielded over blacks, the strength that blacks have gained when they united against white injustice, and the possibilities for an integrated community that can occur when brave people, both black and white, challenge hurtful traditions by acknowledging their mutual humanity. The excerpt from Anne Moody's autobiography, *Coming of Age in Mississippi*, reveals that working for the civil rights movement sometimes meant rebelling against family prohibitions even when you were black. Although Anne Moody worried that whites would retaliate against her family because of her political activism, she defied her mother's demands that she drop out of the movement at the same time that she braved white violence to fight for equal rights. Joan Williams's "Spring Is Now" explores the apprehensions aroused when the public schools were desegregated. The only blacks whom white teenager Sandra knows are field hands, maids, and janitors. Although her family and friends often speculate about what blacks are really like, Sandra only begins to find out when she turns her back on tradition and gets to know a new black male classmate. In a chapter from his memoir, *Colored People,* about growing up in the 1950s and 1960s in West Virginia, Henry Louis Gates, Jr., recounts how the personal became political during his first year in college, when he not only dated a white girl but integrated the Swordfish, a weekend hangout where college kids listened to live bands. The many ways in which southern traditions are challenged in the stories and memoirs in Part IV reveal one crucial and complex similarity. Rebellion necessitates not just challenging the "other" group's definition of one's own group, but often means calling into question the beliefs of family and friends who narrowly define themselves by a group identity. In each of the stories and memoirs in Part IV, formal education plays a crucial role in the process of broadening horizons, crossing color lines, and seeing self and others in new ways.

Although the South of Ernest Gaines, Ellen Gilchrist, Randall Kenan, and Jill McCorkle is not the South of William Faulkner, Richard Wright, Eudora Welty, and Elizabeth Spencer, these stories reveal what it means and what it meant to grow up in the South—what southern literary critic Carol Manning has called "that interesting middle ground between the universality of the process of growing up and the particularity of each individual's experience."

—Suzanne W. Jones

PART I

—◆—

Remembering Southern Places

Elizabeth Spencer

Elizabeth Spencer was born in 1921 in Carrollton, Mississippi, where her father was a prosperous farmer and businessman. Her early memories are of small-town life and a large extended family in which books were a staple of conversation. She attended Belhaven College in Jackson, Mississippi, and became friends with Eudora Welty, who later wrote the foreword to Spencer's collected stories, *The Stories of Elizabeth Spencer* (1981). Spencer received her M.A. at Vanderbilt and went on to teach at the University of Mississippi. She received recognition from the American Academy of Arts and Letters for her second novel, *This Crooked Way* (1952), and an award from the Academy for her third novel, *The Voice at the Back Door* (1956). Spencer's greatest commercial success was a novella set in Italy, *The Light in the Piazza* (1960), which was made into a movie by MGM. After setting several other works in Italy, where she lived for many years, Spencer once again used the South as the fictional setting for the novels *The Snare* (1972) and *The Salt Line* (1984). By this time Spencer was living in Montreal. Married to educator John Rusher, she taught creative writing at Corcordia University from 1976 to 1986, but in 1986 she returned to the South to live, moving to Chapel Hill to teach at the University of North Carolina. The recipient of numerous prizes and awards over the years, she received yet another, the Dos Passos Award, in 1992, the year of her retirement. Writer and reviewer Garrett Epps has said that "her art has been shaped by exile." She told *Publishers Weekly* that in coming to terms with her status as an expatriate, she decided: "There wasn't any need in sitting at home in the cottonfield just to be southern, that you could be southern elsewhere, in Florence, or Paris, or anywhere you found yourself." As this excerpt from her memoir *Landscapes of the Heart* (1998) shows, Spencer's writing reveals her mastery of idiomatic speech and her love of the landscape of her youth.

The Gulf Coast

If I could have one part of the world back the way it used to be, I would not choose Dresden before the firebombing, Rome before Nero, or London before the Blitz. I would not resurrect Babylon, Carthage, or San Francisco. Let the Leaning Tower lean and the Hanging Gardens hang. I want the Mississippi Gulf Coast back as it was before Hurricane Camille, that wicked killer which struck in August 1969.

All through my childhood and youth, north of Jackson, up in the hills, one happy phrase comes down intact: "the coast." *They've just been to the coast . . . They're going to the coast next week . . . They're fishing at the coast . . . They own a house at the coast . . . Let's go to the coast . . . When? For spring holidays? Next week? . . . Now!*

What was magical about it? In the days I speak of, it did not have a decent beach. Strictly speaking, it was not even a seacoast. The islands that stood out in the Gulf of Mexico—Horn Island, Ship Island, Cat Island, and the rest—took the Gulf surf on their sandy shores; what we called the coast was left with a tide you could measure in inches, and a gradual silted, sloping sea bottom, shallow enough to wade out in for half a mile without getting wet above the waist. A concrete seawall extended for miles along the beach drive, shielding the road and houses and towns it ran past from high water that storms might bring, also keeping the shoreline regular.

Compared with the real beaches of Southern California or Florida or the Caribbean islands, all this might seem not much to brag about: what was there besides the seawall, the drive along it, the palms and old lighthouses, the spacious mansions looking out on the water, with their deep porches and outdoor stairways, their green latticework, their moss-hung oaks and sheltered gardens, the crunch of oyster shells graveling side roads and parking lots . . . why was this so grand?

Well, it wasn't "grand," let that be admitted. Natchez was grand. New Orleans had its seductive charms securely placed in a rich Creole history. Still, nothing gave Mississippians quite the same feeling as our own Gulf Coast.

We would come down to it driving through plain little towns, some pretty, some not, south of Jackson through Hattiesburg. The names come back: Mendenhall, Magee, Mount Olive, Collins, Wiggins, Perkinston. Somewhere along the way was D'Lo, curiously pronounced Dee-Lo. In all of these, people of an Anglo-Saxon sameness in admirable (and not so admirable) qualities were pursuing life patterns thought out so long ago they could never be questioned. A day or two to piece the relationships together, learn a few names of Scottish or English origin, discover a cousin or two, and anyone from Carrollton or Winona or Pickens or Vaiden could pick up the same routine of life there as in the ancestral home.

But soon the thrilling smell of salt was on the breeze, increasing until suddenly we were in Gulfport and straight ahead lay the harbor with its big ships at rest, and to either side the long arms of the beach drive stretching east to Biloxi, west to Pass Christian and Bay St. Louis. Here were people with names foreign to our ears; and the mystery of these almost foreign places, easy in their openness, leaning toward the flat blue water, seemed serene beneath the huge floating clouds. That first thin breath of sea air had spread to a whole atmosphere.

What to do in a car crowded with friends on holiday from school but drive straight to the water's edge and sit breathless, not knowing which way to go first, but ready to discover.

I must have come first with girls from around home, or friends from college in Jackson. Someone would have borrowed the family car. Occasions blur into one long sighing memory of live oaks green the year round, and the pillared white houses the trees sheltered, set along the sweep of beach drive, boxes of saltwater taffy to chew on, and little screened restaurants advertising SHRIMP! ALL YOU CAN EAT FOR $1. Gumbo, too, "made fresh every day." Jax beer.

Prohibition lingered for a long time inland, but the coast never paid it much attention. Names alone would tell you they wouldn't. French and Spanish were here from the first, but Poles and Yugoslavs and Czechs had come long ago to work in the fishing industries, while the French traded and the Spanish built ships. But we wouldn't have thought of looking up their history. It was the feeling those names breathed that stirred us: Ladnier, Saucier, Legendre, Christovich, Benachi, Lameuse, Lopez, Toledano.

Religion here was foreign to us too: churches like Our Lady of the Gulf stood proclaiming it, with a statue of the Virgin in the wide paved entrance court, and a bare but graceful façade, facing boldly out to sea. Those who ran the restaurants, and went out in the shrimp boats, worshiped here, as did no doubt the men who waded the shallow water at night with flambeaux blazing, spears ready for flounder, and the women, too, who sat talking through the long afternoons on latticed porches.

We learned that annually at Biloxi, before the shrimp boats go out to their deep-sea fishing grounds, an outdoor mass is held to bless the fleet. It is a fine

occasion and one of general rejoicing. These were ancient ways. Above, the white clouds mounted high,
the gulls on broad white wings soared and tacked,
tilting into the wind. The pelicans stroked toward land
in flawless formation. Midafternoon in spring. Intense
heat had not yet taken over, but a stillness came on,
a sense of absolute suspension. The camellias were
long finished, the azaleas, lingering, but past their
height. Magnolia blooms starred green branches. Jasmine breathed in the back gardens. The moss hung
breezeless. Time stood still.

We were used to staying at the Edgewater Gulf, a
wonderful hotel between Gulfport and Biloxi. Its
grounds were ample. I remember a cool lobby of
gently turning ceiling fans, plants in white recesses,
and rooms designed each facing on the sea but with
a long entrance passage to draw a constant breeze
through latticed doors.

Parting admonitions—"Don't talk to strangers,"
"Be careful where you swim," "Be sure to call Sally
the minute you get there"—may have sounded in our
girlish ears for a while on the way down, but vanished
after Gulfport. Yet I cannot recall any serious mischief
we ever got ourselves into.

Grown beyond all that and long out of school I was
to return to the coast many times over. A nagging
sense began to persist that the coast was withholding
something; I'd something yet to solve. Then I took the
boat one summer and went out to Ship Island.

Ship Island is the largest and best known of the
coastal islands, and the only one that excursion boats
go out to. It takes these little tourist ferries well over
an hour to make the twelve miles or so to the island.
But who is in a hurry? Someone in the pilothouse will
be playing a harmonica. Cold drinks and snacks are
sold in the galley. The island is low and white, like a
sandbar with dunes. Once we are ashore, the dunes
seem higher: they mount up before the visitor, low

hills fringed with sea oats, which blow in the steady breeze. Wooden walkways climb among them. There are signs to an old fort to the west, dating from Civil War days. History will be related on the dutiful markers. An old weathered lighthouse, wooden, four-sided, gray, stands guard.

The first visit I made to this spot was during the summer of 1951. Already it seemed part of my own personal geography. Everyone had been to Ship Island. Picnics were talked of, summer days recalled.

On that first time for me, I walked ahead of friends (a man I went with, two friends of his) straight south, taking the walk through the dunes. Then, cresting, I saw before me what I'd come for without knowing it: the true Gulf, no horizon to curb its expanse, spread out infinite and free, restless with tossing whitecaps, rushing in to foam up the beach, retreating, returning, roaring. Out there, I thought, astonished, is Mexico, the Caribbean, South America. We are leaning outward to them. Everybody back on land, all along the coast, feels this presence, whether they consciously know it or not. What was it but distance, the leaning outward, the opening toward far-off, unlikely worlds? The beyond.

Here at the Mississippian's southernmost point of native soil, one had to recall what inland Mississippi was like, how people in its small towns (or even in larger towns like Meridian and Jackson and Columbus) related inward, to family life, kinfolks, old friendships and hatreds. How hospitably newcomers were welcomed, but how slowly accepted. Once I heard this remark: "The H——s haven't lived here but thirty years, but look how everybody likes them!" In talk of the outside world, not much was to be accepted, nothing could be trusted to be "like us." There were Yankees "up there," we said to ourselves, looking north; the other southern states, like neighboring counties, offered names that could be traced in and out among one's connection and might prove acceptable.

In such towns people lived on stories of one another's sayings and doings, repeating and checking for the facts, speculating and measuring and fitting together the present to the past, the known to the suspected, weaving numberless patterns. It was a complex and at times beautiful society; much fine literature has been created to do it justice; but the smell of salt air did not reach it, and none can deny that it was confined and confining.

So one from those places comes to stand, in memory fixed forever like a monument or a snapshot, on a Ship Island dune staring out to sea.

I wrote a story named for the island. In it a young girl comes to it with her summer lover, and in the sight and feel of the sea discovers her own true nature—good or bad, she finds it there, like a wonderful shell dug out of the sand. In Walker Percy's book *The Moviegoer,* we read: "You come over the hillock and your heart lifts up; your old sad music comes into the major." That's another way of saying it. But it may be that the only way of knowing it is to go there.

* * *

Many years later, Ship Island, the very spot where I had caught my breath to see the Gulf in all its expanse and glory, found itself in the target eye of a destruction so complete that the coast as we knew it could never be restored. Its name was Hurricane Camille.

Other hurricanes, memorable ones, had struck the area. One in 1947 burst the seawall to bits; it was replaced by a man-made beach of white sand. Betsy, in 1965, swept the beach away; it was built up again. But to Camille, all such efforts might have been sand castles left by a child. The statement was repeated too often to be false that here was the most powerful hurricane ever to strike the continent; none stronger was to be found in any record or in human memory.

In 1969 I was living in Montreal, but I saw more than enough of it on TV. I saw the few cars that crept through a world that was not falling down but bursting apart horizontally, trees, buildings, and telephone poles fighting like wildcats through the haze of wind and water to remain, slowly losing a night-long battle. I saw evacuation moving massively north along the highways, heard stations fading from the air, until all communication, like threads snipped one by one, was cut. I was left, in the distant northern night, to dream of other horrors still—my favorite old mansions crashing to flinders, piers lifted from their pilings to coil like whips in the storm's fury, giant oaks with their roots nakedly exposed. But whatever I could imagine would still be less than the actual disasters of August 17, 1969.

I returned to the area in the summer of 1970 to do a reading at Gulf Park, a junior college whose solid concrete buildings had survived the holocaust. I flew to New Orleans and rode to Gulfport on the bus. As we approached the coast through the marshy land west of New Orleans, I heard a woman talking behind me to someone she was sitting by. She had had to wait out the hurricane in Biloxi, at the hospital bedside of her father, who was too ill to be moved. "It was something more than natural," she kept repeating. "It was like one of them bomb experiments done got loose. It was just a lot more awful than anything natural could be." The tremor in her voice made me think that what had come that night would not leave her.

Not that I could blame her. The bus reached Bay St. Louis and crossed the bridge. To the right was open water, calm and innocent, but everything that had stood between the road and the water had vanished. The shoreline and the road were at least twenty yards higher than before. A wonderful alley of oaks, a cool tunnel of bearded moss, was simply gone, as were the noble white houses just beyond them, and all their gardens. Double staircases, high verandas like a dream of long summer afternoons, tall white-painted fences with wrought-iron gates, all were gone. Only walkways remained.

Back of the bare rerouted beach drive, I later saw whole groves of pine trees reduced to blackened stumps, as though the land had been burned over. I was told that sand driven by winds that had reached two hundred miles an hour (and probably much more: instruments at the time could go no higher) had blackened whatever it struck. How far back did the monster range, how far along the coast had it foraged? Sickened by the loss, I didn't want to hear any more statistics. The real message was written already in the ragged shoreline, the disappearance of the Pass Christian Yacht Club with its brave flags and trim marina, the few stricken and displaced houses that had somehow got through. This place was finished. "Gone with the wind" was waiting to be wryly said here. It may be in order to observe that Camille, with her demure name like a southern belle's, did a better job than Sherman.

I knew I must write about all this someday. I had already done a number of stories about various points along the Gulf or in the Caribbean. The writer A. J. Leibling, who loved the area, insisted that the Caribbean was this hemisphere's Mediterranean Sea. I agree. Its ways of life, its mystery, belong to the sea and create lifestyles and outlooks that are totally, rhythmically different from what we think of as our own "normal" ways of living.

But it was the hurricane itself, its wild force and aftermath, that stayed with me and finally grew into the novel *The Salt Line,* which took many years in writing. I made a number of trips to the coast, lingering for weeks at a time. I heard hundreds of stories from people I knew who lived there. I read through innumerable accounts in the all-new library in Gulfport. I even went out once more to Ship Island. The lighthouse was gone, no victim of Camille, which she had somehow gallantly weathered, but burned down, I was told, by some boys on a lark. The island itself had been split in two parts by the storm. Now land that had offered the first harbor the French explorers had found and had been the scene of historic wartime events, decades of Sunday school picnics, and countless romantic afternoons was now two diminished little islands with the sea flowing between.

Back at Pass Christian the Gothic-style white-painted Episcopal church in its grove of oaks was gone—the rector, I learned, had seen his wife and child drowned in the tidal wave while he held to the front steps and reached out vainly to bring them in.

Ocean Springs, however, I found to my delight, was hardly touched. Best of all, Shearwater Pottery had been spared. It was still to be reached by its shaggy winding road, and there I discovered what others had found after the death of Walter Anderson. A hidden treasure was in a small cottage adjacent to the main house and the pottery, where he had lived in later years quite alone, his place of refuge.

This singular man had died soon after sitting through Hurricane Betsy in 1965 on Horn Island. He had gone out on purpose to get as close as possible to the invader. It is well known that Horn Island, like the cottage, was his special province. He rowed to it often, stayed there for weeks at a time, kept a journal about his experiences, and, of course, painted and drew its creatures, plants, flowers, sand, and sea. The hurricane to him must have been one more visiting live thing. He died soon after the experience of it, though not before rejoicing in his log:

> Never has there been a hurricane more respectable, provided with all the portents, predictions, omens, etc., etc. The awful sunrise—no one could fail to take a warning from it—the hovering black spirit bird (man o'war)—only one—*(comme il faut)* . . .

The cottage where he painted has now been entirely moved to the new Walter Anderson Museum in Ocean

Springs. There one finds the walls set up as they were when he covered them entirely in brilliantly colored murals, all revealing his vision of the coast, its flora and fauna, its myth and its reality. The book that reproduces this astonishing work is called *A Painter's Psalm*. I know of no greater work anywhere in this country—it is safe to say that we must go to Europe for achievement to compare with it.

The character central in my novel *The Salt Line*, Arnold Carrington, also has a vision of the coast. Regretting Camille's destruction, he tries to restore by building anew what was typical of the old. Many of his feelings are echoes of my own:

> . . . the old pre-hurricane Coast: shrimp boats and ancient oaks, camellias in bloom, flags flying from the old white lighthouse, moonlight on the Sound, softly blowing curtains of Spanish moss . . . where to find this unity of house, shade and sun . . . the brick walk, the moss barely stirring to its familiar breeze of this hour, this peace and precious past . . .

But "gone are the days" is something all southerners have had to get used to. Days are going all the time, taking with them places and times, leaving memories good and bad. I had taken a lot from the coast. For others to come, the sound is still there and the sea beyond the islands, opening toward unknown worlds.

Harry Crews

Born in 1935, Harry Crews, the son of a poor tenant farmer, never lived in one place very long so he did not have the anchor of a family "home place," which he, like many other southerners, defines as "that single house where you were born, where you lived out your childhood, where you grew into young manhood." In his autobiography, *A Childhood: The Biography of a Place,* from which the following selection is taken, he writes, "But because we were driven from pillar to post when I was a child, there is nowhere I can think of as the home place. Bacon County is my home place, and I've had to make do with it. If I think of where I come from, I think of the entire county. I think of all its people and its customs and all its loveliness and all its ugliness." In Bacon County Crews learned that "Nothing is allowed to die in a society of storytelling people. It is all—the good and the bad—carted up and brought along from one generation to the next. And everything that is brought along is colored and shaped by those who bring it." Harry Crews acquired this gift for storytelling and has written many novels, all with a nod to the southern gothic tradition, but transformed by his own unique humor and satiric bent. Among them are *The Gospel Singer* (1968), *Car* (1972), *The Hawk Is Dying* (1973), *A Feast of Snakes* (1976), *Body* (1990), *Scar Lover* (1992), and *Celebration* (1998). His novel *The Mulching of America* (1995) satirizes corporate America. Author of the column "Grits" for *Esquire,* Crews has been a frequent contributor to

Sewanee Review, *Georgia Review*, and *Playboy*. After enlisting in the U.S. Marines at age seventeen, Crews graduated from the University of Florida, only to return there in 1968 to become a professor of creative writing.

from A Childhood:
The Biography of a Place

It has always seemed to me that I was not so much born into this life as I awakened to it. I remember very distinctly the awakening and the morning it happened. It was my first glimpse of myself, and all that I know now—the stories, and everything conjured up by them, that I have been writing about thus far—I obviously knew none of then, particularly anything about my real daddy, whom I was not to hear of until I was nearly six years old, not his name, not even that he was my daddy. Or if I did hear of him, I have no memory of it.

I awoke in the middle of the morning in early summer from the place I'd been sleeping in the curving roots of a giant oak tree in front of a large white house. Off to the right, beyond the dirt road, my goats were trailing along in the ditch, grazing in the tough wire grass that grew there. Their constant bleating shook the warm summer air. I always thought of them as my goats although my brother usually took care of them. Before he went to the field that morning to work, he had let them out of the old tobacco barn where they slept at night. At my feet was a white dog whose name was Sam. I looked at the dog and at the house and at the red gown with little pearl-colored buttons I was wearing, and I knew that the gown had been made for me by my Grandma Hazelton and that the dog belonged to me. He went everywhere I went, and he always took precious care of me.

Precious. That was my mama's word for how it was

between Sam and me, even though Sam caused her
some inconvenience from time to time. If she wanted
to whip me, she had to take me in the house, where
Sam was never allowed to go. She could never touch
me when I was crying if Sam could help it. He would
move quietly—he was a dog not given to barking very
much—between the two of us and show her his teeth.
Unless she took me somewhere Sam couldn't go,
there'd be no punishment for me.

The house there just behind me, partially under the
arching limbs of the oak tree, was called the Williams
place. It was where I lived with my mama and my
brother, Hoyet, and my daddy, whose name was Pas-
cal. I knew when I opened my eyes that morning that
the house was empty because everybody had gone to
the field to work. I also knew, even though I couldn't
remember doing it, that I had awakened sometime in
midmorning and come out onto the porch and down
the steps and across the clean-swept dirt yard through
the gate weighted with broken plow points so it would
swing shut behind me, that I had come out under the
oak tree and lain down against the curving roots with
my dog, Sam, and gone to sleep. It was a thing I had
done before. If I ever woke up and the house was
empty and the weather was warm—which was the only
time I would ever awaken to an empty house—I always went out under the oak tree to finish my nap. It
wasn't fear or loneliness that drove me outside; it was
just something I did for reasons I would never be able
to discover.

I stood up and stretched and looked down at my
bare feet at the hem of the gown and said: "I'm almost
five and already a great big boy." It was my way of
reassuring myself, but it was also something my daddy
said about me and it made me feel good because in
his mouth it seemed to mean I was almost a man.

Sam immediately stood up too, stretched, reproduc-
ing, as he always did, every move I made, watching
me carefully to see which way I might go. I knew I

ought not to be outside lying in the rough curve of root in my cotton gown. Mama didn't mind me being out there under the tree, but I was supposed to get dressed first. Sometimes I did; often I forgot.

So I turned and went back through the gate, Sam at my heels, and across the yard and up the steps onto the porch to the front door. When I opened the door, Sam stopped and lay down to wait. He would be there when I came out, no matter which door I used. If I went out the back door, he would somehow magically know it and he would be there. If I came out the side door by the little pantry, he would know that, too, and he would be there. Sam always knew where I was, and he made it his business to be there, waiting.

I went into the long, dim, cool hallway that ran down the center of the house. Briefly I stopped at the bedroom where my parents slept and looked in at the neatly made bed and all the parts of the room, clean, with everything where it was supposed to be, just the way mama always kept it. And I thought of daddy, as I so often did because I loved him so much. If he was sitting down, I was usually on his lap. If he was standing up, I was usually holding his hand. He always said soft funny things to me and told me stories that never had an end but always continued when we met again.

He was tall and lean with flat high cheekbones and deep eyes and black thick hair which he combed straight back on his head. And under the eye on his left cheek was the scarred print of a perfect set of teeth. I knew he had taken the scar in a fight, but I never asked him about it and the teeth marks in his cheek only made him seem more powerful and stronger and special to me.

He shaved every morning at the water shelf on the back porch with a straight razor and always smelled of soap and whiskey. I knew mama did not like the whiskey, but to me it smelled sweet, better even than the soap. And I could never understand why she resisted it so, complained of it so, and kept telling him

over and over again that he would kill himself and
ruin everything if he continued with the whiskey. I did
not understand about killing himself and I did not
understand about ruining everything, but I knew the
whiskey somehow caused the shouting and screaming
and the ugly sound of breaking things in the night.
The stronger the smell of whiskey on him, though, the
kinder and gentler he was with me and my brother.

I went on down the hallway and out onto the back
porch and finally into the kitchen that was built at the
very rear of the house. The entire room was dominated by a huge black cast-iron stove with six eyes on
its cooking surface. Directly across the room from the
stove was the safe, a tall square cabinet with wide
doors covered with screen wire that was used to keep
biscuits and fried meat and rice or almost any other
kind of food that had been recently cooked. Between
the stove and the safe sat the table we ate off of, a
table almost ten feet long, with benches on each side
instead of chairs, so that when we put in tobacco,
there would be enough room for the hired hands to
eat.

I opened the safe, took a biscuit off a plate, and
pushed a hole in it with my finger. Then with a jar of
cane syrup, I poured the hole full, waited for it to
soak in good, and then poured again. When the biscuit
had all the syrup it would take, I got two pieces of
fried pork off another plate and went out and sat on
the back steps, where Sam was already lying in the
warm sun, his ears struck forward on his head. I ate
the bread and pork slowly, chewing for a long time
and sharing it all with Sam.

When we had finished, I went back into the house,
took off my gown, and put on a cotton undershirt, my
overalls with twin galluses that buckled on my chest,
and my straw hat, which was rimmed on the edges
with a border of green cloth and had a piece of green
cellophane sewn into the brim to act as an eyeshade.
I was barefoot, but I wished very much I had a pair

of brogans because brogans were what men wore and I very much wanted to be a man. In fact, I was pretty sure I already was a man, but the only one who seemed to know it was my daddy. Everybody else treated me like I was still a baby.

I went out the side door, and Sam fell into step behind me as we walked out beyond the mule barn where four mules stood in the lot and on past the cotton house and down the dim road past a little leaning shack where our tenant farmers lived, a black family in which there was a boy just a year older than I was. His name was Willalee Bookatee. I went on past their house because I knew they would be in the field, too, so there was no use to stop.

I went through a sapling thicket and over a shallow ditch and finally climbed a wire fence into the field, being very careful of my overalls on the barbed wire. I could see them all, my family and the black tenant family, far off there in the shimmering heat of the tobacco field. They were pulling cutworms off the tobacco. I wished I could have been out there with them pulling worms because when you found one, you had to break it in half, which seemed great good fun to me. But you could also carry an empty Prince Albert tobacco can in your back pocket and fill it up with worms to play with later.

Mama wouldn't let me pull worms because she said I was too little and might damage the plants. If I was alone in the field with daddy, though, he would let me hunt all the worms I wanted to. He let me do pretty much anything I wanted to, which included sitting in his lap to guide his old pickup truck down dirt roads all over the county.

I went down to the end of the row and sat under a persimmon tree in the shade with Sam and watched as daddy and mama and brother and Willalee Bookatee, who was—I could see even from this distance— putting worms in Prince Albert cans, and his mama, whose name was Katie, and his daddy, whose name was Will, I watched them all as they came toward me, turning the leaves and searching for worms as they came.

The moment I sat down in the shade, I was already wondering how long it would be before they quit to go to the house for dinner because I was already beginning to wish I'd taken two biscuits instead of one and maybe another piece of meat, or else that I hadn't shared with Sam.

Bored, I looked down at Sam and said: "Sam, if you don't quit eatin my biscuit and meat, I'm gone have to cut you like a shoat hog."

A black cloud of gnats swarmed around his heavy muzzle, but I clearly heard him say that he didn't think I was man enough to do it. Sam and I talked a lot together, had long involved conversations, mostly about which one of us had done the other one wrong and, if not about that, about which one of us was the better man. It would be a good long time before I started thinking of Sam as a dog instead of a person. But I always came out on top when we talked because Sam could only say what I said he said, think what I thought he thought.

"If you was any kind of man atall, you wouldn't snap at them gnats and eat them flies the way you do," I said.

"It ain't a thing in the world the matter with eatin gnats and flies," he said.

"It's how come people treat you like a dog," I said. "You could probably come on in the house like other folks if it weren't for eatin flies and gnats like you do."

That's the way the talk went until daddy and the rest of them finally came down to where Sam and I were sitting in the shade. They stopped beside us to wipe their faces and necks with sweat rags. Mama asked if I had got something to eat when I woke up. I told her I had.

"You all gone stop for dinner now?"

"I reckon we'll work awhile longer," daddy said.

I said: "Well then, can Willalee and me go up to his house and play till dinnertime?"

Daddy looked at the sun to see what time it was. He could come within five or ten minutes by the position of the sun. Most of the farmers I knew could.

Daddy was standing almost dead center in his own shadow. "I reckon so," he said.

Then the whole thing had to be done over again. Willalee asked his daddy the same question. Because my daddy had said it was all right didn't mean Willalee's daddy would agree. He usually did, but not always. So it was necessary to ask.

We climbed the fence and went across the ditch and back through the sapling thicket to the three-track road that led up to the shack, and while we walked, Willalee showed me the two Prince Albert tobacco cans he had in his back pockets. They were both filled with cutworms. The worms had lots of legs and two little things on their heads that looked like horns. They were about an inch long, sometimes as long as two inches, and round and fat and made wonderful things to play with. There was no fence around the yard where Willalee lived and the whole house leaned toward the north at about a ten-degree tilt. Before we even got up the steps, we could smell the food already cooking on the wood stove at the back of the house where his grandma was banging metal pots around over the cast-iron stove. Her name was Annie, but everybody called her Auntie. She was too old to work in the field anymore, but she was handy about the house with ironing and cooking and scrubbing floors and canning vegetables out of the field and berries out of the woods.

She also was full of stories, which, when she had the time—and she usually did—she told to me and Willalee and his little sister, whose name was Lottie Mae. Willalee and my brother and I called her Snottie Mae, but she didn't seem to mind. She came out of the front door when she heard us coming up on the porch and right away wanted to know if she could play in the book with us. She was the same age as I and sometimes we let her play with us, but most of the time we did not.

"Naw," Willalee said, "git on back in there and help Auntie. We ain't studying you."

"Bring us the book," I said.

"I git it for you," she said, "if you give me five of them worms."

"I ain't studying you," said Willalee.

She had already seen the two Prince Albert cans full of green worms because Willalee was sitting on the floor now, the lids of the cans open and the worms crawling out. He was lining two of them up for a race from one crack in the floor to the next crack, and he was arranging the rest of the worms in little designs of diamonds and triangles in some game he had not yet discovered the rules for.

"You bring the book," I said, "and you can have two of them worms."

Willalee almost never argued with what I decided to do, up to and including giving away the worms he had spent all morning collecting in the fierce summer heat, which is probably why I liked him so much. Lottie Mae went back into the house, and got the Sears, Roebuck catalogue and brought it out onto the porch. He handed her the two worms and told her to go on back in the house, told her it weren't fitting for her to be out here playing with worms while Auntie was back in the kitchen working.

"Ain't nothing left for me to do but put them plates on the table," she said.

"See to them plates then," Willalee said. As young as she was, Lottie Mae had things to do about the place. Whatever she could manage. We all did.

Willalee and I stayed there on the floor with the Sears, Roebuck catalogue and the open Prince Albert cans, out of which deliciously fat worms crawled. Then we opened the catalogue at random as we always did, to see what magic was waiting for us there.

In the minds of most people, the Sears, Roebuck catalogue is a kind of low joke associated with outhouses. God knows the catalogue sometimes ended up in the outhouse, but more often it did not. All the farmers, black and white, kept dried corncobs beside their double-seated thrones, and the cobs served the purpose for which they were put there with all possible efficiency and comfort.

The Sears, Roebuck catalogue was much better used as a Wish Book, which it was called by the people out in the country, who would never be able to order anything out of it, but could at their leisure spend hours dreaming over.

Willalee Bookatee and I used it for another reason. We made up stories out of it, used it to spin a web of fantasy about us. Without that catalogue our childhood would have been radically different. The federal government ought to strike a medal for the Sears, Roebuck company for sending all those catalogues to farming families, for bringing all that color and all that mystery and all that beauty into the lives of country people.

I first became fascinated with the Sears catalogue because all the people in its pages were perfect. Nearly everybody I knew had something missing, a finger cut off, a toe split, an ear half-chewed away, an eye clouded with blindness from a glancing fence staple. And if they didn't have something missing, they were carrying scars from barbed wire, or knives, or fishhooks. But the people in the catalogue had no such hurts. They were not only whole, had all their arms and legs and eyes on their unscarred bodies, but they were also beautiful. Their legs were straight and their heads were never bald and on their faces were looks of happiness, even joy, looks that I never saw much of in the faces of the people around me.

Young as I was, though, I had known for a long
time that it was all a lie. I knew that under those fancy
clothes there had to be scars, there had to be swellings
and boils of one kind or another because there was
no other way to live in the world. And more than
that, at some previous, unremembered moment, I had
decided that all the people in the catalogue were related, not necessarily blood kin, but knew one another,
and because they knew one another there had to be
hard feelings, trouble between them off and on, violence, and hate between them as well as love. And it
was out of this knowledge that I first began to make
up stories about the people I found in the book.

Once I began to make up stories about them, Willalee and Lottie Mae began to make up stories, too.
The stories they made up were every bit as good as
mine. Sometimes better. More than once we had spent
whole rainy afternoons when it was too wet to go to
the field turning the pages of the catalogue, forcing the
beautiful people to give up the secrets of their lives: how
they felt about one another, what kind of sicknesses they
may have had, what kind of scars they carried in their
flesh under all those bright and fancy clothes.

Willalee had his pocketknife out and was about to
operate on one of the green cutworms because he
liked to pretend he was a doctor. It was I who first
put the notion in his head that he might in fact be a
doctor, and since we almost never saw a doctor and
because they were mysterious and always drove cars
or else fine buggies behind high-stepping mares,
quickly healing people with their secret medicines, the
notion stuck in Willalee's head, and he became very
good at taking cutworms and other things apart with
his pocketknife.

The Sears catalogue that we had opened at random
found a man in his middle years but still strong and
healthy with a head full of hair and clear, direct eyes
looking out at us, dressed in a red hunting jacket and
wading boots, with a rack of shotguns behind him. We

used our fingers to mark the spot and turned the Wish Book again, and this time it opened to ladies standing in their underwear, lovely as none we had ever seen, all perfect in their unstained clothes. Every last one of them had the same direct and steady eyes of the man in the red hunting jacket.

I said: "What do you think, Willalee?"

Without hesitation, Willalee said: "This lady here in her step-ins is his chile."

We kept the spot marked with the lady in the step-ins and the man in the hunting jacket and turned the book again, and there was a young man in a suit, the creases sharp enough to shave with, posed with his foot casually propped on a box, every strand of his beautiful hair in place.

"See, what it is," I said. "This boy right here is seeing that girl back there, the one in her step-ins, and she is the youngun of him back there, and them shotguns behind'm belong to him, and he ain't happy."

"Why he ain't happy?"

"Cause this feller standing here in this suit looking so nice, he ain't nice at all. He's mean, but he don't look mean. That gal is the only youngun the feller in the jacket's got, and he loves her cause she is a sweet child. He don't want her fooling with that sorry man in that suit. He's so sorry he done got hisself in trouble with the law. The high sheriff is looking for him right now. Him in the suit will fool around on you."

"How it is he fool around?"

"He'll steal anything he can put his hand to," I said. "He'll steal your hog, or he'll steal your cow out of your field. He's so sorry he'll take that cow if it's the only cow you got. It's just the kind of feller he is."

Willalee said: "Then how come it is she mess around with him?"

"That suit," I said, "done turned that young girl's head. Daddy always says if you give a man a white shirt and a tie and a suit of clothes, you can find out real quick how sorry he is. Daddy says it's the quickest way to find out."

"Do her daddy know she's messing round with him?"

"Shore he knows. A man allus knows what his youngun is doing. Special if she's a girl." I flipped back to the man in the red hunting jacket and the wading boots. "You see them shotguns behind him there on the wall? Them his guns. That second one right there, see that one, the double barrel? That gun is loaded with double-ought buckshot. You know how come it loaded?"

"He gone stop that fooling around," said Willalee.

And so we sat there on the porch with the pots and pans banging back in the house over the iron stove and Lottie Mae there in the door where she had come to stand and listen to us as we talked even though we would not let her help with the story. And before it was over, we had discovered all the connections possible between the girl in the step-ins and the young man in the knife-creased suit and the older man in the red hunting jacket with the shotguns on the wall behind him. And more than that we also discovered that the man's kin people, when they had found out about the trouble he was having with his daughter and the young man, had plans of their own to fix it so the high sheriff wouldn't even have to know about it. They were going to set up and wait on him to take a shoat hog out of another field, and when he did, they'd be waiting with their own guns and knives (which we stumbled upon in another part of the catalogue) and they was gonna throw down on him and see if they couldn't make two pieces out of him instead of one. We had in the story what they thought and what they said and what they felt and why they didn't think that the young man, as good as he looked and as well as he stood in his fancy clothes, would ever straighten out and become the man the daddy wanted for his only daughter.

Before it was over, we even had the girl in the step-ins fixing it so that the boy in the suit could be shot. And by the time my family and Willalee's family came walking down the road from the tobacco field toward the house, the entire Wish Book was filled with feuds of every kind and violence, maimings, and all the other vicious happenings of the world.

Since where we lived and how we lived was almost hermetically sealed from everything and everybody else, fabrication became a way of life. Making up stories, it seems to me now, was not only a way for us to understand the way we lived but also a defense against it. It was no doubt the first step in a life devoted primarily to men and women and children who never lived anywhere but in my imagination. I have found in them infinitely more order and beauty and satisfaction than I ever have in the people who move about me in the real world. And Willalee Bookatee and his family were always there with me in those first tentative steps. God knows what it would have been like if it had not been for Willalee and his people, with whom I spent nearly as much time as I did with my own family.

There was a part of me in which it did not matter at all that they were black, but there was another part of me in which it had to matter because it mattered to the world I lived in. It mattered to my blood. It is easy to remember the morning I found out Willalee was a nigger.

It was not very important at the time. I do not know why I have remembered it so vividly and so long. It was the tiniest of moments that slipped by without anybody marking it or thinking about it.

It was later in the same summer I awoke to a knowledge of myself in the enormous, curving oak roots. It was Sunday, bright and hot, and we were on the way to church. Everybody except daddy, who was sick from whiskey. But he would not have gone even if he were well. The few times he ever did go he could never stand more than five or ten minutes of the ser-

mon before he quietly went out a side door to stand
beside the pickup truck smoking hand-rolled Prince
Albert cigarettes until it was all over.

An aunt, her husband, and their children had come
by to take us to the meeting in their car. My aunt was
a lovely, gentle lady whom I loved nearly as much as
mama. I was out on the porch waiting for my brother
to get ready. My aunt stood beside me, pulling on the
thin black gloves she wore to church winter and summer. I was talking nonstop, which I did even as a
child, telling her a story—largely made up—about
what happened to me and my brother the last time
he went to town.

Robert Jones figured in the story. Robert Jones was
a black man who lived in Bacon County. Unlike any
other black man I knew of, though, he owned a big
farm with a great shining house on it. He had two
sons who were nearly seven feet tall. They were all
known as very hard workers. I had never heard anybody speak of Robert Jones and his family with anything but admiration.

". . . so me and Hoyet was passing the cotton gin
and Mr. Jones was standing there with his wife
and. . . ."

My aunt leaned down and put her arm around my
shoulders. Her great soft breast pressed warmly at my
ear. She said: "No, son. Robert Jones is a nigger. You
don't say 'mister' when you speak of a nigger. You
don't say 'Mr. Jones,' you say 'nigger Jones'."

I never missed a stroke in my story. ". . . so me
and him was passing the cotton gin and nigger Jones
was standing there with his wife. . . ."

We were all dutiful children in Bacon County,
Georgia.

I don't know what difference it ever made that I
found out Willalee Bookatee was a nigger. But no
doubt it made a difference. Willalee was our friend,
my brother's and mine, but we sometimes used him

like a toy. He was always a surefire cure for boredom
because among other things he could be counted on
to be scared witless at the mention of a bull. How
many afternoons would have been endless if we
couldn't have said to one another: "Let's go get Willalee Bookatee and scare the shit out of him."

It didn't take much encouragement or deception to
get Willalee out in the cornfield with us just after
noon, when it was hot as only a day can be hot in the
middle of an airless field in Georgia.

Hoyet turned to Willalee Bookatee and said: "You
ever seen this here bull?"

"Which air bull?" Willalee rolled his eyes and shuffled his feet and looked off down the long heat-
distorted rows of corn, the corn so green it seemed
almost purple in the sun.

"The bull that stays in this field," I said.

My brother said: "To hook little boys that won't
tote a citron."

Willalee was out in the middle of a twenty-acre field
of corn, equidistant from all fences, brought there by
design by Hoyet and me to see if we could make him
carry a heavy citron to the gate. A citron is a vine
that grows wild in the field, and it puts out a fruit
which is also called a citron and looks in every way
like a watermelon except it's slightly smaller. Its rind
was sometimes pickled and used in fruitcakes, but by
and large, it was a worthless plant and farmers did
everything they could think of to get rid of them, but
they somehow always managed to survive.

"Hook little boys," said Willalee.

It wasn't a question; it was only repeated into the
quiet dust-laden air. There had been no rain in almost
two weeks, and when you stepped between the corn
rows, the dust rose and hung, not falling or blowing
in the windless day, but simply hanging interminably
between the purple shucks of corn.

"No siree, it's got to be bigger than that one," I

said when Willalee rushed to snatch a grapefruit-sized citron off the ground. "That old bull wants you to tote one bigger'n that."

Willalee was scared to death of bulls. He had been trampled and caught on the horns of one when he was about three years old, and he never got over it. At the mention of a bull, Willalee would go gray and his eyes would get a little wild and sometimes he would get out of control with his fear. Willalee was struggling with an enormous citron, staggering in the soft dirt between the corn rows.

"That's better," I said. "That's a lot better. That old bull will never touch you with that in your arms."

Willalee couldn't have weighed more than about sixty-five pounds, and the citron he caught against his skinny chest must have weighed twenty pounds.

"How come it is you ain't got no citron?" said Willalee.

My brother and I walked on either side of him. He could hardly see over the citron he was carrying.

"We already carried ourn," I said. "That bull doesn't make you tote but one. After you tote one citron, you can take and come out here in the field anytime you want to and that bull don't pay no more mind than if you was a goat."

Willalee was a long way from the gate, and he had already started crying, soundlessly, tears tracking down through the dust on his cheeks. That citron was hurting him a lot.

"But you ain't toted your citron yet," I said, "and that big bull looking to hook into your ass if you put it down, that bull looking to hook him some ass, some good tender little-boy ass, cause that the kind he likes the best."

"I know," whispered Willalee through his tears. "I know he do."

And so Willalee made it to the fence with his citron and felt himself forever safe from the bull. He didn't hesitate at the fence but went right over it, still carrying his citron in case the bull was watching, and once over it, he didn't say anything but took off in a wild run down the road.

But Willalee was not entirely helpless, and he gave back about as good as he got. He once took a crab-apple and cut the core out of it, put some cow plop down in the bottom of the hole, and then covered it over all around the top with some blackberry jam his mama had canned.

"Jam in a apple?" I said.

"Bes thing *you* ever put in your mouth," he said.

My brother, who had seen him fix the apple, stood there and watched him offer it to me, did in fact encourage me to take it.

"Had one myself," he said. "That thing is some gooooood eatin."

"I ain't had nair one with jam in it," I said.

"Take you a great big bite," said Willalee.

I not only took a great big bite, I took *two* great big bites, getting right down to the bottom. Anybody else would have known what he was eating after the first bite. It took me two. Even then, I did not so much as taste it as I smelled it.

"I believe this thing is ruint," I said.

"Nawwwww," said Willalee.

"Nawwwww," said my brother.

"It smells just like . . . like . . ." And then I knew what he had fed me.

Willalee was laughing when he should have been running. I got him around the neck and we both went into the dust, where we wallowed around for a while before my brother got tired of watching it and pulled us apart. No matter what we did to one another, though, Willalee and I never stayed angry at each other for more than an hour or two, and I always felt welcome at his family's house. Whatever I am, they had a large part in making.

Eudora Welty

Eudora Welty was born in Jackson, Mississippi, in 1909, and was still living in her childhood home when she died in 2001. After graduating from the University of Wisconsin with a major in English, she attended Columbia University Graduate School of Business. During the Depression she worked in Mississippi for newspapers and radio stations and as a publicity agent for the Works Progress Administration from 1933–1936, a job that took her all over the state. She wrote feature stories, took photographs, and talked and listened to people—thereby gathering material for the stories she would write, becoming interested in the importance of place in fiction, and attuning her ear to the rhythms of southern speech. A member of the American Academy and Institute of Arts and Letters, she received numerous grants and awards for her fiction. Among them are three O. Henry awards for her short stories, the William Dean Howells medal from the American Academy of Arts and Letters for *The Ponder Heart* (1954), a National Book Award nomination for *Losing Battles* (1970), and a Pulitzer Prize for *The Optimist's Daughter* (1972). She won an American Book Award for *The Collected Stories of Eudora Welty* (1980), and a Christopher Book Award for *One Time, One Place: Mississippi in the Depression; A Snapshot Album* (1971), her collection of photographs, mostly of Mississippi sharecropper families. Although she lectured and taught at a number of colleges and universities in the United States and in England, she always returned to Jackson. Welty thinks that affinity with place gives southerners a "narrative sense of human destiny." In a 1972 interview, she explained, "There's someone to remember a man's whole life, every bit of the way along. I think that's a marvelous thing, and I'm glad I got to know something of it. In New York you may have the greatest and most congenial friends, but it's extraordinary if you ever know anything about them except that little wedge of their life that you meet with the little wedge of your life. You don't get that sense of a continuous narrative line. You never see the full circle. But in the South, where people don't move about as much, even now, and where they once hardly ever moved at all, the pattern of life was always right there." Welty's first novel, *Delta Wedding* (1946), was inspired by her memories of growing up, and her last book, *One Writer's Beginnings* (1984), which won an American Book Award, traces her development as a writer back to childhood experiences. The following excerpts from the "Listening" section of this memoir are meditations on the development of the distinctive narrative voices in her fiction.

from One Writer's Beginnings

Evangelists visited Jackson then; along with the Redpath Chautauqua and political speakings, they seemed to be part of August. Gypsy Smith was a great local favorite. He was an evangelist, but the term meant nothing like what it stands for today. He had no "team," no organization, no big business, no public address system; he wasn't a showman. Billy Sunday, a little later on, who preached with the athletics of a baseball player, threw off his coat when he got going, and in his shirtsleeves and red suspenders, he wound up and pitched his punchlines into the audience.

Gypsy Smith was a real Gypsy; in this may have lain part of his magnetism, though he spoke with sincerity too. He was so persuasive that, as night after night went by, he saved "everybody in Jackson," saved all the well-known businessmen on Capitol Street. They might well have been churchgoers already, but they never had been saved by Gypsy Smith. While amalgamated Jackson church choirs sang "Softly and Tenderly Jesus Is Calling" and "Just as I Am," Gypsy Smith called, and being saved—standing up and coming forward—swept Jackson like an epidemic. Most spectacular of all, the firebrand editor of the evening newspaper rose up and came forward one night. It made him lastingly righteous so that he knew just what to say in the *Jackson Daily News* when one of our fellow Mississippians had the unmitigated gall to publish, and expect other Mississippians to read, a book like *Sanctuary*.

Gypsy Smith may have been a Methodist; I don't know. At any rate, our Sunday school class was expected to attend, but I did not go up to be saved. Though all my life susceptible to anyone on a stage, I never would have been able to hold up my hand in front of the crowd at the City Auditorium and "come forward" while the choir leaned out singing "Come home! Come home! All God's children, come home, come home!" And I never felt anything like the pang of secular longing that I'd felt as a much younger child to go up onto the stage at the Century Theatre when the magician dazzlingly called for the valuable assistance of a child from the audience in the performance of his next feat of magic.

Neither was my father among the businessmen who were saved. As if the whole town were simply going through a temperamental meteorological disturbance, he remained calm and at home on Congress Street.

My mother did too. She liked reading her Bible in her own rocking chair, and while she rocked. She considered herself something of a student. "Run get me my Concordance," she'd say, referring to a little book bound in thin leather, falling apart. She liked to correct herself. Then from time to time her lips would twitch in the stern books of the Bible, such as Romans, providing her as they did with memories of her Grandfather Carden who had been a Baptist preacher in the days when she grew up in West Virginia. She liked to try in retrospect to correct Grandpa too.

I painlessly came to realize that the reverence I felt for the holiness of life is not ever likely to be entirely at home in organized religion. It was later, when I was able to travel farther, that the presence of holiness and mystery seemed, as far as my vision was able to see, to descend into the windows of Chartres, the stone peasant figures in the capitals of Autun, the tall sheets of gold on the walls of Torcello that reflected the light of the sea; in the frescoes of Piero, of Giotto; in the shell of a church wall in Ireland still standing on a floor of sheep-cropped grass with no ceiling other than the changing sky.

I'm grateful that, from my mother's example, I had found the base for this worship—that I had found a love of sitting and reading the Bible for myself and looking up things in it.

How many of us, the South's writers-to-be of my generation, were blessed in one way or another, if not blessed alike, in not having gone deprived of the King James Version of the Bible. Its cadence entered into our ears and our memories for good. The evidence, or the ghost of it, lingers in all our books.

"In the beginning was the Word."

In that vanished time in small-town Jackson, most of the ladies I was familiar with, the mothers of my friends in the neighborhood, were busiest when they were sociable. In the afternoons there was regular visiting up and down the little grid of residential streets. Everybody had calling cards, even certain children; and newborn babies themselves were properly announced by sending out their tiny engraved calling cards attached with a pink or blue bow to those of their parents. Graduation presents to high-school pupils were often "card cases." On the hall table in every house the first thing you saw was a silver tray waiting to receive more calling cards on top of the stack already piled up like jackstraws; they were never thrown away.

My mother let none of this idling, as she saw it, pertain to her; she went her own way with or without her calling cards, and though she was fond of her friends and they were fond of her, she had little time for small talk. At first, I hadn't known what I'd missed.

When we at length bought our first automobile, one of our neighbors was often invited to go with us on the family Sunday afternoon ride. In Jackson it was counted an affront to the neighbors to start out for

anywhere with an empty seat in the car. My mother
sat in the back with her friend, and I'm told that as a
small child I would ask to sit in the middle, and say
as we started off, "Now *talk*."

There was dialogue throughout the lady's accounts
to my mother. "I said" . . . "He said" . . . "And I'm
told she very plainly said" . . . "It was midnight before
they finally heard, and what do you think it *was*?"

What I loved about her stories was that everything
happened in *scenes*. I might not catch on to what the
root of the trouble was in all that happened, but my
ear told me it was dramatic. Often she said, "The crisis
had come!"

This same lady was one of Mother's callers on the
telephone who always talked a long time. I knew who
it was when my mother would only reply, now and
then, "Well, I declare," or "You don't say so," or
"Surely not." She'd be standing at the wall telephone,
listening against her will, and I'd sit on the stairs close
by her. Our telephone had a little bar set into the
handle which had to be pressed and held down to
keep the connection open, and when her friend had
said goodbye, my mother needed me to prize her fingers loose from the little bar; her grip had become
paralyzed. "What did she say?" I asked.

"She wasn't *saying* a thing in this world," sighed my
mother. "She was just ready to talk, that's all."

My mother was right. Years later, beginning with
my story "Why I Live at the P.O.," I wrote reasonably
often in the form of a monologue that takes possession
of the speaker. How much more gets told besides!

This lady told everything in her sweet, marveling
voice, and meant every word of it kindly. She enjoyed
my company perhaps even more than my mother's.
She invited me to catch her doodlebugs; under the
trees in her backyard were dozens of their holes.
When you stuck a broom straw down one and called,
"Doodlebug, doodlebug, your house is on fire and all
your children are burning up," she believed this is why

the doodlebug came running out of the hole. This was why I loved to call up her doodlebugs instead of ours.

My mother could never have told me her stories, and I think I knew why even then: my mother didn't believe them. But I could listen to this murmuring lady all day. She believed everything she heard, like the doodlebug. And so did I.

This was a day when ladies' and children's clothes were very often made at home. My mother cut out all the dresses and her little boys' rompers, and a sewing woman would come and spend the day upstairs in the sewing room fitting and stitching them all. This was Fannie. This old black sewing woman, along with her speed and dexterity, brought along a great provision of up-to-the-minute news. She spent her life going from family to family in town and worked right in its bosom, and nothing could stop her. My mother would try, while I stood being pinned up. "Fannie, I'd rather Eudora didn't hear that." "That" would be just what I was longing to hear, whatever it was. "I don't want her exposed to gossip"—as if gossip were measles and I could catch it. I did catch some of it but not enough. "Mrs. O'Neil's oldest daughter she had her wedding dress *tried on,* and all her fine underclothes feather-stitched and ribbon run in and then—" "I think that will do, Fannie," said my mother. It was tantalizing never to be exposed long enough to hear the end.

Fannie was the worldliest old woman to be imagined. She could do whatever her hands were doing without having to stop talking; and she could speak in a wonderfully derogatory way with any number of pins stuck in her mouth. Her hands steadied me like claws as she stumped on her knees around me, tacking me together. The gist of her tale would be lost on me, but Fannie didn't bother about the ear she was telling it to; she just liked telling. She was like an author. In fact, for a good deal of what she said, I daresay she *was* the author.

Long before I wrote stories, I listened for stories.

Listening *for* them is something more acute than listening *to* them. I suppose it's an early form of participation in what goes on. Listening children know stories are *there*. When their elders sit and begin, children are just waiting and hoping for one to come out, like a mouse from its hole.

It was taken entirely for granted that there wasn't any lying in our family, and I was advanced in adolescence before I realized that in plenty of homes where I played with schoolmates and went to their parties, children lied to their parents and parents lied to their children and to each other. It took me a long time to realize that these very same everyday lies, and the stratagems and jokes and tricks and dares that went with them, were in fact the basis of the *scenes* I so well loved to hear about and hoped for and treasured in the conversation of adults.

My instinct—the dramatic instinct—was to lead me, eventually, on the right track for a storyteller: the *scene* was full of hints, pointers, suggestions, and promises of things to find out and know about human beings. I had to grow up and learn to listen for the unspoken as well as the spoken—and to know a truth, I also had to recognize a lie.

Bobbie Ann Mason

Bobbie Ann Mason was born in Mayfield, Kentucky, in 1940, the daughter of a dairy farmer. After she graduated from the University of Kentucky, she moved to New York City to write for television and movie fan magazines. Later she received an M.A. from the State University of New York at Binghamton and a Ph.D. from the University of Connecticut. Her stories appear regularly in such magazines as *The New Yorker, The Atlantic Monthly,* and *Redbook,* and they have been selected for such anthologies as *Best American Short Stories, The Pushcart Prize,* and *The O. Henry Awards*. Her characters typically are farmers and working-class people who inhabit a contemporary rural southern landscape that is rapidly changing. Bobbie Ann Mason has said, "I think the culture I write about is very distinctly southern. I don't think the people I write about are obsessed with the Past. I don't think they know anything about the Civil War, and I don't think they care. They're kind of naive and optimistic for the most part: they think better times are coming." Although for much of her adult life she lived in Pennsylvania, in her writing she has always captured the colloquial speech of the place where she grew up. Mason has published three story collections, *Zigzagging Down a Wild Trail* (2001), *Love Life* (1989), and *Shiloh and Other Stories* (1982), which won the Ernest Hemingway Foundation Award and the PEN/Faulkner Award for Fiction, as well as three novels, *In Country* (1985), *Spence + Lila* (1988), and *Feather*

Crowns (1993), which won the Southern Book Award. While she sets her fiction in the contemporary South of housing developments, shopping malls, and chain stores, her memoir, *Clear Springs* (1999), takes readers back to the Kentucky of her youth. She is also the author of two works of criticism, *Nabokov's Garden: A Nature Guide to Ada* (1974) and *The Girl Sleuth: A Feminist Guide to the Bobbsey Twins, Nancy Drew, and Their Sisters* (1975). She has written that her interest in childhood "extends all the way from Nancy Drew to Nabokov, whose magnificent childhood permeates all his works. . . . He read Pushkin as a child, whereas I read Nancy Drew. I am interested in that contrast as a literary theme, and in the culture shock one can experience because of geographical and economic isolation."

State Champions

In 1952, when I was in the seventh grade in Cuba, Kentucky, the Cuba Cubs were the state champions in high school basketball. When the Cubs returned from the tournament in Lexington, a crowd greeted them at Eggner's Ferry bridge over Kentucky Lake, and a convoy fourteen miles long escorted them to Mayfield, the county seat. It was a cold day in March as twelve thousand people watched the Cubs ride around the courthouse square in convertibles. The mayor and other dignitaries made speeches. Willie Foster, the president of the Merit Clothing Company, gave the players and Coach Jack Story free suits from his factory. The coach, a chunky guy in a trench coat like a character in a forties movie, told the crowd, "I'm mighty glad we could bring back the big trophy." And All-Stater Howie Crittenden, the razzle-dazzle dribbler, said, "There are two things I'm proud of today. First, we won the tournament, and second, Mr. Story said we made him feel like a young mule."

The cheerleaders then climbed up onto the concrete seat sections of the Confederate monument and led a final fight yell.

> *Chick-a-lacka, chick-a-lacka chow, chow, chow*
> *Boom-a-lacka, boom-a-lacka bow, wow, wow*
> *Chick-a-lacka, boom-a-lacka, who are we?*
> *Cuba High School, can't you see?*

The next day the Cubs took off in the convertibles

again, leading a motorcade around western Kentucky,
visiting the schools in Sedalia, Mayfield, Farmington,
Murray, Hardin, Benton, Sharpe, Reidland, Paducah,
Kevil, La Center, Barlow, Wickliffe, Bardwell, Arlington, Clinton, Fulton, and Pilot Oak.

I remember the hoopla at the square that day, but
at the time I felt a strange sort of distance, knowing
that in another year another community would have
its champions. I was twelve years old and going
through a crisis, so I thought I had a wise understanding of the evanescence of victory.

But years later, in the seventies, in upstate New
York, I met a man who surprised me by actually remembering the Cuba Cubs' championship. He was a
Kentuckian, and although he was from the other side
of the state, he had lasting memories of Howie Crittenden and Doodle Floyd. Howie was a great dribbler,
he said. And Doodle had a windmill hook shot that
had to be seen to be believed. The Cubs were inspired
by the Harlem Globetrotters—Marcus Haynes's ball
handling influenced Howie and Goose Tatum was
Doodle's model. The Cuba Cubs, I was told, were, in
fact, the most incredible success story in the history
of Kentucky high school basketball, and the reason
was that they were such unlikely champions.

"Why, they were just a handful of country boys who
could barely afford basketball shoes," the man told
me in upstate New York.

"They were?" This was news to me.

"Yes. They were known as the Cinderella Cubs.
One afternoon during the tournament they were at
Memorial Coliseum watching the Kentucky Wildcats
practice. The Cubs weren't in uniform, but one of
them called for a ball and dribbled it a few times and
then canned a two-hand set shot from midcourt.
Adolph Rupp happened to be watching. He's another
Kentucky basketball legend—don't you know anything about Kentucky basketball? He rushed to the
player at midcourt and demanded, 'How did you do

that?' The boy just smiled. 'It was easy, Mr. Rupp,' he said. 'Ain't no wind in here.' "

Of course that was not my image of the Cuba Cubs at all. I hadn't realized they were just a bunch of farm boys who got together behind the barn after school and shot baskets in the dirt, while the farmers around complained that the boys would never amount to anything. I hadn't known how Coach Jack Story had started them off in the seventh grade, coaching the daylights out of those kids until he made them believe they could be champions. To me, just entering junior high the year they won the tournament, the Cuba Cubs were the essence of glamour. Seeing them in the gym—standing tall in those glossy green satin uniforms, or racing down the court, leaping like deer— took my breath away. They had crew cuts and wore real basketball shoes. And the cheerleaders dressed smartly in Crayola-green corduroy circle skirts, saddle oxfords, and rolled-down socks. They had green corduroy jackets as well as green sweaters, with a C cutting through the symbol of a megaphone. They clapped their hands in rhythm and orchestrated their elbows in a little dance that in some way mimicked the Cubs as they herded the ball down the court. "Go, Cubs, Go!" "Fight, Cubs, Fight!" They did "Locomotive, locomotive, steam, steam, steam," and "Strawberry shortcake, huckleberry pie." We had pep rallies that were like revival services in tone and intent. The cheerleaders pirouetted and zoomed skyward in unison, their legs straight and clean like jump shots. They whirled in their circle skirts, showing off their green tights underneath.

I never questioned the words of the yells, any more than I questioned the name Cuba Cubs. I didn't know what kind of cubs they were supposed to be—bear cubs or wildcats or foxes—but I never thought about it. I doubt if anyone did. It was the sound of the words that mattered, not the meaning. They were the Cubs. And that was it. Cuba was a tiny community with a

couple of general stores, and its name is of doubtful
origin, but local historians say that when the Cuba
post office opened, in the late 1850s, the Ostend Mani-
festo had been in the news. This was a plan the United
States had for getting control of the island of Cuba in
order to expand the slave trade. The United States
demanded that Spain either sell us Cuba at a fair price
or surrender it outright. Perhaps the founding fathers
of Cuba, Kentucky (old-time pronunciation: Cubie),
were swayed by the fuss with Spain. Or maybe they
just had romantic imaginations. In the Jackson Purchase, the western region of Kentucky and Tennessee
that Andrew Jackson purchased from the Chickasaw
Indians in 1818, there are other towns with faraway
names: Moscow, Dublin, Kansas, Cadiz, Beulah, Paris,
and Dresden.

The gymnasium where the Cuba Cubs practiced was
the hub of the school. Their trophies gleamed in a
glass display case near the entrance of the school, between the principal's office and the gymnasium, and
the enormous coal furnace that heated the gym
hunched in a corner next to the bleachers. Several
classrooms opened onto the gym floor, with the study
hall at one end. The lower grades occupied a separate
building, and in those grades we used an outhouse.
But in junior high we had the privilege of using the
indoor restrooms, which also opened onto the gym.
(The boys' room included a locker room for the team,
but like the outhouses, the girls' room didn't even
have private compartments.) The route from the study
hall to the girls' room was dangerous. We had to walk
through the gym, along the sidelines, under some
basketball hoops. There were several baskets, so many
players could practice their shots simultaneously. At
recess and lunch, in addition to the Cuba Cubs, all the
junior high boys used the gym too, in frantic emulation
of their heroes. On the way to the restroom you had

to calculate quickly and carefully when you could run beneath a basket. The players pretended that they were oblivious to you, but just when you thought you were safe and could dash under the basket, they would hurl a ball out of nowhere and the ball would fall on your head as you streaked by. Even though I was sort of a tomboy and liked to run—back in the fifth grade I could run as fast as most of the boys—I had no desire to play basketball. It was too violent.

Doodle Floyd himself bopped me on the head once, but I doubt if he remembers it.

The year of the championship was the year I got in trouble for running in the study hall. At lunch hour one day, Judy Howell and I decided to run the length of the gym as fast as we could, daring ourselves to run through the hailstorm of basketballs flying at us. We raced through the gym and kept on running, unable to slow down, finally skidding to a stop in the study hall. We were giggling because we had caught a glimpse of what one of the senior players was wearing under his green practice shorts (different from the satin show shorts they wore at the games), when Mr. Gilhorn, the history teacher, big as a buffalo, appeared before us and growled, "What do you young ladies think you're doing?"

I had on the tightest Levi's I owned. When they were newly washed and ironed, they fit snug. My mother had ironed a crease in them. I had on a cowboy shirt and a bandanna.

Mr. Gilhorn went on, "Now girls, do we run in our own living rooms? Does your mama let you run in the house?"

"Yes," I said, staring at him confidently. "My mama always lets me run in the house." It was a lie, of course, but it was my habit to contradict whatever anybody assumed. If I was supposed to be a lady, then I would be a cowboy. The truth in this instance was that it had never occurred to me to run in our house.

It was too small, and the floorboards were shaky. Therefore, I reasoned, my mother had never laid down the law about not running in the house.

Judy said, "We won't do it again." But I wouldn't promise.

"I know what would be good for you girls," said Mr. Gilhorn in a kindly, thoughtful tone, as if he had just had a great idea.

That meant the duckwalk. As punishment, Judy and I had to squat, grabbing our ankles, and duckwalk around the gym. We waddled, humiliated, with the basketballs beating on our heads and the players following our progress with loud quacks of derision.

"This was your fault," Judy claimed. She stopped speaking to me, which disappointed me because we had been playmates since the second grade. I admired her short blond curls and color-coordinated outfits. She had been to Detroit one summer.

During study-hall periods, we could hear the basketballs pounding the floor. We could tell when a player made a basket—that pause after the ball hit the backboard and sank luxuriously into the net before hitting the floor. I visited the library more often than necessary just to get a glimpse of the Cubs practicing as I passed the door to the gym. The library was a shelf at one end of study hall, and it had a couple of hundred old books—mostly hand-me-downs from the Graves County Library, including outdated textbooks and even annuals from Kentucky colleges. That year I read some old American histories, and a biography of Benjamin Franklin, and the "Junior Miss" books. On the wainscoted walls of the study hall were gigantic framed pictures, four feet high, each composed of inset portraits of all the faculty members and the seniors of a specific year. They gazed down at us like kings and queens on playing cards. There was a year for each frame, and they dated all the way back to the early forties.

In junior high, we shared the study hall with the

high school students. The big room was drafty, and in the winter it was very cold. The boys were responsible for keeping the potbelly stove filled with coal from the coal pile outside, near where the school buses were parked. In grade school during the winter, I had worn long pants under my dresses—little starched print dresses with gathered skirts and puffed sleeves. But in junior high, the girls wore blue jeans, like the boys, except that we rolled them up almost to our knees. The Cuba Cubs wore Levi's and green basketball jackets, and the other high school boys—the Future Farmers of America—wore bright blue FFA jackets. Although the FFA jackets didn't have the status of the basketball jackets, they were beautiful. They were royal-blue corduroy and on the back was an enormous gold eagle, embraced by the words "KENTUCKY" and "GRAVES" (for Graves County).

I had a crush on a freshman named Glenn in an FFA jacket. He helped manage the coal bucket in the study hall. Glenn didn't ride my bus. He lived in Dukedom, down across the Tennessee line. Glenn was one of the Cuba Cubs, but he wasn't one of the major Cubs—he was on the B team and didn't yet have a green jacket. But I admired his dribble, and his long legs could travel that floor like a bicycle. When I waited at the edge of the gym for my chance to bolt to the girls' room, I sometimes stood and watched him dribble. Then one day as I ran pell-mell to the restroom, his basketball hit me on the head and he called to me flirtatiously. "I got a claim on her," he yelled out to the world. If a boy had a claim on a girl, it meant she was his girlfriend. The next day in study hall he showed me an "eight-page novel." It was a Li'l Abner comic strip. In the eight-page novel, Li'l Abner peed on Daisy Mae. It was disgusting, but I was thrilled that he showed me the booklet.

"Hey, let me show you these hand signals," Glenn said a couple of days later, out on the playground. "In case you ever need them." He stuck his middle finger

straight up and folded the others down. "That's single
F," he said. Then he turned down his two middle fingers, leaving the forefinger and the little finger upright,
like horns. That's double *F*," he said confidently.

"Oh," I said. At first I thought he meant hand signals used in driving. Cars didn't have automatic turn
signals then.

There were other hand signals. In basketball, the
coach and the players exchanged finger gestures. The
cheerleaders clapped us on to victory. And with lov-
ers, lightly scraping the index finger on the other's
palm meant "Do you want to?" and responding the
same way meant "Yes." If you didn't know this and
you held hands with a boy, you might inadvertently
agree to do something that you had no intention of
doing.

Seventh grade was the year we had a different teacher
for each subject. Arithmetic became mathematics. The
English teacher paddled Frances High and me for
stealing Jack Reed's Milky Way from his desk. Jack
Reed had even told us he didn't mind that we stole
it, that he wanted us to have it. "The paddling didn't
hurt," I said to him proudly. He was cute, but not as
cute as Glenn, who had a crooked grin I thought was
fascinating and later found reincarnated in Elvis. In
the study hall I stood in front of the stove until my
backside was soaked with heat. I slid my hands down
the back of my legs and felt the sharp crease of my
Levi's. I was in a perpetual state of excitement. It was
1952 and the Cuba Cubs were on their way to the
championship.

Judy was still mad at me, but Glenn's sister Willowdean was in my class, and I contrived to go home with
her one evening, riding her unfamiliar school bus
along gravel roads far back into the country. Country
kids didn't socialize much. To go home with someone
and spend the night was a big event, strange and un-
predictable. Glenn and Willowdean lived with three

brothers and sisters in a small house surrounded by bare, stubbled tobacco fields. It was a wintry day, but Willowdean and I played outdoors, and I watched for Glenn to arrive.

He had stayed late at school, practicing ball, and the coach brought him home. Then he had his chores to do. At suppertime, when he came in with his father from milking, his mother handed him a tray of food. "Come on and go with me," he said to me. His Levi's were smudged with cow manure.

His mother said, "Make sure she's got her teeth."

"Have you got your teeth?" Glenn asked me with a grin.

His mother swatted at him crossly. "I meant Bluma. You know who I meant."

Glenn motioned with a nod of his head for me to follow him, and we went to a tiny back room where Glenn's grandmother sat in a wheelchair in a corner with a heater at her feet. She had dark hair and lips painted bright orange and a growth on her neck.

"She don't talk," Glenn said. "But she can hear."

The strange woman jerked her body in a spasm of acknowledgment as Glenn set the supper tray in her lap. He fished her teeth out of a glass of water and poked them in her mouth. She squeaked like a mouse.

"Are you hungry?" Glenn asked me as we left the room. "We've got chicken and dumplings tonight. That's my favorite."

That night I slept with Willowdean on a fold-out couch in the living room, with newspaper-wrapped hot bricks at our feet. We huddled under four quilts and whispered. I worked the conversation around to Glenn.

"He told me he liked you," Willowdean said.

I could feel myself flush. At supper, Glenn had tickled me under the table.

"I'll tell you a secret if you promise not to tell," she said.

"What?" I loved secrets and usually didn't tell them.

"Betty Jean's going to have a baby."

Willowdean's sister Betty Jean was a sophomore.
On the school bus her boyfriend Roy Matthews had
kept his arm around her during the whole journey,
while she cracked gum and looked pleased with herself. That evening at the supper table, Glenn and his
brothers had teased her about Roy's big feet.

Willowdean whispered now, "Did you see the way
she ate supper? Like a pig. That's because she has to
eat for two. She's got a baby in her stomach."

"What will she do?" I asked, scared. The warmth
of the bricks was fading, and I knew it would be a
freezing night.

"Her and Roy will live with us," said Willowdean.
"That's what my sister May Lou did at first. But then
she got mad and took the baby off and went to live
with her husband's folks. She said they treated her
better."

The high school classes were small because kids
dropped out, to have babies and farm. They seemed
to disappear, like our calves going off to the slaughterhouse in the fall, and it was creepy.

"I don't want to have a baby and have to quit
school," I said.

"You don't?" Willowdean was surprised. "What do
you want to go to school for?"

I didn't answer. I didn't have the words handy. But
she didn't seem to notice. She turned over and pulled
the quilts with her. In the darkness, I could hear a
mouse squeaking. But it wasn't a mouse. It was Willowdean's grandmother, in her cold room at the back
of the house.

That winter, while basketball fever raged, a student
teacher from Murray State College taught Kentucky
history. She was very pretty and resembled a picture
of Pocahontas in one of the library books. One time
when she sat down, flipping her large gathered skirt
up, I saw her panties. They were pink. She was so

soft-spoken she didn't know how to make us behave well enough to accomplish any classwork. Daniel Boone's exploits were nothing, compared to Doodle Floyd's. During the week the Cubs were at the tournament Pocahontas couldn't keep us quiet. The school was raising money for next year's basketball uniforms, and each class sold candy and cookies our mothers had made. Frequently there was a knock at the door, and some kids from another grade would be there selling Rice Krispies squares wrapped in waxed paper, or brownies, or sometimes divinity fudge. One day, while Pocahontas was reading to us about Daniel Boone and the Indians, and we were throwing paper wads, there was a sudden pounding on the door. I was hoping for divinity, and I had a nickel with me, but the door burst open and Judy Howell's sister Georgia was there, crying, "Judy Bee! Mama's had a wreck and Linda Faye's killed."

Judy flew out of the room. For one moment the class was quiet, and then it went into an uproar. Pocahontas didn't know what to do, so she gave us a pop quiz. The next day we learned that Judy's little sister Linda Faye, who was three years old, had been thrown into a ditch when her mother slammed into a truck that had pulled out in front of her. The seventh-grade class took up a collection for flowers. I was stunned by the news of death, for I had never known a child to die. I couldn't sleep, and my mind went over and over the accident, imagining the truck plowing into the car and Linda Faye pitching out the door or through the window. I created various scenes, ways it might have happened. I kept seeing her stretched out stiff on her side, like the dead animals I had seen on our farm. At school I was sleepy, and I escaped into daydreams about Glenn, imagining that I had gone to Lexington too, to watch him in triumph as he was called in from the sidelines to replace Doodle Floyd, who had turned his ankle.

It was a sober, long walk from the study hall to the

restroom. The gymnasium seemed desolate, without the Cubs practicing. I walked safely down the gym, remembering the time in the fourth grade when I was a flower girl in the court of the basketball queen. I had carried an Easter basket filled with flower petals down the center of the gym, scattering rose petals so the queen could step on them as she minced slowly toward her throne.

I was too scared to go to the funeral, and my parents didn't want me to go. My father had been traumatized by funerals in his childhood and he didn't think they were a good idea. "The Howells live so far away," Mama said. "And it looks like snow."

That weekend, the tournament was on the radio, and I listened carefully, hoping to hear Glenn's name. The final game was crazy. In the background, the cheerleaders chanted:

> *Warren, Warren, he's our man*
> *If he can't do it—*
> *Floyd can*
> *Floyd, Floyd, he's our man*
> *If he can't do it*
> *Crittenden can—*

The announcer was saying, "Crittenden's dribbling has the crowd on its feet. It's a thrilling game! The Cubs were beaten twice by this same Louisville Manual squad during the season, but now they've just inched ahead. The Cubs pulled even at 39–39 when Floyd converted a charity flip, and then Warren sent them ahead for the first time with a short one-hander on Crittenden's pass. The crowd is going wild!"

Toward the end of the game the whole Coliseum—except for a small Manual cheering section—was yelling, "Hey, hey, what do you say? It looks like Cuba all the way!"

As I listened to the excited announcer chatter about huddles and timeouts and driving jumps and hook shots, I forgot about Judy, but then on Sunday, when I went to the courthouse square to welcome the Cubs home, her sister's death struck me again like fresh news. Seeing so many people celebrating made me feel uncomfortable, as if the death of a child always went unnoticed, like a dead dog by the side of the road. It was a cold day, and I had to wear a dress because it was Sunday. I wanted to see Glenn. I had an audacious plan. I had been thinking about it all night. I wanted to give him a hug, of congratulations. I would plant a big wet kiss on his cheek. I had seen a cheerleader do this to one of the players once after he made an unusual number of free throws. It was at a home game, one of the few I attended. I wanted to hug Glenn because it would be my answer to his announcement that he had a claim on me. It would be silent, without explanation, but he would know what it meant.

I managed to lose my parents in the throng and I headed for the east side of the square, where the dime store was. Suddenly I saw Judy, with her mother, in front of a shoe store. I knew the funeral had been the day before, but here they were at the square, in the middle of a celebration. Judy and her mother were still in their Sunday church clothes. Judy saw me. She looked straight at me, then turned away. I pretended I hadn't seen her and I hurried to the center of the square, looking for Glenn.

But when I finally saw him up ahead, I stopped. He looked different. The Cubs, I learned later, had all gone to an Army surplus store and bought themselves pairs of Army fatigue pants and porkpie hats. Glenn looked unfamiliar in his basketball jacket—now he had one—and the baggy Army fatigues instead of his Levi's. The hat looked silly. I thought about Judy, and how her sister's death had occurred while Glenn was away playing basketball and buying new clothes. I wanted to tell him what it was like to be at home when such a terrible thing happened, but I couldn't, even though I saw him not thirty feet from me. As I hesitated, I saw his parents and Willowdean and one of his brothers crowd around him. Playfully Willowdean knocked his hat off.

The tournament was over, but we were still wild with our victory. Senior play practice started then, and we never had classes in the afternoon because all the teachers were busy coaching the seniors on their lines in the play. Maybe they had dreams of Broadway. If the Cubs could go to the tournament, anything was possible. Judy returned to school, but everyone was afraid to speak to her. They whispered behind her back. And Judy began acting aloof, as though she had some secret knowledge that lifted her above us.

On one last cool day in early spring we had cleanup day, and there were no classes all day. Everyone was supposed to help clean the school grounds, picking up all the discarded candy wrappers and drink bottles. There was a bonfire, and instead of a plate lunch in the lunchroom—too much like the plain farm food we had to eat at home—we had hot dogs, boiled outside in a kettle over the fire. The fat hot dogs in the cold air tasted heavenly. They steamed like breath.

Just as I finished my hot dog and drank the last of my RC (we had a choice between RC Cola and Orange Crush and I liked to notice which people chose which—it seemed to divide people into categories), Judy came up behind me and whispered, "Come out there with me." She pointed toward the graveyard across the road.

I followed her, and as we walked between solemn rows of Wilcoxes and Ingrahams and Morrisons and Crittendens, the noise of the playground receded. Judy located a spot of earth, a little brown heap that was not grassed over, even though the dandelions had already come up and turned to fluff. She knelt beside the dirt pile, like a child in a sandbox, and fussed with a pot of artificial flowers. She straightened them and poked them down into the pot, as if they were real.

As she worked tenderly but firmly with the flowers, she said, "Mama says Linda Faye will be waiting for us in heaven. That's her true home. The preacher said we should feel special, to think we have a member of our family all the way up in heaven."

That was sort of how I had felt about Glenn, going to Lexington to the basketball tournament, and I didn't know what to say. I couldn't say anything, for we weren't raised to say things that were heartfelt and gracious. Country kids didn't learn manners. Manners were too embarrassing. Learning not to run in the house was about the extent of what we knew about how to act. We didn't learn to congratulate people; we didn't wish people happy birthday. We didn't even address each other by name. And we didn't jump up and spontaneously hug someone for joy. Only cheerleaders claimed that talent. We didn't say we were sorry. We hid from view, in case we might be called on to make appropriate remarks, the way certain old folks in church were sometimes called on to pray. At Cuba School, there was one teacher who, for punishment, made her students write "I love you" five hundred times on the blackboard. "Love" was a dirty word, and I had seen it on the walls of the girls' restroom—blazing there in ugly red lipstick. In the eight-page novel Glenn showed me, Li'l Abner said "I love you" to Daisy Mae.

Gustavo Pérez Firmat

Gustavo Pérez Firmat was born in Havana in 1949, but after the Castro Revolution his family left Cuba for Miami. At the age of eleven he became a member of what has been called the "one-and-a-half" generation, Cuban-Americans who were born in Cuba but raised in America. In his memoir *Next Year in Cuba: A Cubano's Coming-of-Age in America* (1995), which I have excerpted here, Firmat explains, "As a one-and-a-halfer, I'm too old to be entirely American, but too young to be anything else—a condition that I share with many other Hispanic Americans as well as with immigrants from other cultures and lands. Born in Cuba but made in the U.S.A., I can no longer imagine living outside American culture and the English language. And yet Cuba remains my true home, the place that decisively shaped my character and my values. My life is a delicate balancing act between two countries, two cultures, two languages. Ask me where I really belong, in Cuba or in America, and I wouldn't be able to tell you, because I belong in both." After undergraduate work at the University of Miami and graduate work at the University of Michigan, Firmat became a professor at Duke University. Since then he has published many works of literary and cultural criticism, among them *The Cuban Condition: Translation and Identity in Modern Cuban Literature* (1988), *Life on the Hyphen: The Cuban-American Way* (1994), and *My Own Private Cuba: Essays on Cuban Literature and Culture* (1999), as well as volumes of poetry,

Carolina Cuban (1988), *Equivocaciones* (1989), and *Bilingual Blues* (1995), and most recently a novel, *Anything but Love* (2000). As the titles suggest, both Firmat's scholarly writing and his creative writing reflect his "delicate balancing act." Living has become a balancing act as well, as he now divides his time between North Carolina and New York, where he is David Feinson Professor in the Humanities at Columbia University.

Mooning over Miami

Little Havana, 1960s and beyond

When I entered ninth grade in 1963, La Salle High School in Southwest Miami already had many Cuban students, but it was still predominantly American. American kids starred on the sports teams, ran the student council, edited the newspaper and the yearbook. But by the time I became a senior, La Salle had metamorphosed into "Lah-Sah-yeh," an exile franchise of my old Havana academy, with some American Brothers and lay teachers, but also with some of the same Brothers and students from Cuba. At La Salle I had classmates whom I had known since the first grade in Cuba. My Spanish teacher in high school, Hermano Andrés, was the same teacher who had taught third grade in Cuba; he now taught Spanish because he didn't know any English. Elio the bus driver, who drove the La Salle varsity teams to their games, had driven a bus at the Cuban school.

The chemistry teacher at La Salle, Hermano Ramón, was another transplant from Havana. Everyone called him Plátano, because his curved, elongated body and head made him look like a banana. Unlike the other Cuban Brothers, Plátano was a loner who always wore a pained, doleful expression on his face. I never saw him without his black habit. If you ran into Plátano in the hall, he would acknowledge your existence by lifting his drooping head an inch or two and curling his lips ever so slightly, but without stopping or saying a word. Inside the classroom, he was all business—I should say, all chemistry, a subject he loved but that he didn't seem to have mastered. What happened to the Spanish Armada sometimes happened to him—he was defeated by the elements. Although Plátano set up every experiment carefully and deliberately, at times the anticipated chemical reaction did not take place, or worse, an unanticipated one did. When something blew up or fizzled out, he was just as startled as the rest of us, although he quickly regained his composure. He accepted failure with a kind of resignation, as if it were a consequence of exile. The sad expression on his long face seemed to say, "In Cuba. sulfur and magnesium would not have reacted this way; in Cuba the elements did what they were supposed to." If anyone made fun of the botched experiment, he would issue a reprimand in Spanish, the only time he lapsed from his heavily accented but fluent English. *"Oye, chico,"* he would say sharply to the culprit, "we didn't come to this country to fool around."

As more and more exiles arrived in Miami, La Salle became known as the "Cuban" high school in the diocese. Although many Americans still attended—kids with names such as Perantoni and Pascawicz and Mac-Swiggan and Koziol—the dominant culture of the school quickly changed. At the sock hops and dances in the school cafeteria, even if we began with the music of Wilson Pickett, we ended up with Beny Moré. Sooner or later, someone would start a conga line. Although many of us went by the American version of our names—Gus (Pérez), Willie (Díaz), Charlie (Castillo), Joe (Martínez), Manny (Álvarez)—we mostly spoke Spanish and considered ourselves unassailably Cuban. Even as we absorbed American culture, we tended to "Cubanize" things we came in touch with. In football a tackle was *un palo* (the same word was used to denote a drink, a home run, and sexual intercourse); in basketball a blocked shot was *un tapón.* A nerd was *un mechero,* a drunk *un curda,* and a good-looking American girl was a *yegua* (but Cuban ones were *jebitas*). The school's signature cheer was one I had learned in Cuba: *"Bon-bon-chíe-chíe-chíe./Bon-bon-chíe-chíe-chá./Lah-Sah-yeh, Lah-Sah-yeh,/ rrah-rrah-rrah!"* The emotional high points of each basketball game came when the cheerleaders, who were American, started into a *bon-bon-chíe.* (Although many girls in our sister school, Immaculata, were also Cuban, they considered it vaguely slutty to parade in front of a crowd in a tight sweater and short skirt.) It was wonderful to see perky Catholic girls like Marti and Nancy lead a throng of rowdy Cuban teenagers in a *bon-bon-chíe.* Here we were, Cuban exiles in a foreign country, playing a sport like football or basketball and screaming in Cuban, being led by American cheerleaders in the same cheers we would have chanted in Havana. For the duration of the cheer, it seemed that we had never left, that our lifelines had not veered to the north. Screaming *bon-bon-chíe* in the Columbus High gym, where the La Salle Royals played home games, we were defying distance, denying discontinuity.

If the other students resented the *bon-bon-chíe,* I didn't notice. They seemed to launch into it with the same gusto that we did. What I remember is the American parents and kids and teachers looking upon us with a mixture of amusement and benevolence. Since we were as smart, as Catholic, as good-looking, and often as athletic as the Americans, there didn't seem to be any reason for condescension or disdain. If anything, *we* pitied the Americans because they weren't lucky enough to have been born Cuban. The only difference between the two groups was that the American kids had more money and nicer homes. They drove Mustangs and GTOs and lived in places like Coral Gables or South Miami; we lived in Little Havana and felt fortunate if we got our hands on a 1956 Olds. I search my memory now and I cannot come up with one single example of feeling ostracized or discriminated against because I was Cuban. I recall coming back in the team bus from a football or basketball game with everybody—at least I thought it was everybody—singing Cuban songs like "Los Elefantes" and "Guantanamera." Not once did I hear any of the Americans complain about the loud Cubans or their music. One Cuban guy on the team, Carlos Ziegenhirt (we called him Ziggy), had a beautiful tenor voice. When we got tired of singing in unison, Ziggy would serenade us with *boleros*. The darkened bus seemed a perfect setting for his romantic melodies. While Ziggy sang, our imaginations roamed free. Johnny Mathis had nothing on him.

At La Salle *los americanos* and *los cubanos* went their separate ways, but without friction or hostility. Each group had its customs, its coteries, its hangouts, its language. When we partied, we partied among ourselves. When we fought, we fought among ourselves. Although the Cubans sometimes dated American girls (the converse—a *cubana* with an *americano*—was very rare, because most Cuban girls required chaperones), almost everyone I hung out with eventually settled into a same-culture *novia* (girlfriend). Sometimes Cuban teenagers did American things—went to beach parties and drive-ins. Other times we hewed to old-country mores and learned the *danzón*—a ballroom dance—so that we could perform it at the *quinces,* the traditional coming-out ball for Cuban teenage girls. The convention of sticking to our own kind was not formal or explicit, and nobody ever told me or any of my friends to socialize with Cubans or stay away from Americans. It was just how we liked it.

The Chinatowns and Little Italys of large American cities suggest that most immigrants, upon first arriving in the U.S., tend to stick together. We were no different. A clannish people, Cubans seek out other Cubans. Not surprisingly (given that we are islanders), we like to insulate ourselves. When I was at La Salle, the American girls were enticing but the *cubanitas* were more comfortable. Yes, the Cuban girls expected (and got) more attention and commitment, but in return they looked after you in ways that the American girls didn't. For every pretty blonde there was an equally pretty, dark-haired girl like Ana María, my *novia* of several years.

For most of us, the *americanas* were a lark, a hobby, a sometimes dangerous adventure in foreign relations. For a while during my senior year, my best friend was a guy called Grifolito (Cubans are big on diminutives—Grifolito was the younger of two brothers whose last name was Grifol). On Friday nights Grifolito and I would go to dances sponsored by the Police Benevolent Association. Held in an auditorium somewhere in South Miami and attended almost entirely by Americans, these dances provided happy hunting grounds for young Cuban charmers like us looking to meet and pick up *americanas,* an endeavor at which Grifolito excelled. Our word for picking up girls was *ligar,* literally to fasten or bind, and Grifolito was quite a *ligador.* In fact, he was a blonde-binding dynamo. I could never figure out Grifolito's secret—whether it was his clear complexion, his baby-blue eyes, his macho swagger, or his fearlessness—but whatever it was, it worked time after time. After the dances ended, I often had to wait in the car for half an hour while Grifolito, our Cuban goodwill-ambassador-in-exile, finished getting acquainted with his sweetheart for the night. On a good night, he didn't have to dance more than one or two songs before spending the rest of the evening outside, embracing a foreign culture.

One Friday I was milling around in the crowd, trying to hide from Grifolito the fact that I wasn't getting anywhere with any of the girls, when I brushed shoulders with some American guy. As usually happened with me, the brush led to a bump and the bump led to a face-off. Suddenly, I found myself surrounded by a horde of six-foot-tall, crew-cut, football-playing Charles Atlases. Although I was a football player myself—starting half-back on La Salle's varsity team, which won our conference my junior year—I was no match for my formidable gringo foes. Several inches short of six feet, I never could push my weight above 157 pounds, no matter how many barbells I lifted or how much food I ate (Spam isn't particularly rich in protein). Grifolito, who was heftier, came to my rescue, but the odds didn't look good for us. It would have been like the Spanish-American War all over again. I didn't mind rumbles, and the gang I belonged to (we called it a fraternity) started a few of them, but always against other Cubans, who may have been meaner or stronger than I was, but who weren't nearly as big as these action-figure types.

Just as Grifolito and I were about to get our army-surplus lunches handed back to us, I saw an apparition (remember, we were Catholic)—actually two apparitions—from my past, Pete Apeland and Buzzy Horne, who had been in Mrs. Myers's class at Dade Elementary and with whom I had played sports at the Boys Club. Although I hadn't run into them in years, I remembered Pete well, for he wasn't only the quarter-back on our team but Brigitte Johnson's cousin as well. Pete and Buz had been short and skinny when we had played together in the 115-pound-and-under league, but as teenagers they had sprouted into muscle-bound behemoths. Pete was a full head taller than I and had a scar that ran from his forehead to his cheek (the result of a motorcycle accident), and Buzzy was even bigger. He looked like Ray Nietzsche with hair. When Pete spotted me, he pushed his way through the crowd, with Buzzy right behind. Getting between me and the guy I had bumped shoulders with, Pete told the guy, "Gus is a friend of mine. If you want to fight him, you're going to have to fight me first." God bless *americanos*! The Rough Riders backed off, no Cuban blood was spilled that night, and Grifolito and I gratefully went back to our pursuit of the American dream.

Randall Kenan

Born in 1963 in Brooklyn, New York, Randall Kenan grew up in Chinquapin, North Carolina, which resembles the fictional Tims Creek of his novel and stories. A reviewer for the *Washington Post* said that in his descriptions of Tims Creek Kenan manages to conjure a place "at once specific to one imaginary corner of the South and yet somehow evocative of the entire region and period." The following excerpt from *Walking on Water: Black American Lives at the Turn of the Twenty-First Century* (1999) is a meditation on the small rural town where he grew up and the changes in Chinquapin since his boyhood. After graduating from the University of North Carolina at Chapel Hill with a degree in English, Kenan began his career as an editor at Knopf. When his novel, *A Visitation of Spirits,* was published in 1989, he turned his full attention to writing and to teaching writing. He is also the author of a biography of James Baldwin (1994) and a collection of short stories, *Let the Dead Bury Their Dead and Other Stories,* which was nominated for the 1992 National Book Critics Circle Award and which won a Lambda Literary Award in 1993. In 2002 he received the Dos Passos Award. He has taught at Columbia University, Duke University, Sarah Lawrence College, the University of Memphis, the University of Mississippi, the University of North Carolina at Chapel Hill, and Vassar College.

Where Am I Black?

Or, Something About My Kinfolks

Cyberspace, North Carolina

During the academic year of 1994–95, I was honored to be a guest lecturer at my alma mater, the University of North Carolina at Chapel Hill, and its perpetual academic rival, Duke University. It was a bracing experience. Or, to paraphrase Marianne Moore, I laughed too much and was afraid of snakes.

Many revelations presented themselves to me that year, and some were daunting, and some were tender, and some I would like to forget, but probably never will, not without work. I became reacquainted with my family in a way that geography heretofore had made not possible; and I became reacquainted with a young black man, really a boy, ten years in the past, who made the first important move of his life, when he left a small village on the coastal plains of North Carolina, and matriculated at a major university, in an area later described by the national news media to be among the most civilized in the country. And not the least of all my discoveries and rediscoveries was my fervent return to the computer.

The reasons I never got any good at basketball are fourfold: (a) I didn't really have a place or anyone to play with; (b) I didn't play and practice when I had the opportunity; (c) I was so pitiful when I did attempt to play that I was roundly discouraged and ridiculed; and (d) I really didn't care. Actually I did, but it helped me deal with the fact that I was so bad, by feigning indifference until that feigning became real. In fact, not playing basketball gave me as much identity as it gave those black teens who did. If they were to become superb dribblers, slam dunkers, passers, shooters—I would become superb as something other. Or that's what my twelve- and thirteen-year-old mind told itself. My being drummed out of the corps of future NBA wanna-bes was so draconian. And it is for a great number of black males. Mine was in junior high school during school tournaments. We had a varsity high school player as a coach for a week. I was at the bottom of the lineup. I played for two shakes of a dog's tail near the end of the game when the outcome was inevitable, and even then I got laughed at and eyes rolled at by fellow players. For a while, I carted around something like contempt in my heart for all athletics, seeing supreme hypocrisy operating under the guise of sportsmanship. And being a boy, I could not get my mind round the conflation of commerce and recreation and "education" and, let's just face it, fun. I had not yet developed the ability to see and think on more than a few levels and could not understand how a particle could contain the truth and a lie and remain whole. I was a sensitive lad.

Now many will say that this trial by fire, as harmless as it is, ultimately builds character, not unlike what some folk say the military will do for adolescents. I don't know about that. But I will weigh in with the observation that to be a young black male in the public school system is to experience a weird, outsized pressure to excel at this now-national pastime. Young boys such as myself are weeded out of the process early. Most, unlike myself, try and try again, and deepen their affection and admiration for the sport and for the Michael Jordans and Dennis Rodmans and Horace Grants of the world. And, to quote B.B. King: "I'm not saying it's wrong; and I'm not saying it's right." Suffice it to say that today I watch my fellow schoolmates from UNC burn up the court and amaze the world (and draw down huge checks) with the rest of them. I cheer the Bulls and lament the Knicks. I see the game whole and for what it is. No longer is my ego bound up in my sorry inability to put a big orange ball through a metal hoop.

It was on this very subject that I would stumble upon what was to be my penultimate inquiry into the nature of blackness: haphazardly and unexpectedly, a discussion of basketball on the Internet.

Someone said it takes a village to raise a child. I do not doubt that piece of West African wisdom. But in my case, it was largely done by four people, with a village to back them up.

I was born illegitimate and male and black to a poor woman in Brooklyn, New York, in 1963. Luckily for both of us, my father acknowledged me as his issue, and he happened to possess a kindhearted father, who offered to raise me with his family in Wallace, North Carolina. My grandfather had been born in 1914, and had by the early sixties built himself a thriving dry-cleaning establishment; his wife was a seamstress. From the very beginning, they doted on me. I came to live with them at the age of six weeks.

My grandfather's sister, Mary Flemming, still lived in my grandfather's hometown, just fourteen miles east of Wallace, a village called Chinquapin, unincorporated and rural, largely tobacco fields and cornfields and hog farms.

My great-aunt Mary took a shine to me straight-away, and would often take me from Wallace to Chinquapin on the weekends, to spend time with her and her husband who ran the family farm. I'm not certain how many weekends she did take me back to Wallace, but one weekend she simply didn't bring me back, and there I remained. My grandfather, who drove one of his own delivery trucks, came by Chinquapin every Monday, so he saw me each week.

Three years later, on a mild September day, my

great-uncle Redden died of a blood clot. I remember this vividly, for he died right next to me, on the porch of a pack-house, where my great-aunt and other women were grading cured tobacco. My grandfather suggested, now that my great-aunt Mary was a widow and alone, that I remain with her, which I did for the next fifteen years. I did, and I continue to call her Mama.

It took me years to appreciate the accident of my winding up in a place like Chinquapin during my developing years. For in many ways, Duplin County, fairly remote, off the beaten path from any metropolitan area of consequence, forty miles from the ocean, rich with history, was in a time warp. During the years that I was learning the English language, and figuring out the basic realities of the world, the United States was going through some of its most tumultuous events: Vietnam, Woodstock, Watergate, rashes of assassinations, civil rights marches and boycotts and sit-ins, the Black Panther Party, free love, flower children, Kent State, Jackson State, men walking on the moon, the Great Society. In Chinquapin, all those events could have been happening in Thailand. Not to say that folk were ignorant of the goings-on in the wide world; rather, folk were simply focused on more pressing matters: getting crops in, getting their children fed, grown and married, caring for the elderly, going to church and trying to be good, with occasional missteps. Chinquapin from 1963 to 1981 could have been Chinquapin in 1920, with the exception of a few welcome new gadgets. Mama had an old Admiral television set, which was situated in a handsome walnut cabinet, the screen about the size of a letter; a set which broke down before my uncle died. She didn't get a new one until I was in kindergarten—something on which I always blame my addiction to print, although she, who worked in kindergarten, taught me to read when I was four.

Moreover, I was surrounded by folk who had been

on the planet for the entire century, and their view of the world began before any of these newfangled machines were even invented. There was my cousin Norman, who lived right across the dirt road from us, who was in his seventies when I was born. He knew an awful lot about the land and raised hogs and chickens, and had an admirable orchard adjacent to his and his wife, Miss Alice's, house. There was my great-great-aunt Erie, who was the youngest daughter of my great-great-grandfather. (Only years later did I discover how rare it is for a person to know a great-great-aunt. Indeed, both my maternal great-grandmothers were living when I went to high school.) Aunt Erie had over ten children, most of whom were away, but all were colorful people, and they would descend on Chinquapin during the holidays and the town would feel like a festival. There was my aunt Lillian, who lived in a big two-story house down the road, and her multitude of daughters, and her sons, Herman and Irving, who had worked to send many of the girls to college, and Herman's nine children with whom I went to school . . . and that's just one limb on one branch of one side of the tree of the extended family in which I grew up, surrounded by stories and antics and foibles and gossip and artifacts and something like love, though the many feelings engendered by life in a small town are much more complex and tangled than most people who've never lived in one, belonged to one, could ever imagine.

There was church. Two churches in fact. First Baptist and St. Louis. Both Baptist, and to this day I cannot say why Chinquapin never had an AME church. My mama was zealous about my going to church, and I remember too many sermons to be in my right mind, and the pastors Hestor, and Lassiter the younger, who succeeded Lassiter the senior. There were revivals in September and Vacation Bible School in June, when the blueberry season came, and Sunday school each and every Sunday—even on fifth Sunday when nobody

had church services. Church remained an indelible
mark on my growing up, and, no matter how far or
how fast I run, the lessons of Baptist protestantism
and southern Calvinism will be etched on my brain—
probably my soul—the way circuits are hardwired to
a motherboard.

There was school, which I truly enjoyed. And all
the black women who taught me (I actually had more
black teachers than white teachers before I went to
high school), women who had known me and my
mother their entire lives; women who watched me and
all the other black boys and black girls like sentient
hawks, and who would report any crime or misde-
meanor with the rapidity of lightning. Getting away
with wrongdoing or occasional mischief was doomed
to fail. I remember feeling completely watched, and
always felt that was one of the many reasons I couldn't
wait to say goodbye to the hamlet. Not that I wanted
to do anything particularly evil; I just didn't want my
business known to every Myrtle, Blanche and Willie
Earl.

I will not be romantic about Chinquapin. From as
early as I can remember, I always wanted to get the
hell out of there. After all, it was what it was: a very
small backwoods North Carolina village. The schools
were not desegregated until 1969; a great many roads
were unpaved; medical care was twenty-five miles
away and then not particularly competent; water was
pumped from private wells, and many folk had no
running water. As soon as I could read newspapers
and magazines, I had a clue that the world was wide
and far different from what I had seen day in and day
out in Duplin County, and something like resentment
grew in my breast. I resented people who were elsewhere. Though I would not know the phrase for decades to come, like Milan Kundera's poor artists in the
novel *Life Is Elsewhere,* I figured real life was going
on somewhere else.

Of course that was a boy thinking, feeling. And

though I think that this feeling, inchoate and arch, was the origin of my wanderlust, I now see those elements of Chinquapin that were so fundamental in making me a fairly good citizen, a fairly decent person, a fairly respectful human being, and, probably, a writer. Though, in truth, all those years, there was nothing I wanted to do more than become a scientist.

*   *   *

In 1994, Chinquapin had finally been thrust—more like yanked—into the heady whorl of the postmodern era. The ambulance was state-of-the-art. The town had city water. There was cable television and a supermarket and two convenience stores, at which one could rent videos of movies that had, in some cases, been released in the last six months. Less than twenty miles down the road was Ellis Airport with a landing sleeve and a rotating luggage belt. Interstate 40 had been completed only a few years before, which effectively created a line all the way from Barstow, California, to Wilmington, North Carolina, and, for the good folk of Duplin County, cut an hour off the drive to the Raleigh/Durham/Chapel Hill area, which in that year had been assessed by *Money* magazine as the most livable place in the country. My grandfather now used a microwave, and cultivated a taste for *Die Hard* and *Lethal Weapon,* while my mother watched *Montel* and *Oprah* and was receiving medical care that, in 1963, would have been essentially the stuff of science fiction.

To be sure, these things seem minor to most folk in the country, but the way they changed the complexion and the quality and the quantity of life bewitched me. For in my mind, Chinquapin was still backwoods and out of step, yet, thanks to satellite dishes and faxes and e-mail, was not so far away from the rest of America, and not so quaint and Tobacco Road.

Nevertheless, for me, Chinquapin was very much a land of specters, so many of the people I had known as a boy now dead and gone. I could not help but hear their ghosts about the rooms and fields and barns, now empty and relic-like. And, as sentimental and shamefully nostalgic as it may sound, groups of folk no longer sat about on porches and just talked; now they watched HBO and Cinemax. Most farms had been bought out by larger farms; church congregations seemed sparse. The old folks who remained seemed older, more frail, halting, almost ethereal, some from Alzheimer's, some from neglect and being forgotten. My running buddies were practically all gone, like me.

All of which is not to say that any of these changes are in and of themselves bad, and I am the last person on the planet Earth who will lament the passage of an era. Chinquapin did, and probably still does, abound with a multitude of hateful truths, dirty laundry, murders, substance abuse, strife of every manner, small-mindedness, racism, boredom, and downright inertia.

During my year back home, I could make the drive in less than two hours, go from Chapel Hill's squeaky clean, high-tech, Ph.D.-laden opulence, to Chinquapin's postmodern present, where hog farms were running riot, and the chopped barbecue was good, and I could get chitlins and run from snakes and attend the Daughters of Zion's annual event at the church, and go home and watch BET, and check my e-mail after calling a friend in Japan.

I was not so much bothered as disquieted by the changes that were occurring in Chinquapin, for in a way, those changes were at the foundation of the changes that were taking place in America. Chances were that the young folk in the elementary schools and the high schools of Duplin County were not having the same sorts of experiences that I had had in school. In fact, their experiences were probably very close to those of young folk growing up in Alaska or Maine or Wyoming or Arizona. Yes, there was a local flavor, a local color, but the information they were receiving, there in no-longer-quite-so-remote Chinquapin, was not very different from the information being received by kids, black kids, in Seattle and Madison and Salt Lake City and New York.

More to the point, those things that I had taken so for granted about being black, which had come from my mama and my grandfather and Uncle Roma and Aunt Lillian and Aunt Mildred in third grade, and Reverend Raynor and Miss Ruth, were now being dictated by the *Martin Lawrence Show* and *Moesha* and Snoop Doggy Dogg and Dr. Dre and Russell Simmons and *Vibe* magazine and, yes, Paramount. Chinquapin was becoming more like the rest of America. It was being absorbed by the vast cultural soup of consumeristic we-think.

The problem, as I saw it, had to do with the idea that blackness was not so easily beamed through a satellite or through an optic fiber. After all this travel and bother, I had, in many ways, arrived back in Chinquapin with the same question: What is blackness?

I have argued that Internet experiences help us to develop models of psychological well-being that are in a meaningful sense postmodern: They admit multiplicity and flexibility. They acknowledge the constructed nature of reality, self, and other. The Internet is not alone in encouraging such models. There are many places within our culture that do so. What they have in common is that they all suggest the value of approaching one's "story" in several ways and with fluid access to one's different aspects. We are encouraged to think of ourselves as fluid, emergent, decentralized, multiplicitous, flexible, and ever in process. The metaphors travel freely among computer science, psychology, children's games, cultural studies, artificial intelligence, literary criticism, advertising, molecular biology, self-help, and artificial life. They reach deep into the popular culture. The ability of the Internet to change popular understandings of identity is heightened by the presence of these metaphors.

—Sherry Turkle, *Life on the Screen: Identity in the Age of the Internet*

* * *

Here I was in my room in North Carolina, talking to folk in New Zealand, in Nigeria, in China, in Passaic, New Jersey. I say talk, but what we were doing was typing at one another; who they were, who I was, was largely immaterial; in truth, at the time, I deeply believe we were all, essentially, in love with the concept. We were netizens.

One fine night, I found myself on America Online, chatting with a man who said he was black and living in Los Angeles. We fell into a typersation about this and that. By and by, why I don't now remember, we began to discuss basketball. I allowed as how I was no good at the game, and probably went on too long about my feelings of insecurity, especially after having gone to a basketball-crazy place like UNC. Without preamble or warning, this cyberNegro typed: "Well, I got to get outta here and git wit some real niggas." And blipped off on his merry way.

Now objectively there is nothing remarkable about this minor incident. Folk on the Internet tended, and still tend, to be ruder to folk than they would be face to face; there is something about the electronic anonymity engendered by the beast that makes people insensitive. No, the thing that got my goat, stuck in my craw, angered the hell out of me, was the content of his aspersion. Here, after years of seeking out the nature of blackness, after talking to so many black folk, after reading, discussing, debating, investigating, the nature of blackness, here I was being accused of not being black. That stung. That hurt.

But what fascinated me—after I realized how silly it had been to allow my feathers to get ruffled by somebody I did not know—was how quicksilver and fast was my reaction; how subjective the idea had been on the one hand; and how, on the other hand, the very nature of what this cyberfellow expected to be black had fallen into question. Indeed, how could you be black on a computer screen? To be sure, he meant more than skin color, but how, qualitatively, could anyone adjudge how black you were or even if one were black? This silly incident led me once again, like a snake chasing its tail, right back to my original dilemma. What is blackness? Where does it exist? How can one person be more authentic in his being than another?

My grandfather is now eighty-four. He rises each morning between six o'clock and seven. Most months of the year he first goes out and tends his garden, which is almost half an acre. He still works six days a week, and his hobbies are still renovating houses and restoring furniture, and he cleans carpets sometimes on the side. George Washington Kenan seems to have more energy every year.

He owns a 1964 Park Lane Mercury, which is red, has less than 100,000 miles on its odometer, and runs like a dream. That car is one of his most prized possessions.

I enjoy sitting and talking with my grandfather for hours, and he seems to enjoy waxing nostalgic. I was surprised to learn a few years ago that he almost regrets not having become a farmer; he learned many things about farming as a teenager, and knows in his soul that he could have produced bountiful crops. Once, in the 1950s, he owned a farm for twelve years, and farmed while he ran his business. He sold the land at a profit in the 1960s. (Ironically, that land is now the site of a new luxury housing development.)

My grandfather tells me stories of his father and his father's father, of his days working at the shipyard, and of building his business from practically nothing;

he talks of Chinquapin, which, in his day, was home to more people than it is now. Much of today's technology baffles my grandfather, and he coexists in a world with it, paying computers and faxes next to no attention. Air travel astonishes him, and new cars amaze him, but he knows his old Park Lane remains something special; and he only flew on a plane once when his older brother was sick and dying, and otherwise has no real use for flying.

I remember once discussing nursing homes with my grandfather, who remains grateful that at his age he has maintained his independence. He marvels at the paradox of how much medical science has done to prolong life; and yet, once when a member of the family fell sick, he or she became the focus of an entire family, not the nuclear family of the 1950s television dreams, but of uncles and aunts and cousins. He remembered when his own father fell ill, how people would take turns sitting by his side, the women taking care of him.

"No," he said, "it ain't like it used to be. People just don't seem to care about people the way they once did."

The truth is that I am very different from my grandfather, and we both know this for a fact. I can no more imagine such a world as he describes, than he can imagine jacking into cyberspace. I am a creature of network television and books and music and cyberdreams; I am the inheritor of not only his vision, but of the ultimate dream of the American: individualism. I am not surrounded by family and bound by codes of caring and closeness. At the age of thirty-four, I am as itinerant as the fabled Wandering Jew. I have changed my address more in one year than my grandfather has in his entire life. I could easily live in California or Brazil or Japan or Ireland or South Africa. My friends come from all over the world, and some of my closest friends I have not seen for years, though we keep up over the phone and through the computer.

In this way, in many ways, I am emblematic of my generation. Despite my rural background, I am now a netizen, a paradoxically rootless American whose home is reluctantly the world. We have exchanged the village for the globe, yet, despite what Mr. McLuhan predicted, the global village can be a cold, impersonal place.

And whence blackness in this strange happenstance we find ourselves? After this long march across the country, I now see that the era in which I came of age was the era in which the concept of being black or Negro or African American changed indelibly. During my grandfather's time, the construct was at once political (Jim Crow), cultural (language, food, clothing, music), and spiritual (black Baptist). Now Jim Crow is no more, one can bridge the distances between Protestant, Catholic, Islam and agnostic, and this thing called culture, once specific to so many regions, has become a postmodern amalgam of this and that, borrowings and findings and newfangled creations like Kwanzaa, and media manipulations of street lingo, innocent of its origins and only interested in style, newness, the expression of being other, being black. But what is black anymore? Who is authentically black in a country, within a culture, where one's very existence has always been the shifting identity of survival?

Black American culture was always a Creole culture, a mixture of remembered African ways, of European impositions and influences and inflections, of Native American wisdom, and of the stubborn will to survive. Long before the term was coined, black culture was a postmodern culture; folk made it up as they went along. Therefore, who can be authentically black, when every black person holds the codes and the blueprints of that blackness?

Not only do I march to the beat of a different drummer, but sometimes I fail to make out the beat. It seems at times I'm making it up as I go along. I think of those black folk in the 1860s who had none of the modern baggage my contemporaries and I lug around. As deprived as they were, they were also lucky. They knew exactly who they were. There was no jangling television set, no blasting boom boxes, no candy-colored magazines, no Wal-Marts, Tower Records, Web pages, billboards. Marketing had yet to be invented, and consumerism was a mere glint in Rockefeller's eye. We—black, white, indifferent, but American—must now disentangle ourselves from the garbage of the information age; we must pioneer a new way of seeing ourselves; we must reinvent humanity.

Who I am and who the world wants me to be will not jibe. So much of this disease is caused by peer pressure, the perceived notion that one is not "black" enough; the hints and clues that somehow I, he, she, wishes to be other than other, and therefore a traitor.

Traitor. A strong word. But a traitor to what? Traitor to the race? Most countries punish treachery by the most severe means available. But how do you betray that which has yet to be truly defined?

Going back to Chapel Hill resurrected a great many of my personal specters, many of which I was certain I had laid to rest years ago. But walking down the halls of the English building, down the long green mall, down Franklin Street, into the massive Davis Library, I was accompanied always by the kid from Chinquapin, ten years before, and, like those patients of charlatan psychotherapists, I began remembering those things that I didn't want to remember.

After polyglot and polycolored Brooklyn and Queens and Manhattan, it struck me how homogeneous and largely white Chapel Hill was in 1994, and how much more it had to have been in 1984. All those Scots, Irish, English and German faces, blond, brunette and red hair all seemed to weigh on me more, and I wondered then how I had coped with that sea. I remembered how often I joined groups of black folk out of the sheer need to see black folk; how I volunteered at soup kitchens and tutored black kids, perhaps more out of a personal need than out of a desire to help.

I remembered incidents of being singled out as a Negro, like the time I was almost ejected from a frat party, being the only black person there; or the time the police stopped me while I was running down Rosemary Street near a number of sorority houses, because I "fit the description" of someone who had mugged a woman the day before. I remembered trying to express my outrage to my white housemates at the time, and their baffled inability to say anything at all, which made all of us feel inexpressibly worse and alienated from one another.

I remembered, as a freshman, having gone to a mixer at one of the tony North Campus female dorms, and being introduced by one of my roommates to a young lady friend of his. She asked me where I was from, and I said, Chinquapin. Her eyes grew wide, and she exclaimed, "Oh, you mean in *Africa*?" Everyone laughed, primarily at her profound ignorance, but somehow I felt the laughter aimed at me. I felt marked.

Perhaps, most damningly, the thing that came back to me with such a wave of psychic force was the remembrance of how very much I disliked myself. I was not white, rich, socially in; I felt excluded, and subconsciously unacceptable.

I never wanted to be white; I never felt ashamed of being black. Indeed, until my school had been integrated in the first grade, it never occurred to me that anyone was any different from me and my folks. Over the years, increasingly, as I watched more television, read more, thought more, became exposed to more and more of the insidious social microcosm of high school, I did become more and more dissatisfied with my own personal lot. I believed everything my family told me about what one had to do to succeed in this world, that, as a young black man, I had to make certain my house was in order, that I had to eschew the more frivolous activities my white contemporaries indulged in. I had to hit the books; I had to prove myself.

By college, I remembered ten years later, this pressure had become acute. Often, in those years, I was not only uncomfortable but depressed. I now remembered that I did not often have a good time as an undergraduate. I felt myself on the outside looking in.

Many of the black guys I knew in those years made a fetish of whiteness. They coveted white women, and cultivated white attitudes, white clothing, white manners and mores. Was I one of those misled young men?

Sometimes I think I was; sometimes, most times, I know I was not. This conundrum being, at its base, the basis of my questioning. The question becomes not whether I, a young black man, an "affirmative action baby" (whatever that means), a child of the dream, wished to shed my skin, exchange my nappy head for blond tresses, expunge my chitlins and collard greens past, and adopt a New England clenched-teeth speech, eradicate all folkways and knowledge of the Veil, and blissfully slip into a country-club future unhampered by the shadow of the Other. No, the question becomes: Did I, in my attempts to learn and to experience another world, somehow lose, divest, mitigate or disavow who or what I was? Did I, in mingling and comingling with white folks, dilute or pollute or weaken my legacy as a son of a son of a son of a son of slaves stolen from Africa?

By 1994, I had moved a long way from that way of thinking. Like Lorri Hewett, I had come to realize that being black is not something to grab; like the Reverend Swift in Utah, I understood that being black was more than love, peace and hair grease. I had remedied the confusion of politics, economics, social class and skin color; I had come to understand that other people's notions of me could only influence me as much as I allowed them to do; I had come to the unshatterable conclusion that being black was indeed a willed affirmation, a recognition of my past, my beliefs and my most secret dreams.

> We Americans have lived in a country that's been very successful technologically, and we instinctively think that every problem must have a technological solution.
>
> —I. F. Stone, National Public Radio,
> April 12, 1983

I met Richard Elias Wimberly, III, the first day I arrived at Chapel Hill as a freshman; he roomed right across the hall from me in one of the older dorms on what is called the North Campus of the university.

The first black student was admitted to Chapel Hill in 1951 to the medical school; in fact, Chapel Hill was the first southern university to voluntarily accept black students, though it did not gracefully tear down the barricade for most black folk for decades. In 1981, most of the 800 or so black students (out of 20,000) lived in what was known as South Campus, at the southernmost edge of the school, where four of the newest, high-rise dorms had been erected. It was understood that South Campus was where the black folk were largely housed, and those who chose to live elsewhere were considered somehow different. And though it was not an instant badge of oreo-dom (for instance, Michael Jordan and most of the other basketball players lived on a special floor of a privately owned and operated "dorm" called Granville, north of North Campus), one was open to being suspect. Or, to be more specific, folk would wonder where you were at.

When I chose Grimes Dormitory, I was blissfully ignorant of all these territorial imperatives; it merely seemed logical to be close to most of my classes. There were a number of other black guys in my dorm, twelve or fifteen out of about a hundred students. It took me

a while, but gradually I came to realize what some of
the folk on South Campus thought of the black folk
who lived on North Campus. The truth is they were
right about a number of those people; that is to say,
some of those black men and women who sojourned
on North Campus did so because they wanted little if
anything to do with other black folk, while for some
there were other reasons; and some, like me, had
given it little, if any, thought.

For many people on South Campus, the few who
knew him, Richard Wimberly fell into the former category. Richard was from a prosperous upper-middle-
class family from Raleigh, which belonged to one of
the oldest and most affluent black churches in the
state; his father owned his own business, and Richard
had gone to one of the more competitive high schools
in the state capital. Richard was beautiful, athletic,
articulate, a gentleman and a preppie; funny, good
spirited, a history major. Richard enjoyed playing
basketball, and was good at it. He had an eye for the
ladies, and loved pepperoni pizza, and Richard was
deeply, deeply religious.

Richard had white friends, Richard had black
friends, Richard had Chinese friends, Richard had
Japanese friends. And fairly quickly, the two of us
became fast friends. I often wonder if the proximity
in which we lived for a year was the basis of our
friendship, plus the fact that being black together, surrounded largely by white folk, forced us to seek one
another out. And of course, the answer is partly yes.
However, we had so much in common that I feel it
was inevitable that we would get along so famously.
Our interest in history, sociology, theology, and in
Dungeons and Dragons, led us to spend hours just
talking. And yes, our interest in *Star Trek* and science
fiction as well.

In the fullness of time, we spoke more and more
about our specific circumstances, about the specula-

tions folk had made about him, about us. One of our mutual friends actually told Richard to his face that for months he had assumed Richard to be an "uppity nigger"; one who didn't want anything to do with black folk; one who thought he was better than other black folk; one who had few black friends by design. This friend later asked for Richard's forgiveness, saying, after getting to know him, that Richard was "all right." These ideas intrigued both Richard and me, and we shared our feelings of insecurity, of doubt, of the possibility of self-hate, of the doublethink that goes on in one's own mind when people who don't know you cast aspersions about your inner self; the second-guessing that breeds discontent. These ideas led us to ask questions about blackness. What is it?

I remember one night in particular, one which seems too good to be true, though it is true nonetheless. Richard and I had started talking after studying late; somewhere around ten or eleven, we were in the hall, on the landing, talking. At one point, we looked up, and the sun was peeking up. Neither of us was tired. We talked about many things that night: personhood, faith, history, economics, Hegel, Martin Luther King, sex, death, manifest destiny.

At one point, Richard said something to the effect of:

I would love to just travel all over the country and study black people. Try to figure out what exactly it is we talk about when we talk about blackness.

I remember, as the sun came up that morning, as we said good night and went to our own beds, agreeing with him, thinking, somehow, I would try to do just that.

Richard went on to Duke Divinity School, and then on to become an ordained minister, and then chaplain at Central Prison in Raleigh. When I told Richard my plans, to do what he himself had suggested, he was perhaps more excited than I. I suggested that for the final chapter, I would go with him to the prison and interview him and some of the inmates. He thought that would be a grand idea.

Richard married a beautiful black woman named Denise in the summer of 1993. He died almost exactly a year later of cancer.

Life, love, work, service, death.

I remember most fondly how fervently Richard Wimberly applied his mind to the conundrum of being. The issue of being black was no singular, isolatable question for him. He saw it always within the context of faith, of humanity. It never mattered to Richard what others thought of him; rather, it mattered what he thought of himself. He refused to allow himself to be dictated to about what or who he was, for, like Ralph Ellison's Invisible Man, he stubbornly examined each and every particle of his life; he questioned it, not on the basis of what he was supposed to think about it, but on the basis of what he actually thought of it. This, of course, is a wearisome, tiring, frustrating exercise, and when anyone questioned him or became impatient with his dogged analysis, he would just smile his infectious smile, and say, Now just bear with me . . .

Now just bear with me . . .

Now you've been told, so you ought to know. But maybe, after all the Negro doesn't really exist. What we think is a race is detached moods and phases of other people walking around. What we have been talking about might not exist at all. Could be the shade patterns of something else thrown on the ground—other folks, seen in shadow. And even if we do exist it's all an accident anyway. God made everybody else's color. We took ours by mistake. The way the old folks tell it, it was like this . . .

—Zora Neale Hurston, *Dust Tracks on a Road*

PART II

—

Experiencing Southern Families

William Hoffman

William Hoffman was born in 1925 in Charleston, West Virginia, but most of his fiction is set in Virginia where he went to college and now lives. He received a B.A. from Hampden-Sydney College and began law school at Washington and Lee University. There he took a creative writing course, "just as a lark" he told a *McCall's* interviewer, but became "trapped" by writing, and decided to give up law school and attend the University of Iowa's Writers' Workshop for a year. Afterward he worked for a newspaper in Washington, D.C., and a bank in New York City, but eventually returned to Hampden-Sydney to teach English. In 1967 he was playwright-in-residence at the Barter Theatre in Abingdon, Virginia, where he wrote *The Love Touch*. Hoffman is the author of twelve novels, among them *Godfires* (1985), *Furors Die* (1989), *Tidewater Blood* (1998), and *Blood and Guile* (2000), and four collections of stories, *Virginia Reels* (1979), *By Land, by Sea* (1988), *Follow Me Home* (1994), and *Doors* (1999). Reviewers routinely praise his ability to evoke distinctive places. He lives at Wynyard Farm in Charlotte County, Virginia, where he breeds horses.

Amazing Grace

The way we knew was that Nana, my grandmother, stopped making bread and instead of running the kitchen like a drill sergeant she walked out into the front yard and sat on a bench under the Indian cigar-tree.

"Maybe she's tired," my father said when he and I came in from changing the tire on the John Deere. "There's times I'd like to sit under that tree."

"That's not it," my mother said and slapped at me for reaching to get a hot corn-dodger from the stove.

My mother had to drive to the store to buy us bread. None of us remembered how sorry store-boughten tasted because Nana baked three times a week ever since I could remember—biscuits, rolls, and loaves, some of the loaves salt-rising bread which smelled up the house, and she had a cool dusky pantry with wooden shelves where she set her dough and bread, covering them with clean white cloths. Though there was a GE electric stove in the kitchen now, she still liked the old wood-burning Kalamazoo for her baking, or had until she walked out to sit under the Indian cigar-tree.

She sat and looked past the plank fence to the meadow and past the meadow to the barbed-wire fence at the road. Beyond the road the valley sloped up to a ridge, and on the other side of that ridge was Virginia, but here in the valley it was West Virginia, not the coal-mining part, but farming. The grassy hills had outcroppings of limestone, and sometimes it was hard to see the difference between the limestone and sheep grazing the slopes.

"It's Henry," my mother said to my father on Wednesday night after Nana went to bed. My mother and father were sitting in the kitchen, at the metal table that had paper towels for mats, their arms on the table, sitting not to eat or drink but to talk. My father was tall, which was unusual for us Sharps, who ran to heft, yet he had their blond hair and heaviness of jaw, like me. My mother, a Henson, was a small woman, though strong, and her hair and eyes were dark brown.

"What about Henry?" my father asked.

"He's not been to the river," my mother said. "None of his has."

My daddy's two sisters, Aunt Henrietta and Aunt Cornelia, were both older than him. They and their husbands, Albert and Asa, came the next night to the kitchen, again after Nana was in bed. It was agreed my father should speak to Henry in person since that would be more effective than just a letter or a phone call. Early Friday Daddy put on his gray suit and drove the Ford pickup to Pittsburgh.

The night he came back I was scrubbing my hair. Every Saturday night I had to wash my hair, and my mother inspected it, parted the hair to look at my scalp the way a person would search for a dime lost in the grass.

"They own a house out of town now," my father said. "Place called Sewickley, kind of in the country."

"Smoke and grit?" my mother asked.

"Not yesterday and today when I left, though Henry never minded smoke and grit," my father said. "Henry always claims smoke and grit shakes off money. You can live clean and pure in the desert where the air's perfect, Henry says, but that's all you got except sand. Where people do honest work, there's going to be some smoke and grit, Henry says."

"Dale Blue still have the same color hair?" my mother asked about Henry's wife.

"That's enough," my father said.

Uncle Henry was the member of the family who'd left. He first played football for West Virginia University, right tackle, and afterwards he became a mining engineer. His job took him to the southwest part of the state near Kentucky, and while he was driving a shaft into a seam of bituminous coal a steel company bought the seam, and he found himself in the steel business. Now he had an office in Pittsburgh overlooking the Monongahela River and barges carrying his money.

"That's not coal in those barges," he told me when he came back to the farm and showed snapshots. "Those are black lumps of money being shoved to my bank."

That's the way I thought of him, sitting up high in his shiny office watching the tugs nose his money to the bank. I guess the bank had a rear door on the river to take the money through.

During the summer Nana sat under the Indian cigar-tree. One afternoon she lifted her chin, and I saw the car glint a long ways off. The road was paved, but the speed of the car still raised tan dust along both shoulders. The horn started honking. It had to be.

"It's him!" I shouted, running to Nana. "It's Uncle Henry!"

"Drives too fast," she said.

I'd seen pictures of Nana when she was a girl in high school, and she'd been thin, like my daddy, and smiling, her head lowered, her dark hair parted in the middle and pulled back, her eyes raised, her feet set a little pigeon-toed. It'd been graduation time, and she'd worn a white dress and black slippers.

Over the years she'd grown shorter and thicker, not fat because she'd never stayed still long enough to gather fat, but stout the way an oak tree is stout. When I kissed her before she went to bed, I felt the strength in her. She was no puny old woman. Her forearm was as hard as my father's. I'd seen her hit a mule so hard with a hoe handle that he was cross-eyed for ten minutes.

I climbed the plank fence, ran across the meadow, and jumped the ditch to open the gate for Uncle Henry. Naturally he came in his big car. He knew I'd be disappointed if he didn't. One of the things he'd do on visits was to take me in his car and run her up to about a hundred. This time it was a gunmetal Cadillac with white sidewalls and tinted windows.

Dale Blue, his wife, was in front beside him. Like my mother would, the first thing I did was look at her hair, yellowish now, though I'd seen it both black and platinum, sometimes short, sometimes long, now piled on top of her head in a twist. It reminded me of custard on a cone at the Tastee Freeze.

She was the prettiest woman I'd ever seen. We lived in the country, but we had TV, and I'd drive in the truck with Daddy to the livestock market in Lewisburg, so I'd seen some pretty women, but she was the best yet, always licked to a gloss, her jewelry glittering, her clothes bright and fresh, herself sweet-smelling. The last time she was on the farm I walked into the bathroom while she was drying and stepping from the tub, and I saw one of her creamy bosoms. I get hot in the face even thinking about it.

After opening and shutting the gate, I rode in with them. Dale Blue gave me a wet, perfumed kiss. Uncle Henry shook hands and roughed my hair. In the back seat was Dawson, their son and my cousin. He was my age. Though built low and square like the Sharps, he had red hair. As soon as his parents weren't looking, he frogged me on the arm. That frog jumped out at least three inches.

"Oh aw!" I said.

"What's that, hon?" Dale Blue asked, turning and smiling.

"Just clearing my throat," I said.

"Got him a frog in it," Dawson said.

Uncle Henry drove to the house. He didn't wait for Dale Blue or Dawson but was out of the car and vaulting the plank fence before they opened a door. He kissed Nana, hugged her, and knelt on the ground beside her, not caring about grass stain on his peach slacks.

"How come you sitting out here and not fixing me an angel food?" Uncle Henry asked. "You always fix me my angel food cake when I come."

"You going to the river before I die?" Nana asked.

"What, you die? Listen, Momma, I don't want any talk of dying around here, and I been wetted anyhow. I'm a bonafide deacon in the church. I have my own pew every Sunday, and I bought a big window showing Jesus with the twelve."

"You weren't wetted in our river," Nana said.

Dale Blue and Dawson had walked through the gate, and my mother was coming from the porch. My father drove his tractor toward the house. As soon as Uncle Henry was in the county, things happened. The summer air stirred, and our water ran cooler. We touched each other and laughed. No wonder the rich people in Pittsburgh liked him.

"And look here, Momma, here's Dale Blue and little Dawson," Uncle Henry said. "They all want to kiss you."

As she leaned to Nana, one of Dale Blue's diamond earrings got tangled in Nana's white hair. For a minute Dale Blue and Uncle Henry were laughing and calling out as they unsnagged the earring, but Nana wasn't laughing. She stared at Dale Blue and Dawson as if they'd stolen the church.

"None's been to the river," Nana said.

"Ah come on, Momma, forget the river a second, will you?" Uncle Henry said. He ran and jumped the plank fence to reach his Caddy. In the trunk he had presents for everybody. I got me a baseball mitt. My mother was handed a five-pound can of peanut brittle, and Daddy shouldered a big net sack of Florida grapefruits.

For Nana Uncle Henry had a clock, a grandfather clock which he and my daddy lugged in pieces across the grass and put together under the Indian cigar-tree. They leveled it and hooked on golden weights shaped like pinecones. The brass pendulum swung into a shaft of sunshine. When the clock ticked and gonged, the cows stopped grazing and lifted their heads. Two crows spiraled cawing from the corn.

"Eight days," Uncle Henry explained to Nana. "Eight whole days and you don't have to pull the chains to wind her."

Nana eyed the clock. She had an oval face, and her hair was thin, wispy cotton. She adjusted her glasses to peer at the clock. Then she turned away.

"But don't you like it?" Dale Blue asked. "Henry went to lots of trouble to bring it."

"All that clock tells me is my days are running out, and nobody's been to the river," Nana said.

She wouldn't look at the clock again. The men carried it into the hall to set it up a second time, but she went to bed without glancing at it. Uncle Henry and Dale Blue came to the kitchen where they sat around the table with my mother and daddy as well as Aunt Henrietta and Aunt Cornelia and their husbands Albert and Asa.

"She's sure low," Aunt Cornelia said while she poured iced tea from a glass pitcher, her arms brown from helping Uncle Asa in the hayfields. "I've not seen her this far down since lightning hit the heifers."

"Spoiled is what she is," Dale Blue said.

Boy, eyes bugged at Dale Blue as if she was a snake on a rock. She was in the family but not of it. She colored, touched her frozen-custard hair, and shrugged.

"Honey, maybe you better let me do the talking here," Uncle Henry said.

"But she's pouting like a child," Dale Blue said.

"All the work she's done for this family she's got a right to pout until Moses makes sauerkraut out of little sour apples in December," Aunt Henrietta said.

Dale Blue kind of sniffed, crossed her arms, and jiggled a pretty foot in a black-and-white slipper. From time to time while the others talked she'd raise her nose as if she wasn't sure she should be breathing the same air as the rest of us. She came from West Virginia too, from Beckley, but she didn't tell anybody if she could help it.

"Give me another day anyhow," Uncle Henry said, standing. "Maybe I can fun her up tomorrow."

"I know you're tired," my mother said. "The spare room's ready."

"Oh, well, we won't be needing the spare room, thanks," Dale Blue said. "Henry made us a reservation over at White Sulphur. Allows him to combine business with pleasure. The railroad men are having a convention."

Nobody said anything, first because they couldn't imagine a member of the family not staying at the farm and second because no one in our family had ever slept at the resort before—a white hotel covering acres and acres where they had a private airport, golf courses, stables, and foreign servants who wore red jackets. To us in the county the resort and grounds were like another country.

"I don't know whether you ought to do that, Henry," my father said. "Momma might not understand."

"Blame me," Dale Blue said. "I've signed up for a bath."

"You can use the tub here," I said and thought of the time I'd seen her creamy bosom fall over the lilac towel. I again got hot in the face.

"Sh-h-h," my mother said to me, and Dawson snickered.

"What difference does it make except cause you all less trouble?" Dale Blue asked. "Henry and Dawson will come back tomorrow and spend the day."

She led them out to the car. We watched the Caddy's red taillights in the darkness. My mother made me go up to bed, but I sneaked down to hear them talking in the kitchen.

"Henry's changed," Aunt Henrietta said and sighed.

"It's not Henry," Aunt Cornelia said. "Nothing's wrong with Henry."

"I wonder Dale Blue don't make him wear a bib at the table," my daddy said.

I sank to sleep hearing the ticking and gonging of the grandfather clock downstairs, and then I woke because I wasn't hearing it. I peeked over the railing. Nana was at the clock. She held her flashlight, and her hand had stilled the pendulum. She shuffled to her bedroom.

"Can't sleep with all that clanging," she said.

The next morning I was mowing as soon as the sun dried the orchard grass. I drove the small tractor, the Ford, running her in second gear and keeping the swaths neat as the clattering blade felled the grass. My father drove the big tractor, the John Deere, and was pulling the baler over windrows in a seven-acre field we'd cut three days earlier. My uncles loaded bales on the wagon.

When Uncle Henry came, he too threw bales on the wagon. He showed off his strength by tossing the bales like basketballs. He laughed and joked with his brothers. He wasn't dressed for work but wore a red shirt, apricot pants, and what he called shag chukkas, which my daddy asked him to spell. Uncle Henry worked until he was sweat shiny.

He tried everything to cheer up Nana. He tuned the banjo, his old one from the hall closet, and sang "Rye Whiskey," "The Possum's Lament," and "The Coal Miner's Daughter." He stomped as he played, and later, sitting on the bench beside Nana, he told her stories about Pittsburgh and his new house which had doors that opened and closed when he pushed buttons. It had a sauna and a putting green.

"That house'll do everything for you except pick your teeth," he said.

"Will it bake bread?" I asked.

"Sh-h-h," my mother said.

Nana listened and watched. She kept her bluish-gray eyes on him every second, but she never smiled or put out her hand to him, though she loved him so much she'd set his picture on the center of the mantel in her bedroom. She had other pictures, but his was the place of honor, and she sometimes draped a rose or shasta daisy over the frame.

We ate lunch on the grass around the Indian cigar-tree, a picnic in the yard for all the hands—cold chicken, melons, and lemonade. Nana swallowed a bite or two, but not as if she enjoyed it. Mostly she nibbled and looked at the sheep on the sunny slope. She seemed to forget she was eating.

That afternoon Preacher Arbogast came. He drove a Chevy which he parked beside Uncle Henry's Caddy. Preacher Arbogast was a small pop-eyed man always washed to a waxy finish. When he walked, he did it like a person measuring every step. He shook hands around. There was chicken for him, but he wouldn't sit on the grass to eat it the way the rest of the men did. He let my daddy bring him a chair from the house.

"I was hoping to meet your wife this time, Henry," Preacher Arbogast said.

"She's in the bathtub all day," I said.

"Sh-h-h," my mother said, and Dawson again snickered.

After the picnic it was time to go back to haying. Nana, Uncle Henry, and Preacher Arbogast stayed in the yard. I was now driving Uncle Asa's International and pulling the wagon. Dawson rode behind me on the drawbar. He wanted to steer.

"If a hick-freak like you can do it, anybody can," he said.

"Everybody in Pennsylvania got mouths as big as yours?" I asked.

He punched me in the ribs. I almost fell off the seat. My daddy saw us and hollered. Dawson jumped from the drawbar and walked to Daddy who listened to him. Daddy waved to stop me, came over to the tractor, and told me to teach Dawson to drive.

The thing that made me maddest was that after a few minutes Dawson drove the International almost as good as I could, that and the fact he got to sit up there in his new jeans and act like a king while I had to throw bales on the wagon. Those bales weighed fifty or sixty pounds. I was strong for my age, eleven, but it was man's work, and the next time we unloaded at the barn, I snuck to the house to see if I could find some of that picnic lemonade.

Nana, Preacher Arbogast, and Uncle Henry were still in the yard. I tiptoed through the front bedroom to listen at a window screen that flies buzzed around and bumped against.

"But, Momma, I got here an affidavit," Uncle Henry said. "It's signed and sworn to by my pastor in Sewickley. It's duly notarized. It proves I'm a baptized member of the church."

"You've not been baptized like a Sharp in our river," Nana said.

"But it's not required," Uncle Henry said. "Ask the Reverend Arbogast here about it, and he'll tell you I'm genuinely saved."

"Technically I have to agree," Preacher Arbogast said.

"What do you mean 'technically'?" Uncle Henry asked, and he was angry.

"Outside the denomination you've been," Preacher Arbogast said. "We don't know for sure what they're doing up in Pennsylvania."

"You telling me only you and the Greenbrier River Baptists around here can save me?" Uncle Henry asked, flapping his arms.

"All the Sharps has been to our river," Nana said. "You escaped because you were a sickly boy, and for a time we went without a preacher. Then you slipped away from the county before anybody remembered you'd not been in the river."

It's all I was able to hear. My mother came tiptoeing into the same bedroom. She almost jumped out of her shoes when she pulled back the curtain and saw me standing there looking at her. She yelped and chased me off by shoving me on the back. I went, but I knew she stayed and listened.

In the hayfield Dawson was wheeling around on the International. My daddy stared at me and spat because I'd been gone. I again threw bales on the wagon. Each time I lifted I grunted, and sweat stung my eyes. Chaff made me sneeze. Dawson was driving the tractor so fast I had to hurry with the bales. I fell, but he didn't wait. He grinned at me.

When we finally got the field cleared and the bales stacked in the barn, I lay down in the shade of a sycamore tree. I rested and wondered if Uncle Henry was going to be too worried to take me for a fast ride in the gunmetal Caddy. Dawson walked by. He was still clean in his T-shirt, pressed jeans, and white tennis shoes.

"What's the matter, Cousin Willie Hick-freak?" he asked.

"You going to make me get up out of this shade to whip you?" I asked.

"You'd commit suicide just because I called you Willie Hick-freak?" he asked. "Your name's Willie, isn't it, and you got to admit you're a hick. At least that's what my momma says. Tell me this: you ever been on a jet plane or an escalator?"

"No," I admitted.

"You ever eaten in a French restaurant or swum in an Olympic-size pool?"

"No," I said.

"You ever seen the ocean?" he asked.

"No," I said.

"Then how can you claim you're not a hick-freak?" he asked.

"This is how," I said. I stood and punched him in the mouth.

He came back at me. He might be a city boy, but he was strong like Uncle Henry and knew more about boxing than I did. He was hitting me two or three times for every one I got him. I had to rush him, trip him, and close the scissors on him. I also put the stranglehold on him. He was gasping in the grass.

"Tell me how sorry you are," I said.

"Sorry you're a hick-freak," he said.

I tightened up. He flopped around and became sick. I let go fast. My nose was bleeding. I crawled away, lay on my back, and looked at the yellowish sky.

"You don't fight fair," Dawson said, his head hung like a whipped dog. "We were supposed to be boxing."

"You want to fight about what we were supposed to be doing?" I asked.

"At my school you don't rassle and box at the same time," he said.

"At your school the boys probably wear their hair like girls too," I said.

"Yeah, some of them do," he said. "And I've been to a stylist."

He touched his hair like a girl would, and that got me laughing. He started laughing. My nose had stopped bleeding. We walked to the barn to wash ourselves at the spigot. We bowed our heads under the water and blew into it. As to the bruise on my cheek, I told my mother I'd slipped against the hay wagon. She glanced at Dawson and would've questioned him about his torn T-shirt except she was too excited with news of Uncle Henry.

"He's going to do it," she told my daddy. "Him and Dale Blue and little Dawson."

"Little Dawson," I snickered.

"Has Dale Blue been told yet?" my daddy asked.

"Tonight," my mother said. "Give thanks."

"She ought to be clean enough," I said. "All day in a bath."

Dawson kicked me in the leg. Nobody saw him. I hopped around and hollered.

"Sh-h-h," my mother said.

Next morning when I woke, I heard a sound, something more than the birds, the cattle, and the creaking of the tin roof heating under the sun. I walked to the hallway. My mother and daddy were already standing there, she wearing her white nightgown, Daddy in his undershorts. They were smiling, and I smiled too because downstairs Nana was humming a hymn in her bedroom.

Still everybody was nervous Uncle Henry wouldn't be able to persuade Dale Blue. We watched the road from White Sulphur. Daddy looked at his watch. Uncle Asa spat tobacco juice into the geraniums, and Aunt Cornelia fussed at him for it.

When the Caddy came, it raised a whirling rooster-tail of dust. I ran to the gate. Dale Blue was sitting in the car with Uncle Henry and Dawson. Nana had walked out onto the porch. Uncle Henry hurried to her and hugged her.

"It's okay, Momma," he said. "Tell that old river to get itself set because a bunch of sharp Sharps is coming."

Nana held onto him and laughed. I saw how lively and pretty she must've been as a girl. Dale Blue wore a pink scarf and a pink pantsuit. Though Nana didn't like women in breeches, she kept herself from complaining and even offered her face to Dale Blue for a kiss. Dawson, while nobody was watching, tried to frog me. I was ready and elbowed him in the stomach. He moved around bent over. Uncle Asa drove off in his pickup to see if Preacher Arbogast could do the baptizing that afternoon.

"I don't understand how Henry swung it," Daddy whispered to my mother. "Dale Blue's acting almost pleased about going to the water."

I found out about that. Dawson and I ran to the barn to check the tractors and throw clods at the

Hereford bull in the lot. We also punched each other a couple of times. Dawson was excited about the river.

"Will they let me swim?" he asked. "I never swam in anything except an Olympic-size pool and the ocean."

"No, you poor city-freak, Preacher Arbogast won't let you swim," I said. "He'll dunk you three times, but maybe you and me can slip back afterwards."

"If Momma doesn't get too worried about her hair," Dawson said. "I wish they didn't have to wet that."

"They do unless she can take it off first," I said.

"Well she shouldn't holler too loud since Dad's promised her a green Mercedes and a trip to Italy," Dawson said.

We ate lunch on the lawn. Daddy and my uncles carried out tables, and my mother and aunts covered them with Nana's linen cloths. Family arrived not only from Pocahontas County, but also from the other side of the mountain. They were served ham, snaps, deviled eggs, and seven kinds of pie people brought with them, including brown sugar, sweet potato, and lemon chess. Dawson and I gorged until we couldn't breathe except through our mouths. We were too bloated to punch each other. We stretched out on the grass and let flies walk over us.

"But what does one wear to the river?" Dale Blue asked, lifting her palms. "I simply don't have a thing with me."

"We'll supply you with a clean sheet," Aunt Henrietta said. "Everybody wears a sheet, man, woman, or child."

"Is there anything special I should dress in underneath?" Dale Blue asked and giggled.

"You wear underneath what you would to church," Aunt Cornelia said, disapproving.

The time for the baptism was four o'clock, and at three-thirty we filled up cars and started for the Greenbrier. Dale Blue, Dawson, and Uncle Henry had wrapped themselves in their sheets. The river was seven miles from the farm. We left the highway and wound on an unmarked blacktop road through a state forest and into a gorge which was already partly shaded by the west slope of the wooded mountain.

The green river was shallow and fast, no mud in it because the bottom was all stones that had been shaped by the current until they were rounded like Nana's loaves of Jesus bread. On the rocky beach cars were parked.

"If anybody had ever told me I'd be doing a crazy thing like this," Dale Blue said.

"Salvation's not crazy," Nana said.

"What if I get water up my nose?" Dale Blue asked.

"Just breathe out when you go under," Uncle Henry said.

"If I get water up my nose, I might need a trip to Greece too," she said.

She didn't like the crowd, not only kin, but also a good many of the congregation as well as some fishermen and a group of sightseers. The thing that made her buck, though, was the photographers from Lewisburg who'd come because of Uncle Henry's reputation.

"No!" Dale Blue said, refusing to leave the Caddy. "He's not taking my picture! Suppose they see it in Sewickley. I couldn't show my face."

"Please, Dale Blue, for Momma," Uncle Henry pleaded.

"Not for anybody, not Dawson either, and not you if you remember who you are. They'll laugh you out of the Iron and Coal Club!"

She pulled the door shut, rolled up the window, and drew the sheet tight around herself. Uncle Henry circled the car begging her. Dawson was mad because he wanted to get into the river. The skinny photographer angled with his camera. He tried to take a picture of Dale Blue through the tinted windshield. She covered her face with her sheet. Uncle Henry, growing redder every second, ran him off, tripped on his sheet, and fell, showing for an instant his purple-and-white striped drawers, pale legs and wine garters.

"That's enough," Nana, between Uncle Asa and Albert, said. "We'll leave."

"They can do it to me," Uncle Henry said. "I'm ready to go to the water."

"Me too," Dawson said.

"We'll go home," Nana said.

We moved among gawking people to get back into the cars, and like a funeral procession we drove to the farm, all except Uncle Henry who tore off in the Caddy with Dale Blue and Dawson. Nana again sat on the bench under the Indian cigar-tree. Family milled around, picked at the ham, and dribbled away home.

"What'll Henry do to Dale Blue?" my mother asked my daddy that night.

"What'd Henry ever do but turn it so she'd have an easy time kicking it?" my daddy asked.

"Turn what?" I asked.

"Sh-h-h," my mother said. "Go to bed."

Barking dogs woke me. Daddy carried his flashlight and shotgun outside to see about it. He thought a fox or coon was after our chickens, but the henhouse was quiet. Finally the dogs stopped barking, though they whined a while.

I thought Uncle Henry, Dale Blue, and Dawson were gone to Pittsburgh, but the next morning they drove to the farm. They kissed Nana and pretended nothing had happened. Uncle Henry joked with her. She sat under the tree without moving.

Dale Blue hummed and prissed about. She had on earrings shaped like sunflowers, and she wore a yellow shirt, yellow shorts, and yellow tennis shoes. Her legs were the prettiest I'd ever seen, all the hair smoothed off, the skin tan and satiny, like a dancing girl instead of a married woman. I got caught looking at her legs. She smiled at me, and there I was hot in the face again.

"We thought you'd left," my mother said.

"Oh, we're going after while," Uncle Henry said. He was dressed like Dale Blue, yellow shorts, yellow shirt, though his tennis shoes were white. His lumpy muscled legs were funny with hair curled man-thick over them. "I want to show Dale Blue around. She hasn't had much chance to see the farm, especially the view."

"The view?" my daddy asked.

"From the silo," Uncle Henry said. "I told her you can see a lot of the valley from the silo."

My mother looked at my daddy who looked at her as I looked at them, and they looked at me. Not many people would climb our silo. I'd do it, yet the first time and the second time too I'd been scared because the silo, made of reinforced concrete slabs, was a hundred and twenty feet high.

You ducked into a vertical hatch and went up an iron ladder covered by a wooden canopy to protect climbers from wind and weather. It was like rising in a dim upright tunnel, and at the top was a sliding metal door not to see the view from but to blow in silage and for ventilation. Beams and boards had been laid across the slabs just under the galvanized dome. My mother would never climb the silo, and it'd been a long time since my daddy had.

"At least she's got nerve," my daddy said as Uncle Henry, Dawson, and Dale Blue crossed the pasture toward the barn. Uncle Henry slowed to swing a hand down and pick up a pebble. He fingered the pebble.

I ran after them. The hatch on the silo was inside the barn. Dawson, acting brave, claimed he wanted to be the first to go up, but Uncle Henry told him ladies first. Dale Blue was afraid she'd dirty her yellow shirt or shorts. She didn't like putting her hands on the rusty rungs. She made a face.

"I don't think I want to," she said.

"You'll love it," Uncle Henry said. "You can see so far your eyes get tired from the distance."

"Go on without me," she said.

"Hon, you know I like to share everything with you," he said.

Still making a face, she started up. Uncle Henry

went after her, and me after Dawson. Since we were inside the wooden tunnel, we couldn't tell how high we'd climbed. Light came in only from cracks and from the opening at the top. We must've gone up a couple of minutes before Dale Blue got nervous.

"How far now?" she asked.

"We're close," Uncle Henry said, which was a lie.

"I'm tired," Dale Blue said after we climbed a while farther.

"Too much invested to stop now," Uncle Henry said. "Rest at the top."

"I don't think I like this," Dale Blue said. "We must be pretty high."

"You're pretty, high or low," Uncle Henry said. "And you'll forget the climb when you see the view."

Old Dawson wasn't talking much. Earlier he'd bragged about how he'd shinnied a rope up to the steel rafters of his school gym, but now all I heard was his breathing. I accidentally bumped against his leg and felt him trembling.

"Making it all right, city-freak?" I asked.

"Whew!" was the only thing he said.

At the top Dale Blue was really nervous. Her voice quivered.

"I'll help you up on the boards," Uncle Henry said.

"I don't like any of this," she said.

"Just ease on over," Uncle Henry said.

"Don't push!" she said.

He got her up on the boards, but he stayed on the ladder.

"Occurs to me they probably haven't replaced these boards and beams in years," Uncle Henry said. "Have they, Willie?"

"Not that I know about," I said.

"Hope they're not rotten," Uncle Henry said.

"Rotten!" Dale Blue said.

"Just look at that view, will you?" Uncle Henry said.

"The hell with the view!" Dale Blue said.

"You can see the old gristmill," Uncle Henry said.

"The hell with the old gristmill too," she said. "Am I on rotten boards?"

"Just don't move around a whole lot," Uncle Henry said. "It's higher than I remembered up here. Stick your head out the hole and look down, but be careful of the boards."

"No!" Dale Blue said.

"There's another way we can tell how high we are," Uncle Henry said. "I'll drop this pebble, and we'll see how long it takes to hit bottom."

He held out his hand and let go the pebble. I don't know, even for me who was used to the height, the pebble seemed to take about half an hour to hit. It caused a little plunk in the sour silage-mash, the plunk echoing in the hollowness of the dark silo.

"Get me down from here!" Dale Blue said.

"If you don't like the view, we can leave, but be careful of those boards," Uncle Henry said. "Don't move too much on those boards."

"Give me your hand!" Dale Blue said. "Henry?"

"You sound scared," he said.

"My teeth are clicking," she said.

"Momma, don't be afraid," Dawson said, but he was shivering on the ladder.

"Well I guess I'll help you down then," Uncle Henry said. "I forgot about those boards being up here so long they'd rot. Don't move fast now. And there is one thing before I give you my hand. You have to go to the river with me and Dawson."

"Damn you, Henry, don't you fool around with me up here!" she said.

"Who's fooling?" he asked. "Just tell me you'll go, and I'll give you my hand and help you down off those rotten boards which might give under you any second if you move too much."

"Henry, you bastard, you get me down or I'll make you so sorry you'll wish you lived under a rock!"

"I don't think you ought to talk to me like that, Dale Blue, not in the situation you're in."

"The situation you're in is if you don't get me down off here in a hurry I'll bust your ass!" she said.

"Let's climb down, boys," Uncle Henry said.

"You can't just leave her!" Dawson said.

"Henry, goddamn you, I'll go to the lawyers," Dale Blue said. "They'll take you tonsils to toenails."

"Your last opportunity," Uncle Henry said. "I'll help you off the boards and down the ladder if you promise to go to the river with Dawson and me. If you don't, you can come down by yourself. Now I wouldn't start yelling too loud on those boards."

I was already backing when she screamed words at him I never knew a woman could use. She didn't sound like herself, not only the cussing, but her voice in the silo seemed to be coming from ten directions at the same time. Dawson began crying. Uncle Henry had to force him down.

"Go on, boy," Uncle Henry said. "Go on now."

After I reached bottom, she was still shouting. Dawson was carrying on too. My mother and father were running toward the barn. Chickens squawked, cattle stampeded, and pigeons flapped so hard they shed feathers.

"I'm going back up!" Dawson hollered and tried to get on the ladder, but Uncle Henry dragged him away.

"Those beams and boards are all right," Uncle Henry said softly to Dawson. "I climbed up last night. They'll hold."

Daddy and I looked at each other and nodded. The barking dogs were explained.

"But she might fall anyhow!" Dawson said, his face wet, his lips bubbling.

"You know I love her too much to hurt her," Uncle Henry said. "And she thinks too much of herself to fall."

Uncle Henry stayed at the barn but made the rest of us leave. My daddy had to pull Dawson. All morning and afternoon she hollered. At dark she still hadn't come down. Dawson was sent home with Aunt Henri-

etta and Uncle Albert. I lay in my bed hearing Dale
Blue's voice carry over the pasture. She cussed, she
screamed, she cried.

"Henry Sharp, you'll wish you were dead when I'm
finished with you!" she hollered. "You'll wish you
were in a meat grinder!"

Before sunup I was down the back steps on my bare
feet and out the dining room window. I ran among
cornstalks which rattled and bashed me. I snuck
through mist to the barn where I hid behind bales of
the new hay.

Dale Blue wasn't yelling anymore. She wept and
talked pitifully.

"What'd I ever do to make you treat me this way?"
she asked.

"It's for your own good," Uncle Henry said. "Yours
and everybody's own good."

"I bore your child and have tried to be a loving
wife," she said.

"Come to the river with me, and I'll lay the world
at your feet," Uncle Henry said up the silo.

"You go to hell on a Honda!" she wailed.

Daddy came to the barn, but Uncle Henry sent him
back to the house. About midmorning Uncle Henry
called up to Dale Blue, who was sniffling.

"You want me to bring you your comb?" Uncle
Henry called. "The photographer's going to be here
after while."

"Who?" Dale Blue asked, and her voice echoed in
the silo: who? who? who?

"That photographer from the Lewisburg paper,"
Uncle Henry said.

"No!" she sobbed.

"Can't stop the press," Uncle Henry said. "Now
wouldn't it be better just to let me climb up there,
bring you down so you can rest a while, and then we'll
drive to the river?"

She whimpered.

"I love you," Uncle Henry called. "I'd rather die

than be hurting you. Dale Blue, do this one thing for me."

"Henry, please come get me off these goddamn boards!" she cried.

He ran up that ladder after her and half carried her down. All the way she bawled. Her shorts weren't so yellow any longer, but most of her hair was still on top her head, though falling apart.

Uncle Henry kissed her a long time. He helped her across the pasture to the house, washed her off in the bathtub, and put her to bed in the spare room with the shades drawn.

Later my mother, Aunt Henrietta, and Aunt Cornelia got Dale Blue on her feet to dress her in her sheet. She, Dawson, and Uncle Henry were dipped by the Reverend Arbogast in the Greenbrier River at four-thirty. There was to be a party at the house, but Dale Blue wouldn't leave the Caddy. Uncle Henry had to drive her to White Sulphur. She was still hugging the sheet around her, and her wet hair had toppled.

The next morning sunshine and crows woke me. Something was different in the house. Downstairs the grandfather clock ticked and chimed. I sniffed the keen, charred odor of hickory and the warm, fermented scent of buttermilk biscuits rising from the old Kalamazoo. My stomach flip-flopped. Whooping, I kicked the sheet straight up and grabbed for my jeans on the run to the kitchen.

Alice Walker

Alice Walker was born in Eatonton, Georgia, in 1944, the daughter of sharecroppers. Walker celebrated her mother's domestic creativity in her influential essay "In Search of Our Mothers' Gardens" (1983) in a collection of essays with the same title. Walker attended Spelman College and received a B.A. from Sarah Lawrence. She worked in the voter registration drive in Georgia in the 1960s, in a Head Start Program in Mississippi, and for the New York City welfare department. She has taught at Jackson State, Tougaloo, Wellesley, the University of Massachusetts, Berkeley, and Brandeis. A frequent contributor to such periodicals as *Essence, Harper's, Ms., Negro Digest,* the *New York Times,* and *Southern Voices,* she writes in many genres. Alice Walker has published six collections of essays, six collections of poetry, including *Revolutionary Petunias and Other Poems* (1973), which won the Lillian Smith Award, and six novels, including *The Color Purple* (1982), which won the Pulitzer Prize and an American Book Award and which was made into a major motion picture. While Alice Walker's writing is often about the racism and sexism black women experience, writer Gloria Steinem finds a universality in her work: "She speaks the female experience more powerfully for being able to pursue it across boundaries of race and class." At the same time that Walker writes of the tragedies in black women's lives, her vision tends toward affirmation, reconciliation, and transformation. Although she lives in San Francisco, she has said that her roots as a writer go back to the tradition of oral storytelling that has been "respected" in the South. She rarely sets her fiction in the South anymore, but this region of her childhood was the catalyst for her most celebrated work. In "The Black Writer and the Southern Experience" Walker wrote, "No one could wish for a more advantageous heritage than that bequeathed to the black writer in the South: a compassion for the earth, a trust in humanity beyond our knowledge of evil, and an abiding love of justice. We inherit a great responsibility as well, for we must give voice to centuries not only of silent bitterness and hate but also of neighborly kindness and sustaining love." Her story "Everyday Use" is a testament to these mixed emotions.

Everyday Use

for your grandmama

I will wait for her in the yard that Maggie and I made so clean and wavy yesterday afternoon. A yard like this is more comfortable than most people know. It is not just a yard. It is like an extended living room. When the hard clay is swept clean as a floor and the fine sand around the edges lined with tiny, irregular grooves, anyone can come and sit and look up into the elm tree and wait for the breezes that never come inside the house.

Maggie will be nervous until after her sister goes: she will stand hopelessly in corners, homely and ashamed of the burn scars down her arms and legs, eyeing her sister with a mixture of envy and awe. She thinks her sister has held life always in the palm of one hand, that "no" is a word the world never learned to say to her.

You've no doubt seen those TV shows where the child who has "made it" is confronted, as a surprise, by her own mother and father, tottering in weakly from backstage. (A pleasant surprise, of course: What would they do if parent and child came on the show only to curse out and insult each other?) On TV mother and child embrace and smile into each other's faces. Sometimes the mother and father weep, the child wraps them in her arms and leans across the table to tell how she would not have made it without their help. I have seen these programs.

Sometimes I dream a dream in which Dee and I are suddenly brought together on a TV program of this sort. Out of a dark and soft-seated limousine I am ushered into a bright room filled with many people. There I meet a smiling, gray, sporty man like Johnny Carson who shakes my hand and tells me what a fine girl I have. Then we are on the stage and Dee is embracing me with tears in her eyes. She pins on my dress a large orchid, even though she has told me once that she thinks orchids are tacky flowers.

In real life I am a large, big-boned woman with rough, man-working hands. In the winter I wear flannel nightgowns to bed and overalls during the day. I can kill and clean a hog as mercilessly as a man. My fat keeps me hot in zero weather. I can work outside all day, breaking ice to get water for washing; I can eat pork liver cooked over the open fire minutes after it comes steaming from the hog. One winter I knocked a bull calf straight in the brain between the eyes with a sledge hammer and had the meat hung up to chill before nightfall. But of course all this does not show on television. I am the way my daughter would want me to be: a hundred pounds lighter, my skin like an uncooked barley pancake. My hair glistens in the hot bright lights. Johnny Carson has much to do to keep up with my quick and witty tongue.

But this is a mistake. I know even before I wake up. Who ever knew a Johnson with a quick tongue? Who can even imagine me looking a strange white man in the eye? It seems to me I have talked to them always with one foot raised in flight, with my head turned in whichever way is farthest from them. Dee, though. She would always look anyone in the eye. Hesitation was no part of her nature.

"How do I look, Mama?" Maggie says, showing just enough of her thin body enveloped in pink skirt and red blouse for me to know she's there, almost hidden by the door.

"Come out into the yard," I say.

Have you ever seen a lame animal, perhaps a dog run over by some careless person rich enough to own a car, sidle up to someone who is ignorant enough to be kind to him? That is the way my Maggie walks. She has been like this, chin on chest, eyes on ground, feet in shuffle, ever since the fire that burned the other house to the ground.

Dee is lighter than Maggie, with nicer hair and a fuller figure. She's a woman now, though sometimes I forget. How long ago was it that the other house burned? Ten, twelve years? Sometimes I can still hear the flames and feel Maggie's arms sticking to me, her hair smoking and her dress falling off her in little black papery flakes. Her eyes seemed stretched open, blazed open by the flames reflected in them. And Dee. I see her standing off under the sweet gum tree she used to dig gum out of; a look of concentration on her face as she watched the last dingy gray board of the house fall in toward the red-hot brick chimney. Why don't you do a dance around the ashes? I'd wanted to ask her. She had hated the house that much.

I used to think she hated Maggie, too. But that was before we raised the money, the church and me, to send her to Augusta to school. She used to read to us without pity; forcing words, lies, other folks' habits, whole lives upon us two, sitting trapped and ignorant underneath her voice. She washed us in a river of make-believe, burned us with a lot of knowledge we didn't necessarily need to know. Pressed us to her with the serious way she read, to shove us away at just the moment, like dimwits, we seemed about to understand.

Dee wanted nice things. A yellow organdy dress to wear to her graduation from high school; black pumps to match a green suit she'd made from an old suit somebody gave me. She was determined to stare down any disaster in her efforts. Her eyelids would not flicker for minutes at a time. Often I fought off the temptation to shake her. At sixteen she had a style of her own: and knew what style was.

I never had an education myself. After second grade the school was closed down. Don't ask me why: in 1927 colored asked fewer questions than they do now. Sometimes Maggie reads to me. She stumbles along good-naturedly but can't see well. She knows she is not bright. Like good looks and money, quickness passed her by. She will marry John Thomas (who has mossy teeth in an earnest face) and then I'll be free to sit here and I guess just sing church songs to myself. Although I never was a good singer. Never could carry a tune. I was always better at a man's job. I used to love to milk till I was hooked in the side in '49. Cows are soothing and slow and don't bother you, unless you try to milk them the wrong way.

I have deliberately turned my back on the house. It is three rooms, just like the one that burned, except the roof is tin; they don't make shingle roofs anymore. There are no real windows, just some holes cut in the sides, like the portholes in a ship, but not round and not square, with rawhide holding the shutters up on the outside. This house is in a pasture, too, like the other one. No doubt when Dee sees it she will want to tear it down. She wrote me once that no matter where we "choose" to live, she will manage to come see us. But she will never bring her friends. Maggie and I thought about this and Maggie asked me, "Mama, when did Dee ever *have* any friends?"

She had a few. Furtive boys in pink shirts hanging about on washday after school. Nervous girls who never laughed. Impressed with her they worshiped the well-turned phrase, the cute shape, the scalding humor that erupted like bubbles in lye. She read to them.

When she was courting Jimmy T she didn't have much time to pay to us, but turned all her faultfinding power on him. He *flew* to marry a cheap city girl from a family of ignorant flashy people. She hardly had time to recompose herself.

When she comes I will meet—but there they are!

Maggie attempts to make a dash for the house, in her shuffling way, but I stay her with my hand. "Come back here," I say. And she stops and tries to dig a well in the sand with her toe.

It is hard to see them clearly through the strong sun. But even the first glimpse of leg out of the car tells me it is Dee. Her feet were always neat-looking, as if God himself had shaped them with a certain style. From the other side of the car comes a short, stocky man. Hair is all over his head a foot long and hanging from his chin like a kinky mule tail. I hear Maggie suck in her breath. "Uhnnnh," is what it sounds like. Like when you see the wriggling end of a snake just in front of your foot on the road. "Uhnnnh."

Dee next. A dress down to the ground, in this hot weather. A dress so loud it hurts my eyes. There are yellows and oranges enough to throw back the light of the sun. I feel my whole face warming from the heat waves it throws out. Earrings gold, too, and hanging down to her shoulders. Bracelets dangling and making noises when she moves her arm up to shake the folds of the dress out of her armpits. The dress is loose and flows, and as she walks closer, I like it. I hear Maggie go "Uhnnnh" again. It is her sister's hair. It stands straight up like the wool on a sheep. It is black as night and around the edges are two long pigtails that rope about like small lizards disappearing behind her ears.

"Wa-su-zo-Tean-o!" she says, coming on in that gliding way the dress makes her move. The short stocky fellow with the hair to his navel is all grinning and he follows up with "Asalamalakim, my mother and sister!" He moves to hug Maggie but she falls back, right up against the back of my chair. I feel her trembling there and when I look up I see the perspiration falling off her chin.

"Don't get up," says Dee. Since I am stout it takes something of a push. You can see me trying to move a second or two before I make it. She turns, showing white heels through her sandals, and goes back to the car. Out she peeks next with a Polaroid. She stoops down quickly and lines up picture after picture of me sitting there in front of the house with Maggie cowering behind me. She never takes a shot without making sure the house is included. When a cow comes nibbling around the edge of the yard she snaps it and me and Maggie *and* the house. Then she puts the Polaroid in the backseat of the car, and comes up and kisses me on the forehead.

Meanwhile Asalamalakim is going through motions with Maggie's hand. Maggie's hand is as limp as a fish, and probably as cold, despite the sweat, and she keeps trying to pull it back. It looks like Asalamalakim wants to shake hands but wants to do it fancy. Or maybe he don't know how people shake hands. Anyhow, he soon gives up on Maggie.

"Well," I say. "Dee."

"No, Mama," she says. "Not 'Dee,' Wangero Leewanika Kemanjo!"

"What happened to 'Dee'?" I wanted to know.

"She's dead," Wangero said. "I couldn't bear it any longer, being named after the people who oppress me."

"You know as well as me you was named after your aunt Dicie," I said. Dicie is my sister. She named Dee. We called her "Big Dee" after Dee was born.

"But who was *she* named after?" asked Wangero.

"I guess after Grandma Dee," I said.

"And who was she named after?" asked Wangero.

"Her mother," I said, and saw Wangero was getting tired. "That's about as far back as I can trace it," I said. Though, in fact, I probably could have carried it back beyond the Civil War through the branches.

"Well," said Asalamalakim, "there you are."

"Uhnnnh," I heard Maggie say.

"There I was not," I said, "before 'Dicie' cropped up in our family, so why should I try to trace it that far back?"

He just stood there grinning, looking down on me like somebody inspecting a Model A car. Every once in a while he and Wangero sent eye signals over my head.

"How do you pronounce this name?" I asked.

"You don't have to call me by it if you don't want to," said Wangero.

"Why shouldn't I?" I asked. "If that's what you want us to call you, we'll call you."

"I know it might sound awkward at first," said Wangero.

"I'll get used to it," I said. "Ream it out again."

Well, soon we got the name out of the way. Asalamalakim had a name twice as long and three times as hard. After I tripped over it two or three times he told me to just call him Hakim-a-barber. I wanted to ask him was he a barber, but I didn't really think he was, so I didn't ask.

"You must belong to those beef-cattle peoples down the road," I said. They said "Asalamalakim" when they met you, too, but they didn't shake hands. Always too busy: feeding the cattle, fixing the fences, putting up salt-lick shelters, throwing down hay. When the white folks poisoned some of the herd the men stayed up all night with rifles in their hands. I walked a mile and a half just to see the sight.

Hakim-a-barber said, "I accept some of their doctrines, but farming and raising cattle is not my style." (They didn't tell me, and I didn't ask, whether Wangero [Dee] had really gone and married him.)

We sat down to eat and right away he said he didn't eat collards and pork was unclean. Wangero, though, went on through the chitlins and corn bread, the greens and everything else. She talked a blue streak

over the sweet potatoes. Everything delighted her.
Even the fact that we still used the benches her daddy
made for the table when we couldn't afford to buy
chairs.

"Oh, Mama!" she cried. Then turned to Hakim-a-
barber. "I never knew how lovely these benches are.
You can feel the rump prints," she said, running her
hands underneath her and along the bench. Then she
gave a sigh and her hand closed over Grandma Dee's
butter dish. "That's it!" she said. "I knew there was
something I wanted to ask you if I could have." She
jumped up from the table and went over in the corner
where the churn stood, the milk in it clabber by now.
She looked at the churn and looked at it.

"This churn top is what I need," she said. "Didn't
Uncle Buddy whittle it out of a tree you all used to
have?"

"Yes," I said.

"Uh huh," she said happily. "And I want the
dasher, too."

"Uncle Buddy whittle that, too?" asked the barber.

Dee (Wangero) looked up at me.

"Aunt Dee's first husband whittled the dash," said
Maggie so low you almost couldn't hear her. "His
name was Henry, but they called him Stash."

"Maggie's brain is like an elephant's," Wangero
said, laughing. "I can use the churn top as a centerpiece for the alcove table," she said, sliding a plate
over the churn, "and I'll think of something artistic to
do with the dasher."

When she finished wrapping the dasher the handle
stuck out. I took it for a moment in my hands. You
didn't even have to look close to see where hands
pushing the dasher up and down to make butter had
left a kind of sink in the wood. In fact, there were a
lot of small sinks; you could see where thumbs and
fingers had sunk into the wood. It was beautiful light
yellow wood, from a tree that grew in the yard where
Big Dee and Stash had lived.

After dinner Dee (Wangero) went to the trunk at the foot of my bed and started rifling through it. Maggie hung back in the kitchen over the dishpan. Out came Wangero with two quilts. They had been pieced by Grandma Dee and then Big Dee and me had hung them on the quilt frames on the front porch and quilted them. One was in the Lone Star pattern. The other was Walk Around the Mountain. In both of them were scraps of dresses Grandma Dee had worn fifty and more years ago. Bits and pieces of Grandpa Jarrell's Paisley shirts. And one teeny faded blue piece, about the size of a penny matchbox, that was from Great Grandpa Ezra's uniform that he wore in the Civil War.

"Mama," Wangero said sweet as a bird. "Can I have these old quilts?"

I heard something fall in the kitchen, and a minute later the kitchen door slammed.

"Why don't you take one or two of the others?" I asked. "These old things was just done by me and Big Dee from some tops your grandma pieced before she died."

"No," said Wangero. "I don't want those. They are stitched around the borders by machine."

"That'll make them last better," I said.

"That's not the point," said Wangero. "These are all pieces of dresses Grandma used to wear. She did all this stitching by hand. Imagine!" She held the quilts securely in her arms, stroking them.

"Some of the pieces, like those lavender ones, come from old clothes her mother handed down to her," I said, moving up to touch the quilts. Dee (Wangero) moved back just enough so that I couldn't reach the quilts. They already belonged to her.

"Imagine!" she breathed again, clutching them closely to her bosom.

"The truth is," I said, "I promised to give them quilts to Maggie, for when she marries John Thomas."

She gasped like a bee had stung her.

"Maggie can't appreciate these quilts!" she said. "She'd probably be backward enough to put them to everyday use."

"I reckon she would," I said. "God knows I been saving 'em for long enough with nobody using 'em. I hope she will!" I didn't want to bring up how I had offered Dee (Wangero) a quilt when she went away to college. Then she had told me they were old-fashioned, out of style.

"But they're *priceless*!" she was saying now, furiously; for she has a temper. "Maggie would put them on the bed and in five years they'd be in rags. Less than that!"

"She can always make some more," I said. "Maggie knows how to quilt."

Dee (Wangero) looked at me with hatred. "You just will not understand. The point is these quilts, *these* quilts!"

"Well," I said, stumped. "What would *you* do with them?"

"Hang them," she said. As if that was the only thing you *could* do with quilts.

Maggie by now was standing in the door. I could almost hear the sound her feet made as they scraped over each other.

"She can have them, Mama," she said, like somebody used to never winning anything, or having anything reserved for her. "I can 'member Grandma Dee without the quilts."

I looked at her hard. She had filled her bottom lip with checkerberry snuff and it gave her face a kind of dopey, hangdog look. It was Grandma Dee and Big Dee who taught her how to quilt herself. She stood there with her scarred hands hidden in the folds of her skirt. She looked at her sister with something like fear but she wasn't mad at her. This was Maggie's portion. This was the way she knew God to work.

When I looked at her like that something hit me in the top of my head and ran down to the soles of my feet. Just like when I'm in church and the spirit of God touches me and I get happy and shout. I did something I never had done before: hugged Maggie to me, then dragged her on into the room, snatched the quilts out of Miss Wangero's hands and dumped them into Maggie's lap. Maggie just sat there on my bed with her mouth open.

"Take one or two of the others," I said to Dee.

But she turned without a word and went out to Hakim-a-barber.

"You just don't understand," she said, as Maggie and I came out to the car.

"What don't I understand?" I wanted to know.

"Your heritage," she said. And then she turned to Maggie, kissed her, and said, "You ought to try to make something of yourself, too, Maggie. It's really a new day for us. But from the way you and Mama still live you'd never know it."

She put on some sunglasses that hid everything above the tip of her nose and her chin.

Maggie smiled; maybe at the sunglasses. But a real smile, not scared. After we watched the car dust settle I asked Maggie to bring me a dip of snuff. And then the two of us sat there just enjoying, until it was time to go in the house and go to bed.

Lee Smith

As soon as Lee Smith learned to write, she began writing fiction. She wrote her first novel, *The Last Day the Dogbushes Bloomed* (1968), while she was a student at Hollins College, where southern literary critic Louis D. Rubin Jr. was her professor. Born in Grundy, Virginia, in 1944, Lee Smith sets much of her fiction in or near the Appalachian Mountains. She has published three story collections, *Cakewalk* (1980), *Me and My Baby View the Eclipse* (1990), and *News of the Spirit* (1997), as well as ten novels, including the widely acclaimed *Oral History* (1983), *Fair and Tender Ladies* (1988), and *The Last Girls* (2002). She often satirizes what she calls the "rarefied world of the finer things in life," a world she depicts in the story "Artists." Her ability to capture the everyday speech of such a wide variety of characters from turn-of-the-century mountain herbalists to contemporary teenage boys has caused critics to compare her to Eudora Welty and Flannery O'Connor. Lee Smith says that when she is writing, she hears "it all out loud. While I write, I write real fast, and I almost never revise. I have a sense that I'm sort of transcribing something almost." The winner of numerous prizes for her fiction, including several O. Henry awards, Lee Smith teaches English at North Carolina State University in Raleigh.

Artists

It is one of those hot Sunday afternoons that seem to stretch out, all green and gauzy and golden, over the length of my childhood; I walk in my grandmother's garden. The others are back on the porch in the curly wicker chairs, talking. Their voices come to me in little waves, musical and nonsensical like the sound of bees in the garden, across the wide green grass. I hear my mother's laugh. I cannot see her, or the others. They are cool up there on the porch, I know it; they have iced tea in the tall skinny glasses, with mint. But I want none of that. I attain the roses and halt before them, self-consciously. *I am transfixed by beauty,* I think. In fact I like the names of the roses perhaps more than I like the roses themselves—Pink Cloud, Peace, Talisman, Queen Elizabeth—the names unfurl across my mind like a silken banner, like the banner the children carry in the processional on Easter Sunday. I held a corner of that banner then. My grandmother taught me these names. I lean forward, conscious of myself leaning forward, to examine a Peace rose more closely. It is perfect: the pale velvety outer petals wide and graceful, then turning, curling and closing inward to its strange deep crimson center. The leaves are profuse, glossy, and green. There are thorns. I draw back. What I really prefer is the baby's breath along this border, the riot of pinks by the fountain, the snapdragons like a sassy little army at my feet. But my grandmother has told me that these roses are the pride of her heart. And she grows no common flowers here—no zinnias, no marigolds. This baby's breath is so fragile I can see through it and beyond, to where a lizard flashes shining across a stone and is gone in the phlox. I suck in my breath, feeling dizzy. The sun is so hot on my head and my feet hurt a lot in my patent leather pumps with the straps—because I have nearly outgrown them, I guess, just like my mother says. She says it is time for me to buy some more grown-up shoes, but I have been resisting this, finding excuses not to shop. I like these shoes; I hope that the pain will make me a better person and improve my soul.

For I am all soul these days. I have not missed Sunday School in four years, not even on the occasions when my mother hauls me off to Tucson or Florida and I have to attend strange churches where I ask pastors with funny names to sign affidavits concerning my presence. I mail these documents back to Mr. Beech at the First Methodist Church, so that nothing will mar my record. I have earned so many gold bars for good attendance and special merit that they clink when I walk and Daddy says I look like a major general. I have gone forward to the altar so many times during summer revivals that my mother, embarrassed by my zeal, refuses to let me attend them anymore unless I make a solemn pledge that I will not rededicate my life.

"Religious," then, I am also prone to fears and tremblings of a more general nature, and just about anything can set me off: my father when he's in a hurry; my black-headed first cousin Scott who is up in that big old sycamore tree right now, gathering a collection of sycamore balls; anything at all about cripples, puppies, or horses. For instance I had to go to bed for three days after my aunt Dora foolishly read me "The Little Match Girl" a couple of winters ago. I am "sensitive," "artistic," and "delicate," and everybody knows this is how I am, because my grandmother has laid down the law. Rarely does she lay down the law in such definite terms, preferring that her wishes be intuited, but now she has and this is it: *Do not tease Jennifer. Do not cut her hair.*

I wear a white piqué dress in my grandmother's garden this Sunday, a dress my mother ordered from Miller and Rhoads in Richmond, and I love it because I think it makes me look even thinner than I am. I want to be Peter Pan. I also want to be a ballerina, a detective, a missionary among the savages. My pale blond hair, pulled back by a white velvet bow, hangs down to my waist. My bars for good attendance and special merit jangle ever so slightly when I walk. They are calling me now from the porch. I pretend not to hear them, crossing the grass to where the iron marker has been placed near the thicket of willow trees at the edge of the creek. This marker reads

> *The Scent of the Rose for Pardon*
> *The Song of the Birds for Mirth*
> *I am Closer to God in my Garden*
> *Than Anywhere Else on Earth.*

I stop and run my fingers over the raised iron lettering, hot from the sun. "Rose for Pardon" blazes into my palm, and in the back of my mind I see myself in fifteen years or so on a terrible gory battlefield somewhere or maybe it is a dingy tenement, pardoning a man both elegant and doomed—a *rake*. I think he has tuberculosis.

"Jennifer!" My mother stands beside the rose garden, shading her eyes with her hand. "Come on! Your father is ready to go."

My mother wears a red linen dress and black-and-white spectator shoes. She likes golf, bridge, and dancing to jazz music. She hates these Sunday dinners. I follow her back to the porch, pretending not to see Scott, who throws his sycamore balls down with great skill so that they land silently in the grass just close enough to annoy me, too far away for me to complain.

Scott is one of the crosses I have to bear. It's too soon for me to tell whether Sammy, my own little brother, will turn out to be such a cross or not; sometimes he exhibits certain promise, I think. Other times he is awful. When he had a virus, for instance, he threw up all over my diary, eliminating February. Sammy is already in the car when we reach the porch. I can see his blond head bobbing up and down in the rear window. My father stands by the gate in his seersucker suit, waiting for us.

"Let's go!" he calls.

"Hurry and make your manners, now," my mother tells me in an undertone. "I can't wait to get out of this damn dress."

I ignore her vulgarity and head for the porch, as full of relatives as it is every Sunday, where I have to wait for my uncle Carl—my great-uncle, actually—to finish telling a story. The other people on the porch are my cousin Virginia, Scott's pretty older sister, whom I hate; my aunt Lucia, Scott's mother, who holds a certain interest for me because of a nervous breakdown she is rumored to have had in her twenties; Scott's boring father, Bill; my maiden aunts Dora and Fern; my grandfather, sweet and bent over in his chair, whittling; and my grandmother, of course, imperious as a queen in the glider, moving ever so slightly back and forth as if pushed by a personal breeze. My grandmother wears a pink brocade suit and a rhinestone sunburst pin, which I consider beautiful. Her hair, faintly blue, is piled into wispy curls that float above her wide white forehead, above her pale blue milky eyes, which look away from them all and across the river to the mountains where the sun goes down.

"And so I hollered, 'Well, John, start it up,' and John started his up, and I got in and started mine—" My uncle Carl is a famous storyteller even in Richmond, where he is in the Legislature, and he will not be hurried. The story he is telling now is one I've heard about a million times before, but it's one of

Grandaddy's favorites, all about how Uncle Carl and Grandaddy were the first people in this county to consider automobiles, how they went to Richmond on the train and bought themselves an automobile apiece and drove them home, and then—the climax of the story— how they, the owners of the only two cars in the county at that time, went out driving with their new young wives one Sunday ("in the springtime of our lives," as my uncle Carl always put it) and had a head-on collision on the hairpin curve at the bend of the Green River.

Grandaddy claps his knees with both hands and doubles over laughing, scattering wood chips all over the porch. He is the best-humored man in town— everybody says so—and everybody loves him. He could have been in politics himself, like Uncle Carl, if he had had the ambition. But he did not. He laughs so hard he coughs, and then he can't stop coughing. The wood chips fly all over the porch.

"What a display, Mr. Morris," my grandmother says without moving her mouth.

"Daddy, are you all right?" My own father moves from his place at the gate, starts up the concrete walk. My aunt Lucia stands up by her chair.

"Sure, sure," Grandaddy wheezes and laughs. "But do you remember how those cars *looked,* Carl, how they looked all nosed into each other thataway? And old man Rob Pierce asked if we was trying to mate them."

Daddy grins, on the step below, but Grandmother leans forward to examine the undersides of the fern in the pot by her feet.

"Don't you remember that, Mother?" Daddy asks her.

My grandmother sits up very straight. "Oh yes," she says in her whispery voice. "Oh, yes. I was cast into the river," she says, her head turned away from us all. The glider moves back and forth with the slightest of motions so that in her pink brocade suit she appears to shimmer, tiny and iridescent before us, like a rainbow on the verge of disappearing.

"Now, hell, Flo, that didn't happen at all!" Grandaddy says. "We were right there on the curve where Stinson's store is now. Nobody went in the water."

"Cast into the rushing stream," my grandmother says, looking off.

Uncle Carl guffaws, Grandaddy slaps his knee, and everybody else laughs and laughs.

"Come on now, Jenny," my mother calls. She gets in the car.

"Thank you so much for dinner," I say.

"Oh, can't she stay, Roy?" My grandmother suddenly springs to life. "Can't she?"

"Well, sure, I guess so," my daddy says, with an uneasy look back at the car. "That is, if she—"

"Oh please, Daddy, please please please!" I run down the steps and cling to his hand and beg him.

"Have you met my daughter, Sarah Bernhardt?" my mother says to nobody in particular.

"Please," I beg.

"Well, I suppose so, Jenny, but—" my father says.

My mother closes her door.

"I'll bring her home in the morning," Grandaddy calls from the porch. He stands up to wave as they pull off down the long dirt driveway. Sammy sticks his thumbs in his ears and wiggles his fingers, and grins out the car's back window. They round the bend beyond the willows, almost out of sight. I know that right now inside our car, my mother and my father are lighting cigarettes; I know that they will go home and sit on wrought-iron chairs in the yard with gin and tonic, and Sammy will play with the hose. I wave. When the blue Buick has disappeared, I enter my grandmother's house where it is always cool, always fragrant with something like potpourri, where even the air is cool and dense, and the pictures of people I never knew stare out of the gloom at me from the high dark walls.

My grandmother was famous in our town, and her character was widely discussed. Her dedication to what she referred to as the "finer things of life" was admired by many people and ridiculed by others who found her affected or even laughable. I had heard Mrs. Beech, the preacher's wife, refer to her passionately as a "great lady." I had seen my mother's sister Trixie hold her sides laughing as she and my mother recalled incident after incident in which my grandmother played the role of a comic figure, "putting on airs."

In any case everyone knew her. For at least forty years she had been a fixture in the First Methodist Church, taking her place each Sunday in the third row from the front, left-hand side, directly beneath a stained glass window that depicted Jesus casting the moneylenders out of the temple in a fury of vermilion and royal blue. She had headed the Methodist Ladies' Auxiliary and the Garden Club until all the ladies died who had voted for her year after year and these groups were overrun by younger women with pantsuits and new ideas. She still wrote long, complicated letters to local newspapers on the subjects of town beautification, historic preservation, and the evils of drink; she wore hats and white gloves on every possible occasion. Her manner of dress had changed so little over the years that even I could recognize its eccentricity. She *dressed up* all the time. I never saw her in my life without her pale voile or silk or brocade dresses, without her stockings, without her feet crammed into elegant shoes at least two sizes too small for her, so that at the end her feet were actually crippled. I never saw her without her makeup or the flashing rhinestone earrings and brooches and bracelets that finally she came to believe—as I believed then—were real.

I never ate dinner in her kitchen, either. Meals were served in the octagonal dining room with its dark blue velvet draperies held back by the golden tassels, its wallpaper featuring gods and goddesses and nymphs.

Meals there were interminable and complicated, involving courses intended to be brought in and taken away by that long procession of servants my grandmother hired and then dispensed of, big hardy dough-faced country women who could hoe all day but didn't know what to do next when she rang that silver bell. I was present at the table when one of them, after a fatal error that escapes me now, threw her white apron entirely up over her head crying out "Lord God" in a strangled voice, and fled forever out the back door as fast as her feet would take her. (Some people, my grandmother informed me solemnly after this memorable meal, cannot be taught anything and are best left down in the mire.) Of course I looked up "mire." Of course I remember everything on that table, to this day: the roses in the center, in a silver bowl; the pale pink crystal water goblets, beaded with icy drops, sitting on their cut-glass coasters; pale pink linen napkins and mats or maybe pale green ones and on special occasions the white Irish lace tablecloth; the silver salt and peppers, shaped like swans; the little glass basket, wonderfully wrought, which held pickles or mints or nuts. My grandmother declared the round mahogany table itself to be a family heirloom, then an antique, then a priceless antique from France. In any case it was large, dark, and shining, supported by horrible clawed feet with talons three or four inches long. The knowledge of these cruel taloned feet, right there beneath the table, added greatly to my enjoyment of these meals.

One ate only at the table in that house. Sometimes, though, I let my bestial elements get the best of me and snuck down into the kitchen for a snack after I was sure she was asleep. Once I surprised my grandaddy doing the same thing. The light from the refrigerator turned him light blue in his long flannel nightshirt and he broke into a delighted cackle at the sight of me. We ate cold fried chicken and strawberry ice cream together at the kitchen table and he told me about how he had traded a pony for a bicycle one time when he was a boy and how he tried and tried to get it back after his sprocket chain broke. We laughed a lot. I washed our dishes and he dried them and put them away and kissed me good night. His moustache tickled my cheek and I loved him so much at that moment; yet I felt disloyal, too. I climbed up the long stairs in shame.

Grandaddy called my grandmother Flo, but everyone else called her Florence. "Flo," she said severely, "has connotations." I did not know what those were, nor did I inquire. I called her Grandmother, as instructed. Grandmother called Grandaddy "Mr. Morris" in public all her life. Yet despite her various refinements, my grandmother was a country woman herself, born right in this county. Her father had started the First Methodist Church by importing a circuit rider to preach beneath the big sycamore tree, before the house was built. Her father had been by all accounts a hard, dangerous kind of a man, too, who had made a lot of money and had carried a pistol with him at all times. He had not believed in the education of women, so my grandmother never went to school. Eventually he was murdered, but no one ever mentioned this fact in front of my grandmother. She had married my grandaddy when she was only fifteen years old, but we didn't mention this fact either. Grandaddy was a carpenter who refused to elevate himself; he loved his work and he worked only as much as he had to. At least she had inherited the house.

All her ideas of refinement had come from books and from the self-improvement courses she took by mail, many of these deriving from a dubious institution known as the LaGrande University of Correspondence, which figured largely in my mother's and Trixie's glee. My grandmother knew all about these, among other things: Christianity, including particularly the lives of the saints; Greek mythology; English country houses; etiquette; Japanese flower arranging; Henry

VIII and all his wives; crewel embroidery; and the Romantic poets. She wrote poetry herself and locked it away in a silver filigree box. She made Japanese flower arrangements for everyone, strange flat affairs usually involving one large dried flower, a considerable array of sticks, and little porcelain Oriental men with huge sacks on their backs. She had ordered dozens of these little men for her arrangements. My grandmother had read the entire *Encyclopaedia Britannica* cover to cover, or claimed to have read it; even my mother found this admirable, although Trixie did not.

The primary cross my grandmother had to bear was Grandaddy, who steadfastly refused to be drawn into the rarefied world of the finer things in life. He stayed there, in fact, only long enough to eat. Otherwise he was whittling, smoking cigars out back, cracking jokes, drinking coffee in the Rexall drugstore downtown, building cabinets occasionally. He liked to drink bourbon and go hunting with his friends Mr. J.O. McCorkle and Mr. Petey Branch. My grandmother seemed to amuse him, I would say, more than anything else: he liked to "get her going," as he said. My father did not even like to "get her going"; but he was her son, too, in many ways, consumed by all that ambition my grandfather lacked, a man eaten up with the romance of making money. He made a great deal of money, luckily, since my mother was an expensive wife. Very early in their marriage she developed delicate health and terrible sinus allergies that required her removal, for months at a time, to Tucson, where Trixie lived, or to Coral Gables, Florida, where my father bought her a house. My father encouraged these illnesses, which got us all out of town, and in retrospect I can see that they broadened my horizons considerably. At the time, of course, I never wanted to go. I wanted to stay with my grandmother, and sometimes I was allowed to and sometimes not.

*　　*　　*

I am alone in the parlor while my grandmother works on a watercolor at her easel in the garden (her newest enthusiasm) and Grandaddy is off to the barber shop. I love this parlor, mine now; I love the gloom. I love the blackish gnarled voluptuous roses in the patterned carpet, the tufted velvet chairs and the horsehair sofa; I don't care how uncomfortable anything is. I love the doilies on the tables and the stiff antimacassars on the arms and the backs of the chairs, the *Leaves of Gold* book of poems on the table. I consider this the most beautiful room in the world. I move from portrait to portrait—mostly old daguerrotypes—along the walls, looking. There is stern-faced old Willie Lloyd Morris, her father, staring down his hatchet nose at me across the years. *Murdered.* A delicious chill travels from the top of my head down the length of my spine. There is my grandmother herself, a young girl with a face like a flower, seated primly in a wing chair before a painted backdrop of mountains and stormy clouds. She wears white. I see countless babies, my father among them, in stiff embroidered dresses and little caps. My aunt Lucia gazes soulfully out of her gold-leaf frame at me with strangely glistening dark eyes, like a movie star. My father stands at attention in high boots and the uniform he had to wear at military school, a wonderful uniform with at least a hundred shiny buttons on it. He looks furious. I pause before a family portrait that must have been taken just after my father finished at the University and swept my mother off her feet at a debutante ball in Richmond: it includes my aunts Dora and Fern, young then; my uncle Carl with a pipe in his mouth; my grandaddy grinning broadly, his thumbs locked in his suspenders; my grandmother standing slightly to one side; my father, young and impossibly dashing; and my mother with her hair all a tangle of curls. Then it hits me: *I am not there.* I am not anywhere at all in this picture. Looking at this picture is like being *dead.*

"Gotcha." Scott gooses me.

I whirl around, absolutely furious, mainly because I don't know how long he's been in this room. I don't know how long he's been watching me. I jump on him and we fall in a tangle onto the rose-figured carpet; I kick him in the nose until it bleeds.

"Hey," Scott keeps saying. "Hey."

We lie on our backs breathing hard.

"What's the matter with you?" Scott says.

"You can't just come in here like this," I say. "You can't." I start to cry.

Emboldened by my weakness, Scott sits up. "What do you do in here all the time?" he asks. He scoots closer. He looks like an Indian, having inherited my aunt Lucia's dark exotic charm.

"Nothing."

"Come on, Jenny," Scott moves closer still. *He exerts a certain fascination for her,* I think. *Jennifer succumbs to his appeal.*

"It's just so pretty," I falter. "I like to look at everything."

"Like what?" His black eyes shine through the shadows, close to mine.

"Well, like that table over there, like all the stuff on it." In my confusion I indicate what is in truth my favorite piece of furniture in the room, a multitiered mahogany stand that holds my grandmother's figurine collection, a wondrous array of angels, whistling boys, soldiers, Colonial ladies, cardinals and doves, unicorns—a whole world, in fact, topped by her *"pièce de résistance"* as she calls it, a white porcelain replica of Michelangelo's *David* displayed alone on the top tier. She ordered it from the Metropolitan Museum of Art in New York City. I love the *David* best of all because he seems entirely noble as well as beautiful, his left leg thrust forward in pursuit of justice in some doomed and luminous cause.

"I know why you like that one," Scott sneers.

"What one?"

"That one on the top. That naked guy."

"That's not a naked guy, Scott." I am enraged.

"That is Michelangelo's famous statue *David*. It's a work of Art, if you know anything about Art, which you don't, of course." I do not forget to pronounce the statue's name *Daveed*.

"You don't know anything about art either," Scott hollers. "You just like to look at him because he hasn't got any clothes on, that's all."

I stand up shakily. "I'm going to tell Grandmother," I announce.

Scott stands up too. "Go on then. Tell her," he says. "Just go on and tell her. She's even crazier than you are. She's so crazy because Grandaddy has a girl-friend, that's what my mother says. She says it's a good thing Grandmother has an outlet—"

Even in my horror I recognize a certain terrible authenticity in Scott's words; he sounds like his mother, who uses psychological terms with great aplomb—something I have, in fact, admired about my aunt Lucia in the past.

Now I hate her.

"That's a *lie*!" I scream. "Get out of here!"

Instead, Scott grabs me by the shoulders and pulls me to him and kisses me on the mouth until I get my senses together and push him away. "Yuck!" I wipe my mouth with the back of my hand.

Scott is laughing, doubled up with laughing in my grandmother's parlor. "You're crazy, Jenny," he says. "I'm the best kisser in the eighth grade. Everybody says so."

Still laughing he goes out the front door and gets on his bike and rides off down the curving drive. I go upstairs and brush my teeth. Then I go in the bed-room, fling myself down on the bed, and wait to have a nervous breakdown. *In anguish she considers the violation of her person,* I think.

After a while I went out into the garden and asked Grandmother if I could try painting a rose. "Why yes, Jennifer," she said. Her pale blue eyes lit up. She sent me into the house for more paper, a glass of water, and the lap desk, so that my paper might remain, as she told me, absolutely stationary.

"Anything worth doing is worth doing well," she said severely. "Now then." She dipped her brush into the water and I did the same. "Not too much," she cautioned. "There now."

We painted all that afternoon, until the sun was gone. I did three and a half roses. Then we gathered up all our materials and put them away just so. I went ahead of her, carrying the lap desk and the easel into the hall. I came back out to the porch and found that Grandmother had spread my roses out on the glider. She was studying them. I thought they were pretty good, considering. We stood together and looked at them for some time as they glided ever so gently back and forth.

Grandmother turned to me and clasped me violently against her, smashing me into the spiky sunburst brooch on her bosom. "Jennifer, Jennifer," she said. She had grown little and frail by then and we were almost the same size; I couldn't see her face, but I was lost in her lavender perfume. "Jennifer, Jennifer," she was sobbing. "You must live your life, my darling. You must not get caught up in the press of circumstance; you must escape the web of fate."

I couldn't breathe and I had no idea what "web of fate" she referred to, but I felt as though I had received a solemn commission. "I *will*, Grandmother," I said. "I *will*."

"Hello, ladies!" It was my grandaddy, stumbling a bit on the steps. Mr. J.O. McCorkle stood behind him, grinning broadly. They both appeared to be in a wonderful humor.

"Oh, Mr. Morris, you gave me such a turn!" Grandmother whirled around; seeing Mr. J.O. McCorkle, her eyes narrowed. "Well, Mr. Morris!" she said with a certain significance. She swept up my three and a half roses and vanished mysteriously into the house.

"Now Flo, don't you Mr. Morris me!" Grandaddy called after her. He and Mr. McCorkle laughed. Grandaddy came up on the porch and gave me a whiskery kiss. "How about some checkers?" he asked me.

"Not right now." *Jennifer said meaningfully,* I thought. I turned and went into the house.

This was the first indication of my Talent. Spurred on by my grandmother's enthusiasm, I painted more roses and at length a morning glory. I ventured into daisies, then columbine; I mastered Swedish ivy and attempted, at last, a Still Life. This proved somewhat more difficult because Sammy kept eating the apples and spoiling my arrangement. "Never mind," Grandmother told me when I rode my bicycle over to her house to weep after one such disaster. "Never mind. Great art requires great suffering," my grandmother said.

The second indication of my Talent came from school, where I had written a sonnet, which my English teacher, Miss Hilton, praised extravagantly. This sonnet compared life to a carousel ride, in highly symbolic terms. It was named "The Ride of Life." Miss Hilton sent "The Ride of Life" to the local newspaper, which printed it on the book page. My mother drummed her fingers on the tabletop, reading it. "For heaven's sake!" she said, staring at me. My grandmother clipped it and had it framed. I was suddenly so artistic that my only problem came from trying to decide in which direction to focus my Talent. I did not forget to suffer, either, lying on my bed for a while each afternoon in order to do so.

It didn't surprise me at all, consequently, when I came down with a virus, which all turned into bronchitis, then pneumonia. For a long time I was so sick that they thought I might die. The doctor came every day for a while, and everyone tiptoed. A spirit lamp hissed night and day in my bedroom, casting out a wispy blue jet of steam that formed itself into the camphorous blue haze that still surrounds my entire memory of that illness. Grandaddy came every day, bringing little wooden animals and people carved from pine. Once he brought a little chest of drawers he had made for me. It was incredibly intricate; each drawer opened and shut. I dozed in my blue cloud holding the chest in my hand. Every now and then, when I awakened, I would open and close the drawers. Once when I woke up I saw my mother, in tears, standing beside the bed. This shocked me. I asked for Coca-Cola and drank it; then I sat up and ate some soup; and at the end of that illness it was Grandaddy, not me, who died.

He had a heart attack in the Post Office; after examining him, the hospital doctors said there was nothing they could do and sent him home, where he lived for three more days. During this time, my grandmother's house was filled with people—all our relatives, all his friends—in and out. The kitchen was full of food. My grandmother did not enter his bedroom, as she had not entered mine. Illness made her faint and she had always said so; nobody expected her to. She stayed in the Florida room, painting cardinals and doves, while my aunts sat on the divan and watched her.

From the time they brought Grandaddy home, my own father sat by his bed. I have never, before or since, seen my father as upset—*distraught*, actually, is the word—as he was then. On the morning of the second day, Grandaddy raised his head from the pillow and rolled his eyes around the room. Daddy came forward and bent over him, taking his hand. Grandaddy made a horrible gargling kind of noise in his throat; he was trying to talk. Daddy bent closer. Grandaddy made the noise again. The veins in his forehead stood out, awful and blue. Daddy listened. Then he stood up straight and cleared his own throat.

"By God, I'll do it!" my father announced in a ringing voice, like somebody in a movie. He turned and left the room abruptly, and all of the people remaining looked at one another. My grandfather continued to stare wildly around the room, with his breath rattling down in his throat.

Twenty minutes later my father came back bringing Mollie Crews, the woman who had been my grandaddy's lover for twenty-five years. Mollie Crews was a large, heavy woman with curly and obviously dyed red hair; she was a beautician, with a shop over the Western Auto store downtown. Mollie Crews wore her white beautician's uniform, an orange cardigan sweater, and white lace-up shoes with thick crepe soles. Her hands flew up to her face when she saw Grandaddy, and her big shoulders shook. Then she rushed over to take the chair at the side of his bed, dropping her purse on the floor. "Oh, Buddy," she sobbed. *Buddy?* I was stunned. Grandaddy's eyes fastened on her and an expression like a smile came to his face. He sank back into the pillow, closing his eyes. The rattle of his breathing softened. Still firmly holding his hand, Mollie Crews took off her cardigan—awkwardly, with her free hand—and slung it over the back of the chair. She reached down and fumbled around in her purse and got a cigarette and lit it with a gold lighter. She exhaled, crossing her legs, and settled down into the chair. My father brought her an ashtray. Aunt Lucia stood up abruptly, flashing her black eyes at everyone. She started to speak and then did not. Aunt Lucia exited theatrically, jerking me from the room along with her. My cousin Virginia followed. The hall outside Grandaddy's room was full of people, and Aunt Lucia pulled me straight through them all, sailing out of the house. Scott was in the front yard. "What did I tell you?" he said. "What did I tell you?"

Aunt Lucia never returned to Grandaddy's room, nor did my uncle Bill or my cousin Virginia or my old maid aunts. Uncle Carl came back from Richmond that night and stayed with him until the end. So did my father, and my mother was in and out. The whole family had to take sides. I went in and sat dutifully

with Grandmother, working at her easel in the Florida
room. "This is a woodpecker," she said once, exhib-
iting her latest. "Note the pileations." But I couldn't
stay away from Grandaddy's room either, where I was
mesmerized by Mollie Crews with her generous slack
mouth and her increasingly rumpled beautician's uniform. She looked like a nurse. *A fallen woman,* I told
myself, and I watched her sit there hour after hour holding his hand, even when he was in coma and no longer
knew she was there. *A Jezebel,* I thought, watching her.
I wondered whether she would go to hell.

When my grandfather actually died, everyone left
the room except Mollie Crews, and after a long while
she came out too, shaking her curls and throwing her
head back as she opened the door. We were crowded
into the hall. She looked at all of us, and then for
some reason she came back to me. "He was a fine
man," Mollie Crews said. She was not crying. She
looked at everyone again and then she walked out of
the house as abruptly as she had come and sat on
the front porch until somebody in a battered sky blue
Oldsmobile picked her up, and then she was completely and finally gone.

Mollie Crews was the only person in town who did
not attend the funeral. Grandmother wore her black
silk suit with a hat and a veil. She came in like royalty
and sat between Daddy and Aunt Lucia, never lifting
her veil, and she stood straight with my mother and
me under a black umbrella when they buried Grandaddy in the church cemetery afterward, in a fine gray
drizzle that started then and went on for days. Everyone in town paid a call on my grandmother during the
week after that, and she sat in her parlor on the tufted
sofa beside the tiered table and received them. But
her blue eyes had grown mistier, paler than ever, and
sometimes the things she said did not connect.

I am walking by the ocean, alone, on the beach
near my mother's house in Florida. It is a bright, clear

morning. Sometimes I bend down to pick up a shell. Other times I pause and gaze dramatically out to sea, but this Florida sea is not as I would have it: not tempest-tossed, not filled with drowning nobility clutching at shards of ships. This is a shiny blue Florida sea, determinedly cheerful. The waves have all been choreographed. They arch and break like clockwork at my feet, bringing me perfect shells. The weather is perfect, too. Everything in Florida is hot and easy and tropical and I hate it. My mother has yanked Sammy and me out of school and brought us down here to humor her famous allergies, but I can't even see that she has any allergies: all she does in Florida is shop and play bridge. I feel like a deserter from a beautiful sinking ship. I have deserted my grandmother, just when she needs me most.

My mother has arranged for me to have a Cuban tutor who is supposed to teach me Spanish as well as other things. This Cuban tutor is named Dominica Colindres. She is a plump, dark young woman with greasy hair and big sagging bosoms and pierced ears. She sweats under her arms. I hate Dominica Colindres. I refuse to learn anything she tries to teach me, and I refuse to have anything at all to do with any of the other children my age who try to befriend me on the beach. I walk the shoreline, picking up shells. I think about sin, art, heaven, and hell. Since my arrival in Florida I have written two poems I am rather proud of, although no one else has seen them. One is a poem about the ocean, named "The Sea of Life." The other is named "Artifacts of Existence," about shells.

The sun is hot on my back, even through my long-sleeved shirt, so I pick up one last shell and walk back up the beach to our house. I wear a hat and long pants, too, wet now below the knee: I refuse to get a tan.

My mother is entertaining our next-door neighbors, Mr. and Mrs. Donlevy from Indiana, on the patio. She wears a yellow sundress, looks up and smiles. Mr. and Mrs. Donlevy smile. I do not smile, and my mother raises her eyebrows at Mr. and Mrs. Donlevy in a significant manner. I know they've been talking about me. They are drinking bloody marys and reading the morning paper. The hibiscus around the patio is pink and gaudy in the sun.

I go into my room to work on my shell collection. I have classified my shells as to type, and arranged each type in gradations of hue. This means that every time I find a good shell, I have to move *everything,* in order to put the new shell into its proper place. I take a certain pleasure in the difficulty of this arrangement. I am hard at work when the bells begin to ring, and then, of course, it hits me, *Sunday!* Mother and the Donlevys were reading the Sunday *Times!* It's the first time I've missed Sunday school in four years; my perfect attendance record is broken.

I put my last shell, a *Tellina lineata,* carefully in place. I leave my room. Mother is telling Mr. and Mrs. Donlevy goodbye at the front door. It's already hot; the air conditioner clicks on. I cross the white carpet in the living room, the red tile kitchen floor. Once on the patio, I rush toward the round glass table with its striped umbrella and push it violently, overturning it onto the flagstone. The whole glass top shatters. The umbrella crushes the hibiscus. The frosted bloody mary glasses are flung into the grass, and one of them breaks.

I go back in the kitchen and find Sammy, who has just gotten up, eating Wheaties at the kitchen table. He has made a little mess of his own, fixing his cereal, and this gives me extra satisfaction.

"I had a funny dream," Sammy says.

"What was it about?" I sit down with Sammy at the kitchen table. My mother comes through the kitchen humming and goes out into the patio.

"It was real funny," Sammy says. Milk dribbles down his chin.

"But what was it *about*?" I ask. Out on the patio, my mother has started to shriek.

"I can't remember what it was about." Sammy looks at me with his big blue eyes. "But the name of it was 'The Secret of the Seven Arrows.' "

I get up and hug Sammy as hard as I can, laughing. He *is* cute. Maybe he won't be a cross after all. Then I start to cry. I cry for two hours as hard as I can, and then after that I feel fine and my mother takes Sammy and me out to a fancy restaurant for dinner.

My mother never said a word to me about the broken table, although I knew—in the way children know things, almost like osmosis—that she *knew*. Workmen in overalls came the next day and replaced it. The new umbrella was lime green, with a flowered lining. My mother took me shopping and we bought new bathing suits for both of us; eventually I acquired a tan. I even learned a little Spanish, and on the day before we left, Dominica Colindres pierced my ears.

The day we came back—this was in February—I went straight over to my grandmother's house, of course, riding my bicycle through the falling snow; but even though Daddy had told me how it would be there, I was not prepared. Grandmother had "failed considerably"—those were his words—in the eight weeks we had been gone. Daddy had hired two practical nurses to stay with her, one at night and one in the daytime, and he had turned the dining room into a downstairs bedroom since Grandmother could no longer manage the steps. When I arrived, Grandmother was sitting in the tufted rose velvet wing chair where she always sat in the winter, but she seemed to have shrunk by one or two feet. Or maybe I had grown. In any case Grandmother was so small that she looked lost in the chair, and her feet dangled above the floor. She was dressed as carefully as always, though, and this reassured me at first as I stood in the dark hall pulling off my gloves, my boots, my coat. Noise from the television blared out into the hall: this was very unusual, since Grandmother hated television and said that it had been invented to amuse those people who needed such amusements. The parlor looked all different somehow, lit primarily by the glow of the TV. A tall thin woman stood up from where she sat in the rocking chair. "You must be Jennifer," she said. "I'm Mrs. Page." Mrs. Page wore her hair in a bun; she was crocheting a brown-and-white afghan.

"It's so nice to meet you." *Jennifer said mechanically like a windup doll,* I thought as I crossed the flowered carpet to take my grandmother's hand. Her hand was little and frail, her bones like the bones of birds. She would not look at me.

"Grandmother!" I said. "Grandmother! It's me, Jennifer." Grandmother watched the TV. I noticed that she wore three of her huge rhinestone brooches in an uneven row on the front of her dress. "Grandmother," I said.

"Excuse me, miss, but she doesn't know anybody right now. She just doesn't. It takes them that way sometimes." Mrs. Page looked up from her afghan and smiled.

"Well, this is my grandmother and she will know *me*!" I snapped.

But she didn't.

The only response she made came later, in that same awful afternoon. I had been sitting on a footstool beside her while it grew darker outside and more snow fell and the bluish-white light of the television danced off the bones of her face. The program had changed again; this time it was a stock car race, and it seemed to interest her. She leaned forward and said something under her breath.

"Do you like this, Grandmother?" I asked.

"Listen," Mrs. Page said. "She just likes it all. She doesn't even know what she's watching."

This infuriated me. "What are you watching, Grandmother?" I asked. On the television screen, the cars went around and around the track, and one of them turned over and burst into flames.

"Serves him right for driving that thing," Mrs. Page remarked.

"Grandmother," I said.

Grandmother turned to face me, fully, for the first time. Her light blue eyes seemed to have grown larger. They shone in the pale bony planes of her face. In front of her, the numbered cars went around a track somewhere in Georgia. Grandmother opened her mouth and stared back and forth from me to the television screen.

"What are you watching, Grandmother?" I asked again.

"Art," she said. "I'm watching art, Jennifer."

The cars went around and around on the television, and after watching them for a while longer I put on all my things and rode my bike home through the snow. The road had been scraped but it was still icy in spots, and a fine mist of snow covered the asphalt. I should have been careful, riding, but I was not. I pedaled as hard as I could, gulping huge mouthfuls of cold air and falling flakes of snow. I was moving so fast that the snow seemed to rush straight at me, giving me an odd sense of weightlessness, as if I were somehow suspended between the earth and the sky.

This feeling of suspension—a kind of not belonging, a sense of marking time—hung on even after my grandmother died, which happened a few weeks after our return. Her house was bought by a young attorney. Everything in the house was parceled out among the relatives, who insisted that I should have all the art supplies and the entire figurine collection, including *David*. These things sat in two cardboard boxes in my room for a long time, while I remained suspended. Then one Saturday morning in early May, I knew exactly what I wanted to do. I hauled both boxes out to the tool shed, placing them neatly beside the garden tools. I closed the tool shed door. I went inside and took the saved-up allowance money out of my jewelry box; then I got on my bike and rode straight downtown, parking my bicycle in front of the Western Auto store. Mollie Crews cut my hair off in a page boy, which curled softly under my ears. It looked terrific. Then I rode my bike over to see Scott, who turned out to be—exactly as he had promised—a good kisser. So I grew up. And I never became an artist, although my own career has certainly had its ups and downs, like most careers. Like most lives. Now I keep my grandmother's figurine collection on a special low table for my own children, who spend long hours arranging and rearranging all the little figures in their play.

Shirley Ann Grau

Born in 1929, Shirley Ann Grau grew up in New Orleans, Louisiana, and Montgomery, Alabama. She majored in English at Sophie Newcomb College of Tulane University and went on to graduate school there. She published her first collection of stories, *The Black Prince and Other Stories* (1955), when she was only twenty-four. She has written two other story collections, *The Wind Shifting West* (1973), and most recently *Nine Women* (1985), and six novels, one of which, *The Keepers of the House* (1964), won the Pulitzer Prize. Grau sees in her own family "the two strains—New England and southern—that were careful to preserve a sense of family continuity," and her writing often focuses on the southern interest in family history. She also writes about people whose harsh lives are reflected in their violent behavior. Although she resists the label of southern writer as too limiting, her works exhibit a strong sense of place and recognizable southern characters. Grau divides her time between Metairie, Louisiana, and Martha's Vineyard, Massachusetts.

Homecoming

The telegram was in the middle of the dining room table. It was leaning against the cut-glass bowl that sometimes held oranges, only this week nobody had bought any. There was just the empty bowl, lightly dust coated and flecked with orange oil. And the telegram.

"Did you have to put it there?" Susan asked her mother.

"It's nothing to be ashamed of," her mother said.

"I'm not ashamed," she said, "but why did you put it there?"

"It's something to be proud of."

"It looks just like a sign."

"People will want to see it," her mother said.

"Yes," Susan said, "I guess they will."

She took her time dressing, deliberately. Twice her mother called up the stairs, "Susan, hurry. I told people any time after three o'clock."

And they were prompt, some of them anyway. (How many had her mother asked? She'd been such a long time on the phone this morning . . .) Susan heard them come, heard their voices echo in the high-ceilinged hall, heard the boards creak with unaccustomed weight. She could follow their movements in the sounds of the old boards. As clearly as if she were looking at them, she knew that the women had stayed inside and the men had moved to the porches.

Wide porches ran completely around two sides of

the house, south and west. "Porches are best in old houses like this," her mother often said. "Good, useful porches."

The west porch was the morning porch. Its deep overhang kept off the sun even in these July afternoons. There was a little fringe of moonflower vine too, across the eaves, like lace on a doily. The big white moonflowers opened each night like white stars and each morning, like squashed bugs, dropped to the ground. They were trained so carefully on little concealed wires up there that they never once littered the porch . . . The south porch was the winter porch. The slanted winter sun always reached that side, bare and clear, no vines, no planting. A porch for old people. Where the winter sun could warm their thin blood, and send it pumping through knotty blue veins. Her grandmother sat out there, sightless in the sun, all one winter. Every good day, every afternoon until she died . . .

Susan always thought one porch was much bigger until she measured them—carefully, on hands and knees, with a tape measure. How funny, she thought; they seemed so different to be just the same.

On this particular afternoon, as Susan came downstairs—slowly, reluctantly, hesitating at each step—she glanced toward the sound of men's voices on the south porch. Looking through the screen into the light, she saw no faces, just the glaring dazzle of white shirts. She heard the little rattle of ice in their glasses and she smelled the faint musty sweet odor of bourbon.

Like a wake, she thought. Exactly like a wake.

Her mother called: "In the dining room, dear."

There was coffee on the table, and an ice bucket and a bottle of sherry and two bottles of bourbon. "Come in, Susan," her mother said. "The girls are here to see you."

Of course, Susan thought. They had to be first, her mother's best friends, Mrs. Benson and Mrs. Watkins, each holding a sherry glass. Each kissed her, each with a puff of faint flower scent from the folds of their flowered dresses. "We are so sorry, Susan," they said one after the other.

Susan started to say thank you and then decided to say nothing.

Mrs. Benson peered over her sherry glass at the telegram propped on the table next to the good silver coffeepot. "I thought the Defense Department sent them," she said, "that's what I always heard."

Susan's mother said emphatically, her light voice straining over the words, just the way it always did: "They sent me one for my husband."

"That's right." Mrs. Watkins nodded. "I saw it just now when I came in. Right under the steps in the hall. In that little gold frame."

"When I read that telegram," Susan's mother said, "I got a pain in my heart that I never got rid of. I carried that pain in my heart from that day to this."

And Susan said, patiently explaining: "The army told Harold's parents."

"And the Carters sent word to you," her mother said firmly. Her hand with its broad wedding band flapped in the air. "There on the table, that's the word they sent."

All of a sudden Susan's black dress was too hot and too tight. She was perspiring all over it. She would ruin it, and it was her good dress.

"I'm so hot," she said. "I've got to change to something lighter."

Her mother followed her upstairs. "You're upset," she said, "but you've got to control yourself."

"The way you controlled yourself," Susan said.

"You're mocking now, but that's what I mean, I had to control myself, and I've learned."

"I've nothing to control," Susan said. She stripped off the black dress. The wet fabric stuck and she jerked it free. Close to her ear, a couple of threads gave a little screeching rip. "I've got to find something lighter. It's god-awfully hot down there."

"White," her mother said. "White would be correct."

Susan looked at her, shrugged, and took a white piqué out of the closet.

"Are you all right?"

"I'm fine," Susan said. "I'm great."

She put the white piqué dress across a chair and sat down on her bed. Its springs squeaked gently. She stretched out and stared up at the crocheted tester and felt her sweat-moistened skin turn cool in the air. She pulled her slip and her bra down to her waist and lay perfectly still.

Abruptly she thought: If there were a camera right over me, it would take a picture of five eyes: the two in my head, the one in my navel, and the two on my breasts. Five eyes staring up at the ceiling.

She rolled over on her stomach.

It was a foolish thing to think. Very foolish. She never seemed to have the proper thoughts or feelings. Her mother now, she had the right thoughts, everybody knew they were right. But Susan didn't . . .

Like now. She ought to be more upset now. She ought to be in tears over the telegram. She'd found it stuck in the crack of the door this morning. "Have been informed Harold was killed at Quang Tri last Thursday." She should have felt something. When her mother got the news of her father's death in Korea, the neighbors said you could hear her scream for a block; they found her huddled on the floor, stretched out flat and small as she could be with the bulging womb that held an almost completed baby named Susan.

Susan lifted her head and looked at the picture on her night table. It was a colored photograph of her father, the same one her mother had painted into a portrait to hang over the living room fireplace. Susan used to spend hours staring into that small frame, try-

ing to sharpen the fuzzy colored lines into the shape
of a man. She'd never been quite able to do that; the
only definite thing she knew about him was the sharp
white lines of his grave marker in Arlington.

"That picture looks just exactly like him," her
mother would say. "I almost think he'll speak to me.
I'm so glad you can know what your father looked
like."

And Susan never said: I still don't know. I never
will.

And this whole thing now, her mourning for Harold,
it was wrong. All wrong. She hadn't even known him
very well. He was just a nice boy from school, a tall
thin boy who worked in the A & P on Saturdays and
liked to play pool on Sundays, who had a clear light
tenor and sang solo parts with her in the glee club.
His father worked for the telephone company and
they lived on the other side of town on Millwood
Street—she knew that much. He'd finished high school
a year ago and he'd asked her to his senior prom,
though she hadn't expected him to. On the way home,
he offered her his class ring. "You can take it," he
said. She could see his long narrow head in the light
from the porch. "Till I get out of the army."

"Or some other girl wants it."

"Yeah."

Because she couldn't think of anything else, she
said: "Okay, I'll keep it for you. If you want it, just
write and I'll send it to you."

That was how she got the ring. She never wore it,
and he didn't ask for it back. She didn't even see him
again. His family moved away to the north part of the
state, to Laurel, and Harold went there on his leaves.
He didn't come back to town and he didn't call her.
He did send a chain to wear the ring on—it was far
too big for her finger—from California. She wrote him
a thank-you note the very same day. But he didn't
answer, and the ring and the chain hung on the back

of her dresser mirror. He was just a boy she knew who went in the army. He was just a boy whose ring she was keeping.

Maybe he'd told his parents something more. Why else would they wire her? And what had he told them? All of a sudden there were things she couldn't ask. The world had changed while she wasn't looking.

And Harold Carter was killed. Harold was the name of an English king, and he was killed somewhere too. Now there was another Harold dead. How many had there been in between? Thousands of Harolds, thousands of different battles . . .

Her mother opened the door so quickly it slipped from her hand and smashed into the wall. The dresser mirror shivered and the class ring swung gently on its chain. "Susan, I thought, I just thought of something . . ."

What, Susan asked silently. Did you forget the extra ice? Something like that? Will people have to have warm drinks?

"You're acting very strangely. I've never seen you act like this . . . Did something go on that shouldn't have? Tell me."

Susan tossed a hairbrush from hand to hand. "Maybe it's me," she said, "but I just don't know what people are talking about anymore."

"All right," her mother said, "you make me put it this way. Are you going to have a baby?"

Susan stared at the broken edges of the bristles, and she began to giggle. "Harold left a year ago, Mother."

"Oh," her mother said, "oh oh oh." And she backed out the door.

Susan said after her, sending her words along the empty hall where there was nobody to hear them: "That was you who was pregnant. And it was another war."

She put on some more perfume; her flushed skin burned at its touch. She glanced again at the photograph of her father.

You look kind of frozen there. But then I guess you

really are. Frozen at twenty-three. Smile and crooked cap and all.

And Susan remembered her grandmother sitting on the porch in the sun, eyes hooded like a bird's, fingers like birds' claws. Senility that came and went, like a shade going up and down. "He don't look nothing like the pictures," she said. She always called her dead son-in-law he, never used his name. "Never looked like that, not dead, not alive." The one hand that was not paralyzed waved at an invisible fly. "Died and went to glory, that boy. Those pictures your mother likes, they're pictures of him in glory. Nothing more nor less than glory."

The old woman was dead now too. There weren't any pictures of her. She'd gone on so long she fell apart, inch by inch of skin. All the dissolution visible outside the grave . . .

Susan breathed on the glass front of her father's picture and polished it with the hem of her slip. The young glorious dead . . . like Harold. Only she didn't have a picture of Harold. And she didn't really remember what he looked like.

She could hear the creak of cane rockers on the porch, the soft mumbling of men's talk. She stood by the screen to listen.

"I'll tell you." Harry Benson, the druggist, was sitting in the big chair, the one with the fancy scrolled back. "They called us an amphibious unit and put us ashore and they forgot about us. Two weeks with nothing to do but keep alive on that beach."

That would be Okinawa. She had heard about his Okinawa.

"And after a while some of the guys got nervous. If they found a Jap still alive they'd work him over good, shoot him seven or eight times, just to see him jump. They kind of thought it was fun, I guess."

"Hold it a minute, Harry," Ed Watkins, who was the railroad agent, said. "Here's Susan."

They both stood up. They'd never done that before.

"We were talking about our wars, honey," Mr. Benson said. "I'm afraid we were."

"That's all right," Susan said. "I don't mind."

"It was crazy, plain crazy," Mr. Watkins said. "Like that guy, must have been '51 or '52."

"Ed, look," Mr. Benson said. "Maybe we ought to stop talking about this."

"Nothing so bad . . . This guy, I don't think I ever knew his name, he was just another guy. And in those days you remember how they came down in waves from the North. You could hear them miles away, yelling and blowing horns. So this time, you could hear them like always, and this guy, the one I didn't know a name for, he puts a pistol right under his jaw and blows the top of his head off. The sergeant just looked at him, and all he can say is, 'Jesus Christ, that son of a bitch bled all over my gun.'"

"Hard to believe things like that now," Mr. Benson said.

"I believe them," Susan said. "Excuse me, I have something to do in the kitchen."

She had to pass through the dining room. Mrs. Benson still had a sherry glass in her hand, her cheeks were getting flushed and her eyes were very bright. Mrs. Watkins had switched from sherry to whiskey and was putting more ice in her highball. Susan's mother poured herself coffee.

Susan thought: Mrs. Benson's going to have an awful sherry hangover and Mrs. Watkins' ulcer is going to start hurting from the whiskey and my mother's drunk about twenty cups of coffee today and that's going to make her sick . . .

She only said, "I'm just passing through."

But she found herself stopping to look at the telegram. At the shape of the letters and the way they went on the page. At the way it was signed: "Mr. and Mrs. Carter." She thought again how strange that was.

They were both big hearty people—"Call me Mike," Mr. Carter said to all the kids. "We're Mike and Ida here." Now all of a sudden they were formal.

Like a wedding invitation, Susan thought suddenly. Only just the opposite.

She reached out and touched the paper. It crackled slightly under her fingers. She went on rubbing her thumb across the almost smooth surface, watching the sweat of her skin begin to stain the yellow paper. A little stain, a little mark, but one that would grow if she kept at it.

That was the end of Harold Carter, she thought. He ended in the crisp, crunchy feel of a piece of paper. A tall thin boy who'd taken her to a dance and given her a ring that was too big for her. All that was left of him was a piece of paper.

She'd send the ring back to his parents. Maybe they'd like to have it.

Or maybe they'd rather she kept it. But keeping it would be keeping him. All of a sudden she saw the ring hanging on the side of her dresser mirror, and she looked into its blue stone and way down in its synthetic depths she saw a tiny little Harold, germ-sized and far away. As she looked he winked out.

She put the telegram down. "I really was just going to the kitchen."

"You're not wearing your ring," Mrs. Watkins said.

"No," she said, "no, I never did wear it."

"You must be so upset." Mrs. Benson sipped delicately at the edge of the yellow sherry. "Just like your poor mother."

"I wasn't married to him," Susan said. "It's different."

Her mother was standing next to her, hand on her shoulder. "You would have married him."

"No," Susan said, "no, I don't think so."

"Of course you would have." Her mother was firm. "Why else would he have given you the ring?"

Susan started to say: Because he didn't have anybody else to give it to and he couldn't give it to his mother.

Her mother went on patting her shoulder. "We should be proud of them, Susan. Harold was a fine young man."

Was he? She didn't have the heart to say that aloud either. Did he shoot people to see them squirm? Did he pull the trigger against his own head with fear?

"The young men are so heroic," her mother said. The two women murmured consent. Her mother would know; her mother had lost a husband in a war, she would know.

All the brave young men that die in their glory, Susan thought. And leave rings to girls they hardly knew, and pictures on mantels in houses where they never lived. Rings that don't fit and pictures that don't resemble them.

"Harold was an English king," she said aloud.

"Yes, dear," her mother said patiently. "That's history."

Harold Carter didn't get to sit on porches and remember, the way Watkins and Benson were doing now. He hadn't got to do anything, except go to high school and die. But then, you didn't really know that either, Susan thought. You really didn't know what he did out there, what memories he might have brought back inside his head.

Mrs. Watkins repeated, "All the young men are so brave."

"No," Susan said abruptly. "Not my father, and not Harold. They weren't brave, they just got caught."

In the silence she could hear the soft wheeze of their astonished breaths, and, as she turned, the creak of old boards under her heel. "They don't die in glory." The words came out sounding like her speech at the Senior Debating Society. "They just die dead. Anyway, I was on my way to fix a cup of tea."

Nobody followed her to the kitchen, just the little

ribbon of sound from her high heels on the bare boards and the linoleum. She flipped on the fire under the kettle, decided it would take too long and began to heat some water in a pan. Her feet hurt; she kicked off her shoes. The water warmed and she poured it over the instant tea. There were no lemons in the refrigerator; she remembered suddenly that there weren't any oranges on the dining room table either, that today had been marketing day and nobody had gone.

She put sugar in the tea and tasted it. It was barely warm and nasty, salty almost. She'd forgotten to rinse the dishes again. She would drink it anyway, while she made another proper cup. She put the flame back under the kettle. She pushed open the screen door and went out on the kitchen porch.

It was very small, just wide enough for one person to pass between the railing and the garbage can that always stood there. She'd often argued with her mother over that. "Put it in the yard—it just brings flies into the house." "A clean can," her mother said, "does not attract flies." And the can stayed.

She sat down on the railing, wondering if it would leave a stripe on her white dress. She decided she didn't care. She sipped the cold tea and stared out into the backyard, at the sweet peas growing along the wire fence, at the yellow painted boards on the house next door.

She was still staring over there, not seeing anything in particular, not thinking anything at all, when Mr. Benson came around the corner of the house. He walked across the back yard and stopped, finally, one foot on the bottom step.

"You left the girls in quite a state back there," he said.

So they had rushed to the porch to tell the men . . . Susan didn't take her eyes off the sweet peas, the soft gentle colors of the sweet peas. "They get upset real easy."

"I reckon they do," he said, "and they quiet down real easy too."

She began to swing her leg slowly. I shouldn't have left my shoes in the kitchen, she thought. I'll ruin my stockings out here.

"I take it he wasn't even a very good friend of yours," Mr. Benson said.

"You'd take it right." Because that sounded rude, she added quickly: "Nobody understands that. He was just a boy I knew."

"Shouldn't be so hard to understand."

"It's like a wake in there, and that's silly."

"Well," Mr. Benson said, "he was nineteen and maybe when it's somebody that young, you don't even have to know him to mourn after him."

"He was twenty." Susan looked at Mr. Benson then, the short stocky man, with a fringe of black hair around his ears and a sweaty pink skull shining in the heat. His eyes, buried in folds of puffy skin, were small sharp points of blue. My father might have looked like that, she thought.

"Twenty's still pretty young," he said.

"This whole thing is my mother The minute she saw the telegram all she could think of is how history is repeating itself. She's called everybody, even people she doesn't like."

"I know your mother," Mr. Benson said.

"And that dying in glory talk." Susan hopped off the railing and leaned against it, palms pressing the rough wood. "That's all I ever hear. My mother knows those stories—the ones you were telling on the porch—she knows it's awful and stupid and terrible."

"No," Mr. Benson said, "it isn't awful." He pulled a cigarette holder from his pocket and began to suck it. "I gave up smoking and this is all I got left . . . You're wrong, child, but maybe the stories don't say it clear enough."

Susan said slowly, "You talk about it all the time, any time."

He nodded slowly and the empty cigarette holder

whistled in the hot afternoon air. "Because it was the
most glorious thing ever happened to us."

"Too bad you can't tell Harold," she said.

"Take Harold now." Mr. Benson's voice was dull
and monotonous, singsonging in the heat. "He didn't
have to join up right out of high school. Draft calls
been pretty low around here lately."

"He knew he was going to have to, that's why."

"It don't happen like that." He blew through the
cigarette holder again, then tapped it on his palm.
"Always seemed to me like men have got to have
their war. I had to have mine twenty-five years ago.
When you're in it maybe it's different, but you got to
go. Once you hear about it, you got to go to it."

"That doesn't make any sense to me," Susan said.
"None."

"Even when you're in it, you know that if you live,
you're going to remember it all the rest of your life.
And you know that if there was another war and you
were young enough, you'd go again."

"That's stupid," Susan said.

"Maybe. You forget places you've been and you
forget women you had, but you don't forget fighting."

Behind her the teakettle gave a shriek. He glanced
up. "Sounds like your water is boiling."

"Yes," she said, "I'll see to it."

He nodded and walked away, leaving a light smell
of bourbon behind him. He turned once, lifted his
hands, palms up in a little shrugging gesture.

She made her tea. As if she were obeying a set of
rules. Things were beginning to feel less strange to
her. Even the talk about Harold didn't seem as silly
as it had.

I'm beginning not to mind, she thought, but it's still
all mixed up. He was the sort of boy I could have
married, but I didn't even know him. And that's lucky
for me. Otherwise I might be like my mother. His
being dead doesn't really change anything for me. I'll

get married after a while to somebody as good as him or even better . . .

She drank her tea slowly; she was sad and happy at once. Harold was a young man who had died. He didn't leave a memory behind; he didn't leave anything. He was just gone and there wasn't even a mark at the place where he had been.

Her mother stood in the door. "Do you feel well enough to come back in, child?"

Susan chuckled, a quiet little self-contented chuckle.

"Whatever is funny, child?"

"You're having such a good time, Mother. You haven't had such a good time in ages."

"Well, really."

"You're alive and I'm alive and Harold's not alive."

"That's horrible."

"Sure."

She followed her mother across the waxed linoleum. "Wait, I've got to put my shoes on."

There just isn't anything, she thought. I'm sorry, Harold. I hope it wasn't too bad and I hope it didn't hurt too much. You and my father. I bet your parents have your picture on the mantel too.

Her shoes were on now and she straightened up.

"Good-bye," she said in a very light whisper. "You poor bastard."

And she went inside to join the people.

Ellen Gilchrist

Born in Vicksburg, Mississippi, in 1935, Ellen Gilchrist graduated from Millsaps College and later did postgraduate work at the University of Arkansas. A collection of her broadcast commentaries on National Public Radio, *Falling Through Space* (1987), reflects her life as a working writer. Besides receiving awards for her poetry and several Pushcart prizes for her stories, her first collection of stories, *In the Land of Dreamy Dreams* (1981), was named an honor book of the Louisiana Library Association, and her second collection, *Victory over Japan* (1984), won an American Book Award. Since then she has published ten more story collections as well as six novels: *The Annunciation* (1983), *The Anna Papers* (1988), *Net of Jewels* (1992), *Starcarbon: A Meditation of Love* (1994), *Anabasis: A Journey to the Interior* (1994), and *Sarah Conley* (1997). Her screenplay, *A Season of Dreams,* which was based on Eudora Welty's stories, won a National Educational Television Network scriptwriting award. *In the Land of Dreamy Dreams,* from which the following story was taken, focuses on the lives of rich adolescents, most of whom live in New Orleans. Critics have praised Gilchrist's ability to capture the speech patterns of this region. Writer Beverly Lowry has remarked: "The stories are wonderful to tell aloud," and critics have noticed that Gilchrist writes the way she talks. In an interview she said, "I like the feel of words in my mouth and the sound of them in my ears and the creation of them with my hands."

The President of the Louisiana Live Oak Society

The spring that Robert McLaurin was fourteen he had a black friend named Gus who lived underneath a huge live oak tree in Audubon Park. It was a tree so old and imposing that people in New Orleans called it the President of the Louisiana Live Oak Society.

Gus had a regular home somewhere inside the St. Thomas Street project, with a mother and brothers and sisters, but for all practical purposes he lived underneath the two-hundred-year-old tree in front of Dr. Alton Ochsner's palatial stucco house on Exposition Boulevard.

Imagine a brilliant day in early spring. It is the middle of the afternoon and under the low-hanging branches of the oak tree the air is quiet and cool and smells of all the gardens on the boulevard; confederate jasmine, honeysuckle, sweet alyssum, magnolia, every stereotyped southern flower you can imagine has mingled its individual odor into an ardent humid soup.

In the distance traffic is going along the avenue and a snatch of music floats across the street from the conservatory at Loyola University.

There is room under the tree for twenty or thirty kids on a good day. It is a perfect office for the youngest and most successful dope pushers on the river side of St. Charles Avenue.

Those spring afternoons of 1971 Robert would cut his last-period physical education class and come riding up on his bike playing his portable radio at full volume. Station WTIX would be playing a love song by Judy Collins or "American Pie" by Don McLean, the national anthem of 1971.

Gus would be curled up asleep in the roots of the tree. From a distance he looked like an old catcher's mitt. He wore the same thing every day, a brown leather flight jacket and a pair of indefinite-colored plaid pants so worn that the lines of the plaid all ran together at the edges.

"You got any money?" Gus would ask, rubbing the sleep from his eyes with a dirty fist.

"Yeah, I got plenty. Last week they gave me twenty dollars to buy a track suit with. You want to get a mufflelata?"

"Let's smoke first."

Then Gus would open his cigar box, carefully remove a paper from its folder, pour the beautifully manicured dope onto the paper and roll it into a thin cylinder. He was careful, keeping his back to the wind if there was any so as not to spill a piece. He performed his ceremony to perfection, the rank aroma of his slept-in clothes rising to meet the spectacular smell of the marijuana as he lit the joint with dignity and passed it to Robert.

"How much stuff we got?" Robert asked.

"Not much. We got to find Uncle Clarence and hit him up. We hardly got enough for everyone that's coming today."

Roman Catholic girls in plaid uniform skirts rode by on bikes, their legs flashing in the sunlight.

"You know many of them Catholic girls?" Gus asked, making conversation.

"Yeah, I know them, but they don't talk to me. They're pretty stuck-up."

"How come?" Gus said.

"They go out with older guys. See that one over there," and he pointed out Darlene Trilling, riding by on a ten-speed; "she's really Jewish. She loves a senior in high school but her parents won't let her go out with him. She lives next door to me. She's probably going off somewhere to meet him right this minute."

"How come they won't let her?" Gus asked.

"They're probably afraid he'll give her some dope or something."

Gus started laughing his famous laugh. His face lit up like a three-tiered chandelier. He didn't hold anything back when he laughed.

"You should have seen my momma last Saturday," he said. "She outran a black cop. He couldn't catch her for anything and he knows that block as good as she does. She's fast as lightning. I'm fast like her."

"Is she a big woman?" Robert asked politely.

"Naw, she's little like me. One time when I got sick she put me in her nightgown. It just fit."

The oak tree held the boys like a spell. They rolled another joint.

"Someday I'll get a Buick and deal out of it," Gus said.

"What if they make dope legal?"

Gus looked scared. He looked like Robert had suggested they were going to drop a bomb on the park that very afternoon.

"They can't make it legal. The bars won't let them. It would run all the bars out of business."

They smoked in peace, talking about cars.

"Let's go get a mufflelata before the other kids get here," Robert said, stretching and getting up.

Gus hopped on the handlebars of Robert's bike and they rode off to Tranchina's, an Italian restaurant on Magazine Street that sells muffielata sandwiches to go. A muffielata is a plate-sized loaf of wop bread piled high with salami, bologna, pepperoni, mozzarella cheese, and soaked with olive salad. Gus and Robert ate out frequently that spring and this was one of their favorite meals.

"I wish we could get a cold beer to go with the muffielata."

"There's no place will sell us one. I'll steal some out of the refrigerator for tomorrow."

"What about Darby's, the bookie?"

"Naw, he won't take a chance just to sell a couple of beers."

"Well, we can get an Icee at the Tote-Sum store."

A baby-blue Lincoln Continental turned the corner by the Chandlers' white picket fence and nearly ran over them. They were stoned, riding along looking at the red-and-pink azaleas, and didn't see it coming. Gus managed to jump free and landed on his feet still holding the cigar box.

"Robert!" It was his mother. She had just come from the beauty parlor and her hair looked like a helmet for the Los Angeles Rams.

"Robert, come here to me." She pulled his head into the car window. "What are you doing with that black boy?" Robert's mother was a liberal. She never called black people niggers or Negroes even when she was mad at them.

"He's just a kid. I was giving him a ride to the Tote-Sum."

"Why aren't you at practice?" Her helmet moved up and down as she talked.

"They canceled it. The coach is sick. Listen, you almost ran over us, do you know that?" He had her on the defensive. She was very sensitive about her driving.

"Robert, I'm on my way to the grocery. You be home at six."

She drove off wearing her philosophical look. Jean-Paul Sartre couldn't have done it better.

"That was my mother."

"You scared of her?"

"God no. She's scared of me. She's afraid I'll die like my brother. He died when he was four. He had something wrong with him when he was born."

"Only person I'm scared of is my mother. She'll beat the daylights out of me if she finds out I'm dealing. My cousin just got put in jail for dealing. They put him in the House of D for a week."

"The what?"

"The House of D. The House of Detention. It's supposed to be for over eighteen and he ain't but sixteen but that's where he is and he cries every time they talk to him. Somebody stole his towel the first day he was there."

They ate the mufflelata and drank an Icee and rode back to the park and sold the rest of their stuff. Then they decided to ride down to the project and look for Uncle Clarence.

Supplies were a problem. They tried raising a crop on the back side of the levee, but the cops dug it up. They managed to bring in a small crop in Robert's grandmother's backyard while she was on a tour of Scandinavia with her bridge club, but that was a one-shot deal.

They started off for the project. They rode down Tchoupitoulas Street, which runs in a crescent along the levee lined with wharves and warehouses.

It was supposed to be dangerous to go into the project, but from Robert's elevated point of view the project just looked like a lot of old brick apartment buildings with iron balconies hanging off the sides like abandoned birds' nests and aluminum foil on half the windows to keep out the heat.

It was late afternoon and people were sitting on the stoops talking and drinking beer. Some kids were having a war with Coke bottles full of muddy water for ammunition. Robert and Gus went up a flight of stairs in one of the buildings and Gus's oldest sister met them at the door. She was taller and lighter than Gus, dressed in a ruffled white shirt and a short blue skirt.

"Where you think you been?" she demanded. Robert could smell her cool perfume.

"I been out on business," Gus said. "Where's momma?"

"She's gone to the store and you better stay here till she gets back. She sent Uncle Clarence looking for you yesterday."

She gave Robert a haughty look and settled back on the sofa where she was polishing her fingernails and watching a movie on television. She was studying to be a secretary.

The apartment was small and crowded with furniture. In one corner was a brass coatrack with ten or twelve different colored coats on it. It looked like a melted carousel. Robert kept staring at it, pulling in his pupils to make it look weirder and weirder.

"What's wrong with him?" Gus's sister demanded, pointing a newly coated nail at Robert.

"That's Robert. He does business with me uptown. There ain't nothing wrong with him some food won't fix. Where's Uncle Clarence now? You seen him?"

"He's probably still looking for you."

Gus liked to eat all the time when he was high. He made some peanut-butter sandwiches and they went off looking for his uncle.

They found Clarence sitting on the steps of a neighboring building drinking Apple Jack wine and flirting with a girlfriend. He was light-complected and wore a mustache and a carefully ironed African Mau-Mau shirt.

"Good evening." Gus smiled politely at the lady. "Uncle Clarence, you been looking for me?"

"Come here, Gus," Clarence said and pulled the boys out of earshot of the lady. "Gus, you got me in all kinds of trouble with your momma. She yelled at me for an hour yesterday. What you been doing with that stuff, smoking it yourself?"

"No, I ain't. This here is my partner, Robert. We don't do nothing but sell it to rich white kids in the park. Robert lets me keep supplies in his basement when we got anything to keep. And I got the money I owe you too." Gus produced three ten-dollar bills and some crumpled ones and started counting it out to his uncle.

"Well, you ain't getting any more shit off me one way or the other." Clarence was feeling good. He had drunk just the right amount of Apple Jack. He kept his hand on the boy's shoulder as he talked. "I don't feel like having your momma after me and I'm off you for laying out so much. That's what got her so hot."

"Uncle Clarence, you can't do me this way. I got my partner, I got my business, I got my customers. Momma ain't gonna find out anything. I'll stay home every night. I never knew you to be so scared of her before."

Gus was pulling out all the stops. Great tears were forming in the corners of his eyes.

"Oh, for Jesus' sake," Clarence said, not wanting the lady to see him making a kid cry. "I'll give you enough for one more week and we'll see how you stay home and keep her pacified. You come over to my place after dinner and I'll fix you up."

Gus and Robert looked at each other. Their eyes lit up like someone had just dropped a quarter in a pinball machine. They were set for another week.

Robert McLaurin's father, his name was Will, thought the spring of 1971 was the worst time he had ever lived through. He was a management lawyer. All he did at work was try Equal Opportunity Employment cases, and he had lost five in a row. All he did at home was argue with Robert McLaurin's mother, her name was Lelia, about whether or not Robert was taking drugs.

They argued so much about Robert they had stopped being in love with each other. All day long at the office Will thought about the argument from the day before and used his legal mind to think up ways to make his arguments more convincing.

He would drive up in front of his house after work and sometimes it would take him three or four min-

utes to get ready to go inside and start arguing. He
would look up at the fine house he had bought for his
family and wish he was someplace else. Finally he
would pick up his briefcase and go on in.

Lelia would be running around the kitchen in a tennis
skirt trying to get dinner on the table so Will wouldn't
know she hadn't done anything all day but play tennis.
Will would say, "Did you call Robert's coach?"

"I couldn't get him on the phone."

"What do you mean, you couldn't get him on the
phone? They don't have phones anymore at Horace
Green School?"

"Are you accusing me of lying?"

Will McLaurin was not a big man. He was five nine
with broad shoulders and curly red hair and black
eyes. When he started arguing he lit up like an actor
on the stage.

"Lelia, I said did you call the coach or did you not
call the coach. Don't make something up. Just answer
the question."

Lelia McLaurin looked like a blond housewife on a
television commercial. She had a good figure from
playing tennis all the time and she had a bad temper
from getting her way all the time.

"I don't have to listen to this. I don't have to hear
this while I'm cooking dinner. If you keep this up I'll
leave and you can cook your own dinner." She was
furiously buttering French bread to go with the fried
chicken the cook had left warming in the oven.

"Lelia, listen to me. All I'm asking is did you call
Robert's coach or not. I'm not accusing you of anything and I'm not trying to put anything over on you.
Did you call Robert's coach and ask him if Robert
has been showing up for practice?"

"I left a message but he didn't call back."

"Did you go out and see if he was at practice?"

"I'm not going to spy on my own child. Stop ruining
my evening. Have a drink or something. He goes to
practice. He bought a new track suit just last week."

"Lelia, will you look at this for a minute. Just look at this and then we won't discuss it anymore," and Will handed her a yellow legal pad with a list printed on the first page.

"What in the hell is this?" She turned toward him fiercely, her pleated skirt twirling around her legs.

"That is a partial list of the furnishings, decorations, and trinkets in our only son's bedroom. I was hoping you might sit down and read it and think about it."

"This legal garbage. This goddamn lawyer list," and Lelia ripped the page from the legal pad and threw it at the pantry door.

The list read:

1. Black light
2. Two strobe lights for altering perception of light
3. Poster of androgynous figure on motorcycle smoking a marijuana cigarette
4. Poster of Peter Fonda smoking a marijuana cigarette
5. Package of sandwich-size baggies, often used to parcel out marijuana into what are known as "lids"
6. 36 long-playing record albums featuring artists who smoke marijuana and advocate the use of various drugs in the lyrics of their songs
7. Recipe, supposedly a joke, for the manufacture of LSD from sunflower seeds

"You have to stop spying on Robert! That's just their way of being cute. He pretends he's in the revolution. I think you hate him."

"If you call walking in his room spying. That is a list of objects that can be seen by a person of normal eyesight standing in the middle of his room."

"You hate him."

"Lelia, I don't hate him. I hate him hanging around the park all the time. I hate him barely passing at school and never reading a book anymore. Lelia, a madness is stalking this city and I don't want to lose my son to it."

They were out in the hall. Lelia was getting a rain-coat out of a closet. It wasn't raining. She was getting out the raincoat because it is hard to walk out on someone wearing only a tennis skirt and a LaCoste shirt. She was crying.

Will took the raincoat away from her and tried to put his arms around her. They hadn't made love to each other for two weeks.

"Look, tomorrow is Friday. Leave Robert with your mother and we'll drive to Biloxi for the weekend. We can lie around in the sun and talk things over. Let's get out of town and try to love each other and see if we can think straight."

"All right. If you won't talk about it anymore to-night. The other day I saw him riding a little black boy around on his handlebars. You've got me so para-noid I thought there was something wrong with that."

"What time tomorrow could you leave?"

"I'm going to the beauty parlor at four. I'll pick you up at the office at five-thirty and we'll take the expressway from downtown. We can stop in Mande-ville and have dinner at Begue's."

"Sure we can. Bring a shaker of martinis. We'll drink all the way to the coast like the old days."

Then the McLaurins had a peaceful meal for a change and Will and Lelia went up early to bed.

As soon as they disappeared Robert called up Gus and told him the good news that they would have the house to themselves for the weekend. He smoked a joint and drifted off to sleep listening to his radio. *"Drove my Chevy to the levee but the levee was dry, drove my Chevy to the levee but the levee was dry."*

Gus was waiting for Robert in the front yard when Robert came home the next day. Gus was excited. He loved the McLaurins' beautiful old house. He had spent the night there once before when Robert had a baby-sitter. Robert had sneaked him in. What Gus really liked was Robert's father's shower. It had an attachment that gave you a massage while you took a shower. Gus said it felt like little pieces of diamonds hitting your skin.

On this particular Friday Robert felt good to be walking in the front door with his friend. The McLaurin house was built around a wide central hall. At the far end of the hall a staircase five feet wide rose to the second floor. The hall was hung with an amazing assortment of paintings.

"Your momma sure does have a lot of pictures."

"She painted this one herself."

"What's it a picture of?" Gus asked.

"What does it look like to you?"

"A fire. A big field of fire."

"Well, she says it's a picture of the inside of her head when she was going to have me as a baby."

"I wouldn't have guessed it."

The boys went on in the kitchen. They decided to really have a party.

Lelia entered the Magic Slipper Beauty Salon with a sigh. She was exhausted from rushing to get there on time.

"Tim, I'm sorry I'm late. I got in school traffic on the Avenue."

"It's okay, sweetie, but we'll have to skip the manicure. I've got a date at six." He handed her a leopard-printed smock and nodded toward the dressing room. His silver hair was cut in a Prince Valiant. He was vain of his body and his clientele. He put up with a lot from Lelia because she had been named to the list of Beautiful Activists two years in a row before she had turned herself into a tennis-playing machine.

"He's driving me crazy," she said, settling into the shampoo chair. "Between the two of them I don't care if I live or die. I can't even play tennis worth a damn. I lost every important match I played last week. I'm down to six on the ladder."

"Sweetie, you can't let them do that to you. What

does Arthur say?" They shared a psychiatrist. This creates a strange bond between people.

"He says I have to work through it. Will and I are going to the coast for the weekend to talk it over. We may end up sending Robert off to school. Will wants me to treat Robert the way his mother treated him, the old guilt routine. Look what it did to him. He doesn't even know he's neurotic. At least I know I'm neurotic."

"Lelia, is that you?" Danny Adler's mother came up with her hair wrapped in a turban on the way to the back for a pedicure.

"Janet, how are you?"

"Listen, thanks for asking Danny to spend the night. It really worked out beautifully because we are planning on being out late tonight."

"Janet"—Lelia sat up, half-rinsed—"Janet, I didn't ask Danny to spend the night. Will and I are going out of town for the weekend. Robert is staying with Mother. Are you sure he said Robert asked him?"

"Yes, he said you-all were taking them to the movies."

Tim started laughing. "The old mom's-out-of-town game. I'll bet they're shacked up with some charmers in your bedroom right this minute."

"I'm going home," Lelia said. "Tim, get this stuff off my hair and comb me out."

"You can't go home like this."

"I don't care. Just comb out my hair. I mean it, Tim. Janet, I'll call you later."

"Sweetie, take a Valium. You want a Valium?"

"Oh, could you, thanks."

Tim fished a bottle out of his pocket. "One or two?"

"Two."

Lelia parked the car two houses away and walked across the lawn and onto her front porch. She felt like a member of the CIA. She could hear the music playing as she walked across the yard. She could hear the music before she stepped onto the porch. She could hear the music and through the floor-length windows of the living room she could see Robert draped over the beige-and-white-striped loveseat holding a cigarette in one hand and nodding dreamily with his eyes closed. She could see the mirrored cocktail table with the silver champagne bucket and the two-hundred-year-old red crystal Madeira glasses beside it. Robert got up and walked into the next room to change the record.

Lelia stepped into the hall.

Gus came walking down the stairs. He came walking down the carpeted stairs and down the wide walnut hall with its sixteen-foot ceilings. He came walking down the hall wrapped in a plush baby-blue monogrammed towel from the Lylian Shop. Pearls of water were dripping down his face from his thick soft hair. Widely grinning, hugely smiling, Gus came down the hall, down the Aubusson runner, down Lelia's schizophrenic, eclectic art gallery of a hall, past the Walter Andersons, the deCallatays, the Leroy Morais, the Rolland Golden, the Stanford, past the portrait of Robert's grandfather in the robes of a state supreme court justice, past the Dufy. He had just passed the edge of the new Leonor Fini when Lelia stepped into the hall and they spotted each other.

Here Gus came, in the baby-blue towel, black as a walnut tree in winter, draped as a tiny emperor, carrying his empty champagne glass in one hand and using the other for an imperial robe clasp. Expansively, ecstatically pleased to be, delighted to be, charmed to be alive on this, the fourteenth day of April, nineteen hundred and seventy-one; he, Gus, man of parts, friend of white man and black man, friend of oak tree, levee, and river, citizen of New Orleans, Louisiana, dope pusher to the Audubon

Park, dispenser of the new Nirvana. He, Gus, five feet one inches, one hundred and two pounds of pure D Gus, walking down the hall.

Lelia screamed. She screamed six months of unscreamed screaming. She screamed an ancestral, a territorial scream. She screamed her head off.

"What in the name of God are you doing in my house?" she screamed.

"Robert," she screamed, "what is this black child doing in my house? What is this goddamn black pusher doing in my house? Robert," she screamed, "get in here this second."

Gus's eyes met hers at a forty-degree angle. His huge black eyes met her wide aluminum ones down the long hall and held for a moment and then Gus cut and ran back up the stairs to the bedroom, trailing the towel behind him, his tiny black butt shining in the reflected light from the stained-glass window in the stairway alcove.

Robert ran past his mother's screaming and up the stairs behind Gus and the two boys ran into the master bedroom and slammed the door and threw the safety bolt and Robert stood with his back to the door breathing like a runaway mule.

"What are we gonna do now?" Robert said, his heart pushing against his fake soccer shirt.

"I'm getting out of here. That's what I'm doing," Gus said, pulling on his plaid pants and searching for his boots.

"You can't get out of here. There isn't any way out."

"There's that window," Gus said. "There's that window and that's the way I'm going out." He pointed to a double French window that opened onto a false balcony and overlooked the side yard. The top twelve feet of an old crepe myrtle tree pushed against the balcony waving its clusters of soft pink flowers in the breeze.

"You can't get out there. It's forty feet to the ground."

"I'm going down that tree."

"That's a crepe myrtle. You can't climb down a crepe myrtle."

"If it's the only tree I got, I can climb down it," Gus said, putting on his jacket and pushing open the French doors.

Lelia was beating on the door with her fists.

"Robert, if you don't open this door you will never leave this house again. If you don't open this door this minute you will be sent to Saint Stanislaus. I'll call the police. I've already called your father. He'll be here any minute. You might as well open the door. You better hurry and open this door. You better answer me this minute."

"That's the maddest woman I ever heard in my life," Gus said, throwing one leg over the balcony.

"Don't do it, Gus. Gus, don't do it," Robert said, grabbing him. "She won't really call the police. She's just saying that. It will be all right when my father gets here."

"Let go of me, Robert," Gus warned.

"Robert," she screamed, "if you don't open this door you will be the sorriest boy in New Orleans."

Robert turned to look at the door. He looked past the beautiful white-lacquered four-poster bed with Lelia's favorite sun hats hanging gaily from the bedposts.

As he turned to look at the door Gus shook his head and reached down and bit the freckled hand that held him. He bit Robert's hand as hard as he could bite it and Robert let go.

Gus jumped into the heart of the crepe myrtle tree. He dove into the tree and swayed in its branches like a cat. He steadied, grabbed for a larger branch, found a temporary footing, grabbed again, and began to fall through the upthrust branches like a bird shot in flight.

As Robert watched, Gus came to rest upon the ground, his wet black hair festooned with the soft pink blossoms of the crepe myrtle.

Then, as Robert watched, Gus pushed off from the earth. He began to ascend back up through the broken branches like a movie played in reverse, like a wild kite rising to meet the sun, and Robert was amazed and enchanted by the beauty of this feat and jumped from the window high into the air to join Gus on his journey.

And far away in the loud hall Lelia beat on the door and beat on the door and beat on the door.

Mary Hood

Mary Hood was born in Brunswick, Georgia, in 1946, and educated at Georgia State University in Atlanta. Her short stories, set in rural Georgia, have been published in numerous periodicals, including *Harper's, Southern Magazine, Georgia Review, Kenyon Review,* and *Yankee Magazine*. Her first collection, *How Far She Went* (1984), won both the Flannery O'Connor Award and the *Southern Review*/Louisiana State University Press Award, and her second collection, *And Venus Is Blue* (1986), won the Townsend Prize. Mary Hood's characters, often isolated and lonely, have difficulty communicating with each other as this story from her first collection shows. Critic David Baker noted that Hood's South "finds its families falling apart, its women stranded yet struggling individually to grow stronger, and its very past—the history and nostalgia so important to southern tradition—vanishing or vanished." In her first novel, *Familiar Heat* (1995), Hood leaves Georgia for the Florida Keys.

How Far She Went

They had quarreled all morning, squalled all summer about the incidentals: how tight the girl's cutoff jeans were, the "Every Inch a Woman" T-shirt, her choice of music and how loud she played it, her practiced inattention, her sullen look. Her granny wrung out the last boiled dishcloth, pinched it to the line, giving the basin a sling and a slap, the water flying out in a scalding arc onto the Queen Anne's lace by the path, never mind if it bloomed, that didn't make it worth anything except to chiggers, but the girl would cut it by the everlasting armload and cherish it in the old churn, going to that much trouble for a weed but not bending once—unbegged—to pick the nearest bean; she was sulking now. Bored. Displaced.

"And what do you think happens to a chigger if nobody ever walks by his weed?" her granny asked, heading for the house with that sidelong uneager unanswered glance, hoping for what? The surprise gift of a smile? Nothing. The woman shook her head and said it. "Nothing." The door slammed behind her. Let it.

"I hate it here!" the girl yelled then. She picked up a stick and broke it and threw the pieces—one from each hand—at the laundry drying in the noon. Missed. Missed.

Then she turned on her bare, haughty heel and set off high-shouldered into the heat, quick but not far, not far enough—no road was *that* long—only as far as she dared. At the gate, a rusty chain swinging between

two lichened posts, she stopped, then backed up the
raw drive to make a run at the barrier, lofting, clearing
it clean, her long hair wild in the sun. Triumphant,
she looked back at the house where she caught at the
dark window her granny's face in its perpetual eclipse
of disappointment, old at fifty. She stepped back, but
the girl saw her.

"You don't know me!" the girl shouted, chin high,
and ran till her ribs ached.

As she rested in the rattling shade of the willows,
the little dog found her. He could be counted on. He
barked all the way, and squealed when she pulled the
burr from his ear. They started back to the house for
lunch. By then the mailman had long come and gone
in the old ruts, leaving the one letter folded now to
fit the woman's apron pocket.

If bad news darkened her granny's face, the girl
ignored it. Didn't talk at all, another of her distanc-
ings, her defiances. So it was as they ate that the
woman summarized, "Your daddy wants you to cash
in the plane ticket and buy you something. School
clothes. For here."

Pale, the girl stared, defenseless only an instant before blurting out, "You're lying."

The woman had to stretch across the table to leave
her handprint on that blank cheek. She said, not caring if it stung or not, "He's been planning it since he
sent you here."

"I could turn this whole house over, dump it! Leave
you slobbering over that stinking jealous dog in the
dust!" The girl trembled with the vision, with the
strength it gave her. It made her laugh. "Scatter the
Holy Bible like confetti and ravel the crochet into
miles of stupid string! I could! I will! I won't stay
here!" But she didn't move, not until her tears rose
to meet her color, and then to escape the shame of
minding so much she fled. Just headed away, blind. It
didn't matter, this time, how far she went.

*   *   *

The woman set her thoughts against fretting over their bickering, just went on unalarmed with chores, clearing off after the uneaten meal, bringing in the laundry, scattering corn for the chickens, ladling manure tea onto the porch flowers. She listened though. She always had been a listener. It gave her a cocked look. She forgot why she had gone into the girl's empty room, that ungirlish, tenuous lodging place with its bleak order, its ready suitcases never unpacked, the narrow bed, the contested radio on the windowsill. The woman drew the cracked shade down between the radio and the August sun. There wasn't anything else to do.

It was after six when she tied on her rough oxfords and walked down the drive and dropped the gate chain and headed back to the creosoted shed where she kept her tools. She took a hoe for snakes, a rake, shears to trim the grass where it grew, and seed in her pocket to scatter where it never had grown at all. She put the tools and her gloves and the bucket in the trunk of the old Chevy, its prime and rust like an Appaloosa's spots through the chalky white finish. She left the trunk open and the tool handles sticking out. She wasn't going far.

The heat of the day had broken, but the air was thick, sultry, weighted with honeysuckle in second bloom and the Nu-Grape scent of Kudzu. The maple and poplar leaves turned over, quaking, silver. There wouldn't be any rain. She told the dog to stay, but he knew a trick. He stowed away when she turned her back, leaped right into the trunk with the tools, then gave himself away with exultant barks. Hearing him, her court jester, she stopped the car and welcomed him into the front seat beside her. Then they went on. Not a mile from her gate she turned onto the blue gravel of the cemetery lane, hauled the gearshift into reverse to whoa them, and got out to take the idle walk down to her buried hopes, bending all along to

rout out a handful of weeds from between the markers
of old acquaintance. She stood there and read, slow.
The dog whined at her hem; she picked him up and
rested her chin on his head, then he wriggled and
whined to run free, contrary and restless as a child.

The crows called strong and bold MOM! MOM! A
trick of the ear to hear it like that. She knew it was
the crows, but still she looked around. No one called
her that now. She was done with that. And what was
it worth anyway? It all came to this: solitary weeding.
The sinful fumble of flesh, the fear, the listening for
a return that never came, the shamed waiting, the
unanswered prayers, the perjury on the certificate—
hadn't she lain there weary of the whole lie and it
only beginning? and a voice telling her, "Here's your
baby, here's your girl," and the swaddled package
meaning no more to her than an extra anything, something store-bought, something she could take back for
a refund.

"Tie her to the fence and give her a bale of hay,"
she had murmured, drugged, and they teased her, excused her for such a welcoming, blaming the anesthe-
sia, but it went deeper than that; *she* knew, and the
baby knew: there was no love in the begetting. That
was the secret, unforgivable, that not another good
thing could ever make up for, where all the bad had
come from, like a visitation, a punishment. She knew
that was why Sylvie had been wild, had gone to earth
so early, and before dying had made this child in sudden wedlock, a child who would be just like her, would
carry the hurting on into another generation. A matter
of time. No use raising her hand. But she *had* raised
her hand. Still wore on its palm the memory of the
sting of the collision with the girl's cheek; had she
broken her jaw? Her heart? Of course not. She said
it aloud: "Takes more than that."

She went to work then, doing what she could with
her old tools. She pecked the clay on Sylvie's grave,
new-looking, unhealed after years. She tried again,

scattering seeds from her pocket, every last possible one of them. Off in the west she could hear the pulp-wood cutters sawing through another acre across the lake. Nearer, there was the racket of motorcycles laboring cross-country, insectlike, distracting.

She took her bucket to the well and hung it on the pump. She had half filled it when the bikers roared up, right down the blue gravel, straight at her. She let the bucket overflow, staring. On the back of one of the machines was the girl. Sylvie's girl! Her bare arms wrapped around the shirtless man riding between her thighs. They were first. The second biker rode alone. She studied their strangers' faces as they circled her. They were the enemy, all of them. Laughing. The girl was laughing too, laughing like her mama did. Out in the middle of nowhere the girl had found these two men, some moth-musk about her drawing them (too soon!) to what? She shouted it: "What in God's—" They roared off without answering her, and the bucket of water tipped over, spilling its stain blood-dark on the red dust.

The dog went wild barking, leaping after them, snapping at the tires, and there was no calling him down. The bikers made a wide circuit of the church-yard, then roared straight across the graves, leaping the ditch and landing upright on the road again, heading off toward the reservoir.

Furious, she ran to her car, past the barking dog, this time leaving him behind, driving after them, horn blowing nonstop, to get back what was not theirs. She drove after them knowing what they did not know, that all the roads beyond that point dead-ended. She surprised them, swinging the Impala across their path, cutting them off; let them hit it! They stopped. She got out, breathing hard, and said, when she could, "She's underage." Just that. And put out her claiming hand with an authority that made the girl's arms drop from the man's insolent waist and her legs tremble.

"I was just riding," the girl said, not looking up.

Behind them the sun was heading on toward down. The long shadows of the pines drifted back and forth in the same breeze that puffed the distant sails on the lake. Dead limbs creaked and clashed overhead like the antlers of locked and furious beasts.

"Sheeeut," the lone rider said. "I told you." He braced with his muddy boot and leaned out from his machine to spit. The man the girl had been riding with had the invading sort of eyes the woman had spent her lifetime bolting doors against. She met him now, face to face.

"Right there, missy," her granny said, pointing behind her to the car.

The girl slid off the motorcycle and stood halfway between her choices. She started slightly at the *poosh!* as he popped another top and chugged the beer in one uptilting of his head. His eyes never left the woman's. When he was through, he tossed the can high, flipping it end over end. Before it hit the ground he had his pistol out and, firing once, winged it into the lake.

"Freaking lucky shot," the other one grudged.

"I don't need luck," he said. He sighted down the barrel of the gun at the woman's head. "POW!" he yelled, and when she recoiled, he laughed. He swung around to the girl; he kept aiming the gun, here, there, high, low, all around. "Y'all settle it," he said, with a shrug.

The girl had to understand him then, had to know him, had to know better. But still she hesitated. He kept looking at her, then away.

"She's fifteen," her granny said. "You can go to jail."

"You can go to hell," he said.

"Probably will," her granny told him. "I'll save you a seat by the fire." She took the girl by the arm and drew her to the car; she backed up, swung around, and headed out the road toward the churchyard for her tools and dog. The whole way the girl said nothing, just hunched against the far door, staring hard-eyed out at the pines going past.

The woman finished watering the seed in, and collected her tools. As she worked, she muttered, "It's your own kin buried here, you might have the decency to glance this way one time . . ." The girl was finger-tweezing her eyebrows in the side mirror. She didn't look around as the dog and the woman got in. Her granny shifted hard, sending the tools clattering in the trunk.

When they came to the main road, there were the men. Watching for them. Waiting for them. They kicked their machines into life and followed, close, bumping them, slapping the old fenders, yelling. The girl gave a wild glance around at the one by her door and said, "Gran'ma?" and as he drew his pistol, "Gran'ma!" just as the gun nosed into the open window. She frantically cranked the glass up between her and the weapon, and her granny, seeing, spat, "Fool!" She never had been one to pray for peace or rain. She stamped the accelerator right to the floor.

The motorcycles caught up. Now she braked, hard, and swerved off the road into an alley between the pines, not even wide enough for the school bus, just a fire scrape that came out a quarter mile from her own house, if she could get that far. She slewed on the pine straw, then righted, tearing along the dark tunnel through the woods. She had for the time being bested them; they were left behind. She was winning. Then she hit the wallow where the tadpoles were already five weeks old. The Chevy plowed in and stalled. When she got it cranked again, they were stuck. The tires spattered mud three feet up the near trunks as she tried to spin them out, to rock them out. Useless. "Get out and run!" she cried, but the trees were too close on the passenger side. The girl couldn't open her door. She wasted precious time having to crawl out under the steering wheel. The woman waited but the dog ran on.

They struggled through the dusky woods, their pace
slowed by the thick straw and vines. Overhead, in the
last light, the martins were reeling free and sure after
their prey.

"Why? Why?" the girl gasped, as they lunged down
the old deer trail. Behind them they could hear shots,
and glass breaking as the men came to the bogged
car. The women kept on running, swatting their way
clear through the shoulder-high weeds. They could see
the Greer cottage, and made for it. But it was ivied-
over, padlocked, the woodpile dry-rotting under its
tarp, the electric meterbox empty on the pole. No
help there.

The dog, excited, trotted on, yelping, his lips white-
flecked. He scented the lake and headed that way,
urging them on with thirsty yips. On the clay shore,
treeless, deserted, at the utter limit of land, they stood
defenseless, listening to the men coming on, between
them and home. The woman pressed her hands to
her mouth, stifling her cough. She was exhausted. She
couldn't think.

"We can get under!" the girl cried suddenly, and
pointed toward the Greers' dock, gap-planked, its
walkway grounded on the mud. They splashed out to
it, wading in, the woman grabbing up the telltale,
tattletale dog in her arms. They waded out to the far
end and ducked under. There was room between the
foam floats for them to crouch neck-deep.

The dog wouldn't hush, even then; never had yet,
and there wasn't time to teach him. When the woman
realized that, she did what she had to do. She grabbed
him whimpering; held him; held him under till the
struggle ceased and the bubbles rose silver from his
fur. They crouched there then, the two of them, sub-
merged to the shoulders, feet unsteady on the slimed
lake bed. They listened. The sky went from rose to
ocher to violet in the cracks over their heads. The
motorcycles had stopped now. In the silence there was
the glissando of locusts, the dry crunch of boots on

the flinty beach, their low man-talk drifting as they prowled back and forth. One of them struck a match.

"—they in these woods we could burn 'em out."

The wind carried their voices away into the pines. Some few words eddied back.

"—lippy old smartass do a little work on her knees besides praying—"

Laughter. It echoed off the deserted house. They were getting closer.

One of them strode directly out to the dock, walked on the planks over their heads. They could look up and see his boot soles. He was the one with the gun. He slapped a mosquito on his bare back and cursed. The carp, roused by the troubling of the waters, came nosing around the dock, guzzling and snorting. The girl and her granny held still, so still. The man fired his pistol into the shadows, and a wounded fish thrashed, dying. The man knelt and reached for it, chuffing out his beery breath. He belched. He pawed the lake for the dead fish, cursing as it floated out of reach. He shot it again, firing at it till it sank and the gun was empty. Cursed that too. He stood then and unzipped and relieved himself of some of the beer. They had to listen to that. To know that about him. To endure that, unprotesting.

Back and forth on shore the other one ranged, restless. He lit another cigarette. He coughed. He called, "Hey! They got away, man, that's all. Don't get your shorts in a wad. Let's go."

"Yeah." He finished. He zipped. He stumped back across the planks and leaped to shore, leaving the dock tilting amid widening ripples. Underneath, they waited.

The bike cranked. The other ratcheted, ratcheted, then coughed, caught, roared. They circled, cut deep ruts, slung gravel, and went. Their roaring died away and away. Crickets resumed and a near frog *bic-bic-bic*ked.

Under the dock, they waited a little longer to be

sure. Then they ducked below the water, scraped out from under the pontoon, and came up into free air, slogging toward shore. It had seemed warm enough in the water. Now they shivered. It was almost night. One streak of light still stood reflected on the darkening lake, drew itself thinner, narrowing into a final cancellation of day. A plane winked its way west.

The girl was trembling. She ran her hands down her arms and legs, shedding water like a garment. She sighed, almost a sob. The woman held the dog in her arms; she dropped to her knees upon the random stones and murmured, private, haggard, "Oh, honey," three times, maybe all three times for the dog, maybe once for each of them. The girl waited, watching. Her granny rocked the dog like a baby, like a dead child, rocked slower and slower and was still.

"I'm sorry," the girl said then, avoiding the dog's inert, empty eye.

"It was him or you," her granny said, finally, looking up. Looking her over. "Did they mess with you? With your britches? Did they?"

"No!" Then, quieter, "No, ma'am."

When the woman tried to stand up she staggered, lightheaded, clumsy with the freight of the dog. "No, ma'am," she echoed, fending off the girl's "Let me." And she said again, "It was him or you. I know that. I'm not going to rub your face in it." They saw each other as well as they could in that failing light, in any light.

The woman started toward home, saying, "Around here, we bear our own burdens." She led the way along the weedy shortcuts. The twilight bleached the dead limbs of the pines to bone. Insects sang in the thickets, silencing at their oncoming.

"We'll see about the car in the morning," the woman said. She bore her armful toward her own moth-ridden dusk-to-dawn security light with that country grace she had always had when the earth was reliably progressing underfoot. The girl walked close behind her, exactly where *she* walked, matching her pace, matching her stride, close enough to put her hand forth (if the need arose) and touch her granny's back where the faded voile was clinging damp, the merest gauze between their wounds.

PART III

—◆—

Negotiating Southern Communities

Richard Wright

Richard Wright was born in 1908, near Natchez, Mississippi, and was largely self-educated because his family's frequent moves interrupted his formal schooling. After working at odd jobs in Memphis and other cities and clerking at a post office in Chicago, Wright was employed by the Works Progress Administration Federal Writers' Project in Chicago and New York. In 1938 he published a collection of stories, *Uncle Tom's Children,* and won a prize from *Story* magazine. These stories all deal with a cycle of violence that involves white victimization of blacks and black retaliation against whites. Wright's next work was a novel, *Native Son* (1940), which Wright's protégé James Baldwin called "the most powerful and celebrated statement we have yet had of what it means to be a Negro in America." Wright won the Spingarn Medal from the National Association for the Advancement of Colored People for *Native Son,* and the novel was later made into a movie, for which Wright wrote the screenplay. Many critics consider his autobiography, *Black Boy* (1945), to be his most important work. Wright moved to France in 1947 and lived in Paris until his death in 1960. There he met existentialist writers Jean-Paul Sartre and Simone de Beauvoir, whose philosophy appealed to his own feelings of rootlessness and alienation. During this time, he began to write nonfiction about the national independence movements in Africa, such works as *Black Power* (1954), *The Color Curtain* (1956), and *White Man, Listen!* (1957). Critics have called Wright one of the most influential American writers of the twentieth century.

The Man Who Was Almost
a Man

Dave struck out across the fields, looking home-ward through paling light. Whut's the use talking wid em niggers in the field? Anyhow, his mother was putting supper on the table. Them niggers can't un-derstan nothing. One of these days he was going to get a gun and practice shooting; then they couldn't talk to him as though he were a little boy. He slowed, looking at the ground. Shucks, Ah ain scareda them even ef they are biggern me! Aw, Ah know whut Ahma do. Ahm going by ol Joe's sto n git that Sears, Roebuck catlog n look at them guns. Mebbe Ma will lemme buy one when she gits mah pay from ol man Hawkins. Ahma beg her t gimme some money. Ahm ol ernough to hava gun. Ahm seventeen. Almost a man. He strode, feeling his long loose-jointed limbs. Shucks, a man oughta hava little gun aftah he done worked hard all day.

He came in sight of Joe's store. A yellow lantern glowed on the front porch. He mounted steps and went through the screen door, hearing it bang behind him. There was a strong smell of coal oil and mackerel fish. He felt very confident until he saw fat Joe walk in through the rear door; then his courage began to ooze.

"Howdy, Dave! Whutcha want?"

"How yuh, Mistah Joe? Aw, Ah don wanna buy nothing. Ah just wanted t see ef yuhd lemme look at tha catlog erwhile."

"Sure! You wanna see it here?"

"Nawsuh. Ah wans t take it home wid me. Ah'll

bring it back termorrow when Ah come in from the fiels."

"You plannin on buying something?"

"Yessuh."

"Your ma lettin you have your own money now?"

"Shucks. Mistah Joe, Ahm gittin t be a man like anybody else!"

Joe laughed and wiped his greasy white face with a red bandanna.

"Whut you plannin on buyin?"

Dave looked at the floor, scratched his head, scratched his thigh, and smiled. Then he looked up shyly.

"Ah'll tell yuh, Mistah Joe, ef yuh promise yuh won't tell."

"I promise."

"Waal, Ahma buy a gun."

"A gun? Whut you want with a gun?"

"Ah wanna keep it."

"You ain't nothing but a boy. You don't need a gun."

"Aw, lemme have the catlog, Mistah Joe. Ah'll bring it back."

Joe walked through the rear door. Dave was elated. He looked around at barrels of sugar and flour. He heard Joe coming back. He craned his neck to see if he were bringing the book. Yeah, he's got it. Gawd-dog, he's got it!

"Here, but be sure you bring it back. It's the only one I got."

"Sho, Mistah Joe."

"Say, if you wanna buy a gun, why don't you buy one from me? I gotta gun to sell."

"Will it shoot?"

"Sure it'll shoot."

"Whut kind is it?"

"Oh, it's kinda old . . . a left-hand Wheeler. A pistol. A big one."

"Is it got bullets in it?"

"It's loaded."

"Kin Ah see it?"

"Where's your money?"

"Whut yuh wan fer it?"

"I'll let you have it for two dollars."

"Just two dollahs? Shucks, Ah could buy tha when Ah git mah pay."

"I'll have it here when you want it."

"Awright, suh. Ah be in fer it."

He went through the door, hearing it slam again behind him. Ahma git some money from Ma n buy me a gun! Only two dollahs! He tucked the thick catalogue under his arm and hurried.

"Where yuh been, boy?" His mother held a steaming dish of black-eyed peas.

"Aw, Ma, Ah jus stopped down the road t talk wid the boys."

"Yuh know bettah t keep suppah waitin."

He sat down, resting the catalogue on the edge of the table.

"Yuh git up from there and git to the well n wash yosef! Ah ain feedin no hogs in mah house!"

She grabbed his shoulder and pushed him. He stumbled out of the room, then came back to get the catalogue.

"Whut this?"

"Aw, Ma, it's jusa catlog."

"Who yuh git it from?"

"From Joe, down at the sto."

"Waal, thas good. We kin use it in the outhouse."

"Naw, Ma." He grabbed for it. "Gimme ma catlog, Ma."

She held onto it and glared at him.

"Quit hollerin at me! Whut's wrong wid yuh? Yuh crazy?"

"But Ma, please. It ain mine! It's Joe's! He tol me t bring it back t im termorrow."

She gave up the book. He stumbled down the back steps, hugging the thick book under his arm. When he

had splashed water on his face and hands, he groped
back to the kitchen and fumbled in a corner for the
towel. He bumped into a chair; it clattered to the floor.
The catalogue sprawled at his feet. When he had dried
his eyes he snatched up the book and held it again
under his arm. His mother stood watching him.

"Now, ef yuh gonna act a fool over that ol book,
Ah'll take it n burn it up."

"Naw, Ma, please."

"Waal, set down n be still!"

He sat down and drew the oil lamp close. He
thumbed page after page, unaware of the food his
mother set on the table. His father came in. Then his
small brother.

"Whutcha got there, Dave?" his father asked.

"Jusa catlog," he answered, not looking up.

"Yeah, here they is!" His eyes glowed at blue-and-
black revolvers. He glanced up, feeling sudden guilt.
His father was watching him. He eased the book under
the table and rested it on his knees. After the blessing
was asked, he ate. He scooped up peas and swallowed
fat meat without chewing. Buttermilk helped to wash
it down. He did not want to mention money before
his father. He would do much better by cornering his
mother when she was alone. He looked at his father
uneasily out of the edge of his eye.

"Boy, how come yuh don quit foolin wid tha book
n eat yo suppah?"

"Yessuh."

"How you n ol man Hawkins gitten erlong?"

"Suh?"

"Can't yuh hear? Why don yuh lissen? Ah ast yu
how wuz yuh n ol man Hawkins gittin erlong?"

"Oh, swell, Pa. Ah plows mo lan than anybody
over there."

"Waal, yuh oughta keep yo mind on whut yuh
doin."

"Yessuh."

He poured his plate full of molasses and sopped it

up slowly with a chunk of cornbread. When his father and brother had left the kitchen, he still sat and looked again at the guns in the catalogue, longing to muster courage enough to present his case to his mother. Lawd, ef Ah only had tha pretty one! He could almost feel the slickness of the weapon with his fingers. If he had a gun like that he would polish it and keep it shining so it would never rust. N Ah'd keep it loaded, by Gawd!

"Ma?" His voice was hesitant.

"Hunh?"

"Ol man Hawkins give yuh mah money yit?"

"Yeah, but ain no usa yuh thinking bout throwin nona it erway. Ahm keepin tha money sos yuh kin have cloes t go to school this winter."

He rose and went to her side with the open catalogue in his palms. She was washing dishes, her head bent low over a pan. Shyly he raised the book. When he spoke, his voice was husky, faint.

"Ma, Gawd knows Ah wans one of these."

"One of whut?" she asked, not raising her eyes.

"One of these," he said again, not daring even to point. She glanced up at the page, then at him with wide eyes.

"Nigger, is yuh gone plumb crazy?"

"Aw, Ma—"

"Git outta here! Don yuh talk t me bout no gun! Yuh a fool!"

"Ma, Ah kin buy one fer two dollahs."

"Not ef Ah knows it, yuh ain!"

"But yuh promised me one—"

"Ah don care whut Ah promised! Yuh ain nothing but a boy yit!"

"Ma, ef yuh lemme buy one Ah'll *never* ast yuh fer nothing no mo."

"Ah tol yuh t git outta here! Yuh ain gonna toucha penny of tha money fer no gun! Thas how come Ah has Mistah Hawkins t pay yo wages t me, cause Ah knows yuh ain got no sense."

"But, Ma, we needa gun. Pa ain got no gun. We needa gun in the house. Yuh kin never tell whut might happen."

"Now don yuh try to maka fool outta me, boy! Ef we did hava gun, yuh wouldn't have it!"

He laid the catalogue down and slipped his arm around her waist.

"Aw, Ma, Ah done worked hard alla summer n ain ast yuh fer nothing, is Ah, now?"

"Thas whut yuh spose to do!"

"But Ma, Ah wans a gun. Yuh kin lemme have two dollahs outta mah money. Please, Ma. I kin give it to Pa . . . Please, Ma! Ah loves yuh, Ma."

When she spoke her voice came soft and low.

"Whut yu wan wida gun, Dave? Yuh don need no gun. Yuh'll git in trouble. N ef yo pa jus thought Ah let yuh have money t buy a gun he'd hava fit."

"Ah'll hide it, Ma. It ain but two dollahs."

"Lawd, chil, whut's wrong wid yuh?"

"Ain nothing wrong, Ma. Ahm almos a man now. Ah wans a gun."

"Who gonna sell yuh a gun?"

"Ol Joe at the sto."

"N it don cos but two dollahs?"

"Thas all, Ma. Jus two dollahs. Please, Ma."

She was stacking the plates away; her hands moved slowly, reflectively. Dave kept an anxious silence. Finally, she turned to him.

"Ah'll let you git tha gun ef yuh promise me one thing."

"Whut's tha, Ma?"

"Yuh bring it straight back t me, yuh hear? It be fer Pa."

"Yessum! Lemme go now, Ma."

She stooped, turned slightly to one side, raised the hem of her dress, rolled down the top of her stocking, and came up with a slender wad of bills.

"Here," she said. "Lawd knows yuh don need no

gun. But yer pa does. Yuh bring it right back t me, yuh hear? Ahma put it up. Now ef yuh don, Ahma have yuh pa lick yuh so hard yuh won fergit it."

"Yessum."

He took the money, ran down the steps, and across the yard.

"Dave! Yuuuuuh Daaaaave!"

He heard, but he was not going to stop now. "Naw, Lawd!"

The first movement he made the following morning was to reach under his pillow for the gun. In the gray light of dawn he held it loosely, feeling a sense of power. Could kill a man with a gun like this. Kill anybody, black or white. And if he were holding his gun in his hand, nobody could run over him; they would have to respect him. It was a big gun, with a long barrel and a heavy handle. He raised and lowered it in his hand, marveling at its weight.

He had not come straight home with it as his mother had asked; instead he had stayed out in the fields, holding the weapon in his hand, aiming it now and then at some imaginary foe. But he had not fired it; he had been afraid that his father might hear. Also he was not sure he knew how to fire it.

To avoid surrendering the pistol he had not come into the house until he knew that they were all asleep. When his mother had tiptoed to his bedside late that night and demanded the gun, he had first played possum; then he had told her that the gun was hidden outdoors, that he would bring it to her in the morning. Now he lay turning it slowly in his hands. He broke it, took out the cartridges, felt them, and then put them back.

He slid out of bed, got a long strip of old flannel from a trunk, wrapped the gun in it, and tied it to his naked thigh while it was still loaded. He did not go in to breakfast. Even though it was not yet daylight, he started for Jim Hawkins' plantation. Just as the sun was rising he reached the barns where the mules and plows were kept.

"Hey! That you, Dave?"

He turned. Jim Hawkins stood eying him suspiciously.

"What're yuh doing here so early?"

"Ah didn't know Ah wuz gittin up so early, Mistah Hawkins. Ah wuz fixin t hitch up ol Jenny n take her t the fiels."

"Good. Since you're so early, how about plowing that stretch down by the woods?"

"Suits me, Mistah Hawkins."

"O.K. Go to it!"

He hitched Jenny to a plow and started across the fields. Hot dog! This was just what he wanted. If he could get down by the woods, he could shoot his gun and nobody would hear. He walked behind the plow, hearing the traces creaking, feeling the gun tied tight to his thigh.

When he reached the woods, he plowed two whole rows before he decided to take out the gun. Finally, he stopped, looked in all directions, then untied the gun and held it in his hand. He turned to the mule and smiled.

"Know whut this is, Jenny? Naw, yuh wouldn know! Yuhs jusa ol mule! Anyhow, this is a gun, n it kin shoot, by Gawd!"

He held the gun at arm's length. Whut t hell, Ahma shoot this thing! He looked at Jenny again.

"Lissen here, Jenny! When Ah pull this ol trigger, Ah don wan yuh t run n acka fool now!"

Jenny stood with head down, her short ears pricked straight. Dave walked off about twenty feet, held the gun far out from him at arm's length, and turned his head. Hell, he told himself, Ah ain afraid. The gun felt loose in his fingers; he waved it wildly for a moment. Then he shut his eyes and tightened his forefinger. Bloom! A report half deafened him and he thought his right hand was torn from his arm. He heard Jenny whinnying and galloping over the field, and he found himself on his knees, squeezing his fingers hard between his legs. His hand was numb; he jammed it into his mouth, trying to warm it, trying to stop the pain. The gun lay at his feet. He did not quite know what had happened. He stood up and stared at the gun as though it were a living thing. He gritted his teeth and kicked the gun. Yuh almos broke mah arm! He turned to look for Jenny; she was far over the fields, tossing her head and kicking wildly.

"Hol on there, ol mule!"

When he caught up with her she stood trembling, walling her big white eyes at him. The plow was far away; the traces had broken. Then Dave stopped short, looking, not believing. Jenny was bleeding. Her left side was red and wet with blood. He went closer. Lawd, have mercy! Wondah did Ah shoot this mule? He grabbed for Jenny's mane. She flinched, snorted, whirled, tossing her head.

"Hol on now! Hol on."

Then he saw the hole in Jenny's side, right between the ribs. It was round, wet, red. A crimson stream streaked down the front leg, flowing fast. Good Gawd! Ah wuzn't shootin at tha mule. He felt panic. He knew he had to stop that blood, or Jenny would bleed to death. He had never seen so much blood in all his life. He chased the mule for half a mile, trying to catch her. Finally she stopped, breathing hard, stumpy tail half arched. He caught her mane and led her back to where the plow and gun lay. Then he stooped and grabbed handfuls of damp black earth and tried to plug the bullet hole. Jenny shuddered, whinnied, and broke from him.

"Hol on! Hol on now!"

He tried to plug it again, but blood came anyhow. His fingers were hot and sticky. He rubbed dirt into his palms, trying to dry them. Then again he attempted to plug the bullet hole, but Jenny shied away,

kicking her heels high. He stood helpless. He had to
do something. He ran at Jenny; she dodged him. He
watched a red stream of blood flow down Jenny's leg
and form a bright pool at her feet.

"Jenny . . . Jenny," he called weakly.

His lips trembled. She's bleeding t death! He looked
in the direction of home, wanting to go back, wanting
to get help. But he saw the pistol lying in the damp
black clay. He had a queer feeling that if he only did
something, this would not be; Jenny would not be
there bleeding to death.

When he went to her this time, she did not move.
She stood with sleepy, dreamy eyes; and when he
touched her she gave a low-pitched whinny and knelt
to the ground, her front knees slopping in blood.

"Jenny . . . Jenny . . ." he whispered.

For a long time she held her neck erect; then her
head sank, slowly. Her ribs swelled with a mighty
heave and she went over.

Dave's stomach felt empty, very empty. He picked
up the gun and held it gingerly between his thumb
and forefinger. He buried it at the foot of a tree. He
took a stick and tried to cover the pool of blood with
dirt—but what was the use? There was Jenny lying
with her mouth open and her eyes walled and glassy.
He could not tell Jim Hawkins he had shot his mule.
But he had to tell something. Yeah, Ah'll tell em
Jenny started gittin wil n fell on the joint of the
plow. . . . But that would hardly happen to a mule.
He walked across the field slowly, head down.

It was sunset. Two of Jim Hawkins' men were over
near the edge of the woods digging a hole in which to
bury Jenny. Dave was surrounded by a knot of people,
all of whom were looking down at the dead mule.

"I don't see how in the world it happened," said
Jim Hawkins for the tenth time.

The crowd parted and Dave's mother, father, and
small brother pushed into the center.

"Where Dave?" his mother called.

"There he is," said Jim Hawkins.

His mother grabbed him.

"Whut happened, Dave? Whut yuh done?"

"Nothin."

"C'mon, boy, talk," his father said.

Dave took a deep breath and told the story he knew nobody believed.

"Waal," he drawled. "Ah brung ol Jenny down here sos Ah could do mah plowin. Ah plowed bout two rows, just like yuh see." He stopped and pointed at the long rows of upturned earth. "Then somethin musta been wrong wid ol Jenny. She wouldn ack right a-tall. She started snortin n kickin her heels. Ah tried t hol her, but she pulled erway, rearin n goin in. Then when the point of the plow was stickin up in the air, she swung erroun n twisted herself back on it . . . She stuck herself n started t bleed. N fo Ah could do anything, she wuz dead."

"Did you ever hear of anything like that in all your life?" asked Jim Hawkins.

There were white and black standing in the crowd. They murmured. Dave's mother came close to him and looked hard into his face. "Tell the truth, Dave," she said.

"Looks like a bullet hole to me," said one man.

"Dave, whut yuh do wid the gun?" his mother asked.

The crowd surged in, looking at him. He jammed his hands into his pockets, shook his head slowly from left to right, and backed away. His eyes were wide and painful.

"Did he hava gun?" asked Jim Hawkins.

"By Gawd, Ah tol yuh tha wuz a gun wound," said a man, slapping his thigh.

His father caught his shoulders and shook him till his teeth rattled.

"Tell whut happened, yuh rascal! Tell whut . . ."

Dave looked at Jenny's still legs and began to cry.

"Whut yuh do wid tha gun?" his mother asked.

"Whut wuz he doin wida gun?" his father asked.

"Come on and tell the truth," said Hawkins. "Ain't nobody going to hurt you . . ."

His mother crowded close to him.

"Did yuh shoot tha mule, Dave?"

Dave cried, seeing blurred white and black faces.

"Ahh ddinn gggo tt sshooot hher . . . Ah ssswear ffo Gawd Ahh ddin. . . . Ah wuz a-tryin t sssee ef the old gggun would sshoot—"

"Where yuh git the gun from?" his father asked.

"Ah got it from Joe, at the sto."

"Where yuh git the money?"

"Ma give it t me."

"He kept worryin me, Bob. Ah had t. Ah tol im t bring the gun right back t me . . . It was fer yuh, the gun."

"But how yuh happen to shoot that mule?" asked Jim Hawkins.

"Ah wuzn shootin at the mule, Mistah Hawkins. The gun jumped when Ah pulled the trigger . . . N fo Ah knowed anything Jenny was there a-bleedin."

Somebody in the crowd laughed. Jim Hawkins walked close to Dave and looked into his face.

"Well, looks like you have bought you a mule, Dave."

"Ah swear fo Gawd, Ah didn go t kill the mule, Mistah Hawkins!"

"But you killed her!"

All the crowd was laughing now. They stood on tiptoe and poked heads over one another's shoulders.

"Well, boy, looks like yuh done bought a dead mule! Hahaha!"

"Ain tha ershame."

"Hohohohoho."

Dave stood, head down, twisting his feet in the dirt.

"Well, you needn't worry about it, Bob," said Jim Hawkins to Dave's father. "Just let the boy keep on working and pay me two dollars a month."

"Whut yuh wan fer yo mule, Mistah Hawkins?"

Jim Hawkins screwed up his eyes.

"Fifty dollars."

"Whut yuh do wid tha gun?" Dave's father demanded.

Dave said nothing.

"Yuh wan me t take a tree n beat yuh till yuh talk!"

"Nawsuh!"

"Whut yuh do wid it?"

"Ah throwed it erway."

"Where?"

"Ah . . . Ah throwed it in the creek."

"Waal, c mon home. N firs thing in the mawnin git to tha creek n fin tha gun."

"Yessuh."

"Whut yuh pay fer it?"

"Two dollahs."

"Take tha gun n git yo money back n carry it t Mistah Hawkins, yuh hear? N don fergit Ahma lam you black bottom good fer this! Now march yosef on home, suh!"

Dave turned and walked slowly. He heard people laughing. Dave glared, his eyes welling with tears. Hot anger bubbled in him. Then he swallowed and stumbled on.

That night Dave did not sleep. He was glad that he had gotten out of killing the mule so easily, but he was hurt. Something hot seemed to turn over inside him each time he remembered how they had laughed. He tossed on his bed, feeling his hard pillow. *N Pa says he's gonna beat me* . . . He remembered other beatings, and his back quivered. *Naw, naw. Ah sho don wan im t beat me tha way no mo. Dam em all! Nobody ever gave him anything. All he did was work. They treat me like a mule, n then they beat me.* He gritted his teeth. *N Ma had t tell on me.*

Well, if he had to, he would take old man Hawkins that two dollars. But that meant selling the gun. And he wanted to keep that gun. Fifty dollars for a dead mule.

He turned over, thinking how he had fired the gun. He had an itch to fire it again. *Ef other men kin shoota gun, by Gawd, Ah kin!* He was still, listening. *Mebbe they all sleepin now.* The house was still. He heard the soft breathing of his brother. *Yes, now!* He would go down and get that gun and see if he could fire it! He eased out of bed and slipped into overalls.

The moon was bright. He ran almost all the way to the edge of the woods. He stumbled over the ground, looking for the spot where he had buried the gun. *Yeah, here it is.* Like a hungry dog scratching for a bone, he pawed it up. He puffed his black cheeks and blew dirt from the trigger and barrel. He broke it and found four cartridges unshot. He looked around; the fields were filled with silence and moonlight. He clutched the gun stiff and hard in his fingers. But, as soon as he wanted to pull the trigger, he shut his eyes and turned his head. *Naw, Ah can't shoot wid mah eyes closed n mah head turned.* With effort he held his eyes open; then he squeezed. *Blooooom!* He was stiff, not breathing. The gun was still in his hands. Dammit, he'd done it! He fired again. *Blooooom!* He smiled. *Blooooom! Blooooom! Click, click.* There! It was empty. If anybody could shoot a gun, he could. He put the gun into his hip pocket and started across the fields.

When he reached the top of a ridge he stood straight and proud in the moonlight, looking at Jim Hawkins' big white house, feeling the gun sagging in his pocket. *Lawd, ef Ah had just one mo bullet Ah'd taka shot at tha house. Ah'd like t scare ol man Hawkins jusa little . . . jusa enough t let im know Dave Saunders is a man.*

To his left the road curved, running to the tracks of the Illinois Central. He jerked his head, listening. From far off came a faint *hoooof-hoooof; hoooof-hoooof; hoooof-hoooof.* . . . He stood rigid. *Two dollahs a mont. Les see now . . . Tha means it'll take bout two years. Shucks! Ah'll be dam!*

He started down the road, toward the tracks. Yeah, here she comes! He stood beside the track and held himself stiffly. Here she comes, erroun the ben . . . C mon, yuh slow poke! C mon! He had his hand on his gun; something quivered in his stomach. Then the train thundered past, the gray-and-brown boxcars rumbling and clinking. He gripped the gun tightly; then he jerked his hand out of his pocket. Ah betcha Bill wouldn't do it! Ah betcha . . . The cars slid past, steel grinding upon steel. Ahm ridin yuh ternight, so hep me Gawd! He was hot all over. He hesitated just a moment; then he grabbed, pulled atop of a car, and lay flat. He felt his pocket; the gun was still there. Ahead the long rails were glinting in the moonlight, stretching away, away to somewhere, somewhere where he could be a man . . .

Flannery O'Connor

Flannery O'Connor was born in 1925, in Savannah, Georgia, where she grew up and where she attended Catholic schools. She continued her education at Georgia College and the University of Iowa. At age twenty-five she was diagnosed with lupus, the disease that had killed her father. She and her mother moved to a dairy farm outside Milledgeville, Georgia, where she spent the rest of her life. Flannery O'Connor wrote two novels, *Wise Blood* (1952) and *The Violent Bear It Away* (1960), but she is best known for her stories, for which she won three O. Henry prizes. They were collected in *The Complete Short Stories* (1971), a volume that won the National Book Award. Flannery O'Connor's works often deal with theological subjects, but whatever her subject, the fiction is set firmly in the South. Alice Walker was first drawn to her realistic characterizations, "these white folks without the magnolia . . . and these black folks without melons and superior racial patience, these are like the southerners that I know." After O'Connor's death in 1964, Cecil Dawkins produced a two-act play, *The Displaced Person* (1966), based on five of her stories; Sally and Robert Fitzgerald edited her essays, *Mystery and Manners: Occasional Prose* (1969); and John Huston directed the movie version of *Wise Blood* (1980). A creator of eccentric characters and tragicomic circumstances, O'Connor is most well-known as a writer of the "southern grotesque." She reacted to this classification with wry humor: "Whenever I'm asked why southern writers particularly have a penchant for writing about freaks, I say it is because we are still able to recognize one." But she also added an incisive critique of such classifications: "Of course, I have found that anything that comes out of the South is going to be called grotesque by the northern reader, unless it is grotesque, in which case it is going to be called realistic."

Everything That Rises Must Converge

Her doctor had told Julian's mother that she must lose twenty pounds on account of her blood pressure, so on Wednesday nights Julian had to take her downtown on the bus for a reducing class at the Y. The reducing class was designed for working girls over fifty, who weighed from 165 to 200 pounds. His mother was one of the slimmer ones, but she said ladies did not tell their age or weight. She would not ride the buses by herself at night since they had been integrated, and because the reducing class was one of her few pleasures, necessary for her health, and *free*, she said Julian could at least put himself out to take her, considering all she did for him. Julian did not like to consider all she did for him, but every Wednesday night he braced himself and took her.

She was almost ready to go, standing before the hall mirror, putting on her hat, while he, his hands behind him, appeared pinned to the door frame, waiting like Saint Sebastian for the arrows to begin piercing him. The hat was new and had cost her seven dollars and a half. She kept saying, "Maybe I shouldn't have paid that for it. No, I shouldn't have. I'll take it off and return it tomorrow. I shouldn't have bought it."

Julian raised his eyes to heaven. "Yes, you should have bought it," he said. "Put it on and let's go." It was a hideous hat. A purple velvet flap came down on one side of it and stood up on the other; the rest of it was green and looked like a cushion with the stuffing out. He decided it was less comical than jaunty and pathetic. Everything that gave her pleasure was small and depressed him.

She lifted the hat one more time and set it down slowly on top of her head. Two wings of gray hair protruded on either side of her florid face, but her eyes, sky-blue, were as innocent and untouched by experience as they must have been when she was ten. Were it not that she was a widow who had struggled fiercely to feed and clothe and put him through school and who was supporting him still, "until he got on his feet," she might have been a little girl that he had to take to town.

"It's all right, it's all right," he said. "Let's go." He opened the door himself and started down the walk to get her going. The sky was a dying violet and the houses stood out darkly against it, bulbous liver-colored monstrosities of a uniform ugliness though no two were alike. Since this had been a fashionable neighborhood forty years ago, his mother persisted in thinking they did well to have an apartment in it. Each house had a narrow collar of dirt around it in which sat, usually, a grubby child. Julian walked with his hands in his pockets, his head down and thrust forward and his eyes glazed with the determination to make himself completely numb during the time he would be sacrificed to her pleasure.

The door closed and he turned to find the dumpy figure, surmounted by the atrocious hat, coming toward him. "Well," she said, "you only live once and paying a little more for it, I at least won't meet myself coming and going."

"Some day I'll start making money," Julian said gloomily—he knew he never would—"and you can have one of those jokes whenever you take the fit." But first they would move. He visualized a place where the nearest neighbors would be three miles away on either side.

"I think you're doing fine," she said, drawing on

her gloves. "You've only been out of school a year. Rome wasn't built in a day."

She was one of the few members of the Y reducing class who arrived in hat and gloves and who had a son who had been to college. "It takes time," she said, "and the world is in such a mess. This hat looked better on me than any of the others, though when she brought it out I said, 'Take that thing back. I wouldn't have it on my head,' and she said, 'Now wait till you see it on,' and when she put it on me, I said, 'We-ull,' and she said, 'If you ask me, that hat does something for you and you do something for the hat, and besides,' she said, 'with that hat, you won't meet yourself coming and going.' "

Julian thought he could have stood his lot better if she had been selfish, if she had been an old hag who drank and screamed at him. He walked along, saturated in depression, as if in the midst of his martyrdom he had lost his faith. Catching sight of his long, hopeless, irritated face, she stopped suddenly with a grief-stricken look, and pulled back on his arm. "Wait on me," she said. "I'm going back to the house and take this thing off and tomorrow I'm going to return it. I was out of my head. I can pay the gas bill with that seven-fifty."

He caught her arm in a vicious grip. "You are not going to take it back," he said. "I like it."

"Well," she said, "I don't think I ought . . ."

"Shut up and enjoy it," he muttered, more depressed than ever.

"With the world in the mess it's in," she said, "it's a wonder we can enjoy anything. I tell you, the bottom rail is on the top."

Julian sighed.

"Of course," she said, "if you know who you are, you can go anywhere." She said this every time he took her to the reducing class. "Most of them in it are not our kind of people," she said, "but I can be gracious to anybody. I know who I am."

"They don't give a damn for your graciousness," Julian said savagely. "Knowing who you are is good for one generation only. You haven't the foggiest idea where you stand now or who you are."

She stopped and allowed her eyes to flash at him. "I most certainly do know who I am," she said, "and if you don't know who you are, I'm ashamed of you."

"Oh hell," Julian said.

"Your great-grandfather was a former governor of this state," she said. "Your grandfather was a prosperous landowner. Your grandmother was a Godhigh."

"Will you look around you," he said tensely, "and see where you are now?" and he swept his arm jerkily out to indicate the neighborhood, which the growing darkness at least made less dingy.

"You remain what you are," she said. "Your great-grandfather had a plantation and two hundred slaves."

"There are no more slaves," he said irritably.

"They were better off when they were," she said. He groaned to see that she was off on that topic. She rolled onto it every few days like a train on an open track. He knew every stop, every junction, every swamp along the way, and knew the exact point at which her conclusion would roll majestically into the station: "It's ridiculous. It's simply not realistic. They should rise, yes, but on their own side of the fence."

"Let's skip it," Julian said.

"The ones I feel sorry for," she said, "are the ones that are half white. They're tragic."

"Will you skip it?"

"Suppose we were half white. We would certainly have mixed feelings."

"I have mixed feelings now," he groaned.

"Well let's talk about something pleasant," she said. "I remember going to Grandpa's when I was a little girl. Then the house had double stairways that went up to what was really the second floor—all the cooking was done on the first. I used to like to stay down in the kitchen on account of the way the walls smelled.

I would sit with my nose pressed against the plaster and take deep breaths. Actually the place belonged to the Godhighs but your grandfather Chestny paid the mortgage and saved it for them. They were in reduced circumstances," she said, "but reduced or not, they never forgot who they were."

"Doubtless that decayed mansion reminded them," Julian muttered. He never spoke of it without contempt or thought of it without longing. He had seen it once when he was a child before it had been sold. The double stairways had rotted and been torn down. Negroes were living in it. But it remained in his mind as his mother had known it. It appeared in his dreams regularly. He would stand on the wide porch, listening to the rustle of oak leaves, then wander through the high-ceilinged hall into the parlor that opened onto it and gaze at the worn rugs and faded draperies. It occurred to him that it was he, not she, who could have appreciated it. He preferred its threadbare elegance to anything he could name and it was because of it that all the neighborhoods they had lived in had been a torment to him—whereas she had hardly known the difference. She called her insensitivity "being adjustable."

"And I remember the old darky who was my nurse, Caroline. There was no better person in the world. I've always had a great respect for my colored friends," she said. "I'd do anything in the world for them and they'd . . ."

"Will you for God's sake get off that subject?" Julian said. When he got on a bus by himself, he made it a point to sit down beside a Negro, in reparation as it were for his mother's sins.

"You're mighty touchy tonight," she said. "Do you feel all right?"

"Yes I feel all right," he said. "Now lay off."

She pursed her lips. "Well, you certainly are in a vile humor," she observed. "I just won't speak to you at all."

They had reached the bus stop. There was no bus in sight and Julian, his hands still jammed in his pockets and his head thrust forward, scowled down the empty street. The frustration of having to wait on the bus as well as ride on it began to creep up his neck like a hot hand. The presence of his mother was borne in upon him as she gave a pained sigh. He looked at her bleakly. She was holding herself very erect under the preposterous hat, wearing it like a banner of her imaginary dignity. There was in him an evil urge to break her spirit. He suddenly loosened his tie and pulled it off and put it in his pocket.

She stiffened. "Why must you look like *that* when you take me to town?" she said. "Why must you deliberately embarrass me?"

"If you'll never learn where you are," he said, "you can at least learn where I am."

"You look like a—thug," she said.

"Then I must be one," he murmured.

"I'll just go home," she said. "I will not bother you. If you can't do a little thing like that for me . . ."

Rolling his eyes upward, he put his tie back on. "Restored to my class," he muttered. He thrust his face toward her and hissed, "True culture is in the mind, the *mind*," he said, and tapped his head, "the mind."

"It's in the heart," she said, "and in how you do things and how you do things is because of who you *are*."

"Nobody in the damn bus cares who you are."

"I care who I am," she said icily.

The lighted bus appeared on top of the next hill and as it approached, they moved out into the street to meet it. He put his hand under her elbow and hoisted her up on the creaking step. She entered with a little smile, as if she were going into a drawing room where everyone had been waiting for her. While he put in the tokens, she sat down on one of the broad front seats for three which faced the aisle. A thin woman with protruding teeth and long yellow hair was sitting on the end of it. His mother moved up beside her and left room for Julian beside herself. He sat down and looked at the floor across the aisle where a pair of thin feet in red-and-white canvas sandals were planted.

His mother immediately began a general conversation meant to attract anyone who felt like talking. "Can it get any hotter?" she said and removed from her purse a folding fan, black with a Japanese scene on it, which she began to flutter before her.

"I reckon it might could," the woman with the protruding teeth said, "but I know for a fact my apartment couldn't get no hotter."

"It must get the afternoon sun," his mother said. She sat forward and looked up and down the bus. It was half filled. Everybody was white. "I see we have the bus to ourselves," she said. Julian cringed.

"For a change," said the woman across the aisle, the owner of the red-and-white canvas sandals. "I come on one the other day and they were thick as fleas—up front and all through."

"The world is in a mess everywhere," his mother said. "I don't know how we've let it get in this fix."

"What gets my goat is all those boys from good families stealing automobile tires," the woman with the protruding teeth said. "I told my boy, I said you may not be rich but you been raised right and if I ever catch you in any such mess, they can send you on to the reformatory. Be exactly where you belong."

"Training tells," his mother said. "Is your boy in high school?"

"Ninth grade," the woman said.

"My son just finished college last year. He wants to write but he's selling typewriters until he gets started," his mother said.

The woman leaned forward and peered at Julian. He threw her such a malevolent look that she subsided against the seat. On the floor across the aisle there was an abandoned newspaper. He got up and got it and opened it out in front of him. His mother discreetly continued the conversation in a lower tone but the woman across the aisle said in a loud voice, "Well that's nice. Selling typewriters is close to writing. He can go right from one to the other."

"I tell him," his mother said, "that Rome wasn't built in a day."

Behind the newspaper Julian was withdrawing into the inner compartment of his mind where he spent most of his time. This was a kind of mental bubble in which he established himself when he could not bear to be a part of what was going on around him. From it he could see out and judge but in it he was safe from any kind of penetration from without. It was the only place where he felt free of the general idiocy of his fellows. His mother had never entered it but from it he could see her with absolute clarity.

The old lady was clever enough and he thought that if she had started from any of the right premises, more might have been expected of her. She lived according to the laws of her own fantasy world, outside of which he had never seen her set foot. The law of it was to sacrifice herself for him after she had first created the necessity to do so by making a mess of things. If he had permitted her sacrifices, it was only because her lack of foresight had made them necessary. All of her life had been a struggle to act like a Chestny without the Chestny goods, and to give him everything she thought a Chestny ought to have; but since, said she, it was fun to struggle, why complain? And when you had won, as she had won, what fun to look back on the hard times! He could not forgive her that she had enjoyed the struggle and that she thought *she* had won.

What she meant when she said she had won was that she had brought him up successfully and had sent him to college and that he had turned out so well— good looking (her teeth had gone unfilled so that his could be straightened), intelligent (he realized he was too intelligent to be a success), and with a future ahead of him (there was of course no future ahead of him). She excused his gloominess on the grounds that he was still growing up and his radical ideas on his lack of practical experience. She said he didn't yet know a thing about "life," that he hadn't even entered the real world—when already he was as disenchanted with it as a man of fifty.

The further irony of all this was that in spite of her, he had turned out so well. In spite of going to only a third-rate college, he had, on his own initiative, come out with a first-rate education; in spite of growing up dominated by a small mind, he had ended up with a large one; in spite of all her foolish views, he was free of prejudice and unafraid to face facts. Most miraculous of all, instead of being blinded by love for her as she was for him, he had cut himself emotionally free of her and could see her with complete objectivity. He was not dominated by his mother.

The bus stopped with a sudden jerk and shook him from his meditation. A woman from the back lurched forward with little steps and barely escaped falling in his newspaper as she righted herself. She got off and a large Negro got on. Julian kept his paper lowered to watch. It gave him a certain satisfaction to see injustice in daily operation. It confirmed his view that with a few exceptions there was no one worth knowing within a radius of three hundred miles. The Negro was well dressed and carried a briefcase. He looked around and then sat down on the other end of the seat where the woman with the red-and-white canvas sandals was sitting. He immediately unfolded a newspaper and obscured himself behind it. Julian's mother's elbow at once prodded insistently into his ribs. "Now you see why I won't ride on these buses by myself," she whispered.

The woman with the red-and-white canvas sandals had risen at the same time the Negro sat down and had gone further back in the bus and taken the seat of the woman who had got off. His mother leaned forward and cast her an approving look.

Julian rose, crossed the aisle, and sat down in the place of the woman with the canvas sandals. From this position, he looked serenely across at his mother. Her face had turned an angry red. He stared at her, making his eyes the eyes of a stranger. He felt his tension suddenly lift as if he had openly declared war on her.

He would have liked to get in conversation with the Negro and to talk with him about art or politics or any subject that would be above the comprehension of those around them, but the man remained entrenched behind his paper. He was either ignoring the change of seating or had never noticed it. There was no way for Julian to convey his sympathy.

His mother kept her eyes fixed reproachfully on his face. The woman with the protruding teeth was looking at him avidly as if he were a type of monster new to her.

"Do you have a light?" he asked the Negro.

Without looking away from his paper, the man reached in his pocket and handed him a packet of matches.

"Thanks," Julian said. For a moment he held the matches foolishly. A NO SMOKING sign looked down upon him from over the door. This alone would not have deterred him; he had no cigarettes. He had quit smoking some months before because he could not afford it. "Sorry," he muttered and handed back the matches. The Negro lowered the paper and gave him an annoyed look. He took the matches and raised the paper again.

His mother continued to gaze at him but she did not take advantage of his momentary discomfort. Her eyes retained their battered look. Her face seemed to be unnaturally red, as if her blood pressure had risen. Julian allowed no glimmer of sympathy to show on his face. Having got the advantage, he wanted desperately to keep it and carry it through. He would have liked to teach her a lesson that would last her a while, but there seemed no way to continue the point. The Negro refused to come out from behind his paper.

Julian folded his arms and looked stolidly before him, facing her but as if he did not see her, as if he had ceased to recognize her existence. He visualized a scene in which, the bus having reached their stop, he would remain in his seat and when she said, "Aren't you going to get off?" he would look at her as at a stranger who had rashly addressed him. The corner they got off on was usually deserted, but it was well lighted and it would not hurt her to walk by herself the four blocks to the Y. He decided to wait until the time came and then decide whether or not he would let her get off by herself. He would have to be at the Y at ten to bring her back, but he could leave her wondering if he was going to show up. There was no reason for her to think she could always depend on him.

He retired again into the high-ceilinged room sparsely settled with large pieces of antique furniture. His soul expanded momentarily but then he became aware of his mother across from him and the vision shriveled. He studied her coldly. Her feet in little pumps dangled like a child's and did not quite reach the floor. She was training on him an exaggerated look of reproach. He felt completely detached from her. At that moment he could with pleasure have slapped her as he would have slapped a particularly obnoxious child in his charge.

He began to imagine various unlikely ways by which he could teach her a lesson. He might make friends with some distinguished Negro professor or lawyer and bring him home to spend the evening. He would be entirely justified but her blood pressure would rise to 300. He could not push her to the extent of making her have a stroke, and moreover, he had never been successful at making any Negro friends. He had tried

to strike up an acquaintance on the bus with some of
the better types, with ones that looked like professors
or ministers or lawyers. One morning he had sat down
next to a distinguished-looking dark brown man who
had answered his questions with a sonorous solemnity
but who had turned out to be an undertaker. Another
day he had sat down beside a cigar-smoking Negro
with a diamond ring on his finger, but after a few
stilted pleasantries, the Negro had rung the buzzer and
risen, slipping two lottery tickets into Julian's hand as
he climbed over him to leave.

He imagined his mother lying desperately ill and his
being able to secure only a Negro doctor for her. He
toyed with that idea for a few minutes and then
dropped it for a momentary vision of himself participating as a sympathizer in a sit-in demonstration. This
was possible but he did not linger with it. Instead, he
approached the ultimate horror. He brought home a
beautiful suspiciously Negroid woman. Prepare yourself, he said. There is nothing you can do about it.
This is the woman I've chosen. She's intelligent, digni-
fied, even good, and she's suffered and she hasn't
thought it *fun.* Now persecute us, go ahead and persecute us. Drive her out of here, but remember, you're
driving me too. His eyes were narrowed and through
the indignation he had generated, he saw his mother
across the aisle, purple-faced, shrunken to the dwarf-
like proportions of her moral nature, sitting like a
mummy beneath the ridiculous banner of her hat.

He was tilted out of his fantasy again as the bus
stopped. The door opened with a sucking hiss and out
of the dark a large, gaily dressed, sullen-looking colored woman got on with a little boy. The child, who
might have been four, had on a short plaid suit and a
Tyrolean hat with a blue feather in it. Julian hoped
that he would sit down beside him and that the woman
would push in beside his mother. He could think of
no better arrangement.

As she waited for her tokens, the woman was surveying the seating possibilities—he hoped with the idea of sitting where she was least wanted. There was something familiar-looking about her but Julian could not place what it was. She was a giant of a woman. Her face was set not only to meet opposition but to seek it out. The downward tilt of her large lower lip was like a warning sign: DON'T TAMPER WITH ME. Her bulging figure was encased in a green crepe dress and her feet overflowed in red shoes. She had on a hideous hat. A purple velvet flap came down on one side of it and stood up on the other; the rest of it was green and looked like a cushion with the stuffing out. She carried a mammoth red pocketbook that bulged throughout as if it were stuffed with rocks.

To Julian's disappointment, the little boy climbed up on the empty seat beside his mother. His mother lumped all children, black and white, into the common category, "cute," and she thought little Negroes were on the whole cuter than little white children. She smiled at the little boy as he climbed on the seat.

Meanwhile the woman was bearing down upon the empty seat beside Julian. To his annoyance, she squeezed herself into it. He saw his mother's face change as the woman settled herself next to him and he realized with satisfaction that this was more objectionable to her than it was to him. Her face seemed almost gray and there was a look of dull recognition in her eyes, as if suddenly she had sickened at some awful confrontation. Julian saw that it was because she and the woman had, in a sense, swapped sons. Though his mother would not realize the symbolic significance of this, she would feel it. His amusement showed plainly on his face.

The woman next to him muttered something unintelligible to herself. He was conscious of a kind of bristling next to him, a muted growling like that of an angry cat. He could not see anything but the red pocketbook upright on the bulging green thighs. He visualized the woman as she had stood waiting for her tokens—the ponderous figure, rising from the red shoes upward over the solid hips, the mammoth bosom, the haughty face, to the green-and-purple hat.

His eyes widened.

The vision of the two hats, identical, broke upon him with the radiance of a brilliant sunrise. His face was suddenly lit with joy. He could not believe that Fate had thrust upon his mother such a lesson. He gave a loud chuckle so that she would look at him and see that he saw. She turned her eyes on him slowly. The blue in them seemed to have turned a bruised purple. For a moment he had an uncomfortable sense of her innocence, but it lasted only a second before principle rescued him. Justice entitled him to laugh. His grin hardened until it said to her as plainly as if he were saying aloud: Your punishment exactly fits your pettiness. This should teach you a permanent lesson.

Her eyes shifted to the woman. She seemed unable to bear looking at him and to find the woman preferable. He became conscious again of the bristling presence at his side. The woman was rumbling like a volcano about to become active. His mother's mouth began to twitch slightly at one corner. With a sinking heart, he saw incipient signs of recovery on her face and realized that this was going to strike her suddenly as funny and was going to be no lesson at all. She kept her eyes on the woman and an amused smile came over her face as if the woman were a monkey that had stolen her hat. The little Negro was looking up at her with large fascinated eyes. He had been trying to attract her attention for some time.

"Carver!" the woman said suddenly. "Come heah!"

When he saw that the spotlight was on him at last, Carver drew his feet up and turned himself toward Julian's mother and giggled.

"Carver!" the woman said. "You heah me? Come heah!"

Carver slid down from the seat but remained squatting with his back against the base of it, his head turned slyly around toward Julian's mother, who was smiling at him. The woman reached a hand across the aisle and snatched him to her. He righted himself and hung backwards on her knees, grinning at Julian's mother. "Isn't he cute?" Julian's mother said to the woman with the protruding teeth.

"I reckon he is," the woman said without conviction.

The Negress yanked him upright but he eased out of her grip and shot across the aisle and scrambled, giggling wildly, onto the seat beside his love.

"I think he likes me," Julian's mother said, and smiled at the woman. It was the smile she used when she was being particularly gracious to an inferior. Julian saw everything lost. The lesson had rolled off her like rain on a roof.

The woman stood up and yanked the little boy off the seat as if she were snatching him from contagion. Julian could feel the rage in her at having no weapon like his mother's smile. She gave the child a sharp slap across his leg. He howled once and then thrust his head into her stomach and kicked his feet against her shins. "Behave," she said vehemently.

The bus stopped and the Negro who had been reading the newspaper got off. The woman moved over and set the little boy down with a thump between herself and Julian. She held him firmly by the knee. In a moment he put his hands in front of his face and peeped at Julian's mother through his fingers.

"I see yoooooooo!" she said and put her hand in front of her face and peeped at him.

The woman slapped his hand down. "Quit yo' foolishness," she said, "before I knock the living Jesus out of you!"

Julian was thankful that the next stop was theirs. He reached up and pulled the cord. The woman reached up and pulled it at the same time. Oh my God, he thought. He had the terrible intuition that when they got off the bus together, his mother would open her purse and give the little boy a nickel. The gesture would be as natural to her as breathing. The bus stopped and the woman got up and lunged to the front, dragging the child, who wished to stay on, after her. Julian and his mother got up and followed. As they neared the door, Julian tried to relieve her of her pocketbook.

"No," she murmured, "I want to give the little boy a nickel."

"No!" Julian hissed. "No!"

She smiled down at the child and opened her bag. The bus door opened and the woman picked him up by the arm and descended with him, hanging at her hip. Once in the street she set him down and shook him.

Julian's mother had to close her purse while she got down the bus step but as soon as her feet were on the ground, she opened it again and began to rummage inside. "I can't find but a penny," she whispered, "but it looks like a new one."

"Don't do it!" Julian said fiercely between his teeth. There was a streetlight on the corner and she hurried to get under it so that she could better see into her pocketbook. The woman was heading off rapidly down the street with the child still hanging backward on her hand.

"Oh little boy!" Julian's mother called and took a few quick steps and caught up with them just beyond the lamppost. "Here's a bright new penny for you," and she held out the coin, which shone bronze in the dim light.

The huge woman turned and for a moment stood, her shoulders lifted and her face frozen with frustrated rage, and stared at Julian's mother. Then all at once she seemed to explode like a piece of machinery that had been given one ounce of pressure too much. Julian saw the black fist swing out with the red pocketbook. He shut his eyes and cringed as he heard the

woman shout, "He don't take nobody's pennies!"
When he opened his eyes, the woman was disappearing down the street with the little boy staring
wide-eyed over her shoulder. Julian's mother was sitting on the sidewalk.

"I told you not to do that," Julian said angrily. "I
told you not to do that!"

He stood over her for a minute, gritting his teeth.
Her legs were stretched out in front of her and her
hat was on her lap. He squatted down and looked her
in the face. It was totally expressionless. "You got
exactly what you deserved," he said. "Now get up."

He picked up her pocketbook and put what had
fallen out back in it. He picked the hat up off her lap.
The penny caught his eye on the sidewalk and he
picked that up and let it drop before her eyes into the
purse. Then he stood up and leaned over and held his
hands out to pull her up. She remained immobile. He
sighed. Rising above them on either side were black
apartment buildings, marked with irregular rectangles
of light. At the end of the block a man came out of
a door and walked off in the opposite direction. "All
right," he said, "suppose somebody happens by and
wants to know why you're sitting on the sidewalk?"

She took the hand and, breathing hard, pulled heavily up on it and then stood for a moment, swaying
slightly as if the spots of light in the darkness were
circling around her. Her eyes, shadowed and confused,
finally settled on his face. He did not try to conceal
his irritation. "I hope this teaches you a lesson," he
said. She leaned forward and her eyes raked his face.
She seemed trying to determine his identity. Then, as
if she found nothing familiar about him, she started
off with a headlong movement in the wrong direction.

"Aren't you going on to the Y?" he asked.

"Home," she muttered.

"Well, are we walking?"

For answer she kept going. Julian followed along,
his hands behind him. He saw no reason to let the

lesson she had had go without backing it up with an explanation of its meaning. She might as well be made to understand what had happened to her. "Don't think that was just an uppity Negro woman," he said. "That was the whole colored race which will no longer take your condescending pennies. That was your black double. She can wear the same hat as you, and to be sure," he added gratuitously (because he thought it was funny), "it looked better on her than it did on you. What all this means," he said, "is that the old world is gone. The old manners are obsolete and your graciousness is not worth a damn." He thought bitterly of the house that had been lost for him. "You aren't who you think you are," he said.

She continued to plow ahead, paying no attention to him. Her hair had come undone on one side. She dropped her pocketbook and took no notice. He stooped and picked it up and handed it to her but she did not take it.

"You needn't act as if the world had come to an end," he said, "because it hasn't. From now on you've got to live in a new world and face a few realities for a change. Buck up," he said, "it won't kill you."

She was breathing fast.

"Let's wait on the bus," he said.

"Home," she said thickly.

"I hate to see you behave like this," he said. "Just like a child. I should be able to expect more of you." He decided to stop where he was and make her stop and wait for a bus. "I'm not going any farther," he said, stopping. "We're going on the bus."

She continued to go on as if she had not heard him. He took a few steps and caught her arm and stopped her. He looked into her face and caught his breath. He was looking into a face he had never seen before. "Tell Grandpa to come get me," she said.

He stared, stricken.

"Tell Caroline to come get me," she said.

Stunned, he let her go and she lurched forward

again, walking as if one leg were shorter than the other. A tide of darkness seemed to be sweeping her from him. "Mother!" he cried. "Darling, sweetheart, wait!" Crumpling, she fell to the pavement. He dashed forward and fell at her side, crying, "Mamma, Mamma!" He turned her over. Her face was fiercely distorted. One eye, large and staring, moved slightly to the left as if it had become unmoored. The other remained fixed on him, raked his face again, found nothing and closed.

"Wait here, wait here!" he cried and jumped up and began to run for help toward a cluster of lights he saw in the distance ahead of him. "Help, help!" he shouted, but his voice was thin, scarcely a thread of sound. The lights drifted farther away the faster he ran and his feet moved numbly as if they carried him nowhere. The tide of darkness seemed to sweep him back to her, postponing from moment to moment his entry into the world of guilt and sorrow.

Peter Taylor

Peter Taylor was born in Trenton, Tennessee, in 1917, and he often set his fiction in the communities where he grew up: Trenton, Nashville, St. Louis, and Memphis. He studied with several famous southern writers and critics: Allen Tate, John Crowe Ransom, Robert Penn Warren, and Cleanth Brooks. Taylor left Vanderbilt to follow John Crowe Ransom to Kenyon College, where Taylor received his B.A. He went on to become a professor of creative writing at the University of North Carolina at Greensboro and at the University of Virginia, as well as to accept visiting posts at Indiana University, the University of Chicago, Kenyon College, Oxford University, Ohio State University, Harvard University, and the University of Georgia. Although he won a Pulitzer Prize for his novel *A Summons to Memphis* (1986), and wrote two other novels, *A Woman of Means* (1950) and *In the Tennessee Country* (1994), as well as several plays, Taylor is best known for his short stories. Over the years they were repeatedly selected for inclusion in such collections as *The Best American Short Stories* and *The O. Henry Awards.* Many of his early stories were collected in one volume, *The Collected Stories of Peter Taylor* (1969). Then he went on to publish three other collections: *In the Miro District and Other Stories* (1977), *The Old Forest and Other Stories* (1985), and *The Oracle at Stoneleigh Court* (1994). He received numerous prestigious awards, including the Gold Medal for excellence in the arts from the American Academy and

Institute of Arts and Letters (1979) and the PEN/Faulkner Award (1986). Reviewers have called Peter Taylor one of the most accomplished short story writers of our time, comparing him with Anton Chekhov and Henry James. He has been praised for his ear for dialogue and his eye for psychologically complex characterization. Like Eudora Welty, he thought that growing up in a storytelling family inspired his writing. "My theory is that you listen to people talk when you're a child—a southerner does especially—and they tell stories and stories and stories, and you feel those stories must mean something. So really, writing becomes an effort to find out what these stories mean in the beginning." Peter Taylor told an interviewer that he never thought of himself as a regional writer, but rather a writer "about people under certain circumstances": "I'm always concerned with the individual experience and the unique experience of that story. Goodness knows I don't have any political vision for the South, in retrospect or in the future, but I have strong feelings about it. And I think that's the main thing that you have to write about, not only what you have ideas about but what you feel about most keenly." A member of the American Academy and Institute of Arts and Letters, Peter Taylor lived in Charlottesville, Virginia, until his death in 1994.

The Old Forest

I was already formally engaged, as we used to say, to the girl I was going to marry. But still I sometimes went out on the town with girls of a different sort. And during the very week before the date set for the wedding, in December, I was in an automobile accident at a time when one of those girls was with me. It was a calamitous thing to have happen—not the accident itself, which caused no serious injury to anyone, but the accident plus the presence of that girl.

As a matter of fact, it was not unusual in those days—forty years ago and a little more—for a well-brought-up young man like me to keep up his acquaintance, until the very eve of his wedding, with some member of what we facetiously and somewhat arrogantly referred to as the Memphis demimonde. (That was merely to say with a girl who was not in the Memphis debutante set.) I am not even sure how many of us knew what the word "demimonde" meant or implied. But once it had been applied to such girls, it was hard for us to give it up. We even learned to speak of them individually as demimondaines—and later corrupted that to demimondames. The girls were of course a considerably less sophisticated lot than any of this sounds, though they were bright girls certainly and some of them even highly intelligent. They read books, they looked at pictures, and they were apt to attend any concert or play that came to Memphis. When the old San Carlo Opera Company turned up in town, you could count on certain girls of the demimonde being present in their block of seats, and often with a score of the opera in hand. From that you will understand that they certainly weren't the innocent, untutored types that we generally took to dances at the Memphis Country Club and whom we eventually looked forward to marrying.

These girls I refer to would, in fact, very frequently and very frankly say to us that the MCC (that's how we always spoke of the Club) was the last place they wanted to be taken. There was one girl in particular, not so smart as some of the others perhaps and certainly less restrained in the humor she sometimes poked at the world we boys lived in, an outspoken girl, who was the most vociferous of all in her disdain for the Country Club. I remember one night, in one of those beer gardens that became popular in Memphis in the late thirties, when this girl suddenly announced to a group of us, "*I* haven't lost anything at the MCC. That's something you boys can bet your daddy's bottom dollar on." We were gathered—four or five couples—about one of the big wooden beer-garden tables with an umbrella in its center, and when she said that, all the other girls in the party went into a fit of laughter. It was a kind of giggling that was unusual for them. The boys in the party laughed, too, of course, but we were surprised by the way the girls continued to giggle among themselves for such a long time. We were out of college by then and thought we knew the world pretty well; most of us had been working for two or three years in our fathers' business firms. But we didn't see why this joke was so very funny. I suppose it was too broad for us in its reference. There is no way of knowing, after all these years, if it was too broad for our sheltered minds or if the rest of the girls were laughing at the vulgar tone of the girl who had spoken. She was, you see, a little bit coarser than the rest, and I suspect they were laughing at the way she had phrased what she said. For us boys, anyhow, it was pleasant that the demimondaines took the lighthearted view they did about not going to the MCC, because it was the last place most of us would have wished to take them. Our *other* girls would have known too readily who they were and would not willingly or gracefully have endured their presence. To have brought one of those girls to the Club would have required, at any rate, a boy who was a much bolder and freer spirit than I was at twenty-three.

To the liberated young people of today all this may seem a corrupting factor in our old way of life—not our snobbery so much as our continuing to see those demimonde girls right up until the time of marriage. And yet I suspect that in the Memphis of today customs concerning serious courtship and customs concerning unacknowledged love affairs have not been entirely altered. Automobile accidents occur there still, for instance, the reports of which in the newspaper do not mention the name of the driver's "female companion," just as the report of my accident did not. If the driver is a "scion of a prominent local family" with his engagement to be married already announced at an MCC party, as well as in the Sunday newspaper, then the account of his automobile collision is likely to refer to the girl in the car with him only as his "female companion." Some newspaper readers might, I know, assume this to be a reference to the young man's fiancée. That is what is intended, I suppose—*for* the general reader. But it would almost certainly not have been the case—not in the Memphis, Tennessee, of 1937.

The girl with me in my accident was a girl whose origins nobody knew anything about. But she was a perfectly decent sort of girl, living independently in a respectable rooming house and working a respectable job. That was the sort of girl about whom the Memphis newspapers felt obliged to exercise the greatest care when making any reference to her in their columns. It was as though she were their special ward. Such a girl must be protected from any blaze of publicity. Such a girl must not suffer from the misconduct of any Memphis man or group of men—even newspaper publishers. That was fine for the girl, of course, and who could possibly resent it? It was splendid for her, but I, the driver of the car, had to suffer considerable anguish just because of such a girl's presence in the car and suffer still more because of her behavior afterward. Moreover, the response of certain older men in town to her subsequent behavior would cause me still further anguish and prolong my suffering by several days. Those men were the editors of the city's two newspapers, along with the lawyers called in by my father to represent me if I should be taken into court. There was also my father himself, and the father of my fiancée, *his* lawyer (for some reason or other), and, finally, no less a person than the mayor of Memphis, all of whom one would ordinarily have supposed to be indifferent to the caprices of such a girl. They were the civic leaders and merchant princes of the city. They had great matters on their minds. They were, to say the least, an imposing group in the eyes of a young man who had just the previous year entered his father's cotton-brokerage firm, a young man who was still learning how to operate under the pecking order of Memphis's male establishment.

The girl in question was named Lee Ann Deehart. She was a quite beautiful, fair-haired, hazel-eyed girl with a lively manner, and surely she was far from stupid. The thing she did which drew attention from the city fathers came very near, also, to changing the course of my entire life. I had known Lee Ann for perhaps two years at the time, and knew her to be more levelheaded and more reserved and self-possessed than most of her friends among the demi-mondaines. It would have been impossible for me to predict the behavior she was guilty of that winter afternoon. Immediately after the collision, she threw open the door on her side of the car, stepped out onto the roadside, and fled into the woods of Overton Park, which is where the accident took place. And from that time, and during the next four days, she was unheard from by people who wished to question her and protect her. During that endless-seeming period of four days no one could be certain of Lee Ann Deehart's whereabouts.

The circumstances of the accident were rather complicated. The collision occurred just after three o'clock on a very cold Saturday afternoon—the fourth of December. Although at that time in my life I was already a member of my father's cotton firm, I was nevertheless—and strange as it may seem—enrolled in a Latin class out at Southwestern College, which is on the north side of Overton Park. (We were reading Horace's *Odes!*) The class was not held on Saturday afternoon, but I was on my way out to the college to study for a test that had been scheduled for Monday. My interest in Latin was regarded by my father and mother as one of my "anomalies"—a remnant of many "anomalies" I had annoyed them with when I was in my teens and was showing some signs of "not turning out well." It seemed now of course that I had "turned out well" after all, except that nobody in the family and nobody among my friends could understand why I went on showing this interest in Latin. I was not able to explain to them why. Any more than I was able to explain why to myself. It clearly had nothing to do with anything else in my life at that period. Furthermore, in the classroom and under the strict eye of our classics professor, a rotund, mustachioed little man hardly four feet in height (he had to sit on a large Latin dictionary in order to be comfortable at his desk), I didn't excel. I was often embarrassed by having to own up to Professor Bartlett's accusation that I had not so much as glanced at the assigned odes before coming to class. Sometimes other members of the class would be caught helping me with the translation, out in the hallway, when Professor

Bartlett opened his classroom door to us. My real excuse for neglecting the assignments made by that earnest and admirable little scholar was that too many
hours of my life were consumed by my job, by my
courtship of the society girl I was going to marry, and
by my old, bad habits of knocking about town with
my boyhood cronies and keeping company with girls
like Lee Ann Deehart.

Yet I had persisted with my Horace class throughout that fall (against the advice of nearly everyone,
including Professor Bartlett). On that frigid December
afternoon I had resolved to mend my ways as a student. I decided I would take my Horace and go out
to Professor Bartlett's classroom at the college and
make use of his big dictionary in preparing for Monday's test. It was something we had all been urged to
do, with the promise that we would always find the
door unlocked. As it turned out, of course, I was destined not to take the test on Monday and never to
enter Professor Bartlett's classroom again.

It happened that just before I was setting out from
home that afternoon I was filled suddenly with a dread
of the silence and the peculiar isolation of a college
classroom building on a weekend afternoon. I telephoned my fiancée and asked her to go along with
me. At the other end of the telephone line, Caroline
Braxley broke into laughter. She said that I clearly
had no conception of all the things she had to do
within the next seven days before we were to be married. I said I supposed I ought to be helping in some
way, though until now she had not asked me so much
as to help address invitations to the wedding. "No
indeed," said my bride-to-be, "I want to do everything
myself. I wouldn't have it any other way."

Caroline Braxley, this capable and handsome bride-
to-be of mine, was a very remarkable girl, just as
today, as my wife, she seems to me a very remarkable
woman of sixty. She and I have been married for
forty-one years now, and her good judgment in all

matters relating to our marriage has never failed her—
or us. She had already said to me before that Saturday
afternoon that a successful marriage depended in part
on the two persons' developing and maintaining a certain number of separate interests in life. She was all
for my keeping up my golf, my hunting, my fishing.
And, unlike my own family, she saw no reason that I
shouldn't keep up my peculiar interest in Latin,
though she had to confess that she thought it almost
the funniest thing she had ever heard of a man of my
sort going in for.

Caroline liked any sort of individualism in men. But
I already knew her ways sufficiently well to understand that there was no use trying to persuade her to
come along with me to the college. I wished she would
come with me, or maybe I wished even more she
would try to persuade me to come over to her house
and help her with something in preparation for the
wedding. After I had put down the telephone, it even
occurred to me that I might simply drive over to her
house and present myself at her front door. But I
knew what the expression on her face would be, and
I could even imagine the sort of thing she would say:
"No man is going to set foot in my house this afternoon, Nat Ramsey! *I'm* getting married next Saturday,
in case the fact has slipped your mind. Besides, you're
coming here for dinner tonight, aren't you? And there
are parties every night next week!"

This Caroline Braxley of mine was a very tall girl.
(Actually taller than she is nowadays. We have recently measured ourselves and found that each of us
is an inch shorter than we used to be.) One often had
the feeling that one was looking up at her, though of
course she wasn't really so tall as that. Caroline's
height and the splendid way she carried herself were
one of her first attractions for me. It seems to me now
that I was ever attracted to tall girls—that is, when
there was the possibility of falling in love. And I think
this was due in part to the fact that even as a boy I

was half in love with my father's two spinster sisters, who were nearly six feet in height and were always more attentive to me than to the other children in the family.

Anyhow, only moments after I had put down the telephone that Saturday, when I still sat with my hand on the instrument and was thinking vaguely of rushing over to Caroline's house, the telephone underneath my hand began ringing. Perhaps, I thought, it was Caroline calling back to say that she had changed her mind. Instead, it was Lee Ann Deehart. As soon as she heard my voice, she began telling me that she was bored to death. Couldn't I think of something fun she and I could do on this dreary winter afternoon? I laughed aloud at her. "What a shameless wench you are, Lee Ann!" I said.

"Shameless? How so?" she said with pretended innocence.

"As if you weren't fully aware," I lectured her, "that I'm getting married a week from today!"

"What's that got to do with the price of eggs in Arkansas?" She laughed. "Do you think, old Nat, *I* want to marry you?"

"Well," I explained, "I happen to be going out to the college to cram for a Latin test on Monday."

I could hear her laughter at the other end. "Is your daddy going to let you off work long enough to take your Latin test?" she asked with heavy irony in her voice. It was the usual way those girls had of making fun of our dependence on our fathers.

"Ah, yes," I said tolerantly.

"And is he going to let you off next Saturday, too," she went on, "long enough to get married?"

"Listen," I said, "I've just had an idea. Why don't you ride out to the college with me, and fool around some while I do my Latin?" I suppose I didn't really imagine she would go, but suddenly I had thought again of the lonely isolation of Dr. Bartlett's classroom on a Saturday afternoon. I honestly wanted to go ahead out there. It was something I somehow felt I had to do. My preoccupation with the study of Latin poetry, ineffectual student though I was, may have represented a perverse wish to experience the isolation I was at the same time dreading or may have represented a taste for morbidity left over from my adolescence. I can allow myself to speculate on all that now, though it would not have occurred to me to do so at the time.

"Well," said Lee Ann Deehart presently, to my surprise and delight, "it couldn't be more boring out there than sitting here in my room is."

"I'll pick you up in fifteen minutes," I said quickly. And I hung up the telephone before she could possibly change her mind. Thirty minutes later, we were driving through Overton Park on our way to the college. We had passed the Art Gallery and were headed down the hill toward the low ground where the Park Pond is. Ahead of us, on the left, were the gates to the Zoo. And on beyond was the point where the road crossed the streetcar tracks and entered a densely wooded area which is actually the last surviving bit of the primeval forest that once grew right up to the bluffs above the Mississippi River. Here are giant oak and yellow poplar trees older than the memory of the earliest white settler. Some of them surely may have been mature trees when Hernando de Soto passed this way, and were very old trees indeed when General Jackson, General Winchester, and Judge John Overton purchased this land and laid out the city of Memphis. Between the Art Gallery and the pond there used to be, in my day, a little spinney of woods which ran nearly all the way back to what was left of the old forest. It was just when I reached this spinney, with Lee Ann beside me, that I saw a truck approaching us on the wrong side of the icy road. There was a moderately deep snow on the ground, and the park roads had, to say the least, been imperfectly cleared. On the ice and the packed snow, the driver of the truck had clearly lost control of his vehicle. When he was within about seventy-five feet of us, Lee Ann said, "Pull off the road, Nat!"

Lee Ann Deehart's beauty was of the most feminine sort. She was a tiny, delicate-looking girl, and I had noticed, when I went to fetch her that day, in her fur-collared coat and knitted cap and gutta-percha boots she somehow seemed smaller than usual. And I was now struck by the tone of authority coming from this small person whose diminutive size and whose role in my life were such that it wouldn't have occurred to me to heed her advice about driving a car—or about anything else, I suppose. I remember feeling something like: This is an ordeal that I must, and that I want, to face in my own way. It was as though Professor Bartlett himself were in the approaching truck. It seemed my duty not to admit any weakness in my own position. At least I *thought* that was what I felt.

"Pull off the road, Nat!" Lee Ann urged again. And my incredible reply to her was "He's on *my* side of the road! Besides, trucks are not allowed in the park!" And in reply to this Lee Ann gave only a loud snicker.

I believe I did, in the last seconds, try to swing the car off onto the shoulder of the road. But the next thing I really remember is the fierce impact of the two vehicles' meeting.

It was a relatively minor sort of collision, or seemed so at the moment. Since the driver of the truck, which was actually a converted Oldsmobile sedan—and a rather ancient one at that—had the good sense not to put on his brakes and to turn off her motor, the crash was less severe than it might have been. Moreover, since I *had* pulled a little to the right it was not a head-on meeting. It is worth mentioning, though, that it was sufficiently bad to put permanently out of commission the car I was driving, which was not my own car (my car was in the shop, being refurbished for the honeymoon trip) but an aging Packard limousine of my mother's, which I knew she would actually be happy to see retired. I don't remember getting out of the car at all and I don't remember Lee Ann's getting out. The police were told by the driver of the truck, however, that within a second after the impact Lee Ann had thrown open her door, leaped out onto the snow-covered shoulder, jumped the ditch beyond, and run up the incline and into the spinney. The truck driver's account was corroborated by two ice skaters on the pond, who also saw her run through the leafless trees of the spinney and on across a narrow stretch of the public golf course which divides the spinney from the old forest. They agreed that, considering there was a deep snow on the ground and that she was wearing those gutta-percha boots, she traveled at a remarkable speed.

I didn't even know she was out of the car until I got around on the other side and saw the door there standing open and saw her tracks in the snow, going down the bank. I suppose I was too dazed even to follow the tracks with my eyes down the bank and up the other side of the ditch. I must have stood there for several seconds, looking down blankly at the tracks she had left just outside the car door. Presently I looked up at the truck driver, who was standing before me. I know now his eyes must have been following Lee Ann's progress. Finally he turned his eyes to me, and I could tell from his expression that I wasn't a pleasant sight. "Is your head hurt bad?" he asked. I put my hand up to my forehead and when I brought it down it was covered with blood. That was when I passed out. When I came to, they wouldn't let me get up. Besides the truck driver, there were two policemen and the two ice skaters standing over me. They told me that an ambulance was on the way.

At the hospital, the doctor took four stitches in my forehead; and that was it. I went home and lay down for a couple of hours, as I had been told to do. My parents and my two brothers and my little sister and even the servants were very much concerned about

me. They hovered around in a way I had never before
seen them do—not even when somebody was desperately sick. I suppose it was because a piece of violence
like this accident was a very extraordinary thing in our
quiet Memphis life in those years. They were dis-
turbed, too, I soon realized, by my silence as I lay
there on the daybed in the upstairs sitting room and
particularly by my being reticent to talk about the
collision. I had other things on my mind. Every so
often I would remember Lee Ann's boot tracks in the
snow. And I would begin to wonder where she was
now. Since I had not found an opportunity to telephone her, I could only surmise that she had somehow
managed to get back to the rooming house where she
lived. I had not told anyone about her presence in the
car with me. And as I lay there on the daybed, with
the family and servants coming and going and making
inquiries about how I felt, I would find myself wondering sometimes how and whether or not I could tell
Caroline Braxley about Lee Ann's being with me that
afternoon. It turned out the next day—or, rather, on
Monday morning—that the truck driver had told the
two policemen and then, later, repeated to someone
who called from one of the newspapers that there had
been a girl with me in the car. As a matter of fact, I
learned that this was the case on the night of the accident, but as I lay there in the upstairs sitting room
during the afternoon I didn't yet know it.

Shortly before five o'clock Caroline Braxley arrived
at our house, making a proper sick call but also with
the intention of taking me back to dinner with her
parents and her two younger sisters. Immediately after
she entered the upstairs sitting room, and almost before she and I had greeted each other, my mother's
houseboy and sometime chauffeur came in, bringing
my volume of Horace. Because Mother had thought
it might raise my spirits, she had sent him down to
the service garage where the wrecked car had been
taken to fetch it for me. Smiling sympathetically, he

placed it on a table near the daybed and left the room. Looking at the book, Caroline said to me with a smile that expressed a mixture of sympathy and reproach, "I hope you see now what folly your pursuit of Latin poetry is." And suddenly, then, the book on the table appeared to me as an alien object. In retrospect it seems to me that I really knew then that I would never open it again.

I went to dinner that night at Caroline's house, my head still in bandages. The Braxley family treated me with a tenderness equal to that I had received at home. At table, the servingman offered to help my plate for me, as though I were a sick child. I could have enjoyed all this immensely, I think, since I have always been one to relish loving, domestic care, if only I had not been worrying and speculating all the while about Lee Ann. As I talked genially with Caroline's family during the meal and immediately afterward before the briskly burning fire at the end of the Braxleys' long living room, I kept seeing Lee Ann's boot tracks in the snow. And then I would see my own bloody hand as I took it down from my face before I fainted. I remember still having the distinct feeling, as I sat there in the bosom of the Braxley family, that it had not been merely my bloody hand that had made me faint but my bloody hand plus the tracks in the deep snow. In a way, it is strange that I remember all these impressions so vividly after forty years, because it is not as though I have lived an uneventful life during the years since. My Second World War experiences are what I perhaps ought to remember best—those, along with the deaths of my two younger brothers in the Korean War. Even worse, really, were the deaths of my two parents in a terrible fire that destroyed our house on Central Avenue when they had got to be quite old, my mother leaping from a second-story window, my father asphyxiated inside the house. And I can hardly mention without being overcome with emotion the accidental deaths that took two of my and

Caroline's children when they were in their early teens. It would seem that with all these disasters to remember, along with the various business and professional crises I have had, I might hardly be able to recall that earlier episode. But I think that, besides its coming at that impressionable period of my life and the fact that one just does remember things better from one's youth, there is the undeniable fact that life *was* different in those times. What I mean to say is that all these later, terrible events took place in a world where acts of terror are, so to speak, all around us—everyday occurrences—and are brought home to us audibly and pictorially on radio and television almost every hour. I am not saying that some of these ugly acts of terror did not need to take place or were not brought on by what our world was like in those days. But I am saying that the context was different. Our tranquil, upper-middle-class world of 1937 did not have the rest of the world crowding in on it so much. And thus when something only a little ugly did crowd in or when we, often unconsciously, reached out for it, the contrasts seemed sharper. It was not just in the Braxleys' household or in my own family's that everything seemed quiet and well ordered and unchanging. The households were in a context like themselves. Suffice it to say that though the Braxleys' house in Memphis was situated on East Parkway and our house on Central Avenue, at least two miles across town from each other, I could in those days feel perfectly safe, and *was* relatively safe, in walking home many a night from Caroline's house to our house at two in the morning. It was when we young men in Memphis ventured out with the more adventurous girls of the demimonde that we touched on the unsafe zones of Memphis. And there were girls still more adventurous, of course, with whom some of my contemporaries found their way into the very most dangerous zones. But we did think of it that way, you see, thought of it in terms of the girls' being the adventurous ones, whom we followed or didn't follow.

Anyhow, while we were sitting there before the fire, with the portrait of Caroline's paternal grandfather peering down at us from above the mantel and with her father in his broad-lapelled, double-breasted suit standing on the marble hearth, occasionally poking at the logs with the brass poker or sometimes kicking a log with the toe of his wing-tipped shoes, suddenly I was called to the telephone by the Negro servingman who had wanted to help my plate for me. As he preceded me the length of the living room and then gently guided me across the hall to the telephone in the library, I believe he would have put his hand under my elbow to help me—as if a real invalid—if I had allowed him to. As we passed through the hall, I glanced through one of the broad, etched sidelights beside the front door and caught a glimpse of the snow on the ground outside. The weather had turned even colder. There had been no additional snowfall, but even at a glance you could tell how crisply frozen the old snow was on its surface. The servingman at my elbow was saying, "It's your daddy on the phone. I'd suppose he just wants to know how you'd be feeling by now."

But I knew in my heart it wasn't that. It was as if that glimpse of the crisp snow through the front-door sidelight had told me what it was. When I took up the telephone and heard my father's voice pronouncing my name, I knew almost exactly what he was going to say. He said that his friend the editor of the morning paper had called him and reported that there had been a girl in the car with me, and though they didn't of course plan to use her name, probably wouldn't even run the story until Monday, they would have to *know* her name. And would have to assure themselves she wasn't hurt in the crash. And that she was unharmed after leaving the scene. Without hesitation I gave my father Lee Ann Deehart's name, as well as her address and telephone number. But I made no further explanation to Father, and he asked me for none. The only other thing I said was that I'd be home in a little while. Father was silent a moment after that. Then he said, "Are you all right?"

I said, "I'm fine."

And he said, "Good. I'll be waiting for you."

I hung up the telephone, and my first thought was that before I left Caroline tonight I'd have to tell her that Lee Ann had been in the car with me. Then, without thinking almost, I dialed Lee Ann's rooming-house number. It felt very strange to be doing this in the Braxleys' library. The woman who ran the rooming house said that Lee Ann had not been in since she left with me in the afternoon.

As I passed back across the wide hallway and caught another glimpse of the snow outside, the question arose in my mind for the first time: *Had* Lee Ann come to some harm in those woods? More than the density of the underbrush, more than its proximity to the Zoo, where certain unsavory characters often hung out, it was the great size and antiquity of the forest trees somehow and the old rumors that white settlers had once been ambushed there by Chickasaw Indians that made me feel that if anything had happened to the girl, it had happened there. And on the heels of such thoughts I found myself wondering for the first time if all this might actually lead to my beautiful, willowy Caroline Braxley's breaking off our engagement. I returned to the living room, and at the sight of Caroline's tall figure at the far end of the room, placed between that of her mother and that of her father, the conviction became firm in me that I would have to tell her about Lee Ann before she and I parted that night. And as I drew nearer to her, still wondering if something ghastly had happened to Lee Ann there in the old forest, I saw the perplexed and even suspicious expression on Caroline's face and presently observed similar expressions on the faces of her two parents. And from that moment began the gnawing wonder which would be with me for several days ahead: What precisely would Caroline consider sufficient provocation for breaking off our engagement to be married? I had no idea, really. Would it be sufficient that I had had one of those unnamed "female companions" in the car with me at the time of the accident? I knew of engagements like ours which had been broken with apparently less provocation. Or would it be the suspicious-seeming circumstances of Lee Ann's leaping out of the car and running off through the snow? Or might it be the final, worst possibility—that of delicate little Lee Ann Deehart's having actually met with foul play in that infrequently entered area of underbrush and towering forest trees?

Broken engagements were a subject of common and considerable interest to girls like Caroline Braxley. Whereas a generation earlier a broken engagement had been somewhat of a scandal—an engagement that had been formally announced at a party and in the newspaper, that is—it did not necessarily represent that in our day. Even in our day, you see, it meant something quite different from what it had once meant. There was, after all, no written contract and it was in no sense so unalterably binding as it had been in our parents' day. For us it was not considered absolutely dishonorable for either party to break off the plans merely because he or she had had a change of heart. Since the boy was no longer expected literally to ask the father for the girl's hand (though he would probably be expected to go through the form, as I had done with Mr. Braxley), it was no longer a breach of contract between families. There was certainly nothing like a dowry any longer—not in Memphis—and there was only rarely any kind of property settlement involved, except in cases where both families were extraordinarily rich. The thought pleased me—that is,

the ease with which an engagement might be ended.
I suppose in part I was simply preparing myself for
such an eventuality. And there in the Braxleys' long
living room in the very presence of Caroline and Mr.
and Mrs. Braxley themselves, I found myself indulging
in a perverse fantasy, a fantasy in which Caroline had
broken off our engagement and I was standing up
pretty well, was even seeking consolation in the arms,
so to speak, of a safely returned Lee Ann Deehart.

But all at once I felt so guilty for my private indis-
cretion that actually for the first time in the presence
of my prospective in-laws I put my arm about Caroline
Braxley's waist. And I told her that I felt so fatigued
by events of the afternoon that probably I ought now
to go ahead home. She and her parents agreed at
once. And they agreed among themselves that they
each had just now been reflecting privately that I
looked exhausted. Mrs. Braxley suggested that under
the circumstances she ought to ask Robert to drive
me home. I accepted. No other suggestion could have
seemed so welcome. Robert was the same servingman
who had offered to help my plate at dinner and who
had so gently guided me to the telephone when my
father called. Almost at once, after I got into the front
seat of the car beside him—in his dark chauffeur's
uniform and cap—I fell asleep. He had to wake me
when we pulled up to the side door of my father's
house. I remember how warmly I thanked him for
bringing me home, even shaking his hand, which was a
rather unusual thing to do in those days. I felt greatly
refreshed and restored and personally grateful to Robert for it. There was not, in those days in Memphis,
any time or occasion when one felt more secure and
relaxed than when one had given oneself over completely to the care and protection of the black servants
who surrounded us and who created and sustained for
the most part the luxury which distinguished the lives
we lived then from the lives we live now. They did so
for us, whatever their motives and however degrading

our demands and our acceptance of their attentions may have been to them.

At any rate, after my slumber in the front seat beside Robert I felt sufficiently restored to face my father (and his awareness of Lee Ann's having been in the car) with some degree of equanimity. And before leaving the Braxleys' house I had found a moment in the hallway to break the news to Caroline that I had not been alone in the car that afternoon. To my considerable surprise she revealed, after a moment's hesitation, that she already knew that had been the case. Her father, like my father, had learned it from one of the newspaper editors—only he had learned it several hours earlier than my father had. I was obliged to realize as we were saying good night to each other that she, along with her two parents, had known all evening that Lee Ann had been with me and had fled into the woods of Overton Park—that she, Caroline, had as a matter of fact known the full story when she came to my house to fetch me back to her house to dinner. "Where is Lee Ann now?" she asked me presently, holding my two hands in her own and looking me directly in the eye. "I don't know," I said. Knowing how much she knew, I decided I must tell her the rest of it, holding nothing back. I felt that I was seeing a new side to my fiancée and that unless I told her the whole truth there might be something of this other side of her that wouldn't be revealed to me. "I tried to telephone her after I answered my father's call tonight. But she was not in her room and had not been in since I picked her up at two o'clock." And I told Caroline about Lee Ann's telephoning me (after Caroline and I had talked in the early afternoon) and about my inviting her to go out to the college with me. Then I gave her my uncensored version of the accident, including the sight of Lee Ann's footprints in the snow.

"How did she sound on the telephone?" she asked.

"What do you mean by that?" I said impatiently. "I just told you she wasn't home when I called."

"I mean earlier—when she called you."

"But why do you want to know that? It doesn't matter, does it?"

"I mean, did she sound depressed? But it doesn't matter for the moment." She still held my hands in hers. "You do know, don't you," she went on after a moment, "that you are going to have to *find* Lee Ann? And you probably are going to need help."

Suddenly I had the feeling that Caroline Braxley was someone twenty years older than I; but, rather than sounding like my parents or her parents, she sounded like one or another of the college teachers I had had—even like Dr. Bartlett, who once had told me that I was going to need outside help if I was going to keep up with the class. To reassure myself, I suppose, I put my arm about Caroline's waist again and drew her to me. But in our good-night kiss there was a reticence on her part, or a quality that I could only define as conditional or possibly probational. Still, I knew now that she knew everything, and I suppose that was why I was able to catch such a good nap in the car on the way home.

Girls who had been brought up the way Caroline had, in the Memphis of forty years ago, knew not only what was going to be expected of them in making a marriage and bringing up a family there in Memphis— a marriage and a family of the kind their parents had had—they knew also from a fairly early time that they would have to contend with girls and women of certain sorts before and frequently after they were married: with girls, that is, who had no conception of what it was to have a certain type of performance expected of them, or girls of another kind (and more like themselves) who came visiting in Memphis from Mississippi or Arkansas—pretty little plantation girls, my mother called them—or from Nashville or from the old towns of West Tennessee. Oftentimes these other girls were their cousins, but that made them no less dangerous. Not being on their home ground—in their own country, so to speak—these Nashville or Mississippi or West Tennessee or Arkansas girls did not bother to abide by the usual rules of civilized warfare. They were marauders. But girls like Lee Ann Deehart were something else again. They were the Trojan horse, more or less, established in the very citadel. They were the fifth column, and were perhaps the most dangerous of all. At the end of a brilliant debutante season, sometimes the most eligible bachelor of all those on the list would still remain uncommitted, or even secretly committed to someone who had never seen the inside of the Memphis Country Club. This kind of thing, girls like Caroline Braxley understood, was not to be tolerated—not if the power of moral woman included the power to divine the nature of any man's commitment and the power to test the strength and nature of another kind of woman's power. Young people today may say that that old-fashioned behavior on the part of girls doesn't matter today, that girls don't have those problems anymore. But I suspect that in Memphis, if not everywhere, there must be something equivalent even nowadays in the struggle of women for power among themselves.

Perhaps, though, to the present generation these distinctions I am making won't seem significant, after all, or worth my bothering so much about—especially the present generation outside of Memphis and the Deep South. Even in Memphis the great majority of people might say, Why is this little band of spoiled rich girls who lived here forty years ago so important as to deserve our attention? In fact, during the very period I am writing about it is likely that the majority of people in Memphis felt that way. I think the significant point is that those girls took themselves seriously—girls like Caroline—and took seriously the forms of the life they lived. They imagined they knew quite well who they were and they imagined that that was important. They were what, at any rate, those girls like Lee Ann were not. Or they claimed to be what

those girls like Lee Ann didn't claim to be and what
very few people nowadays claim to be. They considered themselves the heirs to something, though most
likely they could not have said what: something their
forebears had brought to Memphis with them from
somewhere else—from the country around Memphis
and from other places, from the country towns of
West Tennessee, from Middle Tennessee and East
Tennessee, from the Valley of Virginia, from the
Piedmont, even from the Tidewater. Girls like Caroline thought they were the heirs to something, and
that's what the other girls didn't think about themselves, though probably they were, and probably the
present generation, in and out of Memphis—even the
sad generation of the sixties and seventies—is heir to
more than it thinks it is, in the matter of manners, I
mean to say, and of general behavior. And it is of
course because these girls like Caroline are regarded
as mere old-fashioned society girls that the present
generation tends to dismiss them, whereas if it were
their fathers we were writing about, the story would,
shocking though it is to say, be taken more seriously
by everyone. Everyone would recognize now that the
fathers and grandfathers of these girls were the sons
of the old plantation South come to town and converted or half-converted into modern Memphis businessmen, only with a certain something held over from
the old order that made them both better and worse
than businessmen elsewhere. They are the authors of
much good and much bad in modern Memphis—and
modern Nashville and modern Birmingham and modern Atlanta, too. The good they mostly brought with
them from life in cities elsewhere in the nation, the
thing they were imitating when they constructed the
new life in Memphis. And why not judge their daughters and wives in much the same way? Isn't there a
need to know what they were like, too? One thing
those girls did know they were heirs to was the old,
country manners and the insistence upon old, country

connections. The first evidence of this that comes to mind is the fact that they often spoke of girls like Lee Ann as "city girls," by which they meant that such girls didn't usually have the old family connections back in the country on the cotton farms in West Tennessee, in Mississippi, in Arkansas, or back in Nashville or in Jonesboro or in Virginia.

When Robert had let me out at our side door that night and I came into the house, my father and mother both were downstairs. It was still early of course, but I had the sense of their having waited up for me to come in. They greeted me as though I were returning from some dangerous mission. Each of them asked me how the Braxleys "seemed." Finally Mother insisted upon examining the stitches underneath the bandage on my forehead. After that, I said that I thought I would hit the hay. They responded to that with the same enthusiasm that Mr. and Mrs. Braxley had evidenced when I told them I thought I should go ahead home. Nothing would do me more good than a good night's sleep, my parents agreed. It was a day everybody was glad to have come to an end.

After I got upstairs and in my room, it occurred to me that my parents both suddenly looked very old. That seems laughable to me now almost, because my parents were then ten or fifteen years younger than I am today. I look back on them now as a youngish couple in their early middle age, whose first son was about to be married and about whose possible infidelity they were concerned. But indeed what an old-fashioned pair they seemed to me in the present day, waiting up for their children to come in. Because actually they stayed downstairs a long while after I went up to bed, waiting there for my younger brothers and my little sister to come in, all of whom were out on their separate dates. In my mind's eye I can see them there, waiting as parents had waited for hundreds of years for their grown-up children to come home at night. They would seem now to be violating the rights of young individuals and even interfering with the maturing process. But in those times it seemed only natural for parents to be watchful and concerned about their children's first flight away from the nest. I am referring mainly to my parents' waiting up for my brothers and my sister, who were in their middle teens, but also as I lay in my bed I felt, myself, more relaxed knowing that they were downstairs in the front room speculating upon what Lee Ann's disappearance meant and alert to whatever new development there might be. After a while, my father came up and opened the door to my room. I don't know how much later it was. I don't think I had been to sleep, but I could not tell for sure even at the time—my waking and sleeping thoughts were so much alike that night. At any rate, Father stepped inside the room and came over to my bed.

"I have just called down to the police station," he said, "and they say they have checked and that Lee Ann has still not come back to her rooming house. She seems to have gone into some sort of hiding." He said this with wonderment and with just the slightest trace of irritation in his voice. "Have you any notion, Nat, why she *might* want to go into hiding?"

The next day was Sunday, December 5. During the night it had turned bitterly cold, the snow had frozen into a crisp sheet that covered most of the ground. At about nine o'clock in the morning another snow began falling. I had breakfast with the family, still wearing the bandage on my forehead. I sat around in my bathrobe all morning, pretending to read the newspaper. I didn't see any report of my accident, and my father said it wouldn't appear till Monday. At ten o'clock, I dialed Lee Ann's telephone number. One of the other girls who roomed in the house answered. She said she thought Lee Ann hadn't come in last night and she giggled. I asked her if she would make sure about it. She left the phone and came back presently to say in a whisper that there was no doubt about it: Lee Ann had not slept in her bed. I knew she was whispering so that the landlady wouldn't hear. . . . And then I had a call from Caroline, who wanted to know how my head was this morning and whether or not there had been any word about Lee Ann. After I told her what I had just learned, we were both silent for a time. Finally she said she had intended to come over and see how I was feeling but her father had decreed that nobody should go out in such bad weather. It would just be inviting another automobile wreck, he said. She reported that her parents were not going to church, and I said that mine weren't either. We agreed to talk later and to see each other after lunch if the weather improved. Then I could hear her father's voice in the background, and she said that he wanted to use the telephone.

At noon the snow was still falling. My father stood at a front window in the living room, wearing his dark smoking jacket. He predicted that it might be the deepest snowfall we had ever had in Memphis. He said that people in other parts of the country didn't realize how much cold weather came all the way down the Mississippi Valley from Minneapolis to Memphis. I had never heard him pay so much attention to the weather and talk so much about it. I wondered if, like me, he was really thinking about the old forest out in Overton Park and wishing he were free to go out there and make sure there was no sign of Lee Ann Deehart's having come to grief in those ancient woods. I wonder now if there weren't others besides us who were thinking of the old forest all day that day. I knew that my father, too, had been on the telephone that morning—and he was on it again during a good part of the afternoon. In retrospect, I am certain that all day that day he was in touch with a whole circle of friends and colleagues who were concerned about Lee Ann's safety. It was not only the heavy snow that checked his freedom—and mine, too, of course—to go

out and search those woods and put his mind at rest
on the possibility at least. It was more than just this
snow, which the radio reported as snarling up and
halting all traffic. What prevented him was his own
unwillingness to admit fully to himself and to others
that this particular danger was really there; what prevented him and perhaps all the rest of us was the fear
that the answer to the gnawing question of Lee Ann's
whereabouts might really be out there within that im-
memorial grove of snow-laden oaks and yellow pop-
lars and hickory trees. It is a grove, I believe, that
men in Memphis have feared and wanted to destroy
for a long time and whose destruction they are still
working at even in this latter day. It has only recently
been saved by a very narrow margin from a great
highway that men wished to put through there—saved
by groups of women determined to save this last bit
of the old forest from the axes of modern men. Perhaps in old pioneer days, before the plantation and the
neoclassic towns were made, the great forests seemed
woman's last refuge from the brute she lived alone
with in the wilderness. Perhaps all men in Memphis
who had any sense of their past felt this, though they
felt more keenly (or perhaps it amounts to the same
feeling) that the forest was woman's greatest danger.
Men remembered mad pioneer women, driven mad
by their loneliness and isolation, who ran off into the
forest, never to be seen again, or incautious women
who allowed themselves to be captured by Indians and
returned at last so mutilated that they were unrecog-
nizable to their husbands or who at their own wish
lived out their lives among their savage captors. I
think that if I had said to my father (or to myself),
"What is it that's so scary about the old forest?", he
(or I) would have answered, "There's nothing at all
scary about it. But we can't do anything today because
of the snow. It's the worst snow in history!" I think
that all day long my father—like me—was busily not
letting himself believe that anything awful had hap-

pened to Lee Ann Deehart, or that if it had it certainly hadn't happened in those woods. Not just my father and me, though. Caroline's father, too, and all their friends—their peers. And the newspapermen and the police. If they waited long enough, it would come out all right and there would be no need to search the woods even. And it turned out, in the most literal sense, that they—we—were right. Yet what guilty feelings must not everyone have lived with—lived with in silence—all that snowbound day.

At two o'clock, Caroline called again to say that because of the snow, her aunt was canceling the dinner party she had planned that night in honor of the bride and groom. I remember as well as anything else that terrible day how my father and mother looked at each other when they received this news. Surely they were wondering, as I had to also, if this was but the first gesture of withdrawal. There was no knowing what their behavior or the behavior of any of us that day meant. The day simply dragged on until the hour when we could decently go to bed. It was December, and we were near the shortest day of the year, but that day had seemed the longest day of my life.

On Monday morning, two uniformed policemen were at our house before I had finished my breakfast. When I learned they were waiting in the living room to see me, I got up from the table at once. I wouldn't let my father go in with me to see them. Mother tried to make me finish my eggs before going in, but I only laughed at her and kissed her on the top of the head as I left the breakfast room. The two policemen were sitting in the very chairs my parents had sat in the night before. This somehow made the interview easier from the outset. I felt initially that they were there to help me, not to harass me in any way. They had already, at the break of dawn, been out to Overton Park. (The whole case—if case it was—had of course been allowed to rest on Sunday.) And along with four

other policemen they had conducted a full-scale search
of the old forest. There was no trace of Lee Ann
Deehart there. They had also been to her rooming
house on Tutwiler Avenue and questioned Mrs. Troxler, whose house it was, about all of Lee Ann's friends
and acquaintances and about the habits of her daily
life. They said that they were sure the girl would turn
up but that the newspapers were putting pressure on
them to explain her disappearance and—more particularly—to explain her precipitate flight from the scene
of the accident.

I spent that day with the police, leaving them only
for an hour at lunchtime, when they dropped me off
at my father's office on Front Street, where I worked.
There I made a small pretense of attending to some
business for the firm while I consumed a club sandwich and milk shake that my father or one of my
uncles in the firm had had sent up for me. At the end
of the hour, I jogged down the two flights of steep
wooden stairs and found the police car waiting for me
at the curb, just outside the entrance. At some time
during the morning, one of the policemen had suggested that they might have a bulldozer or some other
piece of machinery brought in to crack the ice on the
Overton Park Pond and then drag the pond for Lee
Ann's body. But I had pointed out that the two skaters had returned to the pond after the accident and
skated there until dark. There was no hole in the ice
anywhere. Moreover, the skaters had reported that
when the girl left the scene she did not go by way of
the pond but went up the rise and into the wooded
area. There was every indication that she had gone
that way, and so the suggestion that the pond be
dragged was dismissed. And we continued during the
rest of the morning to make the rounds of the rooming
houses and apartments of Lee Ann's friends and acquaintances, as well as the houses of the parents with
whom some of them lived. In the afternoon we

planned to go to the shops and offices in which some of the girls worked and to interview them there concerning Lee Ann's whereabouts and where it was they last had seen her. It seemed a futile procedure to me. But while I was eating my club sandwich alone in our third-floor walkup office I received a shocking telephone call.

Our offices, like most of the other cotton factors' offices, were in one of the plain-faced, three- and four-story buildings put up on Front Street during the middle years of the last century, just before the Civil War. Cotton men were very fond of those offices, and the offices did possess a certain rough beauty that anyone could see. Apparently there had been few, if any, improvements or alterations since the time they were built. All the electrical wiring and all the plumbing, such as they were, were "exposed." The wooden stairsteps and the floors were rough and splintery and extremely worn down. The walls were whitewashed and the ceilings were twelve or fourteen feet in height. But the chief charm of the rooms was the tall windows across the front of the buildings—wide sash windows with small windowlights, windows looking down onto Front Street and from which you could catch glimpses of the brown Mississippi River at the foot of the bluff, and even of the Arkansas shoreline on the other side. I was sitting on a cotton trough beside one of those windows, eating my club sandwich, when I heard the telephone ring back in the inner office. I remember that when it rang my eyes were on a little stretch of the Arkansas shoreline roughly delineated by its scrubby trees and my thoughts were on the Arkansas roadhouses where we often went with the demimonde girls on a Saturday night. At first I thought I wouldn't answer the phone. I let it ring for a minute or two. It went on ringing—persistently. Suddenly I realized that a normal business call would have stopped ringing before now. I jumped down from my perch by the window and ran back between the cotton troughs to the office. When I picked up the receiver, a girl's voice called my name before I spoke.

"Yes," I said. The voice had sounded familiar, but I knew it wasn't Caroline's. And it wasn't Lee Ann's. I couldn't identify it exactly, though I did say to myself right away that it was one of the city girls.

"Nat," the voice said, "Lee Ann wants you to stop trying to trail her."

"Who is this?" I said. "Where is Lee Ann?"

"Never mind," the girl on the other end of the line said. "We're not going to let you find her, and you're making her very uncomfortable with your going around with the police after her and all that."

"The police aren't 'after her,'" I said. "They just want to be sure she's all right."

"She'll be all right," the voice said, "if you'll lay off and stop chasing her. Don't you have any decency at all? Don't you have a brain in your head? Don't you know what this is like for Lee Ann? We all thought you were her friend."

"I am," I said. "Just let me speak to Lee Ann."

But there was a click in the telephone, and no one was there any longer.

I turned back into the room where the cotton troughs were. When I saw my milk-shake carton and the sandwich paper up by the window, and remembered how the girl had called my name as soon as I picked up the telephone, I felt sure that someone had been watching me from down in the street or from a window across the way. Without going back to my lunch, I turned quickly and started down the stairs toward the street. But when I looked at my watch, I realized it was time for the policemen to pick me up again. And there they were, of course, waiting at the entrance to our building. When I got into the police car, I didn't tell them about my call. And we began our rounds again, going to the addresses where some of Lee Ann's friends worked.

Lee Ann Deehart and other girls like her that we went about with, as I have indicated, were not literally ladies of any Memphis demimonde. Possibly they got called that first by the only member of our generation in Memphis who had read Marcel Proust, a literary boy who later became a college professor and who wanted to make his own life in Memphis—and ours— seem more interesting than it was. Actually, they were girls who had gone to the public high schools, and more often than not to some school other than Central High, which during those Depression years had a de- gree of acceptance in Memphis society. As anyone could have observed on that morning when I rode about town with the policemen, those girls came from a variety of backgrounds. We went to the houses of some of their parents, some of whom were day labor- ers who spoke in accents of the old Memphis Irish, descendants of the Irish who were imported to build the railroads to Texas. Today some of the girls would inevitably have been black. But they were the daugh- ters also of bank clerks and salesmen and of profes- sional men, too, because they made no distinction among themselves. The parents of some of them had moved to Memphis from cities in other sections of the country or even from southern small towns. The girls were not interested in such distinctions of origin, were not conscious of them, had not been made aware of them by their parents. They would have been highly approved of by the present generation of young peo- ple. Like the present generation in general, these girls—Lee Ann included—tended to be bookish and artistic in a middle-brow sort of way, and some of them had real intellectual aspirations. They did not care who each other's families were or where they had gone to school. They met and got to know each other in roadhouses, on double dates, and in the offices and stores where they worked. As I have said, they tended to be bookish and artistic. If they had found them- selves in Proust's Paris, instead of in our Memphis of

the 1930s, possibly they would have played some role
in the intellectual life of the place. But of course this
is only my ignorant speculation. It is always impossible
to know what changes might have been wrought in
people under circumstances of the greatest or slightest
degree of difference from the actual.

The girls we saw that afternoon at their places of
work were generally more responsive to the policemen's questions than to my own. And I became aware
that the two policemen—youngish men in their late
thirties, for whom this special assignment was somehow distasteful—were more interested in protecting
these girls from any embarrassment than in obtaining
information about Lee Ann. With all but one of the
half-dozen girls we sought out, the policemen sent me
in to see the girl first, to ask her if she would rather
be questioned by them in her place of business or in
the police car. In each case the girl treated my question concerning this as an affront, but always she finally sent word back to the policemen to come inside.
And in each case I found myself admiring the girl not
only for her boldness in dealing with the situation
(they seemed fearless in their talk with the police and
refused absolutely to acknowledge close friendship
with Lee Ann, insisting—all of them—that they saw
her only occasionally at night spots, sometimes with
me, sometimes with other young men, that they had
no idea who her parents were or where she came to
Memphis from) but also for a personal, feminine
beauty that I had never before been fully aware of.
Perhaps I saw or sensed it now for the first time because I had not before seen them threatened or in
danger. It is true, I know, that the effect of all this
questioning seemed somehow to put them in jeopardy.
Perhaps I saw now how much more vulnerable they
were than were the girls in the set my parents more
or less intended me to travel in. There was a delicacy
about them, a frailty even, that didn't seem to exist in
other girls I knew and that contrasted strangely—and

disturbingly—with the rough surroundings of the road-houses they frequented at night and the harsh, businesslike atmosphere of the places where they worked. Within each of them, moreover, there seemed a contrast between the delicate beauty of their bodies, their prettily formed arms and legs, their breasts and hips, their small feet and hands, their soft natural hair—hair worn so becomingly, groomed, in each case, on their pretty little heads to direct one's eyes first of all to the fair or olive complexion and the nicely proportioned features of the face—a contrast, that is to say, between this physical beauty and a bookishness and a certain toughness of mind and a boldness of spirit which were unmistakable in all of them.

The last girl we paid a call on that afternoon was one Nancy Minnifee, who happened to be the girl who was always frankest and crudest in making jokes about families like my own and who had made the crack that the other girls had laughed at so irrepressibly in the beer garden: "I haven't lost anything at the MCC." Or it may not have been that she just happened to be the last we called on. Perhaps out of dread of her jokes I guided the police last of all to the farm-implement warehouse where Nancy was a secretary. Or perhaps it wasn't so much because of her personality as because I knew she was Lee Ann's closest friend and I somehow dreaded facing her for that reason. Anyway, at the warehouse she was out on the loading platform with a clipboard and pencil in her hands when we drove up.

"That's Nancy Minnifee up there," I said to the two policemen in the front seat. I was sitting in the backseat alone. I saw them shake their heads. I knew that it was with a certain sadness and a personal admiration that they did so. Nancy was a very pretty girl, and they hated the thought of bothering this lovely creature with the kind of questions they were going to ask. They hated it without even knowing she was Lee Ann's closest friend. Suddenly I began seeing all

those girls through the policemen's eyes, just as next
day, when I would make a similar expedition in the
company of my father and the newspaper editor, I'd
see the girls through their eyes. The worst of it, somehow, for the policemen, was that the investigation
wasn't really an official investigation but was something the newspapers had forced upon the police in
case something had happened which they hadn't reported. The girl hadn't been missing long enough for
anyone to declare her "officially" missing. Yet the police, along with the mayor's office and the newspaper
editor, didn't want to risk something's having happened to a girl like Lee Ann. They—all of them—
thought of such girls, in a sense, as their special wards.
It would be hard to say why they did. At any rate,
before the police car had fully stopped I saw Nancy
Minnifee up there on the platform. She was wearing
a fur-collared overcoat but no hat or gloves. Immediately she began moving along the loading platform
toward us, holding the clipboard up to shield her eyes
from the late-afternoon winter sun. She came down
the steps to the graveled area where we were stopped,
and when the policeman at the wheel of the car ran
down his window she bent forward and put her arm
on his door. The casual way she did it seemed almost
familiar—indeed, almost provocative. I found myself
resenting her manner, because I was afraid she would
give the wrong impression. The way she leaned on the
door reminded me of the prostitutes down on Pontotoc Street when we, as teenage boys, used to stop in
front of their houses and leave the motor running because we were afraid of them.

"I've been expecting you two gentlemen," Nancy
said, smiling amiably at the two policemen and point-
edly ignoring my presence in the backseat. The policemen broke into laughter.

"I suppose your friends have been calling ahead,"
the driver said. Then Nancy laughed as though he had
said something very funny.

"I could draw you a map of the route you've taken this afternoon," she said. She was awfully polite in her tone, and the two policemen were awfully polite, too. But before they could really begin asking her their questions she began giving them her answers. She hadn't seen Lee Ann since several days before the accident. She didn't know anything about where she might be. She didn't know anything about her family. She had always understood that Lee Ann came from Texas.

"That's a big state," the policeman who wasn't driving said.

"Well, I've never been there," she said, "but I'm told it's a mighty big state."

The three of them burst into laughter again. Then the driver said quite seriously, "But we understand you're her best friend."

"I don't know her any better than most of the other girls do," she said. "I can't imagine who told you that." Now for the first time she looked at me in the backseat. "Hello, Nat," she said. I nodded to her. I couldn't imagine why she was lying to them. But I didn't tell her, as I hadn't told the other girls or the police, about the call I had had in the cotton office. I knew that she must know all about it, but I said nothing.

When we had pulled away, the policeman who was driving the car said, "This Lee Ann must be all right or these girls wouldn't be closing ranks so. They've got too much sense for that. They're smart girls."

Presently the other policeman turned his head halfway around, though not looking directly at me, and asked, "She wouldn't be pregnant by any chance, would she?"

"Uh-uh," I said. It was all the answer it seemed to me he deserved. But then I couldn't resist echoing what he had said. "They've got too much sense for that. They're smart girls." He looked all the way around at me now and gave me what I am sure he thought was a straight look.

"Damn right they are," said the driver, glancing at
his colleague with a frown on his forehead and speaking with a curled lip. "Get your mind out of the gutter,
Fred. After all, they're just kids, all of them."

We rode on in silence after that. For the first time
in several hours, I thought of Caroline Braxley, and
I wondered again whether or not she would break
our engagement.

When the policemen let me off at my office at five
o'clock, I went to my car and drove straight to the
apartment house at Crosstown where Nancy Minnifee
lived. I was waiting for Nancy in the parking lot when
she got home. She invited me inside, but without a
smile.

"I want to know where Lee Ann is," I said as soon
as she had closed the door.

"Do you imagine I'd tell you if I knew?" she said.

I sat myself down in an upholstered chair as if I
were going to stay there till she told me. "I want to
know what the hell's going on," I said with what I
thought was considerable force, "and why you told
such lies to those policemen."

"If you don't know that now, Nat," she said, sitting
down opposite me, "you probably won't ever know."

"She wouldn't be pregnant by any chance, would
she?" I said, without really having known I was going
to say it.

Nancy's mouth dropped open. Then she laughed
aloud. Presently she said, "Well, one thing's certain,
Nat. It wouldn't be any concern of yours if she were."

I pulled myself up out of the big chair and left without another word's passing between us.

Lee Ann Deehart and Nancy Minnifee and that
whole band of girls that we liked to refer to as the
girls of the Memphis demimonde were of course no
more like the ladies of the demimonde as they appear
in French literature than *they* were like some band of
angels. And I hardly need say—though it does some-

how occur to me to say—their manners and morals bore no resemblance whatsoever to those of the mercenary, filthy-mouthed whores on Pontotoc Street. I might even say that their manners were practically indistinguishable from those of the girls we knew who had attended Miss Hutchison's School and St. Mary's and Lausanne and were now members of the debutante set. The fact is that some of them—only a few perhaps—were from families that were related by blood, and rather closely related, to the families of the debutante set, but families that, for one reason or another, now found themselves economically in another class from their relatives. At any rate, they were all freed from old restraints put upon them by family and community, liberated in each case, so it seems to me, by sheer strength of character, liberated in many respects, but above all else—and I cannot say how it came about—liberated sexually. The most precise thing I can say about them is that they, in their little band, were like hordes of young girls today. It seems to me that in their attitude toward sex they were at least forty years ahead of their time. But I cannot say how it came about. Perhaps it was an individual thing with each of them—or partly so. Perhaps it was because they were the second or third generation of women in Memphis who were working in offices. They were not promiscuous—not most of them—but they slept with the men they were in love with and they did not conceal the fact. The men they were in love with were usually older than we were. Generally speaking, the girls merely amused themselves with us, just as we amused ourselves with them. There was a wonderful freedom in our relations which I have never known anything else quite like. And though I may not have had the most realistic sense of what their lives were, I came to know what I did know through my friendship with Lee Ann Deehart.

She and I first met, I think, at one of those dives where we all hung out. Or it may have been at some

girl's apartment. I suspect we both would have been
hard put to it to say where it was or exactly when.
She was simply one of the good-looking girls we ran
around with. I remember dancing with her on several
occasions before I had any idea what her name was.
We drifted into our special kind of friendship because,
as a matter of fact, she was the good friend of Nancy
Minnifee, whom my own close friend Bob Childress
got very serious about for a time. Bob and Nancy may
even have been living together for a while in Nancy's
apartment. I think Bob, who was one of six or eight
boys of approximately my background who used to go
about with these girls, would have married Nancy if
she'd consented to have him. Possibly it was at Nancy's apartment that I met Lee Ann. Anyway, we did
a lot of double dating, the four of us, and had some
wonderful times going to the sort of rough night spots
that we all liked and found sufficiently exciting to return to again and again. We would be dancing and
drinking at one of those places until about two in the
morning, when most of them closed. At that hour
most of us would take our girls home, because we
nearly all of us had jobs—the girls and the boys, too—
which we had to report to by eight or nine in the
morning.

Between Lee Ann and me, as between most of the
boys and their girls, I think, there was never a serious
affair. That is, we never actually—as the young people
today say—"had sex." But in the car on the way home
or in the car parked outside her rooming house or
even outside the night spot, as soon as we came out,
we would regularly indulge in what used to be known
as "heavy necking." Our stopping at that I must attribute first of all to Lee Ann's resistance, though also,
in part, to a hesitation I felt about insisting with such
a girl. You see, she was in all respects like the girls
we called "nice girls," by which I suppose we really
meant society girls. And most of us accepted the re-

striction that we were not to "go to bed" with society girls. They were the girls we were going to marry. These girls were not what those society girls would have termed shopgirls. They had much better taste in their clothes and in their general demeanor. And, as I have said, in the particular group I speak of there was at least an intellectual strain. Some of them had been to college for as much as a year or two, whereas others seemed hardly to have finished high school. Nearly all of them read magazines and books that most of us had never heard of. And they found my odd addiction to Latin poetry the most interesting thing about me. Most of them belonged to a national book club, from which they received a new book each month, and they nearly all bought records and listened to classical music. You would see them sometimes in groups at the Art Gallery. Or whenever there was an opera or a good play at the city auditorium they were all likely to be there in a group—almost never with dates. If you hadn't known who they were, you might easily have mistaken them for some committee from the Junior League or for an exceptionally pretty group of schoolteachers—from some fashionable girls' school probably.

But mostly, of course, one saw them with their dates at one of the roadhouses, over in Arkansas or down in Mississippi or out east on the Bristol Highway, or yet again at one of the places we called the "town joints." They preferred going to those roadhouses and town joints to going to the Peabody Hotel Roof or the Claridge—as I suppose nearly everyone else did, really, including society girls like Caroline. You would, as a matter of fact, frequently see girls like Caroline at such places. At her request, I had more than once taken Caroline to a town joint down on Adams Street called The Cellar and once to a roadhouse called The Jungle, over in Arkansas. She had met some of the city girls there and said she found them "dead attractive." And she once recognized them at a play I took her to see and afterward expressed interest in them and asked me to tell her what they were like.

The fact may be that neither the roadhouses nor the town joints were quite as tough as they seemed. Or they weren't as tough for the demimonde girls, anyway. Because the proprietors clearly had protective feelings about them. At The Jungle, for instance, the middle-aged couple who operated the place, an extremely obese couple who were forever grinning in our direction and who were usually barefoot (we called them Ma and Pa), would often come and stand by our table—one or the other of them—and sing the words to whatever was playing on the jukebox. Often as not, one of them would be standing there during the entire evening. Sometimes Ma would talk to us about her two little daughters, whom she kept in a private school in Memphis, and Pa, who was a practicing taxidermist, would talk to us about the dogs whose mounted heads adorned the walls on every side of the dimly lit room. All this afforded us great privacy and safety. No drunk or roughneck would come near our table while either Ma or Pa was close by. We had similar protection at other places. At The Cellar, for instance, old Mrs. Power was the sole proprietor. She had a huge goiter on her neck and was never known to smile. Not even in our direction. But it was easy to see that she watched our table like a hawk, and if any other patron lingered near us even momentarily she would begin moving slowly toward us. And whoever it was would catch one glimpse of her and move on. We went to these places quite regularly, though some of the girls had their favorites and dislikes among them. Lee Ann would never be taken to The Cellar. She would say only that the place depressed her. And Caroline, when I took her there, felt an instant dislike for The Jungle. She would shake her head afterward and say she would never go back and have those dogs' eyes staring down through the darkness at her.

* * *

On the day after I made the rounds with the policemen, I found myself following almost the same routine
in the company of my father and the editor of the
morning paper, and, as a matter of fact, the mayor of
Memphis himself. The investigation or search was, you
see, still entirely unofficial. And men like my father
and the mayor and the editor wanted to keep it so.
That's why after that routine and off-the-record series
of questionings by the police they preferred to do a
bit of investigation themselves rather than entrust the
matter to someone else. As I have said, that generation of men in Memphis evidenced feelings of responsibility for such girls—for "working girls of a superior
kind," as they phrased it—which I find somewhat difficult to explain. For it wasn't just the men I drove
about town with that day. Or the dozen or so men
who gathered for conference in our driveway before
we set out—that is, Caroline's father, his lawyer, the
driver of the other vehicle, his lawyer, my father's lawyer, ministers from three church denominations, the
editor of the afternoon newspaper, and still others.
That day, when I rode about town with my father and
the two other men in our car, I came as near as I ever
had or ever would to receiving a satisfactory explanation of the phenomenon. They were a generation of
American men who were perhaps the last to grow up
in a world where women were absolutely subjected
and under the absolute protection of men. While my
father wheeled his big Cadillac through the side streets
on which some of the girls lived and then along the
wide boulevards of Memphis, they spoke of the
changes they had seen. In referring to the character
of the life girls like Lee Ann led—of which they
showed a far greater awareness than I would have
supposed they possessed—they agreed that this was
the second or third generation there of women who
had lived as independently, as freely as these girls did.
I felt that what they said was in no sense as derogatory

or critical as it would have been in the presence of
their wives or daughters. They spoke almost affection-
ately and with a certain sadness of such girls. They
spoke as if these were daughters of dead brothers of
their own or of dead companions-in-arms during the
First World War. And it seemed to me that they
thought of these girls as the daughters of men who
had abdicated their authority and responsibility as fathers, men who were not strangers or foreign to them,
though they were perhaps of a different economic
class. The family names of the girls were familiar to
them. The fathers of these girls were Americans of
the great hinterland like themselves, even southerners
like themselves. I felt that they were actually cousins
of ours who had failed as fathers somehow, had been
destined to fail, even required to do so in a changing
world. And so these men of position and power had
to act as surrogate fathers during a transitional period.
It was a sort of communal fatherhood they were acting
out. Eventually, they seemed to say, fathers might not
be required. I actually heard my father saying, "That's
what the whole world is going to be like someday."
He meant like the life such girls as Lee Ann were
making for themselves. I often think nowadays of Father's saying that whenever I see his prediction being
fulfilled by the students in the university where I have
been teaching for twenty years now, and I wonder if
Father did really believe his prediction would come
true.

Yet while he and the other two men talked their
rather sanguine talk that day, I was thinking of a call
I had had the night before after I came back from
seeing Nancy Minnifee. One of the servants answered
the telephone downstairs in the back part of the
house, and she must have guessed it was something
special. Because instead of buzzing the buzzer three
times, which was the signal when a call was for me,
the maid came up the backstairs and tapped gently on

my door. "It's for you, Nat," she said softly. "Do you want to take it downstairs?"

There was nothing peculiar about her doing this, really. Since I didn't have an extension phone in my room, I had a tacit understanding with the servants that I preferred to take what I considered my private calls down in that quarter of the house. And so I followed the maid down the back stairway and shut myself in the little servants' dining room that was behind the great white-tiled kitchen. I answered the call on the wall phone there.

A girl's voice, which wasn't the same voice I had heard on the office telephone at noon, said, "Lee Ann doesn't want another day like this one, Nat."

"Who is this?" I said, lowering my voice to be sure even the servants didn't hear me. "What the hell is going on?" I asked. "Where is Lee Ann?"

"She's been keeping just one apartment or one rooming house ahead of you all day."

"But why? Why is she hiding this way?"

"All I want to say is she's had about enough. You let up on pursuing her so."

"It's not me," I protested. "There's nothing I can do to stop them."

Over the phone there came a contemptuous laugh. "No. And you can't get married till they find her, can you?" Momentarily I thought I heard Lee Ann's voice in the background. "Anyhow," the same voice continued, "Lee Ann's had about as much as she can take of all this. She was depressed as it was when she called you in the first place. Why else do you think she would call you, Nat? She was desperate for some comic relief."

"Relief from what?"

"Relief from her depression, you idiot."

"But what's she depressed about?" I was listening carefully to the voice, thinking it was that of first one girl and then another.

"Nat, we don't always have to have something to be depressed about. But Lee Ann will be all right, if you'll let her alone."

"But what is she depressed about?" I persisted. I had begun to think maybe it was Lee Ann herself on the phone, disguising her voice.

"About life in general, you bastard! Isn't that enough?" Then I knew it wasn't Lee Ann, after all.

"Listen," I said, "let me speak to Lee Ann. I want to speak to Lee Ann."

And then I heard whoever it was I was talking with break off the connection. I quietly replaced the receiver and went upstairs again.

In those days I didn't know what it was to be depressed—not, anyway, about "life in general." Later on, you see, I did know. Later on, after years of being married, and having three children, and going to grown-up Memphis dinner parties three or four times a week, and working in the cotton office six days a week, I got so depressed about life in general that I sold my interest in the cotton firm to a cousin of mine (my father and uncles were dead by then) and managed to make Caroline understand that what I needed was to go back to school for a while so that we could start our life all over. I took degrees at three universities, which made it possible for me to become a college professor. That may be an awful revelation about myself—I mean to say, awful that what decided me to become a teacher was that I was so depressed about life in general. But I reasoned that being an English professor—even if I was relegated to teaching composition and simpleminded survey courses—would be something useful and would throw us in with a different kind of people. (Caroline tried to persuade me to go into the sciences, but I told her she was just lucky that I didn't take up classics again.) Anyway, teaching has made me see a lot of young people over the years, in addition to my own children, and I think it is why, in retrospect, those Memphis girls I'm writing about still seem interesting to me after all these many years.

But the fact is I was still so uneasy about the significance of both those calls from Lee Ann's friends that I was unwilling to mention them to Caroline that night. At first I thought I would tell her, but as soon as I saw her tall and graceful figure in her white, pleated evening dress and wearing the white corsage I had sent, I began worrying again about whether or not she might still break off the engagement. Besides, we had plenty of other matters to discuss, including the rounds I had made with the two policemen that day and her various activities in preparation for the wedding. We went to a dinner that one of my aunts gave for us at the Memphis Country Club that night. We came home early and spent twenty minutes or so in her living room, telling each other how much we loved each other and how we would let nothing on earth interfere with our getting married. I felt reassured, or I tried to feel so. It seemed to me, though, that Caroline still had not really made up her mind. It worried me that she didn't have more to say about Lee Ann. After I got home, I kept waking all night and wondering what if that had not been Lee Ann's voice I had heard in the background and what if she never surfaced again. The circumstances of her disappearance would have to be made public, and that would certainly be too embarrassing for Caroline and her parents to ignore.

Next day, I didn't tell my father and his two friends, the editor and the mayor, about either of the two telephone calls. I don't know why I didn't, unless it was because I feared they might begin monitoring all my calls. I could not tolerate the thought of having them hear the things that girl said to me.

In preference to interviewing the girls whose addresses I could give them, those three middle-aged men seemed much more interested in talking to the

girls' rooming-house landladies, or their apartment
landlords, or their mothers. They did talk to some of
the girls themselves, though, and I observed that the
girls were so impressed by having these older men
want to talk to them that they could hardly look at
them directly. What I think is that the girls were *afraid*
they would tell them the truth. They would reply to their
questions respectfully, if evasively, but they were apt
to keep their eyes on me. This was not the case, however, with the mothers and the landlords and the landladies. There was an immediate rapport between these
persons and the three men. There hardly needed to
be any explanation required of the unofficial nature
of the investigation or of the concern of these particular men about such a girl as Lee Ann. One woman
who told them that Lee Ann had roomed with her for
a time described her as being always a moody sort of
girl. "But lots of these girls living on their own are
moody," she said.

"Where did Miss Deehart come from?" my father
asked. "Who were her people?"

"She always claimed she came from Texas," the
woman said. "But she could never make it clear to
me where it was in Texas."

Later the mayor asked Lee Ann's current landlady,
Mrs. Troxler, where she supposed Lee Ann might
have gone. "Well," Mrs. Troxler said, "a girl, a decent
girl, even among these modern girls, generally goes
to her mother when there's trouble. Women turn to
women," she said, "when there's real trouble."

The three men found no trace of Lee Ann, got no
real clue to where she might have gone. When finally
we were leaving the editor at his newspaper office on
Union Avenue, he hesitated a moment before opening
the car door. "Well," he began, but he sat for a moment beating his leg thoughtfully with a newspaper he
had rolled up in his hand. "I don't know," he said.
"It's going to be a matter for the police, after all, if
we can't do any better than this." I still didn't say

anything about my telephone calls. But the calls were worrying me a good deal, and that night I told Caroline.

And when I had told her about the calls and told her how the police and my father and his friends had failed to get any information from the girls, Caroline, who was then sitting beside me on the couch in her living room, suddenly took my hand in hers and, putting her face close to mine and looking me directly in the eye, said, "Nat, I don't want you to go to work at all tomorrow. Don't make any explanation to your father or to anybody. Just get up early and come over here and get me. I want you to take me to meet some of those girls." Then she asked me which of the girls she might possibly have met on the rare occasions when I had taken her dancing at The Jungle or at The Cellar. And before I left that night she got me to tell her all I knew about "that whole tribe of city girls." I told her everything, including an account of my innocent friendship with Lee Ann Deehart, as well as an account of my earlier relations, which were not innocent, with a girl named Fern Morris. When, next morning, I came to fetch Caroline for our expedition, there were only three girls that she wanted to be taken to see. One of the three was of course Fern Morris.

There was something that had happened to me the day before, when I was going about Memphis with my father and his two friends, that I could not tell Caroline about. You see, I had been imagining, each place we went, how as we came in the front door Lee Ann was hurriedly, quietly going out the back. This mental picture of her in flight I found not merely appealing but strangely exciting. And it seemed to me I was discovering what my true feelings toward Lee Ann had been during the past two years. I had never dared insist upon the occasional advances I had naturally made to her, because she had always seemed too delicate, too vulnerable, for me to think of suggesting a casual sexual relationship with her. She had seemed too clever and too intelligent for me to deceive her about my intentions or my worth as a person. And I imagined I relished the kind of restraint there was between us because it was so altogether personal and not one placed upon us by any element or segment of society, or by any outside circumstances whatever. It kept coming to my mind as we stood waiting for an answer to the pressure on each doorbell that she was the girl I ought and wanted to be marrying. I realized the absolute folly of such thoughts and the utter impossibility of any such conclusion to present events. But still such feelings and thoughts had kept swimming in and out of my head all that day. I kept seeing Lee Ann in my mind's eye and hearing her soft, somewhat husky voice. I kept imagining how her figure would appear in the doorway before us. I saw her slender ankles, her small breasts, her head of ash-blond hair, which had a way of seeming to fall about her face when she talked but which with one shake of her head she could throw back into perfect place. But of course when the door opened there was the inevitable landlady or mother or friend. And when the next day came and I saw Caroline rolling up her sleeves, so to speak, to pitch in and settle this matter once and for all, then my thoughts and fantasies of the day before seemed literally like something out of a dream that I might have had.

The first two girls Caroline had wanted to see were the two that she very definitely remembered having met when I had taken her—"on a lark"—to my favorite night spots. She caught them both before they went to work that morning, and I was asked to wait in the car. I felt like an idiot waiting out there in the car, because I knew I'd been seen from some window as I gingerly hopped out and opened the door for Caroline when she got out—and opened it again when she returned. But there was no way around it. I waited out there, playing the car radio even at the risk of running down the battery.

When she came back from seeing the first girl, whose name was Lucy Phelan, Caroline was very angry. She reported that Lucy Phelan had pretended not to remember ever having met her. Moreover, Lucy had pretended that she knew Lee Ann Deehart only slightly and had no idea where she could be or what her disappearance meant. As Caroline fumed and I started up the car, I was picturing Lee Ann quietly tiptoeing out the backdoor of Lucy's rooming house just as Lucy was telling Caroline she scarcely knew the girl or while she was insisting that she didn't remember Caroline. As Caroline came back down the walk from the big Victorian house to the car, Lucy, who had stepped out onto the narrow porch that ran across the front of the house and around one corner of it, squatted down on her haunches at the top of the wooden porch steps and waved to me from behind Caroline's back. Though I knew it was no good, I pretended not to see her there. As I put the car into second gear and we sped away down the block, I took a quick glance back at the house. Lucy was still standing on the porch and waving to me the way one waves to a little child. She knew I had seen her stooping and waving moments before. And knew I would be stealing a glance now.

For a short time Caroline seemed undecided about calling on the second girl. But she decided finally to press on. Lucy Phelan she remembered meeting at The Cellar. The next girl, Betsy Morehouse, she had met at The Jungle and at a considerably more recent time. Caroline was a dog fancier in those days and she recalled a conversation with Betsy about the mounted dogs' heads that adorned the walls of The Jungle. They both had been outraged. When she mentioned this to me there in the car, I realized for the first time that by trying to make these girls acknowledge an acquaintance with her she had hoped to make them feel she was almost one of them and that they would thus be more likely to confide in her. But she

failed with Betsy Morehouse, too. Betsy lived in an
apartment house—an old residence, that is, converted
into apartments—and when Caroline got inside the
entrance-hall door she met Betsy, who was just then
coming down the stairs. Betsy carried a purse and was
wearing a fur coat and overshoes. When Caroline got
back to the car and told me about it, I could not help
feeling that Betsy had had a call from Lucy Phelan
and even perhaps that Lee Ann was hiding in her
apartment, having just arrived there from Lucy's. Because Betsy didn't offer to take Caroline back upstairs
to her apartment for a talk. Instead, they sat down on
two straight-backed chairs in the entrance hall and
exchanged their few words there. Betsy at once denied
the possibility of Caroline's ever having met her before. She denied that she had, herself, ever been to
The Jungle. I knew this to be a lie, of course, but I
didn't insist upon it to Caroline. I said that perhaps
both she and I were mistaken about Betsy's being
there on the night I had taken Caroline. As soon as
Caroline saw she would learn nothing from Betsy, she
got up and began to make motions of leaving. Betsy
followed her to the door. But upon seeing my car out
at the curb—so Caroline believed—she turned back,
saying that she had remembered a telephone call she
had to make. Caroline suspected that the girl didn't
want to have to face me with her lie. That possibly
was true. But my thought was that Betsy just might,
also, have a telephone call she wanted to make.

There was now no question about Caroline's wanting to proceed to the third girl's house. This was the
girl I had told her about having had a real affair
with—the one I had gone with before Lee Ann and I
had become friends. Caroline knew that she and Fern
Morris had never met, but she counted on a different
psychology with Fern. Most probably she had hoped
it wouldn't be necessary for her to go to see Fern. She
had been sure that one of those two other girls would
give her the lead she needed. But as a last resort she

was fully prepared to call on Fern Morris and to take me into the house with her.

Fern was a girl who still lived at home with her mother. She was in no sense a mama's girl or even a home-loving girl, since she was unhappy unless she went out on a date every night of her life. Perhaps she was not so clever and not so intellectual as most of her friends—if reading books, that is, on psychology and on China and every new volume of Andre Maurois indicated intellectuality. And though she was not home-loving, I suppose you would have to say she was more domestic than the other girls were. She had never "held down" a job. Rather, she stayed at home in the daytime and kept house for her mother, who was said to "hold down" a high-powered job under Boss Crump down at City Hall. Mrs. Morris was a very sensible woman, who put no restrictions on her grown-up daughter and was glad to have her as a housekeeper. She used to tell me what a good cook and housekeeper Fern was and how well fixed she would leave her when she died. I really believe Mrs. Morris hoped our romance might end in matrimony, and, as a matter of fact, it was when I began to suspect that Fern, too, was entertaining such notions that I stopped seeing her and turned my attentions to Lee Ann Deehart.

Mrs. Morris still seemed glad to see me when I arrived at their bungalow that morning with Caroline and when I proceeded to introduce Caroline to her as my fiancée. Fern herself greeted me warmly. In fact, when I told her that Caroline and I were going to be married (though she must certainly have already read about it in the newspaper) she threw her arms about my neck and kissed me. "Oh, Natty," she said, "I'm so happy for you. Really I am. But poor Lee Ann." And in later life, especially in recent years, whenever Caroline has thought I was being silly about some other woman, usually a woman she considers her mental and social inferior, she has delighted in addressing

me as "Natty." On more than one such occasion I
have even had her say to me, "I am so happy for you,
Natty. Really I am."

The fact is, Mrs. Morris was just leaving the house
for work when we arrived. And so there was no delay
in Caroline's interview with Fern. "I assume you know
about Lee Ann's disappearance?" Caroline began as
soon as we had seated ourselves in the little front
parlor, with which I was very familiar.

"Of course I do," said Fern, looking at me and
laughing gleefully.

"You think it's a laughing matter, then?" Caroline
asked.

"I do indeed. It's all a big joke," Fern said at once.
It was as though she had her answers all prepared.
"And a very successful joke it is."

"Successful?" both Caroline and I asked. We
looked at each other in dismay.

"It's only my opinion, of course. But I think she
only wants to make you two suffer."

"Suffer?" I said. This time Caroline was silent.

Fern was now addressing me directly. "Everybody
knows Caroline is not going to marry you until Lee
Ann turns up safe."

"Everybody?" Both of us again.

"Everybody in the world practically," said Fern.

Caroline's face showed no expression. Neither, I believe, did mine.

"Fern, do you know where Lee Ann is?" Caroline
asked gently.

Fern Morris, her eyes on me, shook her head,
smiling.

"Do you know where her people are?" Caroline
asked. "And whether she's with them or hiding with
her friends?"

Fern shook her head again, but now she gazed directly at Caroline. "I'm not going to tell you anything!" she asserted. But after a moment she took a
deep breath and said, still looking at Caroline, "You're

a smart girl. I think you'll likely be going to Lee Ann's room in that place where she lives. If you do go there, and if you are a smart girl, you'll look in the left-hand drawer of Lee Ann's dressing table." Fern had an uneasy smile on her face after she had spoken, as if Caroline had got her to say something she hadn't really meant to say, as if she felt guilty for what she had just done.

Caroline had us out of there in only a minute or so and on our way to Lee Ann's rooming house.

It was a red-brick bungalow up in north Memphis. It looked very much like the one that Fern lived in but was used as a rooming house. When Mrs. Troxler opened the front door to us, Caroline said, "We're friends of Lee Ann's, and she wants us to pack a suitcase and bring it to her."

"You know where she is, then?" Mrs. Troxler asked. "Hello, Nat," she said, looking at me over Caroline's shoulder

"Hello, Mrs. Troxler," I said. I was so stunned by what I had just heard Caroline say that I spoke in a whisper.

"She's with her mother—or with her family, at least," Caroline said. By now she had slipped into the hallway, and I had followed without Mrs. Troxler's really inviting us in.

"Where are her family?" Mrs. Troxler asked, giving way to Caroline's forward thrust. "She never volunteered to tell me anything about them. And I never think it's my business to ask."

Caroline nodded her head at me, indicating that I should lead the way to Lee Ann's room. I knew that her room was toward the back of the house and I headed in that direction.

"I'll have to unlock the room for you," said Mrs. Troxler. "There have been a number of people coming here and wanting to look about her room. And so I keep it locked."

"A number of people?" asked Caroline casually.

"Yes. Nat knows. There were the police. And then there were some other gentlemen. Nat knows about it, though he didn't come in. And there were two other girls. The girls just seemed idly curious, and so I've taken to locking the door. Where do her people live?"

"I don't know," said Caroline. "She's going to meet us downtown at the bus station and take a bus."

When Mrs. Troxler had unlocked the door she asked, "Is Lee Ann all right? Do you think she will be coming back here?"

"She's fine," Caroline said, "and I'm sure she'll be coming back. She just wants a few things."

"Yes, I've wondered how she's been getting along without a change of clothes. I'll fetch her suitcase. I keep my roomers' luggage in my storage closet down the hall." We waited till she came back with a piece of plaid luggage, and then we went into the room and closed the door. Caroline went to the oak dresser and began pulling things out and stuffing them in the bag. I stood by, watching, hardly able to believe what I saw Caroline doing. When she had closed the bag, she looked up at me as if to say, "What are you waiting for?" She had not gone near the little mahogany dressing table, and I had not realized that was going to be my part. I went over and opened the left-hand drawer. The only thing in the drawer was a small snapshot. I took it up and examined it carefully. I said nothing to Caroline, just handed her the picture. Finally I said, "Do you know who that is? And where the picture was taken?" She recognized the woman with the goiter who ran The Cellar. The picture had been taken with Mrs. Power standing in one of the flower beds against the side of the house. The big cut stones of the house were unmistakable. After bringing the snapshot up close to her face and peering into it for ten seconds or so, Caroline looked at me and said, "That's her family."

By the time we had stopped the car in front of The

Cellar, I had told Caroline all that I knew about Lee Ann's schooling and about how it was that, though she had a "family" in Memphis, no one had known her when she was growing up. She had been to one boarding school in Shreveport, Louisiana, to one in East Texas, and to still another in St. Charles, Missouri. I had heard her make references to all of those schools. "They kept her away from home," Caroline speculated. "And so when she had finished school she wasn't prepared for the kind of 'family' she had. That's why she moved out on them and lived in a rooming house."

She reached that conclusion while I was parking the car at the curb, near the front entrance to the house. Meanwhile, I was preparing myself mentally to accompany Caroline to the door of the old woman's living quarters, which were on the main floor and above The Cellar. But Caroline rested her hand on the steering wheel beside mine and said, "This is something I have to do without you."

"But I'd like to see Lee Ann if she's here," I said.

"I know you would," said Caroline. "Of course you would."

"But, Caroline," I said, "I've made it clear that ours was an innocent—"

"I know," she said. "That's why I don't want you to see her again." Then she took Lee Ann's bag and went up to the front entrance of the house.

The main entrance to The Cellar was to the side of and underneath the high front stoop of the old house. Caroline had to climb a flight of ten or twelve stone steps to reach the door to the residence. From the car I saw a vague figure appear at one of the first-floor windows. I was relatively certain that it was Lee Ann I saw. I could barely restrain myself from jumping from the car and running up that flight of steps and forcing myself past Caroline and into the house. During the hundred hours or so since she had fled into the woods of Overton Park, Lee Ann Deehart had come to represent feelings of mine that I didn't try to comprehend. The notion I had had yesterday that I was in love with her and wanted to marry her didn't really adequately express the emotions that her disappearance had stirred in me. I felt that I had never looked at her really or had any conception of what sort of person she was or what her experience in life was like. Now it seemed I would never know. I suddenly realized—at that early age—that there was experience to be had in life that I might never know anything about except through hearsay and through books. I felt that this was my last moment to reach out and understand something of the world that was other than my own narrow circumstances and my own narrow nature. When, nearly fifteen years later, I came into a comfortable amount of money—after my father's death—I made my extraordinary decision to go back to the university and prepare myself to become a teacher. But I knew then, at thirty-seven, that I was only going to try to comprehend intellectually the world about me and beyond me and that I had failed somehow at some time to reach out and grasp direct experience of a larger life which no amount of intellectualizing could compensate for. It may be that the moment of my great failure was when I continued to sit there in the car and did not force my way into the house where the old woman with the goiter lived and where it now seemed Lee Ann had been hiding for four days.

I was scarcely aware of the moment when the big front door opened and Caroline was admitted to the house. She was in there for nearly an hour. During that time I don't know what thoughts I had. It was as though I ceased to exist for the time that Lee Ann Deehart and Caroline Braxley were closeted together. When Caroline reappeared on the high stone stoop of the house, I was surprised to see she was still carrying Lee Ann's suitcase. But she would soon make it all clear. It *was* Lee Ann who received her at the door.

No doubt she had seen that Caroline was carrying her own piece of luggage. And no doubt Caroline had counted on just that mystification and its efficacy, because Caroline is an extremely clever psychologist when she sets her mind to it. At any rate, in that relatively brief interview between them Caroline learned that all she had surmised about Lee Ann was true. Moreover, she learned that Lee Ann had fled the scene of the accident because she feared that the publicity would reveal to everyone who her grandmother was.

Lee Ann had crossed the little strip of snow-covered golf course and had entered the part of the woods where the old-forest trees were. And something had made her want to remain there for a while. She didn't know what it was. She had leaned against one of the trees, feeling quite content. It had seemed to her that she was not alone in the woods. And whatever the other presences were, instead of interfering with her reflections they seemed to wish to help her clear her thoughts. She stood there for a long time—perhaps for an hour or more. At any rate, she remained there until all at once she realized how cold she had grown and realized that she had no choice but to go back to the real world. Yet she wasn't going back to her room or to her pretty possessions there. That wasn't the kind of freedom she wanted any longer. She was going back to her grandmother. But still she hoped to avoid the publicity that the accident might bring. She decided to go, first of all, and stay with some of her friends, so that her grandmother would not suppose she was only turning to her because she was in trouble. And while making this important change in her life she felt she must be protected by her friends. She wanted to have an interval of time to herself and she wanted, above all, not to be bothered during that time by the silly society boy in whose car she had been riding.

During the first days she had gone from one girl's

house to another. Finally she went to her grandmother. In the beginning she had, it was true, been mightily depressed. That was why she had telephoned me to start with, and had wanted someone to cheer her up. But during these four days she had much time for thinking and had overcome all her depression and had no other thought but to follow through with the decision to go and live openly with her old grandmother in her quarters above The Cellar.

Caroline also, in that single interview, learned other things about Lee Ann which had been unknown to me. She learned that Lee Ann's own mother had abandoned her in infancy to her grandmother but had always through the years sent money back for her education. She had had—the mother—an extremely successful career as a buyer for a women's clothing store in Lincoln, Nebraska. But she had never tried to see her daughter and had never expressed a wish to see her. The only word she ever sent was that children were not her dish, but that she didn't want it on her conscience that, because of her, some little girl in Memphis, Tennessee, had got no education and was therefore the domestic slave of some man. When Caroline told me all of this about the mother's not caring to see the daughter, it brought from her her first emotional outburst with regard to the whole business. But that was at a later time. The first thing she had told me when she returned to the car was that once Lee Ann realized that her place of hiding could no longer be concealed, she was quickly and easily persuaded to speak to the newspaper editor on the telephone and to tell him that she was safe and well. But she did this only after Caroline had first spoken to the editor herself, and obtained a promise from him that there would be no embarrassing publicity for Lee Ann's grandmother.

The reason Caroline had returned with Lee Ann's suitcase was that Lee Ann had emptied it there in her grandmother's front parlor and had asked that we return to her rooming house and bring all of her possessions to her at her grandmother's. We obliged her in this, making appropriate, truthless explanations to her landlady, whom Lee Ann had meanwhile telephoned and given whatever little authority Mrs. Troxler required in order to let us remove her things. It seemed to me that the poor woman scarcely listened to the explanations we gave. Another girl was already moving into the room before we had well got Lee Ann's things out. When we returned to the grandmother's house with these possessions in the car, Caroline insisted upon making an endless number of trips into the house, carrying everything herself. She was firm in her stipulation that Lee Ann and I not see each other again.

The incident was closed then. I could be certain that there would be no broken engagement—not on Caroline's initiative. But from that point—from that afternoon—my real effort and my real concern would be to try to understand why Caroline had not been so terribly enraged or so sorely wounded upon first discovering that there had been another girl with me in the car at the time of the accident, and by the realization that I had not immediately disclosed her presence, that she had not at least once threatened to end the engagement. What her mental processes had been during the past four days, knowing now as I did that she was the person with whom I was going to spend the rest of my life, became of paramount interest to me.

But at that age I was so unquestioning of human behavior in general and so accepting of events as they came, and so without perception or reflection regarding the binding and molding effect upon people of the circumstances in which they are born, that I actually might not have found Caroline's thoughts of such profound interest and so vitally important to be understood had not Caroline, as soon as we were riding down Adams Street and were out of sight of The Cel-

lar and of Mrs. Power's great stone house above it,
suddenly requested that I drive her out to the Bristol
Highway, and once we were on the Bristol Highway
asked me to drive as fast and as far out of town as I
could or would, to drive and drive until she should
beg me to turn around and take her home; and had
she not, as soon as we were out of town and beyond
city speed limits, where I could press down on the
accelerator and send us flying along the three-lane
strip of concrete which cut through the endless expanse of cotton fields and swamps on either side, had
she not then at last, after talking quietly about Lee
Ann's mother's sending back the money for her education, burst into weeping that began with a kind
of wailing and grinding of teeth that one ordinarily
associates more with a very old person in very great
physical pain, a wailing that became mixed almost immediately with a sort of hollow laughter in which there
was no mirth. I commenced slowing the car at once.
I was searching for a place where I could pull off to
the side of the road. But through her tears and her
harsh, dry laughter she hissed at me, "Don't stop!
Don't stop! Go on. Go on. Go as far and as fast as
you can, so that I can forget this day and put it forever
behind me!" I obeyed her and sped on, reaching out
my right hand to hold her two hands that were resting
in her lap and were making no effort to wipe away
her tears. I was not looking at her—only thinking
thoughts of a kind I had never before had. It was the
first time I had ever witnessed a victim of genuine
hysteria. Indeed, I wasn't to hear such noises again
until six or seven years later, during the Second World
War. I heard them from men during days after a battle, men who had stood with great bravery against the
enemy—particularly, as I remember now, men who
had been brought back from the first onslaught of the
Normandy invasion, physically whole but shaken in
their souls. I think that during the stress of the four
previous days Caroline Braxley had shed not a tear of

self-pity or of shame and had not allowed herself a moment of genuine grief for my possible faithlessness to her. She had been far too busy with thinking—with thinking her thoughts of how to cope with Lee Ann's unexplained disappearance, with, that is, its possible effect upon her own life. But now the time had come when her checked emotions could be checked no longer.

The Bristol Highway, along which we were speeding as she wept hysterically, was a very straight and a very wide roadway for those days. It went northeast from Memphis. As its name implied, it was the old road that shot more or less diagonally across the long hinterland that is the state of Tennessee. It was the road along which many of our ancestors had first made their way from Virginia and the Carolinas to Memphis, to settle in the forest wilderness along the bluffs above the Mississippi River. And it occurred to me now that when Caroline said go as fast and as far as you can she really meant to take us all the way back into our past and begin the journey all over again, not merely from a point of four days ago or from the days of our childhood but from a point in our identity that would require a much deeper delving and a more radical return.

When we had got scarcely beyond the outskirts of Memphis, the most obvious signs of her hysteria had abated. Instead, however, she began to speak with a rapidity and in tones I was not accustomed to in her speech. This began after I had seen her give one long look over her shoulder and out the rear window of the car. Sensing some significance in that look and sensing some connection between it and the monologue she had now launched upon, I myself gave one glance into the rearview mirror. What met my eye was the skyline of modern Memphis beyond the snow-covered suburban rooftops—the modern Memphis of 1937, with its two or three high-rise office buildings. It was not clear to me immediately what there was in that skyline to inspire all that followed. She was speaking to me openly about Lee Ann and about her own feelings of jealousy and resentment of the girl—of *that* girl and of all those other girls, too, whose names and personalities and way of life had occupied our thoughts and had seemed to threaten our future during the four-day crisis that had followed my accident in the park.

"It isn't only Lee Ann that disturbs me," she said. "It began with her, of course. It began not with what she might be to you but with her freedom to jump out of your car, her freedom *from* you, her freedom to run off into the woods—with her capacity, which her special way of living provided her, simply to vanish, to remove herself from the eyes of the world, literally to disappear from the glaring light of day while the whole world, so to speak, looked on."

"*You* would like to be able to do that?" I interrupted. It seemed so unlike her role as I understood it.

"*Any*body would, wouldn't they?" she said, not looking at me but at the endless stretch of concrete that lay straight ahead. "*Men* have always been able to do it," she said. "In my own family, for as many generations back as our family stories go, there have been men who seemed to disappear from the face of the earth just because they wanted to. They used to write 'Gone to Texas' on the front door and leave the house and the farm to be sold for taxes. They walked out on dependent old parents and on sweethearts or even on wives and little children. And though they were considered black sheep for doing so, they were something of heroes, too. It seemed romantic to the rest of us that they had gone Out West somewhere and got a new start or had begun life over. But there was never a woman in our family who did that! There was no way it could happen. Or perhaps in some rare instance it did happen and the story hasn't come down to us. Her name simply isn't recorded in our family annals or reported in stories told around the fire. The assumption of course is that she is a streetwalker in Chicago or she resides in a red-plush whorehouse in Cheyenne. But with girls like Lee Ann and Lucy and Betsy it's all different. They have made their break with the past. Each of them had had the strength and intelligence to make the break for herself. But now they have formed a sort of league for their own protection. How I do admire and envy them! And how little you understand them, Nat. How little you understand Lee Ann's loneliness and depression and bravery. She and all the others are wonderful—even Fern. They occupy the real city of Memphis as none of the rest of us do. They treat men just as they please. And not the way men are treated in *our* circles. And men like them better for it. Those girls have learned to enjoy life together and to be mutually protective, but they enjoy a protection also, I hope you have observed, a kind of communal protection, from men who admire their very independence, from a league of men, mind you, not from individual men, from the police and from men like my father and your father, from men who would never say openly how much they admire them. Naturally we fear them. Those of us who are not like them in temperament—or in intelligence, because there is no use in denying it—we must fear them and find a means to give delaying action. And of course the only way we know is the age-old way!"

She became silent for a time now. But I knew I was going to hear what I had been waiting to hear. If I had been the least bit impatient with her explanation of Lee Ann and her friends, it was due in part to my impatience to see if she would explain *herself* to me. We were now speeding along the Bristol Highway at the very top speed the car would go. Except when we were passing through some crossroad or village I consciously kept the speed above ninety. In those days there was no speed limit in Tennessee. There were merely signs placed every so often along the roadside saying "Speed Limit: Please Drive Carefully." I felt

somehow that, considering Caroline's emotional state
and my own tension, it would be altogether unreason-
able, it would constitute careless and unsafe driving,
for me to reduce our speed to anything below the
maximum capability of the car. And when we did of
necessity slow down for some village or small town it
was precisely as though we had arrived at some at
once familiar and strange point in the past. And on
each occasion I think we both experienced a sense of
danger and disappointment. It was as though we expected to experience a satisfaction in having gone so
far. But the satisfaction was not to be had. When we
had passed that point, I felt only the need to press on
at an even greater speed. And so we drove on and
on, at first north and east through the wintry cotton
land and cornland, past the old Orgill Plantation, the
mansion house in plain view, its round brick columns
on which the plaster was mostly gone, and now and
then another white man's antebellum house, and always at the roadside or on the horizon, atop some
distant ridge, a variety of black men's shacks and cab-
ins, each with a little streamer of smoke rising from
an improvised tin stovepipe or from an ill-made brick
chimney bent away from the cabin at a precarious
angle.

We went through the old villages of Arlington and
Mason and the town of Brownsville—down streets of
houses   with   columned   porticoes   and   double
galleries—and then we turned south to Bolivar, whose
very name told you when it was built, and headed
back to Memphis through Grand Junction and La
Grange. (Mississippi towns really, though north of the
Tennessee line.) I had slowed our speed after Bolivar,
because that was where Caroline began her second
monologue. The tone and pace of her speech were
very different now. Her speech was slow and deliber-
ate, her emotions more under control than usual, as
she described what she had felt and thought in the
time since the accident and explained how she came

to reach the decision to take the action she had—that is, action toward searching out and finding Lee Ann Deehart. Though I had said nothing on the subject of what she had done about Lee Ann and not done about our engagement, expressed no request or demand for any explanation unless it was by my silence, when she spoke now it was almost as though Caroline were making a courtroom defense of accusations hurled at her by me. "I finally saw there was only one thing for me to do and saw why I had to do it. I saw that the only power in the world I had for saving myself lay in my saving you. And I saw that I could only save you by 'saving' Lee Ann Deehart. At first, of course, I thought I would have to break our engagement, or at least postpone the wedding for a year. That's what *every*body thought, of course—everybody in the family."

"Even your father and mother?" I could not help interjecting. It had seemed to me that Caroline's parents had—of all people—been most sympathetic to me.

"Yes, even my mother and father," she went on, rather serenely now. "They could not have been more sympathetic to you personally. Mother said that, after all, you were a mere man. Father said that, after all, you were only human. But circumstances were circumstances, and if some disaster had befallen Lee Ann, if she was murdered or if she was pregnant or if she was a suicide or whatever other horror you can conjure up, and it all came out, say, on our wedding day or came out afterward, for that matter—well, what then? *They* and *I* had to think of that. On the other hand, as I kept thinking, what if the wedding *was* called off? What then for me? The only power I had to save myself was to save you, and to save you by rescuing Lee Ann Deehart. It always came to that, and comes to that still. Don't you see, it was a question of how very much I had to lose and how little power I had to save myself. Because *I* had not set *my*self free the

way those other girls have. One makes that choice at
a much earlier age than this, I'm afraid. And so I
knew already, Nat, and I know now what the only
kind of power I can ever have must be."

She hesitated then. She was capable of phrasing
what she said much more precisely. But it would have
been indelicate, somehow, for her to have done so.
And so I said it for her in my crude way: "You mean
the power of a woman in a man's world."

She nodded and continued. "I had to protect *that*.
Even if it had been *I* that broke our engagement, Nat,
or even if you and I had been married before some
second scandal broke, still I would have been a jilted,
a rejected girl. And some part of my power to protect
myself would be gone forever. Power, or strength, is
what everybody must have some of if he—if she—is
to survive in any kind of world. I have to protect and
use whatever strength I have."

Caroline went on in that voice until we were back
in Memphis and at her father's house on East Parkway. She kissed me before we got out of the car there,
kissed me for my silence, I believe. I had said almost
nothing during the whole of the long ride. And I think
she has ever since been grateful to me for the silence
I kept. Perhaps she mistook it for more understanding
than I was capable of at the time. At any rate, I cannot
help believing that it has much to do with the support
and understanding—rather silent though it was—
which she gave me when I made the great break in
my life in my late thirties. Though it clearly meant
that we must live on a somewhat more modest scale
and live among people of a sort she was not used to,
and even meant leaving Memphis forever behind us,
the firmness with which she supported my decision,
and the look in her eyes whenever I spoke of feeling
I must make the change, seemed to say to me that
she would dedicate her pride of power to the power
of freedom I sought.

Gail Godwin

Born in Birmingham, Alabama, in 1937, Gail Godwin grew up in Asheville, North Carolina. Her mother, a reporter and a writer of romantic fiction, was an early literary influence. After Godwin graduated from the University of North Carolina with a degree in English, she received an M.A. and a Ph.D. from the University of Iowa, where Kurt Vonnegut was her teacher. She went on to teach English and creative writing at a number of colleges and universities, including Vassar, Columbia, and the University of Iowa. She has written ten novels and two collections of stories, work for which she has received a number of awards and grants. Her novels *The Odd Woman* (1974), *Violet Clay* (1978), and *The Finishing School* (1985) concern the relationship between life and art, whereas the novels *A Mother and Two Daughters* (1982), *A Southern Family* (1987), and *Father's Melancholy Daughter* (1991) focus on small-town life in the South and intense family relationships. Literary critic Frances Taliaferro has called the character of Justin in *The Finishing School* "one of the most trustworthy portraits of an adolescent in current literature." Gail Godwin has defined her story collection *Mr. Bedford and the Muses* (1983), from which the following story is taken, as "revisionist autobiography." Godwin, who has achieved both popular and critical acclaim, lives in Woodstock, New York.

The Angry Year

It was 1957, when the Big Bopper and Albert Camus still walked the earth and the Russians sent a dog into space. It was the year I was angry. The whole of my junior year, I went around angry. I had transferred at last from the modest junior college in my hometown to the big, prestigious university with the good program in English. My family was poor, they couldn't afford to send me, so I'd got there with a scholarship based on my freshman and sophomore grades. Yet, once I'd arrived where I'd slaved to get, I seethed from morning till night with a hot, unspecific anger. Everything infuriated me. I went through registration glaring at the coveys of girls with summer tans who welcomed one another back with shrill, delighted cries. I hated their skittish convertibles with the faded tops, bolting the orange traffic lights. I loathed the conformity of their Weejun loafers (though I wore them myself) and the little jeweled pins swinging saucily from their breasts. There was an enemy here who might destroy me unless I routed him out and destroyed him first, but I could not discover his identity.

I did a strange thing, under a sort of compulsion. I went out for sorority rush, although I knew perfectly well I could not afford to join one, even if asked. I dressed myself up and attended the Pan-Hellenic tea and signed the register as a rushee. I went to the first round of parties, hurrying from house to house under the autumn stars. My attitude was a queer blend of arrogance and obsequiousness. At the Chi Omega house I gulped my paper cup of cider and heard myself tell the most astonishing lies. At the Tri Delt house I ate too many cookies and insulted one of the sisters. I was calmer at the other four houses and managed to participate in the established ritual of chitchat without further incidents. Walking back to my dorm afterward, I concluded that I had done no worse than others, though—with the possible exception of the first two houses—I had not made myself memorable. I went over the evening and decided that most of the girls were shallow fools. I made out a budget in my journal to see if I could squeeze sorority dues out of the scholarship, even though there was a clause in the scholarship saying the holder could not join a fraternity or a sorority. I envisioned all six houses bidding for me, and my polite rejection of them. I would remain inscrutably independent. My roommate was a cheerful, sensible girl, a Christian Scientist. She was lying hunched on the floor of our room that evening, "working on" an injury she'd received at basketball tryouts. She said her parents had given her the choice of a sorority or a Volkswagen and she'd taken the VW, of course.

Before rush began, I had met the president of the Dekes, the big fraternity on campus, at a Get Acquainted Dance at the Armory. I was offhand and rather rude to him, and he kept asking me out. I had told him I might go through rush "just for the experience." He seemed pleased, but then Graham seemed pleased by most things. He was a slow, courtly boy from Danville, Virginia. His family owned a textile mill. I never saw him get excited about anything.

The second day of rush, he waited for me beneath a shedding oak while I ran into the Union to check my rushee mailbox. The first day, everyone got six white invitations. The second day, the serious weeding-out began. I came out of the Union enraged, my hands full of tiny bits of white paper. With Graham as my witness, I flung these into the wire trash basket beside the walk. They floated down, like languid snow, upon crumpled newsprint, paper cups, and apple cores.

"I've dropped out of rush," I said. "I've torn up all my silly invitations. There was this poor girl in there. She made me see what a cruel, stupid farce it is. There wasn't a single invitation in her box. She opened it and it was empty and there was this terrible look on her face. Sort of . . . stunned, like those newspaper pictures of people who have just been told their whole family has been wiped out. I refuse to be part of such a thing. You're looking at an Independent, Graham."

Agreeably, he hurried along the leaf-strewn path beside me. It was a splendid, crisp fall day, full of colors, the kind you breathe in exultantly if you're not preoccupied by anger. "Even though I'm a fraternity man myself," he said, "I admire you for taking a stand. Of course you must, feeling the way you do about that girl in there." He never knew how utterly alone his praise made me feel. For Graham really believed that girl existed. His world contained no necessity for inventing such lies, or for raiding a trash basket upstairs in order to have six invitations to tear up and throw away. He continued to take me out. His peaceful personality seemed to bask in the flames of my rebellion. I continued to be amazed that the president of the Dekes would want me as his girl. I never asked myself did I want him.

My second foray into the extracurricular was a visit to the student newspaper, which was published daily. I was curt and defiant. I said there were a lot of hypocrisies in the system I would love to expose. I asked for a personal column. The editor was a wild-eyed, brilliant Jewish boy from New York. He later became a well-known writer. "A mean Mary McCarthy type, that's what we need," he said. He agreed to give me a trial run: three eight-hundred-word columns a week. "And we'll run a half-column shot of you, with your hair flying, like it is now."

I worked very hard on the first three columns. They were titled, in order of appearance: "Worst of Bugs, Extracurricularalysis" (exhorting harassed freshmen not to load themselves down with band and basketball and chorus and student politics until they'd found their true and central interests); "Spit on Me or I on Thee" (a sermon, lifted in liberal chunks from Camus, in which I cautioned fellow students to judge not that they be not judged); and "The Mythical Booked-Up Maiden" (which put forth the proposition to campus males, who outnumbered the females ten to one, that dozens of beautiful coeds sat home on Saturday evenings because the boys assumed they were dated up for months in advance).

The first two columns were ignored. The third drew an amazing barrage of fan mail from the men's dorms. They offered various, sometimes unprintable, kinds of services to these stay-at-home maidens. The editor was pleased by the response and said I could keep my column. From then on I had my weapon: the powerful Fourth Estate. I titled my column "Without Restrictions," and set about avenging my private frustrations in vitriolic prose, beneath the photo of my flying hair.

Weekends I sat on the comfortable sofa at the Deke house and studied the enemy at close hand. I drank their Scotch and smiled my Mary McCarthy smile. I was surprised to discover that all the Dekes were a little scared of me. The house read "Without Restrictions" faithfully. Graham had told them about my stand that memorable fall day. To him, I was the girl who couldn't stop for fripperies when the world was smothering under a blanket of hypocrisy. The girls who came to the Deke house were another matter. Although they were friendly and polite to me, I couldn't decipher their true feelings. Most of them

came from the three top sororities out of the five that
hadn't asked me back. They sat draped over the arms
of their boyfriends' chairs, or, with their Weejuns
tucked chastely beneath their skirts, on the rug. Their
faces were composed, above their jeweled pins, shutting out all disquiet. What was their secret? I asked
myself. Had their wealth bought them their unshakable serenity, as it had bought their cashmere sweaters
and their perfect even teeth? Was it that simple? Or
was their poise due to some secret inner powers, such
as the Rosicrucians advertised, powers denied me forever because of my innately angry heart? I watched
these girls, fascinated; I looked forward to the weekends not because of Graham but because of them. I
sat in the circle of Graham's arm and said witty, icy
things, while my eyes darted back and forth, observing
their languid, seamless gestures, the way they made
a special art out of lighting a cigarette, their glossy,
lacquered nails cupping the flame, the charms on their
bracelets faintly jingling. Were they silently, en masse,
smiling at me while condemning me as a fraud?

I was never sure, and my unsureness whetted my
vituperation.

"Without Restrictions" dealt with second-semester
rush under the subhead *John Paul Jones Had Better
Be Your Friend*. The column ran a "tape recording"
of a typical rush dialogue.

SISTER: And what is *youah* name?
RUSHEE: Mary Kathleen Jones.
SISTER: Jones! Are you by any chance related to
    John Paul?
RUSHEE: I don't believe so. There are lots of Joneses
    where I come from.
SISTER: And where is that?
RUSHEE: Bent Twig.
SISTER: Bent Twig! Why didn't you say so! Then you

must be good friends with the Twigs who own the bank and the funeral parlor and the newspaper and the fish market.

RUSHEE: Well, I don't know them personally, but of course everybody's heard of the Twigs.

SISTER: Uh-huh. Well, Mary Catherine—oh, excuse me, Kath*leen*—it's been just grand talking to you. I'd like you to meet Attalee Hunt, our sister from Savannah. Attie, I think Mary Catherine might like a fresh glass of ice water. She seems to have eaten all her ice.

Not long after this, I received the following letter among my fan mail:

Dear Miss Lewis,
Your farce is ridiculous and futile. Why this endless stream of poison from a girl who professes to keep late-night company with Kierkegaard and Camus? Why waste your eye for the delicate and obscure detail on such passing, boring trivia during your short-term lease among the stars? Where is the discrepancy? Your ambivalence haunts me. Do you know who you are? If you did, I think you would be less angry.

Jack Krazowski
211 Kerr Dorm

The letter upset me briefly. I put it out of my mind. I sipped rum punch after the basketball game, in front of a roaring fire at the Deke house. Suzanne Pinkerton, the Chi O who, it was rumored, once loved Graham, studied me curiously over the rim of her steaming mug and asked softly, "Janie, why do you hate us so?" Graham squeezed my shoulder proudly. "Better watch out for this one," he said. He was always saying about me, "Look out, now," or, "Better watch out for this one." That night, his lack of originality annoyed me.

* * *

At midterm, I got my first C. The sight of the letter-grade gave me a shock. I remembered my former industrious scholarship, the feeling I'd had for years that A's were my birthright. Now my mental sharpness was blurred by this constant association with people who demanded little of my mind. All my energy went into planning my next printed tirade against some small or imagined slight. Graham took me to the Interfraternity Ball. Before the dance, we were inconvenienced by a new state liquor law that made it necessary for us to drive twenty miles into the next county in order to purchase our bottles of J&B. Several days later, "Without Restrictions" presented a scathing diatribe against redneck Baptist legislators who could not hold their liquor and therefore assumed we students at the university could not be trusted, either.

A second letter came from Kerr Dorm.

Dear Miss Lewis,
  Have you ever read Ben Franklin's story of the tin whistle? You probably have—you seem to have read everything—so I won't bore you by retelling it. But your latest column put me in mind of little Ben racing about the house in manic despair, blowing stubbornly on the useless whistle for which he had given all his money.
                                    Yours truly,
                                    Jack Krazowski

I went to the library that evening for the first time in weeks. It was a balmy evening, almost spring, and I looked forward to browsing among shelves of books once more. In a *Benjamin Franklin Reader,* I tracked down the story of the tin whistle, how when Ben as a child had been given a gift of money and sent off to a toy store he had been "charmed" by the sound of another boy's whistle and given all his money for it at once.

I then came home and went whistling all over the house, much pleased by my whistle, but disturbing all the family. My brothers and sisters and cousins, understanding the bargain I had made, told me I had given four times as much for it as it was worth; put me in mind what good things I might have bought with the rest of my money; and laughed at me so much for my folly, that I cried with vexation; and the reflection gave me more chagrin than the whistle gave me pleasure.

I left the library and walked slowly back to my dorm. I passed students, some in groups, others solitary, whom I did not know. I wondered who they were and whether their private thoughts were poems or diatribes. Perhaps the one I had just passed would become very famous someday, and someone would say to me, "Oh did you know —— at your university? You were there at the same time." "No, I hung out mainly with the Dekes," I would answer.

I walked past Kerr Dorm nervously. It was the oldest men's dormitory, built of limestone and covered with ivy. It cost less to live there because there was no air conditioning. Which room on the second floor was 211? A pair of feet in white socks hung out of one of the lighted windows. From another came the sound of Brahms's Violin Concerto. I stood beneath the window, listening to the poignant solo of the violin. The stars were out and I was pleased I could recognize so many constellations. Then I heard footsteps and people coming along the walk laughing and I hurried away, not wanting to be discovered mooning outside Jack Krazowski's dorm.

WITHOUT RESTRICTIONS

"Night Sounds"

Last night, about nine, I walked home from the library. The air had that peculiar spring quality which clarifies a drowsy mind and conducts important sounds. As I passed my fellow students I seemed to hear the rhythms of their thoughts: some quick and angry, others slow and meditative. I heard voices out of the future speak to me and I heard my own voice, also in a future time, trying to explain, to justify, the way in which I'd used my short-term lease among the stars . . .

Dear Miss Janie Lewis,
   Stick to your tirades, hon. "Night Sounds" are just not you at your best.
   Your beer-drinking, frat-hating, establishment-stomping, ever-lovin' buddies from
                                        Bingham Quad

It was Graham's twenty-first birthday. I gave up on men's stores. He had as many cuff links, sweaters, and pocket flasks as they stocked. Also, I had a limited amount to spend, and did not want to risk choosing the wrong brand, an inferior label. I went to the bookstore because here I knew I could trust my taste. Usually, for people I liked, I simply chose a book I wanted myself. Would Graham like a Kierkegaard anthology? The complete poetry of John Donne? I couldn't be sure. I went on to the hobby shelves and examined a glossy volume entitled *A Complete Guide to the World's Firearms.*

"Looking for new ammunition for your column, Miss Lewis?" asked an ironic male voice behind me. Somehow I knew who it was. I turned at last to see what Jack Krazowski looked like. He was tall, but otherwise a disappointment. Pale, hawklike face. Horn-rims, faded Levi's, and muddy combat boots. He was holding the Modern Library edition of *Thus Spake Zarathustra.* His hands were surprisingly graceful and clean.

"I'm looking for a birthday present," I said. "A person I know is being given a surprise birthday party tonight."

"What sort of person?" he asked familiarly. His eyes were such a light blue, he looked as though he were perpetually squinting into the sun.

"One of those persons who have everything already." My sarcastic tone surprised me.

"Oh," he said, not very interested. He was looking at me, rather pleased about something. "You're a lot prettier than that bitchy picture of you they run," he said at last.

"I don't expect you to like my picture any better than you like my column."

"It's getting better. The one about the night sounds showed promise."

"I'm glad you think I have literary promise."

"Oh, that's never been in question. I wasn't referring to that kind of promise when I said you were getting better. Would you like a cup of coffee?"

"I can't. I have to go home and wash my hair for this party. And I haven't even bought a present."

"Let me help you. The purely impersonal shopper's guide. What is your friend like?"

"He's soft-spoken," I said, noting the flicker of disappointment at the masculine pronoun. "Well dressed," I added, looking down at his caked boots. I was being terrible. I couldn't help myself.

"Buy him this." He held up an ornate copy of the *Inferno,* with Doré engravings, on sale for $4.50. "It's a good book, if he wants to read it. And the pictures are nice if he doesn't. He'll be flattered to think that you think he'll read it, anyway."

I caught the implicit snub, but it did seem, somehow, the perfect choice. And the price was certainly right. I bought the book.

"If he likes it, you have to go to dinner with me sometime," said Jack, who then walked me back to the dorm. He had a loping long-distance walk; I had to run along awkwardly to keep up.

"Were you in the army?" I said. "You walk like you're on a long march."

"Nope. Marines."

"For how long?"

"Four years."

"Good grief, you must be ancient."

"A decrepit twenty-seven in June. I had to get somebody to pay for law school. My old man's a miner. I have nine brothers and sisters."

"Well, I'm an only child. But my father has this problem with his temper and keeps losing jobs. I had these war bonds, luckily, my aunt and uncle used to send me every Christmas, and I cashed them in so I could go to this measly little college in my hometown as a day student. The only reason I'm here is because I made straight A's for two years and did nothing but grind, grind, grind. Now I intend to have some fun." I was shocked at myself. I had not even told my Christian Scientist roommate the whole truth.

We were standing, by this time, at the entrance to my dorm. Jack suddenly gave me a paternal pat on top of my head. "That explains a lot," he said. "Yes. Well, after all my fan mail, I guess you know where I live now. Call me when you're ready to go out to dinner. Any night except Tuesday. That's my night to collect dorm laundry."

I hurried upstairs to wash my hair. I was annoyed at Jack for telling me to call him. Where were his manners? I was sorry I had talked to him about my family, but it had poured out before I could stop it. Under the shower I closed my eyes and luxuriated in thoughts of the evening to come. I felt in control of my life here at last. And Jack had said I was pretty. Maybe we could be friends. We could go off occasionally by ourselves and have quiet conversations. He was not exactly a showpiece, but I had my showpiece already. These were those pre-"Liberation" years, before girls felt guilty about treating men like objects because turnabout is fair play.

Graham liked his present. He said, "This is one classic I have always wanted to read. This is the kind of

book you can keep for a lifetime." (And I am sure
Graham still has the book.)

In the days that followed I became unusually depressed. All the anger had suddenly gone out of me.
I read in the newspaper about a student from Texas
who had jumped from the tower due to "pressures
from overwork," and every time I thought of this I
cried. In fact, I tried to think about it so I could cry.
I wrote a column entitled "The Pressures That Bear
Us Away," a disconnected, overwrought piece that,
when it was published, prompted a call to the newspaper from the Director of Student Health, who pronounced it an irresponsible romanticizing of suicide.
The editor called me into his office and more or less
issued an ultimatum: Get funny again, or get out. I
quickly redeemed myself by "crashing" the sororities'
Spring Fashion Show. My next "Without Restrictions"
was called "A Visitor from Mars Reports on Pan-
Hellenic Couture," and put this shallow annual event
in its cosmic place. Graham telephoned, sounding un-
characteristically sad. "I know these things don't seem
important to you, Janie, but Suzanne Pinkerton devoted hours of work organizing that show, and she felt
your column was unfair." He was as courteous and
soft-spoken as ever, but I felt the censure in his words,
and imagined his alliance with Suzanne against my
clumsy fury.

That afternoon, I called Kerr Dorm, second floor.
The phone rang for a long time. At last a boy answered. There was a great commotion in the background, shouts echoing and shower water running.
"Who is it you want?" he kept repeating. "You'll have
to speak up louder."

"I want Jack Krazowski!" I shouted.

"She wants Jack Krazowski!" he shouted. There
was a lot of male laughter. I was getting ready to hang
up in embarrassment.

"Hello," he said. "Don't mind them."

"This is Janie Lewis, from the bookstore," I said.

"I know that. When are we going to dinner? How about tonight?"

"That would be fine. Actually, I've been . . . it will be nice to talk to you."

"I'll be over in about an hour," he said. "I'll shave and put on a suit so you won't be ashamed of me."

"I look forward to it," I said, feeling better.

"I'm glad you finally got around to calling," he said. Was he laughing? I couldn't tell.

When I looked for him in the dorm parlor, I skipped right over him at first. I looked at the boys lounging self-consciously against armchairs and walls, huddling together in groups. One of these boys I recognized as a new Deke, who'd pledged in January. Jack, in a dark suit, turned from the window where he'd been standing. He'd been there all the time, but I had been looking for a boy, not a man.

"I didn't recognize you, all dressed up," I said, hurrying along beside his long-march strides into the early-spring evening. The new Deke looked after us. I supposed it would get back to Graham but I didn't care.

"It's only my charisma," said Jack. "You'll get used to it."

He took me to a steak house on the highway. None of the Greeks ever went there. Everything seemed strangely and pleasantly adult. Jack had borrowed a car, a pedestrian black Plymouth with the radio missing from the dashboard.

"What did you want to talk about?" he said.

"Oh nothing. Everything. I just feel I can be myself around you."

"Can't you be with your other friends? Your friend that had the birthday, for instance?"

"Oh God!" I laughed wildly. Then I amended, "It's

just that . . . with a lot of people, I seem to be able to present only certain sides of myself. But with you, I can just let go."

"Knowing what I think I know," he said, "I'm not sure that's a compliment from you."

"What do you mean?"

"Oh, let's pass on that one. If you don't know, it's because you don't want to know yet. Besides, I'm glad you called." He reached over and tapped the back of my neck lightly with his finger, and a queer thing happened to my stomach.

The atmosphere of the steak house had a liberating effect on me. It seemed we were decades away from the college campus. Sitting across from each other in the dark little restaurant, eating our charcoaled steaks and drinking our beers, we might have been two highway travelers going anywhere. "I haven't felt so relaxed all year," I said. "If you only knew how much time I spend talking about nothing with people I don't even like."

"Why do you do it?" Jack asked, watching me closely. The way he had tapped my neck in the car: I hoped he would touch me again.

I said, "When I was growing up, all my friends belonged to a country club. Or, rather, their parents did. This club had the only swimming pool in town. There was another place, a sort of walled-in lake, but a girl had been molested there—a bunch of local hoodlums stood in a circle around her and made her let them feel under her bathing suit—and my mother wouldn't let me go. I was allowed into the country club pool, as a guest, twice a month. Once, a friend tried to sneak me in a third time and the lifeguard caught us and made me leave. My friend decided to stay on. I remember she gave me this sort of pitying look through the fence and said, very cool and sweet, 'We'll have better luck next time, Janie.' I walked back home, over the golf course, and I felt so ashamed."

"It was your so-called friend who should have felt

ashamed," said Jack. "Did that ever cross your mind?"

"No, I guess it didn't. Not until now. How funny that it shouldn't have, until now."

"That's because you're in a rut," said Jack. "Do you want to be accepted by people just because they remind you of those rich kids in your hometown? Shouldn't you ask yourself, first of all, whether you accept *them*?"

"I don't know," I said. "It's not that simple. These people do have something. This kind of unshakable quality. I'm so . . . shakable. There's a mystery about these people I need to decipher."

"Mystery!" scoffed Jack. He drummed his long fingers on the checkered tablecloth.

"You have wonderful hands," I said, wanting an excuse to touch him. "Have you ever taken piano?"

"Coal miners' sons aren't in the habit of taking piano lessons," he replied, and I hated the smugness in his voice.

"Why do you play up your proletarian role?" I said.

"I don't know. Do I play it up? Perhaps it's my Budapest defense. Do you know chess? No? I'll have to teach you. It will develop your unshakable powers." He picked up my hand.

"What is a Budapest defense?" I said rapturously.

"A gambit. A sort of counterattack. Get them before they have a chance to get you. You of all people ought to understand."

"I wish you would teach me," I said. "Chess, I mean. No, I don't. I wish you could teach me everything." I did not have to ask myself whether I accepted Jack. There were other ways of knowing.

"Janie," he said. "Too bad we didn't meet earlier."

"But we've got now," I said recklessly. "We've got two more months." I pushed it too quickly, promising more than I was sure I could give.

"We have, if you want it," he said, looking at me carefully.

As soon as we got back to the car, in the dark parking lot behind the steak house, we began kissing. Now and then, a car or a truck would hurtle down the highway, beaming its headlights momentarily on the tall yellow grasses growing wild. Then there was darkness and the stars scattered liberally across a black sky. Suddenly the world was so much bigger. Jack and I existed alone under that sky. We were members of the universe, and anything smaller was a bore.

But when we drove back again, into the lights of the town, and saw students coming out of the movies in pairs, and convertibles skimming around corners, my old paltry fear returned. Jack asked whether I would like to stop off at Harry's, a popular campus hangout, for a cup of coffee, but I said no. I was afraid for his charisma, under the fluorescent lights. It might dissolve, and I would be stuck in Harry's with a coal miner's son and his Budapest defense, and I was not ready yet. He seemed to understand, and drove me to the dorm.

At the front door, he took me by the shoulders and looked searchingly into my face. "Janie, there isn't unlimited time for all there is to do," he said. "Don't waste it. Don't be afraid of doing what you want."

"I enjoyed the dinner," I said, in a turmoil.

He sighed. "Well, you call me when you want another one," he said. "Only it probably won't be steak next time. I'm a poor man, remember."

The spring went quickly, like a 33 record somebody had turned up to 78. Graham became hyperattentive. He'd obviously been told of my stepping out by the new Deke trying to score a few Brownie points. Graham didn't pry. That was not his way. He asked me to accept his pin. I had hoped for this for a long time; it had seemed the answer to so many things. With a dry mouth, feeling a stranger to myself, I accepted the pin in an impressive candlelight ceremony. The brothers stood in a circle around us. Even Suzanne Pinkerton came up to me afterward and took my hand and said, as though she meant it, "I'm so happy for you, Janie."

I saw Jack only once more, at the bookstore. I had gone there to browse, hoping I might meet him.

"That's an elegant pin you've got on," he said, looking straight at my eyes and not at the pin. "Does it mean you're engaged?"

"Not exactly. Kind of engaged to be engaged."

"Hmm. What are those, rubies?"

"They're not tin," I said, without thinking, and could have bitten off my tongue.

"No, I can see that," he said quietly. A remote look came into his face. I remembered how we had kissed under the stars. It would be unthinkable, never to do it again. And yet his remoteness clearly proclaimed we wouldn't.

"Oh well," I said, "things happen. But they also unhappen. Will you be back in the fall?"

"I'm finishing up in June," he said. "I get my law degree in June. Then back to West Virginia, to study for the bar."

"Oh." There was nothing else I could think of to say, yet there was so much going on between us.

He broke the silence. "Well, take care, Janie." Then he went out of the bookstore, bouncing up and down on the balls of his feet, in his long-march style. I had an impulse to run after him. But what would I say when I caught up with him?

After finals, Graham gave a houseparty at his parents' summer cottage at the beach. There was much beer-drinking and water-skiing and necking, and I was so integral a part of the group that I found I could dispense altogether with my Mary McCarthy smile. I shared a bedroom with Suzanne Pinkerton and was able to penetrate her mystique at last. She worried terribly about her small breasts and had sent off se-

cretly for a chest developer, which she used morning
and night. She slept with a yellow rabbit, whose fur
had come off in patches, which she'd been given as a
child. She confided that she was not really in love with
the boy who was her date for this houseparty.
"There's someone . . . he's in Maine . . . in some ways
he reminds me of you, Janie."

"Oh? In what ways?"

"Well, he's real smart, like you . . . and at first he
seems, you know, kind of critical. But after you get
to know him, he's a wonderful person."

We were lying on the beach one morning, doing our
nails from the same bottle of polish. She said to me,
"Marietta Porter is transferring to William and Mary
in the fall. There'll be a vacancy at the Chi O house.
I could speak to the others if you're interested, Janie."

I was lying on my stomach, listening to the dull,
even plash of the sea at low tide, watching Suzanne's
polish harden to a fine porcelain sheen on my fingernails. I pretended Jack Krazowski was within listening
distance, hearing me utter the finale to that wasted
year. But no one was listening as I thanked Suzanne
and explained about the clause in my scholarship. No
one at all, not even the Spirit of the Times, who had
turned her back on us to scan the horizon. There were
new things on the way for people to join or to be
angry about. The sixties were coming.

Suzanne said, well, she hoped I'd come around to
the house and have dinner sometime, she hoped we
could get to know each other better. Then she started
on her second coat of polish. I lay there beside her,
staring at my own nails, getting angrier by the minute
because I couldn't love them, even now that I'd made
them love me.

Then the boys came back, carrying their surfboards,
waving at us while they were still some distance away.
Without my glasses I was not sure which of them, in
their look-alike plaid bathing trunks, was Graham.
The closer they came, the angrier I got, not with the

deflected anger that went into the columns of "Without Restrictions," but with a deep, abiding, central anger at the real culprit, the crass conformist who'd been harboring inside the rebel all along. I dug my nails into the sand, ruining the careful polish job. What was the proper procedure for returning a fraternity pin without hurting anyone's feelings?

I don't remember the actual returning of Graham's pin. He must have been hurt, or baffled at the very least. What happened to him later I don't know.

The fall of my senior year I spent ministering to the almost constant anger of a new man, a young psychiatrist in the blackest depths of his training analysis. We spent most of our time together confusing me with his mother. In the spring I rallied and helped to found a new literary magazine on campus. It was called *Shock!!!* and had one triumphant issue before being quashed by the local postmaster. Then I graduated, with no *laudes,* and went out into the world, where I found new people to love and plenty of new things to be angry about.

But ever since the Angry Year, I have reserved my most energetic fury for the Culprit. Though her powers have diminished as I've grown more sure of mine, she still keeps quarters for herself in some unreachable part of my psyche. She bores from inside at the braver scaffoldings erected by my imagination, and her favorite trick is posing as other people whom I hate until I realize I'm hating myself. She is forever trying to constrain me to the well-trodden paths of expression, even as I write this story. For every mental mile I succeed in traveling without her restrictions, she leadens my heart with her ceaseless plaint: *What are the others thinking? What will others think?*

Michael Malone

Michael Malone was born in North Carolina in 1942 and was educated at the University of North Carolina at Chapel Hill and at Harvard. He is the author of a play, several screenplays, and eight novels, ranging from mysteries like *Uncivil Seasons* (1983) to comic novels like *Handling Sin* (1986) to thrillers like *Foolscap* (1991). He has written articles and reviews for magazines such as *The Nation, Human Behavior, Playboy, Mademoiselle*, and *The New York Times Magazine*. He taught creative writing at Yale, Connecticut College, the University of Pennsylvania, and Swarthmore College, and he wrote for television soap operas. Having lived for years in Connecticut, he has returned home to North Carolina. More than one reviewer has noticed that Malone has a gift for comedy and a talent for creating a distinctive narrative voice. These signature characteristics of his writing are both on display in "Fast Love."

Fast Love

It was love at first sight out of the corner of my eye as she flew past the showroom window where I stood eating a double cheeseburger and trying not to hear Merle Longfielder bore our only customer with exaggerations about his racing a 560 horsepower Mustang down in South Carolina last Sunday. It was love in a blur, too. At first I thought maybe something rabid or mentally defective was after her. I didn't think of muggers; we don't have crime in Toomis. (As our billboard for some reason brags, "Toomis is the Smallest Industrial Town in Piedmont, North Carolina." The industries are the state mental hospital and a snuff factory. If you live here, you don't notice the smell.)

So she ran by, and when nothing else followed her, I did. Destiny can't be ignored, no matter how unlikely it may look at first sight—as my grandmother told me when she bought her bus ticket to go march with Martin Luther King, and my father caught her and put her in the (mental) Hospital. This running object of my sudden affection looked unlikely because the women of Toomis walked, on the few occasions when they weren't driving their cars, and in mid-October—whether it was forty degrees or eighty degrees—they wore wool plaid skirts with cardigan sweaters looped over their shoulders. *She* had on white shorts with red stripes and red shoes with white stripes and a sleeveless T-shirt with a picture of Margaret Mead the anthropologist on it. Her red hair in

its ponytail leapt all over the place like a fire chasing
her down the street.

She wasn't wearing a bra either; I don't mind mentioning that I noticed, because I'd already decided to
marry her. We Wintrip males have a long family tradition of choosing a bride in the twinkling of an eye,
though I believe I was the first to spot one on the run.
My grandfather saw his future wife threatening a bully
with a pitchfork as she stood atop a hayrick with her
skirts tucked up. My father first glimpsed my mother
as she and her fiancé were winning a Tri-Delta jitter-
bug contest. And I fell in love in a flash with the first
jogger anyone ever saw in Toomis, North Carolina. I
had loved only once before—unhappily—and now as
I panted towards the town limits, a stitch in my side,
a throb in my back, fear tingled through me: would
this girl break my heart as Betsy Creedmoor had
long ago?

I lost her just on the ridge of the first long upgrade
of Route 55. The double cheeseburger and knee-high
Frye boots did me in. After the spasms ended, I
crawled along the shoulder until I felt well enough to
walk back to Wintrip Motors where Merle Longfielder, my dad's other vice-president, amused himself
by hurling me to the ground on the pretense that he'd
already called an ambulance to rush me off for rabies
shots. He'd seen the girl, too. "Nice bod," was all the
oaf could think of to say.

Merle is my sex, race, and age. So much for what
we have in common. His brain is thick and porous.
He sports a forty-eight-long maroon polyester blazer,
a crew cut, and ought to clip the hairs in his nostrils.
In the summer my father and Merle lie side by side
together under cars in our driveway; their legs stick
out like those of Greek soldiers making love. In their
time, they say, they both crunched a lot of cartilage
playing high school football. I suspect Dad wishes
Merle was his son. So do I. The truth is, during my
youth, team sports were never that compelling. I had

a weakness for learning; chess, debating, and bicycling were also favorite pastimes—all enthusiasms that struck my dad like a collapsed lung.

My senior year, when my life was in shambles over Betsy Creedmoor, the track coach lured me into a letter sweater. As it happened, I was good. But I'd always been a runner. From childhood on, wherever I was supposed to be, I ran there fast. I ran after the schoolbus. I ran after the footballs my father was always kicking at me in the backyard. I ran like the wind out of necessity. Toughs in my neighborhood, murderous with the baffled envious rage that the stupid sometimes feel for the intelligent, would occasionally bolt out at me from behind bushes or cars and try to destroy my body. When we were twelve, Merle Longfielder chased me through the Baptist nursery school playground with a branch of poison sumac he planned to rub into my eyes. I was jumping three-year-olds as if they were hurdles.

So you might say life trained me as a sprinter; now I planned to use that training to win a wife. Sunday night I pawed my old tennis shoes out from under my bed. Wearing them Monday, I was on the watch for my future bride as soon as I had finished my "real" job and hurried over to Wintrip Motors where from five to eight weekdays and all day Saturday I worked for my dad as one of his two vice-presidents. I did it for the money and for my mother who begged me. Maybe she thought that if my dad's only child refused his offer, he'd put me in the Hospital too, like he did his mother. When he first heard about my real job—state social work—he told me I was nuts. As soon as I tried to explain (on the way home from my college graduation), he let me know *social* meant socialist and *worker* meant Red Square. Then he jackknifed to a stop, swelled into a frenzy, and announced he was going to beat the Commie crap out of my head with his pistol butt. By the time he got the glove compartment opened, I'd done the quarter mile in four sec-

onds less than my old coach's best hopes. Plus done
it wearing an academic gown.

My father's response didn't surprise me. He was a
man of the fifties, and in the fifties people all over the
country were scared to death that the Communists
might take over and brainwash Americans into thinking they had a right to other people's property—
especially that property belonging to these people who
were scared to death of the Communists. Nearly all
the parents in Toomis were afraid their children were
going to *catch* Communism; they thought it was like
polio, only there wasn't a vaccine. So when I was nine,
I sold glitter-dusted Christmas cards door-to-door and
the money went to help fight the Red Menace. From
my father's point of view I obviously hadn't sold
enough, for Russia had gotten me in the end and mesmerized me into preferring social services to the showroom of Wintrip Motors. And so, for my mother's
sake, to allow him to hold up his gray (flattop) head
in Toomis, and to help pay my apartment rent so I
wouldn't have to live at home with him, I moonlighted
at Wintrip Motors.

Thank God I did, and that Wintrip Motors hogged
the side of Main Street where Meredith Krantzsky
jogged. Meredith Krantzsky was her name, though
horribly enough it was Merle Longfielder who formally introduced her to me. My own first try was interrupted. Wearing my sneakers, I was in a nonchalant
crouch by the showroom door at six o'clock Monday
when she flashed around the corner of Parritt's Diner
and flew towards me. By the time we reached the end
of the block I could see there were gold specks in the
green irises of her eyes. She was altogether as beautiful as I'd suspected from my original blurred impression.

I tried to be casual. "Mind if I run along with you
for a little bit?"

She turned, arching a copper brown eyebrow at my
seersucker jacket and best paisley tie.

"My name's Blake Wintrip. Felt like. Little exercise. Just happen to notice . . ."

But then I tripped to avoid a baby in a stroller, and while I spiraled about to catch my balance, old Mrs. Etherege spied me from her bus stop bench. She clawed me to a standstill to tell me she'd spent the morning visiting my grandmother at the Hospital. By the time I could unclench her tiny relentless fingers, my bride-to-be was floating like a sunset through the intersection of Culloden and Main. But suddenly she turned, smiled at me; and then she ran on. My heart burst.

Mrs. Etherege pushed up my eyelids and stared. "Blake, are you all right? Heaven's sake. What's the matter? Your face is a deep plum purple. Almost heliotrope." (Mrs. Etherege has been an amateur painter since southern primitivism became fashionable; she and my grandmother—original founders of the Ladies Art League to which Mother also belonged—used to take their canvases up into the Appalachians where the gift galleries would sell them to tourists.) "Are you sick, son?"

"I'm in love," I told her. "I'm about to propose."

"Oh well, isn't that wonderful? Your folks must be so relieved. Who's the lucky girl?"

"There she goes." I pointed with a sigh as Meredith Krantzsky bounced away towards the horizon.

Mrs. Etherege's tactless remark about my parents' relief was a reference to a sorrow from which only time and an inadvertent discovery of the truth had cured me. My high school sweetheart Betsy Creedmoor temporarily lost her mind senior year under the pressure of being forced by her mother to pretend to be stupid for popularity's sake. Betsy was brainy, and in our region the intellectual life was frowned upon for females. (For males, too, as far as that goes.) Betsy's breakdown—she would sit with her bare feet in the gutter outside Toomis High, drawing designs on her legs with lipstick—was my fall from innocence. The sight of her beautiful vacant eyes was the sword that drove me from the garden into a life of social work among children of Cain. That was almost how my grandmother put it when I went to the Hospital to ask her what I ought to do. She sat at her potter's wheel, hummed her old marching song, "We Shall Overcome," while she thought. Finally, she told me to go to the state university and study injustice. Just be warned, she added, the world felt no obligation to make sense, much less be fair. Grandma was in a position to know. Here she was, perfectly sane, locked away to weave place mats. Here was Betsy Creedmoor deteriorating beyond repair, and her mother accused me of cruelty when I pleaded that her daughter needed medical help. "Blake, Blake, why do you persecute me and my Betsy so? Why are you trying day and night to lock our little girl away in a snake pit with old nutty trashy types, when you yourself have been so crazy about her ever since fifth grade and followed her around like a little puppy dog?"

Mrs. Creedmoor had never liked me; her feelings were requited. She had blue hair and leathery arms as brown as her golf bag. She smoked five packs of cigarettes a day; even when she was doing the dishes she would pinch her cigarette with a sudsy hand and stick it in a plastic ashtray over the sink. I told her Betsy was getting sicker. She'd sigh. "Oh Blake, darling, what makes you talk that ugly way? Manic-depressive? Why, Betsy's just worked too hard being a silly old bookworm, *like you,* and got herself a little run-down." And as this woman was speaking, her sixteen-year-old daughter stood weeping at her reflection in the hall mirror, then stuck her fingers in her mouth and stretched it into a grin howling pig Latin.

Betsy missed so much school because of her nervous breakdown that her grades slipped into the norm. This did, in fact, enhance her popularity. She gave up debate club and playing chess with me at lunch; instead she'd wander about the high school grounds with other girls, collecting, as she wafted by, a huddle of large retarded boyfriends—among them Merle Long-fielder. With her mother's blessing, Merle escorted Betsy to the Senior Prom. There, all misty in her trance, she was elected prom queen, and by midnight she lay thrashing like a silverfish in the backseat of Merle's stripped-down Ford. A "friend" told me he saw them. At commencement Betsy was awarded the "Most Popular Girl" trophy. Eventually I began to realize that although Betsy really had lost her mind, it wasn't going to make any difference to people; the man she eventually married, a Sigma Chi predental booze-hound, never even noticed.

Betsy and I both enrolled in the state university. She went, according to her mother's instructions, to work on an M.R.S. degree. I went on my grandmother's recommendation. After my arrival, my father mailed me a local editorial calling the college a "radical-infested swamp of subversives, a compost heap where budding Communist homosexuals meet by night to hide their shameful scheming from God's all-seeing eye." But the truth is we were pitiably behind the times. While everywhere else they had hippies in the sixties, we had beatniks. While the New Left was ripping the ragged social fabric into headbands, we lay on the campus green playing Pete Seeger songs on our bongos. By the time we got around to burning the Marine recruiting stand in front of the dining hall, everywhere else they were back to toga parties and panty raids. I gave up running, except to the john, and passed the time drinking beer and studying injustice.

Betsy Creedmoor said only two things to me throughout our stay. My first year I stood out in the quad listening to a speech by a famous socialist who kept running for president and insisting that somebody arrest him. He told us, "Social reform begins at home. Stand still and look around you!" He went all over the world giving this speech. A group of us were greatly under this man's influence as freshmen. We were cheering him as Betsy ambled by with a weight lifter. She said, "I kid you not. Never take life to heart." That was all. And then our final term I squeezed past her coming out of the bathroom of Slaughterhouse Five, a horribly foul college bar. This time she said, "Check and mate." But her eyes weren't focused, and she may not have even been talking to me. My sole consolation then had been that Betsy had cast off Merle Longfielder for the dentist who wore colored knit shirts with an alligator over his left nipple and who lugged a golf bag to classes.

Yet now three years later all I could wish was that Betsy and Merle were off somewhere in Arizona, upwardly mobile, celebrating their wooden anniversary. The pain might have faded, and arriving at Parritt's Diner I would have been spared the agonizing sight of that hulking body in the maroon blazer leaning across two chili dogs towards Meredith Krantzsky, the girl of my dreams, whom I recognized despite the fact that she was sitting still and wearing a dress. Merle was regaling her with the news that Richard Petty's pit crew could change two tires and fill a gas tank in 12.5 seconds flat when I reached their table. He punched me chummily in the stomach, and after I caught my breath I grabbed the table edge to keep myself from stabbing forks into his cabbage-size hands.

"Merry Krantzsky, I want you to meet Blake Wintrip for about two seconds. Then forget him. He's married with six kids, impotent, queer, and he's got V.D. Say byebye, Blake." (Merle prided himself on his witty urbanity.)

"We've sort of met," she said, and looked up from her tuna salad. "Wintrip? I've got a bone to pick with you. I know your grandmother, I spend a lot of time with her, and . . ."

"How?" My heart cramped with dread. She didn't *look* mad. But of course everyone had let poor Betsy Creedmoor run loose through life, too.

"I work at the Hospital. I'm a psychiatric social worker, and your grandmother shouldn't be in there."

"I know. But I don't think anybody else should be in there either. I'm a social work field coordinator. Nice to meet you."

Right then I could tell she'd decided there was a chance she eventually might like me.

"Merry here's a Yankee. She's been telling me about herself. Just moved down to Toomis from New Hampshire."

"Rhode Island."

"One of those little ones." Merle was holding both his chili dogs in one hand; worse, he was eating them that way as he talked. "I'm pretty sure I drove right through Rhode Island once. I wish I could remember the name of that nice place right off the highway where I ate supper. I bet you'd know it."

I found out (because Merle bragged about it) that he had simply muscled his way into her lunch booth uninvited. That evening in my old high school track shorts I was doing knee bends in front of Parritt's Diner. I'd called in sick; Merle answered the phone and I told him my V.D. was getting worse.

At last through the red and yellow leaves on the trees I saw Meredith Krantzsky jogging towards me. Saw *her,* and in a weaving line behind her, all whooping and sniffling, the eleven members of the Ladies Art League of Toomis—among them old Mrs. Etherege with a stopwatch (high-stepping as an ibis), and my mother in Bermuda shorts, though she still looped the obligatory cardigan sweater over her shoulders. Crouching in the doorway, I pretended to replace my sneaker until this extraordinary procession trotted by. Later I learned from my mother that the ladies of the Art League "just loved Merry to death" and were all crazy about jogging, to which Merry had introduced them when they'd invited her to Newcomer's Day.

Reports (and there were plenty) that my mother was out every evening jogging through the streets of

Toomis with a throng of elderly female marathoners hit my father like a karate chop. She was also serving broiled fish and raw vegetables for supper, and constantly talking about things like biomechanics. Dad told her succinctly, "You've gone nuts, Hattie."

"Then lucky my jogging coach is a mental health expert," replied my mother from the floor where she was doing sit-ups, her feet in their Adidas stuck under the settee.

"And I don't like the sound of that girl's name. Meredith Krantzsky. You know what kind of name that is? Krantzsky? A you-know-what, I bet. And she works in a nuthouse, doesn't she? Some kind of Left Wing nut, I bet."

I asked a question then. "If you don't like the nut house, why'd you put Grandma in there?"

"You're out of line, Mister." He talked as if he thought we were in a western movie.

"I think I'm going to ask Miss Krantzsky to marry me."

"Oh Blake! I love her to death." My mother looked me over. "I'm sure she'll tell you to eat less and get more exercise."

"Marry her and you're fired," my dad promised.

My curtain line I gave skipping backwards. "Hey, you better tell old Merle Longfielder she could be a you-know-what. Because he's after her, too."

Three weeks had now passed since my first sight of my fiancée, and not only were we not engaged, we had never sat down together. But we ran. November flared the trees the bright color of Merry's hair. Indian summer did its best for me, holding back the chill, keeping the evenings crisp and slow. Good jogging weather. I trained, for love, like a fiend. I went on my mother's diet. Whenever Merry wasn't running with the Art League, she and I jogged in the twilight. We exchanged life stories along the way. Her college really had bred all those radical subversives my father itched to pistol-whip. Her version of a Betsy Creedmoor had been a hippie flautist named Matthew who took a charter pilgrimage to Katmandu, where he was arrested for smuggling mescaline. She played chess.

We ran out towards the Hospital where we saw my grandmother and Mrs. Etherege trotting about the grounds as they discussed price hikes they planned to spring on their Appalachian gift galleries. The four of us crossed paths. I said to my grandmother, "What's your advice?"

"Marry this one," she told me.

Merry laughed. I raced to heaven.

That Saturday Merle Longfielder and I walked to Parritt's Diner together for lunch. Inside, he twisted my bicep with his horrible hand. "Now hey! Isn't that that girl from New Hampshire over there? What was her name? Merry? Been saving her for a rainy day. Watch this and learn something, boy."

"Forget it. I don't want you near that girl. Now or ever." I shoved him back. "I catch you around her, I'll shove your jaw up into that cavity where your brain's supposed to be."

Merle stared at me as if I had just stepped out of a UFO. He'd bullied me for more than twenty years. First he started to laugh—it was almost a giggle—then it changed to a puffing snort, and then he swung. I ducked under his basketball of a fist and socked him twice in the gut with a lifetime of injustice behind my punch. By the time he stood back up I was at the door in a prance. Just out of his reach I teased him up that long incline on Route 55. But Merle never even made it to the top.

Meredith Krantzsky and I were married in June. Grandma has the extra bedroom. When the baby comes, we'll move to someplace bigger.

Merle was always quoting Joe Namath: "When you win, nothing hurts." He was right. I feel great.

Jill McCorkle

Jill McCorkle now lives in Boston, but she was born in Lumberton, North Carolina, in 1958. She received a B.A. from the University of North Carolina, where she studied with writer Lee Smith, and an M.A. from Hollins College, where she studied with southern literary critic Louis Rubin Jr. McCorkle began her first novel, *The Cheerleader* (1984), while she was still a student at Hollins and completed her second, *July 7th* (1984), before the first was published. As a result, Algonquin Books issued her first two novels simultaneously, which brought her instant acclaim. She is the author of three other novels, including the coming-of-age novel *Ferris Beach* (1990). McCorkle has said that *Tending to Virginia* (1987), a story of three generations of women, is her favorite. Greg Johnson, reviewing her work for the *Atlanta Journal-Constitution,* wrote that McCorkle "has a deft comic touch and is a keen observer of southern manners, in all their complexity and frequent absurdity." These talents are evident in her short stories as well, which have been published in three volumes: *Crash Diet* (1992), *Final Vinyl Days and Other Stories* (1998), and *Creatures of Habit* (2001). McCorkle has taught creative writing at the University of North Carolina and Duke University; she currently teaches at Bennington College and Harvard University.

Carnival Lights

I never slept with Donnie Wilkins like everybody says I did. I could go and straighten it all out, I guess. I could sit down with the phone book and pick through the names of everybody I know, call and give my speech, my explanation about how they've got the wrong idea about me. I would say, "Hey, this is Lori Lawrence, you know Mr. Lawrence who is co-owner of that new grocery store where everything's all natural? I'm his daughter. I just graduated from the high school. I carried a flag in the marching band. I've helped flip the sausage patties at the Kiwanis pancake supper since I was eleven." And then I'd pause because of course they'd know who I was. It isn't like this is some metropolis we live in. There are no more than eight thousand people here, and so once you figure in marriage and friends of friends, it gets real small. People don't even expect the new grocery store to make it, that's how small it is. Then my dad will be out beating the pavements and I'll have to hear that old *this is why we are so proud you're going to college* speech. There were only seventy-five people in my graduating class, and if I hadn't been one of them (like I honestly feared for a while), my parents would've died fourteen hundred times.

Nobody needs to be told who I am. Everybody knows my mama is Sandy Lawrence. She used to be Sandy Leech and, yes, we have heard *all* of those parasite jokes. We made a bunch of them up ourselves. My mother is the little plump woman who always wears clogs and who will fill in and drive a schoolbus if somebody's sick. Otherwise she is a secretary at the courthouse, vital information at her fingertips. We hear things over the dinner table that don't even get in the paper until the next day. Everybody knows she married my dad the same night she graduated from high school because she was afraid he'd be drafted. Everybody *also* knows that I was born exactly—give or take a day or two—nine months later. She says that though this course of action would *not* be good for a girl like me, it was the best thing she could have done in 1972 and she has never regretted her decision. She says I might think the world was so very different eighteen years ago but within these city limits, except for the fashions and music, it was pretty much the same. The Lions Club was selling light bulbs and brooms and the Civitans were selling fruitcakes. Her parents *made* her go to Methodist Youth Fellowship, which is why she had left me to my own free will. She grew up with old parents and once said that she had decided to break that mold and several others; she didn't want us to be afraid to ask her questions and she didn't want us to have to bury her before we got out of high school. Speaking of her old parents, Granddaddy Leech lives with us; you know him, old Herman Leech, who used to grow tobacco and now doesn't know what day it is or who he is.

I've got a little brother, Bill, who is a royal pain. His way of getting on Mama's nerves is to pick on Granddaddy and call him names even though Granddaddy doesn't know the difference. Daddy says this is Bill's way of dealing with the way Granddaddy has changed. At least that's what Daddy said over the holidays in between learning how to pronounce the various kinds of yuppie lettuce he was suddenly responsible for buying and selling.

"People want more than just iceberg," he said every hour or so. Mama said she didn't know why people were suddenly so hepped up on maroon-colored wilted

lettuce and she didn't know how Granddaddy's falling
off could possibly explain why Bill had draped the old
man's head with a woman's nylon hose and Christmas
tinsel. She also wanted to know where Bill got that
nylon hose. He's just two years younger than I am but
you'd never guess it. He looks like he ought to be in
the seventh grade rather than just out of the tenth. I
sure wouldn't go out with him if I were a girl other
than his sister. We look a lot alike—thick curly hair and
compact bodies, eyes too big and sad for the rest of us.
It's the kind of look that goes better on a girl.

People say that for somebody so short, I've got a
large chest and that I should've made cheering squad
and would've if I hadn't had that fight with Bonita
Inman when I was in the tenth grade and she called
my daddy a fruit pusher (though hoping for a break
in the business, he was still just manager at Food Lion
at the time). You can imagine how everybody took it
from there and got to saying fruit pimp, gigolo. They
made awful jokes about bananas and cucumbers. It
was nothing to take sitting down, and I got sent home
with one-day suspension for fighting at the bus stop.
A clump of Bonita's hair was still in my fist when my
father choked up in that old Chevette. The worst part
was that I couldn't tell him *why* I'd socked Bonita in
the face and made her nose bleed down a blouse
which she had broadcasted all day long was brand new
from that new store in the mall where the mannequins
are painted silver and don't have faces. "Tell me what
happened, Lori," my mother said that night. "You can
tell us the truth." My dad was standing there with her,
and I made up some silly story about Bonita calling
me a name so ugly I couldn't repeat it. You just don't
look your father (or the woman who loves him) in the
face and say he's been the butt of penis jokes for two
days running.

I did *not* sleep with Donnie Wilkins even though I
wanted to. He's a nice guy and I'm a nice girl. I mean,

I've only had one boyfriend other than Donnie. I went with Mike Tyler my junior year for one month, the highlight of our relationship being the Sunday nights I exercised my free will and we stood out behind the Methodist church during youth fellowship and kissed. I told him that if he could keep his mouth shut, I'd go with him, otherwise forget it. Ours was a brief relationship which ended with him telling people that he had given me seven hickeys and had undone my shirt to get a feel three times. Of course that wasn't true, only further proof of his inability to keep his trap shut, but still there it was, the beginning of my reputation being sucked down the drain.

Donnie's dad is the school guidance counselor, a tall skinny man who looks like he's made out of Tinkertoys. It was in late November, around the time everybody was taking the SAT, when he told me that I had a lot of natural talent for putting things together and taking them apart. "If you were a boy," he said and looked over at Donnie's mama who assists him at his job, her little half glasses swinging from a chain around her neck, "I'd tell you to go to trade school, become a mechanic." I keep hoping that women's lib will be what follows the all-natural grocery in my hometown, but as of yet, people are still doing the HIS and HER types of things.

Everybody in school made jokes about the Wilkinses being the guidance counselors (her title is Assistant Guidance Counselor). People said that *really* there's just *one* of them and that he/she has many personalities like in that movie *Sybil*. I tried not to think about all that while I looked at them, their button-down shirts the exact same shade of blue.

"I'd like to be an engineer," I offered. "Or an architect." When he talked of my *natural talent* it wasn't like he was telling me some big news I didn't already know. I knew the first time I ever sat down with a can of Lincoln Logs that I had this special *aptitude,* as they say. Lincoln Logs and Legos are why I stayed in the baby-sitting business as long as I did. I have a special aptitude all right. I could look at him and *know* how many cans of Tinkertoys it would take to duplicate his body. Mrs. Wilkins was harder to figure.

"But you're a girl." Mrs. Wilkins inched her chair closer to her husband's and peered down at my test scores. I know what she was really peering at was the front of my notebook where I'd written her son's name in big block letters. I loved Donnie Wilkins and had for a long time. Even when I was kissing Mike behind the church, I was loving Donnie Wilkins. He had finally started loving me just two months before, when we found ourselves sitting together at a football game. The band wasn't performing because the field was so muddy, but we wore our uniforms anyway. They finally called the game on account of rain, and we were about the only people left in the stands, our heads under his denim jacket and leaned in real close. It could have been a toothpaste or breath mint commercial on TV; it was that good.

"You are a girl with a grade point total that falls just a little above class average, and so I suggest you take the clerical courses out at the Technical Institute and see how you fare in a setting of higher learning before committing yourself," Mr. Wilkins said. His "just a little above class average" was a 93 so I knew he was not telling the whole truth. And everybody knew that I would have had an even higher average except I had received an "F" for everything I missed on that day I was suspended two years before. I knew that what The Counselors were really thinking was that someone like me would need financial assistance to go to college and it was just too damn much trouble to fill out the forms.

"You think I should take a course like you took?" I asked Mrs. Wilkins and watched her bristle, her lips as thin as a paper cut. I turned and watched the principal on the other side of the glass partition. Mr. Sinclair was attractive in an odd way, sort of a prehistoric way. When he first moved here last year, the rumors raced that he'd once had a part on a detergent commercial that was filmed in New York, but he announced, in a joking sort of way, in the first assembly that this was not true. (He had only *tried out* for it.) He was married and had three small children. He had been a wrestler in college and it showed. He had a real thick neck and walked with his legs apart. A lot of the girls like Mr. Sinclair's looks, but I much prefer Donnie Wilkins's type, thin and graceful, smart-looking. Mr. Sinclair is what some people might call a jock. If I had to give an opinion I'd say he's all right for his age, which my best friend, Jennifer Morgan, says must be forty or so. At the ball games his wife just sits there quiet as a mouse with children hanging all over her, while he stands and waves his broad hand at the people in the stand like *he* might've made that eighty-yard touchdown instead of Scooter Clark. My dad says that Mr. Sinclair is much too hard on the fruit in the grocery store and oftentimes eats as much as he buys while shopping. To his credit, though, or so my dad says, he's a man's man, an iceberg lettuce man. No flaccid leaves for him.

"I *was* in a clerical position," Mrs. Wilkins said, again with that strained look. "I've gone back to school for two summers now. It is hard work." She smiled a fake smile.

"She's enrolled in a class right now." Mr. Wilkins looked at her and grinned. "She has to go at night and that's hard work. She's a modern woman."

And you just got voted most desirable fat man on the planet, I was thinking and had to look away.

"That's right." Mrs. Wilkins nodded her head modestly, returned his smile and then continued. "You could start out at Tech and whether or not you pursue school after that . . . well, time will tell." She had one of those faces that is easily forgotten, a powdered white face that looks like a ray of sunshine has never shone her way, mousey, plain, all those words you put with little pointed-looking women, waist cinched in *just so*, cheeks sucked in *just so*. I sat there and imagined her to be somebody who washed her hands and couldn't stop.

While The Guidance Counselors sat there and talked about what I should do with my life, I sat there wondering how this pair had ever come to give birth to my Donnie. I was thinking that Mrs. Wilkins probably had tissue *folded* in tiny squares in some hidden compartment of her purse and she handwashed her underwear (she would say panties) but never touched the crotch when checking to see if they were dry. She was the kind of woman who complained about public toilets and hovered her butt over the john like a helicopter and sprayed without any thoughts about who would come in and want to use that commode next. I hate when women do that, too good just to wipe off the seat or even cover it over several times with toilet paper. I made myself laugh while picturing Mrs. Wilkins's mousey little *panties* pulled down around those snow white ankles while she crouched and sprayed the floor of the girls' bathroom, where the walls tell you to go and do things I've never done but have thought about, and the air is thick with cigarette smoke.

"Is that my Donnie's name you've got on your notebook?" Mrs. Wilkins asked. Her eyes matched her beige skirt, shoes, and hair. Mr. Wilkins shifted in his seat, and it hurt me to think of those knobby bones rolling beneath him.

"Peggy," Mr. Wilkins said. "Let's keep this discussion on Miss Lawrence's test performance."

"Very well," she said. "But you ought to know that Donnie will be going off to school next fall."

"I know that," I told her and pushed my chair back from the table. I could look through the glass partition and see everybody milling around in the hall, getting ready to dash through those big double doors with that three o'clock bell. I was supposed to meet Donnie out in front of the school so we could ride in Red Smith's new Jeep Cherokee. "I'm going off to school, too."

"You are?" Mrs. Wilkins asked and scanned my aptitude test again as if she'd overlooked some major fact. "Where are you going and what in?"

"In what, dear." Mr. Wilkins patted her hand and shook his head. Her cheeks flushed for a second but then she came back around to her natural pasty color and was right back in there with Mr. Tinkertoy. Just as the two of them were closing in on me, the bell sounded and I bolted. I started to tell Donnie how weird I thought his folks were, but by the time we were all alone I decided I'd rather kiss him instead. We were in the backseat of the Jeep, his blue-jean jacket around my shoulders. "So what do your parents think about us going together?" I asked right when Red Smith leaned out the door of the Time Out and motioned for us to come inside—it was our turn for the pinball machine. I could tell by the look on Donnie's face that I'd hit a rough spot. "We've been going together two months, one week, and two days, but they act like they've never heard of me."

"I don't know." He shrugged. "They know we're friends but my parents are kind of weird about those things." There was a pause and then he had all his reasons together and started talking real fast. "You know, they're afraid I'll change my mind about going off next year or something so I just don't tell them a whole lot. You can see that, can't you?" I nodded because he had the purest, clearest emerald green eyes I'd ever seen and nice full lips. He had a mature-looking razor stubble, too, particularly up against somebody like Red, who had skin like a baby's butt. I nodded and leaned in close enough to breathe in the scent of his Obsession, which all the boys in my class were wearing if they could scrape up the money to buy some. I was thinking that for excitement his parents probably sat in ramrod fashion and spanked each other's palms with rulers or something. They probably conjugated verbs over the dinner table. She probably had to get his permission to sit her modern mousey self down. He probably had to floss his teeth before she'd kiss him. I was thinking, *Your parents are queer as a three-dollar bill,* but what I said was, "Of course, Donnie. Why, that makes lots of sense. I really like how you smell."

For Christmas I gave Donnie Obsession body shampoo (which my mother thought was a little personal until I explained how it was no different from what she had once known as *soap on a rope*) and a key chain with his initials (my father's suggestion, something about how a man should always have something jingling in his pocket). That, like everything on the planet, reminded Bill of a dirty joke, and he got sent out of the room even though everybody (including Granddaddy) had laughed. Donnie gave me a pen and pencil set (gift choice of The Counselors, I'm sure). But secretly, what we gave each other was a solemn vow that very soon, as soon as we felt comfortable with the idea, we'd go somewhere where we could be all alone and take our clothes off. We didn't make any promises beyond that.

Over the holidays, Bill and I sat up one whole night watching the "Madonna Marathon" on MTV. I was studying the way she moved and took her clothes off. Bill sat there trying to act like he wasn't about to start drooling. Then we both got distracted by circling headlights in the parking lot across the street from our house. For years that lot had been the meeting spot for people fooling around, or so my parents always joked. They never named names but it was obvious they knew some things. "What do you think we did before we could afford a big television and cable?" my dad often asked, and she grinned at him. It was possible she was grinning about something *else* they did which I couldn't bear to think about. It gave me the creeps to imagine my parents in a hot naked embrace, especially now that I was planning my *own* unvirgining.

Bill and I had sat and waited for cars to come before, but this was the first time we'd actually witnessed a meeting. We didn't have any lights turned on other than the TV, so it was easy enough to kneel by the window and watch the two cars pull into spaces side by side. The dark station wagon's engine cut off, lights out, door opened. Bill was breathing too close to me, his breath like nacho Doritos, and he fogged the glass. By the time we stopped shoving each other, the other car had driven off and we had missed seeing who had moved from one car to another. Bill had the bright idea that we'd sneak out to watch the return, but an hour later we both got caught up in Madonna's "Like a Virgin" video, and while we were trying to figure out why those weird-looking guys were wearing and stroking these really gross-out fake boobs while Madonna writhed on the bed, both cars disappeared. "That was a quickie," Bill said knowingly as he stared out into the empty lot. "Poor guy just couldn't keep going."

"What do you know?" I asked, and he turned to face me just as seriously as if I'd asked him to explain condensation. He turned his head to one side and sighed.

"I know more than you know," he finally said and flipped open his wallet to show me a condom packet.

"Yeah, right," I said and examined the packet. "This must have come with the wallet." It said it was a size *large*, but I didn't say anything about that. Everybody I heard talking about condoms (people like Mike Tyler and Rowland Jones) talked about how they *needed* a size large. Yeah, right; like how have people gone all these years without the jumbo size? What boy is going to walk in and say give me a size *small*? I closed the Doritos and put the bag on the table. Madonna was writhing again to "Express Yourself," and I decided not to challenge Bill on his *knowledge* or his size; it was not a good time for me to be swapping stories, not to mention the fact that if he *had* done something, I didn't want to think about it. My head was already getting filled up with enough thoughts without one of Bill dancing the dance.

Vacation ended and Donnie and I still hadn't taken anything off. The Counselors had given him a long speech over the holidays (probably after they saw his body shampoo) about how he was too young for something serious and shouldn't be dating just one person. Everybody at school *knew* we were going steady, but neither of us ever came right out and said it. The only person who knew all about our plan was Jennifer Morgan, and she was sworn to secrecy. I knew what was going on with her, too, and that's what being best friends is all about. You've got the dirt on each other and it holds you tight like glue. Jennifer took the pill and Rowland Jones had put his hand up her bra right there in Chemistry while they were supposed to be washing some beakers they'd burned up real bad. If that's not insurance, there's no such thing.

It was February when Bill started calling Granddaddy "Paw Paw," all the while rapping and dancing around like M. C. Hammer, which drove my mother up the wall. It was right after the doctor said that Granddaddy would never ever be the same. It didn't matter what Bill called him, Granddaddy grinned great big. Paw Paw, Monterey Jack, Homer Simpson, it didn't make a dab bit of difference, except anything other than Granddaddy Leech made Mama bite her lip and turn away. The worse Granddaddy got, the more my parents talked about me going to college, and before I knew it they had me filling out all kinds

of applications and financial aid forms they had ordered themselves. Nothing like a good sharp contrast
between life and death to make people start planning
out their futures. I knew then more than ever that Bill
(yes, Bill) and I were a big hunk of my parents' future.
It shocked me to think that when my mother was my
very age, she and my dad were talking about their
future together. It was hard to believe that such planning went into me and Bill and all those grocery
store jobs.

Meanwhile Donnie said that he was tired of waiting
for us to be together. He said if something didn't happen soon he'd die. My mother had once told me that
there were lots of stories boys would tell to get what
they wanted: explosions, blindness, wild-seed sowing,
but somehow Donnie's reasons sounded real. There
had been many nights when we could have easily kept
right on going (he sure wanted to), but I just didn't
want my first memory to be of a backseat.

Then we heard the carnival was coming to town,
and we decided *that* was our perfect time. Everybody
got to stay out late those nights since it was a rare
event to have so much entertainment in town. The
carnival came on a Wednesday afternoon, and by
Thursday morning, they were already all set up in the
big vacant lot across from the shopping center. It was
what my daddy called a *snap-to* carnival. He said he'd
stood right there in the grocery window and watched
it all appear out of nowhere. On Friday night the carnival was going to kick off with The Retching
Wretches, a local band whose lead singer was a girl
who had once been our babysitter. Donnie and I had
planned to meet all of our friends at the band's performance and then slip off and go for a drive; he said he
had the perfect place for us to go. I knew it was the
Royal Villa Inn out on Highway 301 (he had talked
to Rowland Jones, who told Jennifer since they had
been there before themselves), but I didn't let on that

I knew. I had a black lace bra and underwear hidden in an empty box of Cheerios in my school locker.

"Those rides can't be safe," Mama said and wheeled Monterey Jack up to the table. This was on Friday morning, right after she'd informed us that we couldn't go to the carnival that night. "It's Granddaddy's birthday," she said and bent to kiss Granddaddy's cheek. "We decided late last night to do something special, have a few of the old neighbors in."

"But the band is playing," Bill said.

"You can go tomorrow night," she said.

"*Old* neighbors is right." Daddy patted Granddaddy's shoulder. He was ignoring our pleas. "Right, Pops?" Granddaddy just grinned great big and then focused on Bill, studied him as if he'd never seen him before. I could tell it made Bill uneasy. He had always been Granddaddy's favorite, and now the old man was looking at him like he had no earthly idea who he was. It was like our grandfather had already died and we were left with this big doll baby to remind us that he'd once been a part of our lives. It was getting hard for me to look at him, and the thought of a whole roomful of old people gave me the creeps.

Bill finally got tired of arguing about going to the carnival and balanced a spoon on Granddaddy's head. I probably would have laughed, but I was upset about having to tell Donnie I couldn't make our date. What if he thought I didn't *want* to take my clothes off with him? What if he thought I was having second thoughts? What if he couldn't get his parents' car a second night, how would we get to the Royal Villa Inn? Where was I going to hide my fancy underwear at home so that I'd have it for *Saturday* night?

I wrote Donnie a quick note while Bill and Jennifer and I waited for the school bus. I made it real mushy so he would believe what was the truth. Then I said that my grandfather, who was old and would probably

die before too long (Bill had suggested I say Granddaddy was circling the drain), was having a birthday
party and I had to be there. As wracked with grief as
I was (Jennifer's suggestion), I couldn't keep our date.
I said that I longed for our moment together, the one
we had planned, the one that filled my every dream
waking and sleeping. I said, "But it'll be worth the
wait! It'll be Grrrrreat, you big bad Tiger" (also Jennifer's suggestion—she was very good at that kind of
letter). He took it all real well, responding with a note
wedged up in the vent slots of my locker that simply
said "Tomorrow is the Day!" It was Jennifer's mission
(if she could keep some sense about her while on a
date with Rowland Jones) to keep an eye on Donnie
just in case somebody decided to move in on my turf.

Granddaddy and his guests didn't know it was his
birthday, but we celebrated all the same. Daddy
brought home a bag of cherry tomatoes and made
them look like little roses; he hollowed out a red cab-
bage and filled it with dip. It was all beautiful and
everybody told him so, but all Granddaddy and his
friends ate were the little pastel butter mints and the
Cheetos that left their hands and mouths bright orange. Mama said that such a birthday celebration is
like a funeral, a ritual for the living, so you'll feel
like you've done the best you could. Bill sang *Happy
Birthday, dear Paw Paw* and when Mama gave him a
dirty look changed his song to *Happy Birthday, dear
Burrhead*. Granddaddy grinned great big and then
cried, his mouth twisting silently. By nine Granddaddy
was tucked in bed and fast asleep.

While my parents shuttled all the guests back where
they'd come from, I cleaned the kitchen. Bill actually
offered to help me, balancing his niceness by calling
me *asshole*. More and more, Bill was trying to get on
my good side. He never would've admitted it, but he
was terrified of girls. He knew that if he didn't hurry

up and grow taller or get some facial or underarm hair, that he was in for a bumpy ride. He had a crush on Tanya Taylor, who was my fellow flag girl, and more than ever, he needed me.

Several times since the "Madonna Marathon," Bill and I had seen those same two cars pull up and park, the station wagon left behind while the other drove off down that dark road that led to Hermit's Crossing. Bill told me a lot of high school people went there, too. He waited for me to say something, and the way he looked at me it was almost like he knew about my plans. Bill said some older boys told him that you could find *things* out there: underwear and stockings and *things* you wouldn't want to touch. I had only seen Hermit's Crossing in the daylight. All it was was a little wooden bridge crossing a stream, but there were lots of stories about how it was haunted.

It was after ten when my parents got home and we all went to bed. I knew that Bill was probably already up and sneaking back in to watch MTV or to call one of those 900 numbers that had mysteriously appeared on our phone bill the month before. "What is this?" my mother had asked and handed the number to my dad. I don't know if she was accusing him or not. She had already called the number to see who answered and had gotten quite a shock. Then they called back for *him* to hear. "Good grief," he said. "You thought I'd called that?" They never even asked Bill about it, just assumed aloud that some *sordid* person had charged his *filth* to our number. Still, I did notice that every night before going to bed my mother adjusted the phone on the table just so; it seemed to me that it was positioned on the phone book in such a way that she'd know if it had been touched. "What kind of young girl takes such a job?" my mother had whispered to my father when she thought I wasn't paying attention. "And I wonder," she continued, "is she reading what she says or making it up right off the

top of her head?" I didn't hear what he said to her
but it was one of those times I wished I hadn't seen.
She just sort of smiled and turned red. She pushed his
arm and said, "Oh really, Jack," and then they kissed
that slow close way that made me feel like I didn't
belong on this earth. It seemed to me that every time
she touched the phone book it was a signal for him
to give her that look.

I lay there that night half waiting to hear Bill dial-
ing. I was trying to picture myself in the act with Donnie, but I kept picturing my parents or the weird guys
from the Madonna video instead. It was like I was
watching a scrambled channel and I couldn't keep it
focused on just me and Donnie. I must have been
lying there for about a half hour when I heard a car
pass and then the engine cut. I tiptoed out into the
living room, expecting to see Bill perched in front of
the window, binoculars up to his eyes, but he had
fallen asleep. The figures on MTV were moving
around in silence. The phone was exactly the same on
the table. I knelt just as the other car drove off. I
started to wake him but then I changed my mind. I
needed some time to myself to think through things.
I'm not one to ever go creeping around at night, so
I'm not quite sure what came over me. It was like I
had a sudden urge to sneak out. The next thing I
knew I had my jacket on and was tiptoeing through
the kitchen.

Quietly, I stepped out the back door and crept
through the side yard, following the edge of the parking lot so that I was always near some high shrubs. I
sat watching the lot for what seemed like an hour. It
was quiet out there, too chilly for any frogs or crickets
to be calling. The station wagon was a Camry, black
or dark blue or burgundy. (My dad said we were about
the only people in town without a car that was made
in Japan.) I tiptoed around, pressing my face against
the windows, but I couldn't see anything. I was about
to squat down and try to read the license number,

when I saw headlights coming down Hermit's Crossing Road. My whole life I'd heard those stories about Hermit's Crossing and how that's where witches had been killed hundreds of years before. They said if you went and stood in front of the huge live oaks you'd hear the creaking of the ropes as they hung, hear the crackling of the fire as they burned. With a rush of gooseflesh I crouched down in the bushes and held my breath. I waited, barely breathing, while the other car pulled up beside the wagon. I couldn't see the driver at all. It was a Honda, but the color was difficult to figure in that light: white, yellow, pale blue. I felt my chest tighten like I might have to scream or laugh or something. I was about to run when the door on the passenger side opened and then I saw him. Mr. Sinclair, just as big and thick-necked as ever. "See ya, babe," he said. Then he clucked his tongue and said, "Mmmmm, mmmmm, mmmmm."

I felt all the blood pumping to my head, and every muscle in my body tensed. He stood there in the dark empty parking lot and watched the Honda pull away, his keys jingling in his hand. The car rolled right by me, the tires kicking up sand. There was a piece of twine hanging out of the trunk like maybe it had been tied down or something, and then I realized that I had studied the twine, its ends painted fluorescent yellow, and had missed my chance to read the license. All I caught was a "booster club" bumper sticker, which everybody in town had bought to support the high school athletic department. It seemed like hours before Mr. Sinclair got in his own car and cranked the engine, the roar vibrating across the empty lot. I sat back and took a deep breath, the fumes from the Camry still in the air. My knees were shaking like they never had before, like rubber, like jelly. I didn't feel normal until I got inside and collapsed on Bill's pallet on the living room floor. "Bill." I shook him and he rolled towards me, let out a deep sigh. I shook him again but he shrugged me away. It took a good ten minutes before he was really awake, and in that time, I decided that I had some leverage and ought to use it. I told Bill everything I'd seen except who it was. He was begging. He was ready to do my household chores for a week, ready to pay me ten dollars.

"What kind of car was it?" he asked.

"A station wagon."

"The other car." He was getting impatient.

"A Honda."

"Oh, great." He sat up and pulled a bag of Doritos out from under the sofa. "Everybody drives a Honda. Was it an Accord or a Civic?"

"What do I look like, a car dealer?" I asked. I was enjoying myself. After all the times he had taped mine and Jennifer's conversations or tried to spy on me and Donnie, I had him where I wanted him.

"I'll just go out there myself," he finally said, tired of begging. "I'll go tomorrow night and every night until they come back." He wanted me to tell the end again, the part about *mmmmm mmmmm mmmmm*.

"Who said that?" he asked quickly, thinking he could trick me into saying, and we both fell out laughing. I had never felt so close to Bill, and I almost reconsidered and told him that it was Mr. Sinclair. There was even a part of me that wanted to tell him about mine and Donnie's plan, how we were in love and ready to make a move, *show* how we loved each other, but I let the moment pass. Bill seemed so vulnerable at night stripped down to a T-shirt and gym shorts, spots of Clearasil on his chin and forehead, but come morning he would be right back to his tricks. As much as we *wanted* to trust each other, we just couldn't. I closed my eyes and tried to conjure Donnie, but all I could see was Mr. Sinclair's thick neck and back moving up and down in a backseat, some unknown *babe* beneath him.

Donnie picked me up in his dad's new Chrysler at six the next night. My face was so flushed with nervousness that Mama kept asking if I was sick and pressing her hand up against my forehead. Bill had already left to go to the carnival with some boys his age, but I knew that he was planning to set up camp in the parking lot later that night. All day long he had talked about it, and all day long I was torn between the sick feeling I had thinking about Mr. Sinclair saying "Mmmmm mmmmm mmmmm" and the nervousness I felt when I put on that lace bra and underwear. I was terrified that my mother would see the lacy outline under my sweater.

"Have fun, kids!" Mama called as Donnie and I got in the car. My dad had gone to rent a movie, which is what they always did (or said they did) when Bill and I were both out. They rented movies we'd never heard of with stars who had either died or gotten real old and fat. I breathed a sigh of relief as I leaned into the plush leather seat. I had made it over the first hurdle. Donnie was all shaved and smelling of Obsession. I watched the key chain I'd given him dangle from the ignition as we drove to Shoney's. We were both nervous. Donnie asked for a booth by the window so we could look out at the carnival, where all the lights were coming on, the Ferris wheel moving in a circle as jumpy as our conversation. Donnie got the fried chicken plate and I got the salad bar. We started to have dessert but then passed as we watched the Bullet in the distance, the passenger cars on either end spinning and twisting. Everybody had talked about the Bullet at school. Dares had been made about who could ride it the most times without getting sick. Scooter Clark had talked about how, the year before, he and Andy Hamilton had found all kinds of money that had flown from pockets to the ground around the ride.

We walked from Shoney's, since it was hard to find a parking spot. Donnie grabbed my hand, and his felt almost as cold and clammy as my own. I kept waiting for him to mention our plans, but instead he kept talking about how pretty the moon was coming up in the distance and was I up for riding the Bullet and did I really believe that there was any such thing as a miniature horse only fourteen inches high. "No, I don't believe it," I said just as we were passing the trailer that said there *was* a fourteen-inch horse.

"What about The Headless Woman?" he asked. We stopped and stood in front of the trailer, the voice on the loudspeaker inviting us to come in and see this medical miracle. The sloppy letters on the side of the trailer said she had been decapitated in a car accident but was still living. Donnie was waiting for me to say whether or not I wanted to go. I shook my head no and we continued, past the Led Zeppelin Laser Light Show (Jennifer had said that it was the best part of the carnival), past the Sky Diver, past the Haunted House where Andy Hamilton was working as a were-wolf. He perched up on the roof and jumped down on each cart as it came out, couples screaming bloody murder at the sight of his hairy mask. We stood there and watched him work for a while. It was so funny we started to loosen up with each other. I was feeling good, warm and happy and almost ready to go some-where and take my clothes off, when Donnie said that he had forgotten something important. I didn't have to be a rocket scientist to know what that *something* was, and the thought of our rendezvous leading to *that* gave me a little shock. All night I had wanted to tell him about Mr. Sinclair but was waiting until the ride home when we'd already done what we were going to do. I didn't want him to think I was making sug-gestions.

I was relieved to find that the *something* I was think-ing (why would he keep them at home anyway?) was not what he meant. His something was that he was supposed to go over and speak to his parents, who had volunteered to oversee the high school booths. "Let's go on and get it over with," he said and pulled me away just as Andy jumped down on top of a middle-aged couple. The man pulled back his fist and was about to sock Andy, but the ticket taker stepped in to explain it was part of the ride.

The high school booths were at the far edge of the parking lot under a big tent that had been donated by Price Funeral Home. We passed by the shop projects and I saw Bill's TV table he had worked on so long. He had said it was a present for Granddaddy, and it made me sad to see it sitting there holding lamps made from Gallo wine jugs. I had wanted to take shop but everybody talked me out of it; I took Latin like a *bona puella* instead, though to hear The Counselors talk I had no business saddling myself with such collegiate courses. And speaking of Ms. *Femina Consilium,* there she was in all of her mousey glory. I saw her take me in from head to toe, and I wished she *could* see my lacy black bra through my sweater, complete with its little foam push-ups. I would have liked to shock her out of ramrod position. Instead I smiled politely and said nothing while Donnie bought some toll house cookies in a Baggie.

"Where's Dad?" Donnie asked.

"Oh, poor man," she said. "He just wasn't feeling well, said that all these lights and things spinning had made him feel sick, so I told him to go on home and rest."

"Oh." Donnie hesitated as if she had him under some kind of spell. "Well, how will you get home?"

"I've got the car," she said. "Your dad got a ride home. Oh, go on now, shoo." She waved her hand, smiling at Donnie and never once looking at me. "Have fun," she said. "Don't stay out too late. I have to close the booth but Dad will be home all night."

"Do you want to swap cars?" Donnie asked, forehead wrinkled.

"No, I'm fine." She was holding the cash box up to her chest like I might be aching to steal it. "Oh, but, Donnie," she called, "if you will, do bring me my seat cushion from the trunk. It's going to be a long night."

She handed him the key, and that's when I saw her look at my breasts. "I'm right beside that Dumpster behind the drugstore."

"Be right back," he called and then pulled me towards the parking lot. "As soon as we take her the cushion, we can go. I'm sorry I've been so quiet, but you know, I knew we had to come over here and I just wanted everything else out of the way." I felt his arm circle around my waist, his hand finding its way up the side of my sweater. "I can't wait," he whispered as we walked in and out of rows of cars. I was about to ask him where we were going when he grabbed me and kissed me like he never had before, my back thrown up against that filthy old Dumpster. I was out of breath and my heart was pounding when he stopped and opened the trunk. He was telling me how as long as he could remember his dad always got sick at things like this and left his mom to fend for herself. He said his mother had sat on a cushion ever since she had an accident and hurt her back. I heard myself asking what kind of accident, but I wasn't really thinking about his answer. I was thinking about that piece of twine dangling from the trunk, its ends flecked with yellow. I knew before looking down at the bumper the exact placement of the booster club sticker. I thought of her then, thin white body beneath Mr. Sinclair, her hands on his broad muscular back, her heart beating like mad. I imagined her planning and scheming, hiding underwear in strange places just like I'd done. Maybe when she kissed her husband it was like kissing Mike Tyler. Maybe she was waiting for the right time to come along when she'd do something. I watched the Ferris wheel circling and circling while Donnie ran the cushion over to his mother, and I felt like I might throw up myself. She looked over as Donnie was walking back to me and she lifted her hand; then she looked over at the shop booth where there was an engine recently reassembled by three guys in my class. Mr. Sinclair was there with his big foot propped up on the table. He was talking to some men but the whole time he was looking at her.

"Let's go," Donnie said suddenly, and I told him that we had to ride at least one ride so that I could tell my parents all about it without lying. He looked reluctant, his mind counting off every second it would take to drive out to the Royal Villa Inn, which was twenty miles away. Finally he gave in and bought two tickets for the Ferris wheel. When we stopped at the very top, our cart rocking back and forth, I could see Mr. Sinclair had made his way over and now was sitting right beside Donnie's mother.

"What was it you wanted to tell me?" Donnie asked. "You said you knew something funny."

"Well, not that I know something," I said and tried to force my brain to think a little faster while I watched Mrs. Wilkins begin to pack up her baked goods like she might be closing shop. It was at that moment I thought of Bill and how he was going to be out there in the parking lot, waiting. All I could think was that if the story got out it would all be my fault. Donnie would never forgive me, not to mention stop loving me. Then we would never have that perfect moment to take our clothes off.

"It's just an idea is all," I said. And then I told him that I had a fantasy of being with him in the *car,* that I'd fought it by saying again and again how cheap and meaningless I thought it was, but that really it was what I wanted more than anything. I said my biggest fantasy was being parked in that lot right behind my very own house. I knew as soon as the words left my mouth that I had ruined our night, that there was no way I'd be showing off my underwear; he moved his arm from around my shoulder and just sat there staring at me. We were stuck at the top again, and now his mother was standing with her purse over her shoulder. I couldn't believe he wasn't watching her, noticing something.

"It's pretty strange," he said. "But okay. I've heard

girls have a lot of ideas about how the first time—"
His sentence was cut short when the machine bolted
and lurched forward, dropping us down and then lifting us back up. Scooter Clark was just a blur below
as he bent to pick up something beneath the Bullet.
When our cart was stopped on the ramp, our safety
bar lifted, Donnie kissed me full on the mouth, then
grabbed my hand and pulled me off towards Shoney's.
He moved faster and faster until I had to run to keep
up with him. I would have been excited out of my
mind if all this other hadn't been going on. We passed
Jennifer, who smiled and gave me the thumbs-up sign
and then turned to whisper something to Rowland and
Mike Tyler, who was standing close by. The story was
starting; like a match head struck against a rough surface, it had leapt to life and now would begin spread-
ing in and among our classmates. I could almost see
it happening, a trail of words cutting through all the
people, reaching all the ears except those of my
brother, who would already be out in the parking
lot, waiting.

Donnie was out of breath when we got to the car,
and just kept grinning at me in that way that made
my heart almost stop. He pulled me over beside him,
his arm around my shoulder while he drove with his
left hand. When we passed by my house, I could see
Granddaddy sitting in the living room, as motionless
as the lamp beside him. Donnie pulled into the far
end of the lot, parked, and leaned over to kiss me.

"Nervous?" he asked when he opened his eyes to
find me staring right back. "You're acting kind of
weird."

"I am?" I asked, and he nodded, laughed.

"But that's okay," he whispered into my neck, his
breath warm on my skin as he fumbled with the buttons on my sweater. I saw the bushes move, and I
knew it was Bill and his friends. They were smoking
cigarettes; I could see the flare of matches and the

tiny red glows marking where they huddled in the shrubbery. Donnie's mouth covered mine, and I quickly pushed him away and moved to my side of the seat. "Can't we talk a little first?" I asked.

"Sure." He tapped his finger on the steering wheel, breathed in and out in puffs. It seemed the longer we were quiet, the more rapid those puffs became. Once I saw Bill peek in the window and then squat quickly; I was going to break his neck. I asked Donnie about his plans to go to Yale. How far was it to Connecticut anyway? Would he be taking a lot of courses? Did he think we'd date other people or keep on going together? How much snow would he see over the winter? Did he think he'd come home often or just on the major holidays? What did he think about the new Madonna video? Did he think his mama liked me or not? He answered everything politely but his answers were getting shorter and shorter, the last one a simple *yes*.

"Why didn't you just say you didn't want to go through with our plan?" he finally asked. I turned to face him and the moment I did, headlights circled and crossed his face. It was the Honda, lights cut as it moved slowly to the side of the lot opposite ours. It was *her*. I imagined how it all worked: Mr. Wilkins goes home and suddenly the evening is convenient after all. She makes a phone call. They are shorthanded at the booths. Who can possibly come now that poor Mr. Wilkins is sick? Poor Mrs. Sinclair can't come. She can't get a baby-sitter on such short notice. Mr. Sinclair will just have to do it. And he says, "Aw, honey, I don't want to go. I have to deal with those crappy people all week long." But it's his duty and in no time there he is meeting his lover in the parking lot behind my house. Does he *really* like her or is he telling stories about how he'll die if they don't meet? Does he catch her in the school hallways and whisper *tonight is the night?*

Bill and his friends had put out their cigarettes and I watched the shrubs move slightly as if by the wind, as the troop made its way around the lot.

"I'm sorry," I said to Donnie.

"So now what happens?" He was watching the car. I was watching Bill getting closer and closer.

"I don't know." I was too scared to cry. My mind was working so fast in so many directions that it was like it stopped functioning, and when I saw Mr. Sinclair's headlights turning into the lot, I jumped out and began running toward the shrubs where Bill was hidden. I still don't know why I felt the need to keep everybody from knowing what they were up to, but I did. It seems like I was thinking about the way my parents looked at each other when they didn't know I was looking, a look that let me know they wanted to be together.

"What are you doing hiding in those bushes?" I kept yelling. "Can't a couple get a little privacy?" I ran right up beside Donnie's mama's window so that I blocked the sight of her, and immediately she cranked her car and screeched backwards. I turned and there was a slow second when I knew we were looking at each other, and then she was gone, almost sideswiping Mr. Sinclair along the way.

"Why'd you do that?" Bill stepped from the bushes, somehow looking older now that he had a group following him. "You messed it all up. They'll never come back now."

I heard a car door slam and then Donnie was walking across the parking lot. I looked to see if my parents were in the window but I couldn't tell. Bill turned and looked at me then. "What are you doing out here?"

"Same as you," I said, the words coming to me quickly. "We're out here spying."

"Yeah, right. That's why you scared them off." Bill was staring first at Donnie and then at my unbuttoned sweater that was hanging off one shoulder. My black lacy bra was showing. His friends were laughing, ready to spread the word. "What are you *really* doing?" Bill asked, his face red, from embarrassment or anger I wasn't sure.

"What do you think?" I asked, the words coming to me quickly. I turned and rubbed my hand up and down Donnie's chest, kissed him on the mouth. My legs were shaking like crazy. "So why don't you leave?" I looked at Bill the way I always looked at him, like he was scum and not worth my breath. "Go on."

"Why?"

"Because you're a jerk," I said, "and you're in our way." There was a brief flicker of feeling on his face, a hurt look that maybe I wouldn't have even noticed if we hadn't felt so close the night before. Now he had no choice but to get me back, to go along with his friends and spread some rumors, or at least to act like he had. "Donnie and I want to be alone . . ." I let my voice trail off with a lilt that implied a lot. Might as well let Donnie's reputation get some mileage out of it. It would be good for him. Boys would elbow him and nod knowingly. His mother would stare at him every morning and be left to wonder how much he knew and what we really did. It would keep her squirming for a long while.

My reputation was dirt by Monday morning, and even though Donnie still walked me to my classes we both knew things would never be the same. After all that teasing in front of Bill and his friends, I had gone back to the car and cried. I don't mean polite little sniffles either. I mean out-and-out sobs, the kind that leave you with red splotches all over and a stuffed-up head. Donnie said he didn't understand me at all. That he didn't think he could take much more of my leading him on. He said that if I was trying to *hook* him permanently, then we weren't thinking the same way. "I was," I told him. "I was trying to get it so you'd marry me." I thought later *that* was a dumb thing to

have said; I mean, if he'd repeated *that* I wouldn't
have had a date for the next century. But he didn't.
As a matter of fact, he didn't say anything at all. Noth-
ing. He made no effort to correct the rumors that we
had *done it* five times in the back of his daddy's
Chrysler, once under an old live oak at Hermit's
Crossing, and yet another time in the Led Zeppelin
Laser Light Show. Be real.

By the time graduation came around and I had
spent two months as a *bona puella* with no dates at
all, things died down a little. I spent most of my time
with Bill, the two of us playing cards or talking while
Granddaddy stared at us. There were so many nights
when I almost told Bill the whole story, but I couldn't
risk it. By then (despite her husband's differing opinion) Mrs. Wilkins had gone out of her way to show
me all kinds of financial aid forms *just in case you
might be interested, a smart young woman such as
yourself.* We never *said* anything about what I knew
but, as they say, a picture paints a thousand words
and we were doing it all with our eyes. Mr. Wilkins
watched her every move like he was waiting for a
mistake. But the worst part of it all was the way my
parents couldn't look me full in the face for a while.

Sometimes when I think about it all, I wish that I
had never crept out that night while Bill was sleeping.
Then I would've just gone on about my business, to
the carnival and then out to the Royal Villa Inn,
where I would've taken my clothes off. Donnie
would've gone off to school and I would've stayed at
home—not a virgin—and worked somewhere like
Pick-a-Chick, ending my day with bunions and a polyester uniform that smelled of grease. I would have
eventually gotten around to going to Tech; I would
have had to take the long route. Would it have been
worth it, that one thrilling moment? Sometimes I think
maybe it would've because I loved Donnie Wilkins

like I'd never loved anybody. Sometimes I still think about kissing him and imagine myself in black lingerie writhing on a bed like Madonna.

Instead, I was called into The Counselors' office one day late in the spring to be told that I had a full scholarship to the state university. "It was very lucky that there was an open spot this late in the year; I'm sure you'll do very, very well," Mrs. Wilkins said and handed me a letter that spelled it all out.

I wanted to say "mmmmm mmmmm mmmmm," as I looked over the letter but instead I said "thank you." Mr. Wilkins was standing there in all his Tinker-toy glory, acting like he was the one who had gotten it for me.

"Thank *you,*" she said, and it was clear that she meant it. It was the first time she ever looked me square in the eye and smiled.

On graduation night, my scholarship and attendance to State were announced along with all the others (including Donnie's acceptance to Yale), and when I walked across the stage to get my diploma from Mr. Sinclair it seemed he held my hand a little longer and a little tighter than he had everyone else's. It was like a silent pact, this scholarship of mine. It was as binding as the one Donnie and I had made to each other even though we'd never seen it through. I looked up at the rows of seats in the auditorium until I found my parents and Bill, all three of them waving at me. I walked under those bright lights while Mr. Sinclair told the whole auditorium that I planned to go to State and become an architect. I figure I've got the rest of my life to fall in love and take my clothes off for a man, but I don't have so long to be my parents' future. I mean, someday they're going to be sitting there like Monterey Jack, staring at me with a blank empty look, and I want to know that I made at least one decision that was right.

PART IV

—

*Challenging
Southern
Traditions*

William Faulkner

William Faulkner was born in 1897 in New Albany, Mississippi, and died in 1962. His great-grandfather, who bears some resemblance to Colonel Sartoris in the story that follows, built railroads, served in the Confederate Army, and wrote a novel called *The White Rose of Memphis* (1880). William Faulkner worked a variety of jobs from postmaster to poet before he took writer Sherwood Anderson's advice and began to write fiction about the region where he grew up. Faulkner created a fictional county, Yoknapatawpha, with a county seat he called Jefferson, which was based on his hometown of Oxford, Mississippi. Returning to Oxford after a year in New Orleans, Faulkner began a period of incredible creativity, during which he wrote his most highly praised work: *Sartoris* (1929, an abridged version of *Flags in the Dust*, 1973), *The Sound and the Fury* (1929), *As I Lay Dying* (1930), *Sanctuary* (1931), *Light in August* (1932), *Absalom, Absalom!* (1936), *The Unvanquished* (1938), *The Hamlet* (1940), and *Go Down, Moses and Other Stories* (1942). More concerned with writing the way he wanted than with writing books that would sell, Faulkner often found himself short of cash. During these times he went to Hollywood to write screenplays for Metro-Goldwyn-Mayer and for Warner Brothers. Elected to the National Institute of Arts and Letters and the American Academy of Arts and Letters, Faulkner is the most honored writer in the United States. He won several O. Henry awards for his stories, two National Book Awards, the Pulitzer Prize, and the Nobel Prize for Literature. During the last years of his life, he was a writer-in-residence at the University of Virginia. The selection from *The Unvanquished* that follows points up several of his key themes: the problem of the past, the young boy's initiation into manhood, the clash between the individual and the community, and the sins of parents being visited on children. The selection also reveals his idiosyncratic style—convoluted sentences, repetition of words, minimal punctuation, and vague pronoun references. Helen Swink has suggested that his sentences, which often withhold meaning from readers, "intensify the emotional experience," and Michael Millgate has observed that they allow Faulkner "to hold a single moment in suspension while its full complexity is explored."

"An Odor of Verbena" is the last section in Faulkner's novel *The Unvanquished* (1938). The narrator, Bayard Sartoris, is a law student at the University of Mississippi and a member of an old family in Jefferson, Mississippi. The Civil War has been over for seven years when his father, Colonel Sartoris, is killed by his business partner, B. J. Redmond. Bayard is under great pressure from the community, from his young stepmother, Drusilla, from his servant Ringo, and from members of his father's Confederate troop to avenge his death. During the war, Bayard's grandmother was killed by a man named Grumby, and Bayard and Ringo found and killed him. But this killing and the brutality of war, so very different from his genteel upbringing, have had a traumatic effect on Bayard.

An Odor of Verbena

1

It was just after supper. I had just opened my *Coke* on the table beneath the lamp; I heard Professor Wilkins' feet in the hall and then the instant of silence as he put his hand to the door knob, and I should have known. People talk glibly of presentiment, but I had none. I heard his feet on the stairs and then in the hall approaching and there was nothing in the feet because although I had lived in his house for three college years now and although both he and Mrs. Wilkins called me Bayard in the house, he would no more have entered my room without knocking than I would have entered his—or hers. Then he flung the door violently inward against the doorstop with one of those gestures with or by which an almost painfully unflagging preceptory of youth ultimately aberrates, and stood there saying, "Bayard. Bayard, my son, my dear son."

I should have known; I should have been prepared. Or maybe I was prepared because I remember how I closed the book carefully, even marking the place, before I rose. He (Professor Wilkins) was doing something, bustling at something; it was my hat and cloak which he handed me and which I took although I would not need the cloak, unless even then I was thinking (although it was October, the equinox had not occurred) that the rains and the cool weather would arrive before I should see this room again and

so I would need the cloak anyway to return to it if I
returned, thinking "God, if he had only done this last
night, flung that door crashing and bouncing against
the stop last night without knocking so I could have
gotten there before it happened, been there when it
did, beside him on whatever spot, wherever it was that
he would have to fall and lie in the dust and dirt."

"Your boy is downstairs in the kitchen," he said. It
was not until years later that he told me (someone
did; it must have been Judge Wilkins) how Ringo had
apparently flung the cook aside and come on into the
house and into the library where he and Mrs. Wilkins
were sitting and said without preamble and already
turning to withdraw: "They shot Colonel Sartoris this
morning. Tell him I be waiting in the kitchen" and
was gone before either of them could move. "He has
ridden forty miles yet he refuses to eat anything." We
were moving toward the door now—the door on my
side of which I had lived for three years now with
what I knew, what I knew now I must have believed
and expected, yet beyond which I had heard the approaching feet yet heard nothing in the feet. "If there
was just anything I could do."

"Yes, sir," I said. "A fresh horse for my boy. He
will want to go back with me."

"By all means take mine—Mrs. Wilkins'," he cried.
His tone was no different yet he did cry it and I suppose that at the same moment we both realised that
was funny—a short-legged deep-barreled mare who
looked exactly like a spinster music teacher, which
Mrs. Wilkins drove to a basket phaeton—which was
good for me, like being doused with a pail of cold
water would have been good for me.

"Thank you, sir," I said. "We won't need it. I will
get a fresh horse for him at the livery stable when I
get my mare." Good for me, because even before I
finished speaking I knew that would not be necessary
either, that Ringo would have stopped at the livery
stable before he came out to the college and attended

to that and that the fresh horse for him and my mare
both would be saddled and waiting now at the side
fence and we would not have to go through Oxford
at all. Loosh would not have thought of that if he had
come for me, he would have come straight to the college, the Professor Wilkins', and told his news and
then sat down and let me take charge from then on.
But not Ringo.

He followed me from the room. From now until
Ringo and I rode away into the hot thick dusty darkness quick and strained for the overdue equinox like
a laboring delayed woman, he would be somewhere
either just beside me or just behind me and I never
to know exactly nor care which. He was trying to find
the words with which to offer me his pistol too. I
could almost hear him: "Ah, this unhappy land, not
ten years recovered from the fever yet still men must
kill one another, still we must pay Cain's price in his
own coin." But he did not actually say it. He just
followed me, somewhere beside or behind me as we
descended the stairs toward where Mrs. Wilkins
waited in the hall beneath the chandelier—a thin gray
woman who reminded me of Granny, not that she
looked like Granny probably but because she had
known Granny—a lifted anxious still face which was
thinking *Who lives by the sword shall die by it* just as
Granny would have thought, toward which I walked,
had to walk not because I was Granny's grandson and
had lived in her house for three college years and was
about the age of her son when he was killed in almost
the last battle nine years ago, but because I was now
The Sartoris. (The Sartoris: that had been one of the
concomitant flashes, along with the *at last it has happened* when Professor Wilkins opened my door.) She
didn't offer me a horse and pistol, not because she
liked me any less than Professor Wilkins but because
she was a woman and so wiser than any man, else the
men would not have gone on with the War for two
years after they knew they were whipped. She just put

her hands (a small woman, no bigger than Granny had been) on my shoulders and said, "Give my love to Drusilla and your Aunt Jenny. And come back when you can."

"Only I don't know when that will be," I said. "I don't know how many things I will have to attend to." Yes, I lied even to her; it had not been but a minute yet since he had flung that door bouncing into the stop yet already I was beginning to realise, to become aware of that which I still had no yardstick to measure save that one consisting of what, despite myself, despite my raising and background (or maybe because of them) I had for some time known I was becoming and had feared the test of it; I remember how I thought while her hands still rested on my shoulders: *At least this will be my chance to find out if I am what I think I am or if I just hope; if I am going to do what I have taught myself is right or if I am just going to wish I were.*

We went on to the kitchen, Professor Wilkins still somewhere beside or behind me and still offering me the pistol and horse in a dozen different ways. Ringo was waiting; I remember how I thought then that no matter what might happen to either of us, I would never be The Sartoris to him. He was twenty-four too, but in a way he had changed even less than I had since that day when we had nailed Grumby's body to the door of the old compress. Maybe it was because he had outgrown me, had changed so much that summer while he and Granny traded mules with the Yankees that since then I had had to do most of the changing just to catch up with him. He was sitting quietly in a chair beside the cold stove, spent-looking too who had ridden forty miles (at one time, either in Jefferson or when he was alone at last on the road somewhere, he had cried; dust was now caked and dried in the tear-channels on his face) and would ride forty more yet would not eat, looking up at me a little red-eyed with weariness (or maybe it was more than just weariness and so I would never catch up with

him) then rising without a word and going on toward
the door and I following and Professor Wilkins still
offering the horse and the pistol without speaking the
words and still thinking (I could feel that too) *Dies
by the sword. Dies by the sword.*

Ringo had the two horses saddled at the side gate,
as I had known he would—the fresh one for himself
and my mare father had given me three years ago,
that could do a mile under two minutes any day and a
mile every eight minutes all day long. He was already
mounted when I realised that what Professor Wilkins
wanted was to shake my hand. We shook hands; I
knew he believed he was touching flesh which might
not be alive tomorrow night and I thought for a second how if I told him what I was going to do, since we
had talked about it, about how if there was anything at
all in the Book, anything of hope and peace for His
blind and bewildered spawn which He had chosen
above all others to offer immortality, *Thou shalt not
kill* must be it, since maybe he even believed that he
had taught it to me except that he had not, nobody
had, not even myself since it went further than just
having been learned. But I did not tell him. He was
too old to be forced so, to condone even in principle
such a decision; he was too old to have to stick to
principle in the face of blood and raising and background, to be faced without warning and made to de-
liver like by a highwayman out of the dark: only the
young could do that—one still young enough to have
his youth supplied him gratis as a reason (not an excuse) for cowardice.

So I said nothing. I just shook his hand and
mounted too, and Ringo and I rode on. We would not
have to pass through Oxford now and so soon (there
was a thin sickle of moon like the heel print of a boot
in wet sand) the road to Jefferson lay before us, the
road which I had travelled for the first time three
years ago with Father and travelled twice at Christmas
time and then in June and September and twice at

Christmas time again and then June and September again each college term since alone on the mare, not even knowing that this was peace; and now this time and maybe last time who would not die (I knew that) but who maybe forever after could never again hold up his head. The horses took the gait which they would hold for forty miles. My mare knew the long road ahead and Ringo had a good beast too, had talked Hilliard at the livery stable out of a good horse too. Maybe it was the tears, the channels of dried mud across which his strain-reddened eyes had looked at me, but I rather think it was the same quality which used to enable him to replenish his and Granny's supply of United States Army letterheads during that time—some outrageous assurance gained from too long and too close association with white people: the one whom he called Granny, the other with whom he had slept from the time we were born until Father rebuilt the house. We spoke one time, then no more:

"We could bushwhack him," he said. "Like we done Grumby that day. But I reckon that wouldn't suit that white skin you walks around in."

"No," I said. We rode on; it was October; there was plenty of time still for verbena although I would have to reach home before I would realise there was a need for it; plenty of time for verbena yet from the garden where Aunt Jenny puttered beside old Joby, in a pair of Father's old cavalry gauntlets, among the coaxed and ordered beds, the quaint and ordorous old names, for though it was October no rain had come yet and hence no frost to bring (or leave behind) the first half-warm half-chill nights of Indian Summer—the drowsing air cool and empty for geese yet languid still with the old hot dusty smell of fox grape and sassafras— the nights when before I became a man and went to college to learn law Ringo and I, with lantern and axe and crokersack and six dogs (one to follow the trail and five more just for the tonguing, the music) would hunt possum in the pasture where, hidden, we had seen our first Yankee that afternoon on the bright horse, where for the last year now you could hear the whistling of the trains which had no longer belonged to Mr. Redmond for a long while now and which at some instant, some second during the morning Father too had relinquished along with the pipe which Ringo said he was smoking, which slipped from his hand as he fell. We rode on, toward the house where he would be lying in the parlor now, in his regimentals (sabre too) and where Drusilla would be waiting for me beneath all the festive glitter of the chandeliers, in the yellow ball gown and the sprig of verbena in her hair, holding the two loaded pistols (I could see that too, who had had no presentiment; I could see her, in the formal brilliant room arranged formally for obsequy, not tall, not slender as a woman is but as a youth, a boy, is motionless, in yellow, the face calm, almost bemused, the head simple and severe, the balancing sprig of verbena above each ear, the two arms bent at the elbows, the two hands shoulder high, the two identical duelling pistols lying upon, not clutched in, one to each: the Greek amphora priestess of a succinct and formal violence).

2

Drusilla said that he had a dream. I was twenty then and she and I would walk in the garden in the summer twilight while we waited for Father to ride in from the railroad. I was just twenty then: that summer before I entered the University to take the law degree which Father decided I should have and four years after the one, the day, the evening when Father and Drusilla had kept old Cash Benbow from becoming United States Marshal and returned home still unmarried and Mrs. Habersham herded them into her carriage and drove them back to town and dug her husband out of his little dim hole in the new bank and made him sign Father's peace bond for killing the two carpet baggers,

and took Father and Drusilla to the minister herself
and saw that they were married. And Father had rebuilt the house too, on the same blackened spot, over
the same cellar, where the other had burned, only
larger, much larger: Drusilla said that the house was
the aura of Father's dream just as a bride's trousseau
and veil is the aura of hers. And Aunt Jenny had
come to live with us now so we had the garden (Drusilla would no more have bothered with flowers than
Father himself would have, who even now, even four
years after it was over, still seemed to exist, breathe,
in that last year of it while she had ridden in man's
clothes and with her hair cut short like any other
member of Father's troop, across Georgia and both
Carolinas in front of Sherman's army) for her to
gather sprigs of verbena from to wear in her hair because she said verbena was the only scent you could
smell above the smell of horses and courage and so it
was the only one that was worth the wearing. The
railroad was hardly begun then and Father and Mr.
Redmond were not only still partners, they were still
friends, which as George Wyatt said was easily a record for Father, and he would leave the house at day-
break on Jupiter, riding up and down the unfinished
line with two saddlebags of gold coins borrowed on
Friday to pay the men on Saturday, keeping just two
cross-ties ahead of the sheriff as Aunt Jenny said. So
we walked in the dusk, slowly between Aunt Jenny's
flower beds while Drusilla (in a dress now, who still
would have worn pants all the time if Father had let
her) leaned lightly on my arm and I smelled the verbena in her hair as I had smelled the rain in it and in
Father's beard that night four years ago when he and
Drusilla and Uncle Buck McCaslin found Grumby and
then came home and found Ringo and me more than
just asleep: escaped into that oblivion which God or
Nature or whoever it was had supplied us with for the
time being, who had had to perform more than should
be required of children because there should be some

limit to the age, the youth at least below which one should not have to kill. This was just after the Saturday night when he returned and I watched him clean the derringer and reload it and we learned that the dead man was almost a neighbor, a hill man who had been in the first infantry regiment when it voted Father out of command: and we never to know if the man actually intended to rob Father or not because Father had shot too quick, but only that he had a wife and several children in a dirt-floored cabin in the hills, to whom Father the next day sent some money and she (the wife) walked into the house two days later while we were sitting at the dinner table and flung the money at Father's face.

"But nobody could have more of a dream than Colonel Sutpen," I said. He had been Father's second-in-command in the first regiment and had been elected Colonel when the regiment deposed Father after Second Manassas, and it was Sutpen and not the regiment whom Father never forgave. He was underbred, a cold ruthless man who had come into the country about thirty years before the War, nobody knew from where except Father said you could look at him and know he would not dare to tell. He had got some land and nobody knew how he did that either, and he got money from somewhere—Father said they all believed he robbed steamboats, either as a card sharper or as an out-and-out highwayman—and built a big house and married and set up as a gentleman. Then he lost everything in the War like everybody else, all hope of descendants too (his son killed his daughter's fiancé on the eve of the wedding and vanished) yet he came back home and set out singlehanded to rebuild his plantation. He had no friends to borrow from and he had nobody to leave it to and he was past sixty years old, yet he set out to rebuild his place like it used to be; they told how he was too busy to bother with politics or anything; how when Father and the other men organised the nightriders to keep the carpet baggers from organising the Negroes into an insurrection, he refused to have anything to do with it. Father stopped hating him long enough to ride out to see Sutpen himself and he (Sutpen) came to the door with a lamp and did not even invite them to come in and discuss it; Father said, "Are you with us or against us?" and he said, "I'm for my land. If every man of you would rehabilitate his own land, the country will take care of itself" and Father challenged him to bring the lamp out and set it on a stump where they could both see to shoot and Sutpen would not. "Nobody could have more of a dream than that."

"Yes. But his dream is just Sutpen. John's is not. He is thinking of this whole country which he is trying to raise by its bootstraps, so that all the people in it, not just his kind nor his old regiment, but all the people, black and white, the women and children back in the hills who don't even own shoes—Don't you see?"

"But how can they get any good from what he wants to do for them if they are—after he has——"

"Killed some of them? I suppose you include those two carpet baggers he had to kill to hold that first election, don't you?"

"They were men. Human beings."

"They were Northerners, foreigners who had no business here. They were pirates." We walked on, her weight hardly discernible on my arm, her head just reaching my shoulder. I had always been a little taller than she, even on that night at Hawkhurst while we listened to the niggers passing in the road, and she had changed but little since—the same boy-hard body, the close implacable head with its savagely cropped hair which I had watched from the wagon above the tide of crazed singing niggers as we went down into the river—the body not slender as women are but as boys are slender. "A dream is not a very safe thing to be near, Bayard. I know; I had one once. It's like a loaded pistol with a hair trigger: if it stays alive long enough, somebody is going to be hurt. But if it's a good dream, it's worth it. There are not many dreams in the world, but there are a lot of human lives. And one human life or two dozen——"

"Are not worth anything?"

"No. Not anything.—Listen. I hear Jupiter. I'll beat you to the house." She was already running, the skirts she did not like to wear lifted almost to her knees, her legs beneath it running as boys run just as she rode like men ride.

I was twenty then. But the next time I was twenty-four; I had been three years at the University and in another two weeks I would ride back to Oxford for the final year and my degree. It was just last summer, last August, and Father had just beat Redmond for the State legislature. The railroad was finished now and the partnership between Father and Redmond had been dissolved so long ago that most people would have forgotten they were ever partners if it hadn't been for the enmity between them. There had been a third partner but nobody hardly remembered his name now; he and his name both had vanished in the fury of the conflict which set up between Father and Redmond almost before they began to lay the rails, between Father's violent and ruthless dictatorial-ness and will to dominate (the idea was his; he did think of the railroad first and then took Redmond in) and that quality in Redmond (as George Wyatt said, he was not a coward or Father would never have teamed with him) which permitted him to stand as much as he did from Father, to bear and bear and bear until something (not his will nor his courage) broke in him. During the War Redmond had not been a soldier, he had had something to do with cotton for the Government; he could have made money himself out of it but he had not and everybody knew he had not, Father knew it, yet Father would even taunt him with not having smelled powder. He was wrong; he knew he was when it was too late for him to stop just as a drunkard reaches a point where it is too late for

him to stop, where he promises himself that he will
and maybe believes he will or can but it is too late.
Finally they reached the point (they had both put
everything they could mortgage or borrow into it for
Father to ride up and down the line, paying the workmen and the waybills on the rails at the last possible
instant) where even Father realised that one of them
would have to get out. So (they were not speaking
then; it was arranged by Judge Benbow) they met and
agreed to buy or sell, naming a price which, in reference to what they had put into it, was ridiculously low
but which each believed the other could not raise—at
least Father claimed that Redmond did not believe he
could raise it. So Redmond accepted the price, and
found out that Father had the money. And according
to Father, that's what started it, although Uncle Buck
McCaslin said Father could not have owned a half
interest in even one hog, let alone a railroad, and not
dissolve the business either sworn enemy or death-
pledged friend to his recent partner. So they parted
and Father finished the road. By that time, seeing that
he was going to finish it, some Northern people sold
him a locomotive on credit which he named for Aunt
Jenny, with a silver oil can in the cab with her name
engraved on it; and last summer the first train ran
into Jefferson, the engine decorated with flowers and
Father in the cab blowing blast after blast on the whistle when he passed Redmond's house; and there were
speeches at the station, with more flowers and a Confederate flag and girls in white dresses and red sashes
and a band, and Father stood on the pilot of the engine and made a direct and absolutely needless allu-
sion to Mr. Redmond. That was it. He wouldn't let
him alone. George Wyatt came to me right afterward
and told me. "Right or wrong," he said, "us boys and
most of the other folks in this county know John's
right. But he ought to let Redmond alone. I know
what's wrong: he's had to kill too many folks, and
that's bad for a man. We all know Colonel's brave as

a lion, but Redmond ain't no coward either and there ain't any use in making a brave man that made one mistake eat crow all the time. Can't you talk to him?"

"I don't know," I said. "I'll try." But I had no chance. That is, I could have talked to him and he would have listened, but he could not have heard me because he had stepped straight from the pilot of that engine into the race for the Legislature. Maybe he knew that Redmond would have to oppose him to save his face even though he (Redmond) must have known that, after that train ran into Jefferson, he had no chance against Father, or maybe Redmond had already announced his candidacy and Father entered the race just because of that, I don't remember. Anyway they ran, a bitter contest in which Father continued to badger Redmond without reason or need, since they both knew it would be a landslide for Father. And it was, and we thought he was satisfied. Maybe he thought so himself, as the drunkard believes that he is done with drink; and it was that afternoon and Drusilla and I walked in the garden in the twilight and I said something about what George Wyatt had told me and she released my arm and turned me to face her and said, "This from you? You? Have you forgotten Grumby?"

"No," I said. "I never will forget him."

"You never will. I wouldn't let you. There are worse things than killing men, Bayard. There are worse things than being killed. Sometimes I think the finest thing that can happen to a man is to love something, a woman preferably, well, hard hard hard, then to die young because he believed what he could not help but believe and was what he could not (could not? would not) help but be." Now she was looking at me in a way she never had before. I did not know what it meant then and was not to know until tonight since neither of us knew then that two months later Father would be dead. I just knew that she was looking at me as she never had before and that the scent of the verbena in her hair seemed to have increased a hundred times, to have got a hundred times stronger, to be everywhere in the dusk in which something was about to happen which I had never dreamed of. Then she spoke. "Kiss me, Bayard."

"No. You are Father's wife."

"And eight years older than you are. And your fourth cousin too. And I have black hair. Kiss me, Bayard."

"No."

"Kiss me, Bayard." So I leaned my face down to her. But she didn't move, standing so, bent lightly back from me from the waist, looking at me; now it was she who said, "No." So I put my arms around her. Then she came to me, melted as women will and can, the arms with the wrist- and elbow-power to control horses about my shoulders, using the wrists to hold my face to hers until there was no longer need for the wrists; I thought then of the woman of thirty, the symbol of the ancient and eternal Snake and of the men who have written of her, and I realised then the immitigable chasm between all life and all print—that those who can, do, those who cannot and suffer enough because they can't, write about it. Then I was free, I could see her again, I saw her still watching me with that dark inscrutable look, looking up at me now across her down-slanted face; I watched her arms rise with almost the exact gesture with which she had put them around me as if she were repeating the empty and formal gesture of all promise so that I should never forget it, the elbows angling outward as she put her hands to the sprig of verbena in her hair, I standing straight and rigid facing the slightly bent head, the short jagged hair, the rigid curiously formal angle of the bare arms gleaming faintly in the last of light as she removed the verbena sprig and put it into my lapel, and I thought how the War had tried to stamp all the women of her generation and class in the South into a type and how it had failed—the suffering, the identical experience (hers and Aunt Jenny's had been almost the same except that Aunt Jenny had spent a few nights with her husband before they brought him back home in an ammunition wagon while Gavin Breckbridge was just Drusilla's fiancé) was there in the eyes, yet beyond that was the incorrigibly individual woman: not like so many men who return from wars to live on Government reservations like so many steers, emasculate and empty of all save an identical experience which they cannot forget and dare not, else they would cease to live at that moment, almost interchangeable save for the old habit of answering to a given name.

"Now I must tell Father," I said.

"Yes," she said. "You must tell him. Kiss me." So again it was like it had been before. No. Twice, a thousand times and never like—the eternal and symbolical thirty to a young man, a youth, each time both cumulative and retroactive, immitigably unrepetitive, each wherein remembering excludes experience, each wherein experience antedates remembering; the skill without weariness, the knowledge virginal to surfeit, the cunning secret muscles to guide and control just as within the wrists and elbows lay slumbering the mastery of horses: she stood back, already turning, not looking at me when she spoke, never having looked at me, already moving swiftly on in the dusk: "Tell John. Tell him tonight."

I intended to. I went to the house and into the office at once; I went to the center of the rug before the cold hearth, I don't know why, and stood there rigid like soldiers stand, looking at eye level straight across the room and above his head and said "Father" and then stopped. Because he did not even hear me. He said, "Yes, Bayard?" but he did not hear me although he was sitting behind the desk doing nothing, immobile, as still as I was rigid, one hand on the desk with a dead cigar in it, a bottle of brandy and a filled and untasted glass beside his hand, clothed quiet and bemused in whatever triumph it was he felt since the last overwhelming return of votes had come in late in the afternoon. So I waited until after supper. We went to the dining room and stood side by side until Aunt Jenny entered and then Drusilla, in the yellow ball gown, who walked straight to me and gave me one fierce inscrutable look then went to her place and waited for me to draw her chair while Father drew Aunt Jenny's. He had roused by then, not to talk himself but rather to sit at the head of the table and reply to Drusilla as she talked with a sort of feverish and glittering volubility—to reply now and then to her with that courteous intolerant pride which had lately become a little forensic, as if merely being in a political contest filled with fierce and empty oratory had retroactively made a lawyer of him who was anything and everything except a lawyer. Then Drusilla and Aunt Jenny rose and left us and he said, "Wait" to me who had made no move to follow and directed Joby to bring one of the bottles of wine which he had fetched back from New Orleans when he went there last to borrow money to liquidate his first private railroad bonds. Then I stood again like soldiers stand, gazing at eye level above his head while he sat half-turned from the table, a little paunchy now though not much, a little grizzled too in the hair though his beard was as strong as ever, with that spurious forensic air of lawyers and the intolerant eyes which in the last two years had acquired that transparent film which the eyes of carnivorous animals have and from behind which they look at a world which no ruminant ever sees, perhaps dares to see, which I have seen before on the eyes of men who have killed too much, who have killed so much that never again as long as they live will they ever be alone. I said again, "Father," then I told him.

"Hah?" he said. "Sit down." I sat down, I looked at him, watched him fill both glasses and this time I knew it was worse with him than not hearing: it didn't even matter. "You are doing well in the law, Judge Wilkins tells me. I am pleased to hear that. I have not needed you in my affairs so far, but from now on I shall. I have now accomplished the active portion of my aims in which you could not have helped me; I acted as the land and the time demanded and you were too young for that, I wished to shield you. But now the land and the time too are changing; what will follow will be a matter of consolidation, of pettifogging and doubtless chicanery in which I would be a babe in arms but in which you, trained in the law, can hold your own—our own. Yes, I have accomplished my aim, and now I shall do a little moral housecleaning. I am tired of killing men, no matter what the necessity nor the end. Tomorrow, when I go to town and meet Ben Redmond, I shall be unarmed."

3

We reached home just before midnight; we didn't have to pass through Jefferson either. Before we turned in the gates I could see the lights, the chandeliers—hall, parlor, and what Aunt Jenny (without any effort or perhaps even design on her part) had taught even Ringo to call the drawing room, the light falling outward across the portico, past the columns. Then I saw the horses, the faint shine of leather and buckle-glints on the black silhouettes and then the men too—Wyatt and others of Father's old troop—and I had forgot that they would be there. I had forgot that they would be there; I remember how I thought, since I was tired and spent with strain, *Now it will have to begin tonight. I won't even have until tomorrow in which to begin to resist.* They had a watchman, a picquet out, I suppose, because they seemed to know at once that we were in the drive. Wyatt met me, I halted the mare, I could look down at him and at the others gathered a few yards behind him with that curious vulture-like formality which Southern men assume in such situations.

"Well, boy," George said.

"Was it—" I said. "Was he——"

"It was all right. It was in front. Redmond ain't no coward. John had the derringer inside his cuff like always, but he never touched it, never made a move toward it." I have seen him do it, he showed me once: the pistol (it was not four inches long) held flat inside his left wrist by a clip he made himself of wire and an old clock spring; he would raise both hands at the same time, cross them, fire the pistol from beneath his left hand almost as if he were hiding from his own vision what he was doing; when he killed one of the men he shot a hole through his own coat sleeve. "But you want to get on to the house," Wyatt said. He began to stand aside, then he spoke again: "We'll take this off your hands, any of us. Me." I hadn't moved the mare yet and I had made no move to speak, yet he continued quickly, as if he had already rehearsed all this, his speech and mine, and knew what I would say and only spoke himself as he would have removed his hat on entering a house or used 'sir' in conversing with a stranger: "You're young, just a boy, you ain't had any experience in this kind of thing. Besides, you got them two ladies in the house to think about. He would understand, all right."

"I reckon I can attend to it," I said.

"Sure," he said; there was no surprise, nothing at all, in his voice because he had already rehearsed this: "I reckon we all knew that's what you would say." He stepped back then; almost it was as though he and not I bade the mare to move on. But they all followed, still with that unctuous and voracious formality. Then I saw Drusilla standing at the top of the front steps, in the light from the open door and the windows like a theatre scene, in the yellow ball gown and even from here I believed that I could smell the verbena in her hair, standing there motionless yet emanating something louder than the two shots must have been— something voracious too and passionate. Then, although I had dismounted and someone had taken the mare, I seemed to be still in the saddle and to watch myself enter that scene which she had postulated like another actor while in the background for chorus Wyatt and the others stood with the unctuous formality which the Southern man shows in the presence of death—that Roman holiday engendered by mist-born Protestant-ism grafted onto this land of violent sun, of violent alteration from snow to heat-stroke which has pro-duced a race impervious to both. I mounted the steps toward the figure straight and yellow and immobile as a candle which moved only to extend one hand; we stood together and looked down at them where they stood clumped, the horses too gathered in a tight group beyond them at the rim of light from the bril-liant door and windows. One of them stamped and blew his breath and jangled his gear.

"Thank you, gentlemen," I said. "My aunt and my—Drusilla thank you. There's no need for you to stay. Goodnight." They murmured, turning. George Wyatt paused, looking back at me.

"Tomorrow?" he said.

"Tomorrow." Then they went on, carrying their hats and tiptoeing, even on the ground, the quiet and resilient earth, as though anyone in that house awake would try to sleep, anyone already asleep in it whom they could have wakened. Then they were gone and Drusilla and I turned and crossed the portico, her hand lying light on my wrist yet discharging into me with a shock like electricity that dark and passionate voracity, the face at my shoulder—the jagged hair with a verbena sprig above each ear, the eyes staring at me with that fierce exaltation. We entered the hall and crossed it, her hand guiding me without pressure, and entered the parlor. Then for the first time I realised it—the alteration which is death—not that he was now just clay but that he was lying down. But I didn't look at him yet because I knew that when I did I would begin to pant; I went to Aunt Jenny who had just risen from a chair behind which Louvinia stood. She was Father's sister, taller than Drusilla but no older,

whose husband had been killed at the very beginning
of the War, by a shell from a Federal frigate at Fort
Moultrie, come to us from Carolina six years ago.
Ringo and I went to Tennessee Junction in the wagon
to meet her. It was January, cold and clear and with
ice in the ruts; we returned just before dark with Aunt
Jenny on the seat beside me holding a lace parasol
and Ringo in the wagon bed nursing a hamper basket
containing two bottles of old sherry and the two jasmine cuttings which were bushes in the garden now,
and the panes of colored glass which she had salvaged
from the Carolina house where she and Father and
Uncle Bayard were born and which Father had set in
a fanlight about one of the drawing room windows for
her—who came up the drive and Father (home now
from the railroad) went down the steps and lifted her
from the wagon and said, "Well, Jenny," and she said,
"Well, Johnny," and began to cry. She stood too,
looking at me as I approached—the same hair, the
same high nose, the same eyes as Father's except that
they were intent and very wise instead of intolerant.
She said nothing at all, she just kissed me, her hands
light on my shoulders. Then Drusilla spoke, as if she
had been waiting with a sort of dreadful patience for
the empty ceremony to be done, in a voice like a
bell: clear, unsentient, on a single pitch, silvery and
triumphant: "Come, Bayard."

"Hadn't you better go to bed now?" Aunt Jenny said.

"Yes," Drusilla said in that silvery ecstatic voice,
"oh yes. There will be plenty of time for sleep." I followed her, her hand again guiding me without pressure;
now I looked at him. It was just as I had imagined
it—sabre, plumes, and all—but with that alteration,
that irrevocable difference which I had known to expect yet had not realised, as you can put food into
your stomach which for a while the stomach declines
to assimilate—the illimitable grief and regret as I
looked down at the face which I knew—the nose, the
hair, the eyelids closed over the intolerance—the face

which I realised I now saw in repose for the first time
in my life; the empty hands still now beneath the invisible stain of what had been (once, surely) needless
blood, the hands now appearing clumsy in their very
inertness, too clumsy to have performed the fatal ac-
tions which forever afterward he must have waked and
slept with and maybe was glad to lay down at last—
those curious appendages clumsily conceived to begin
with yet with which man has taught himself to do so
much, so much more than they were intended to do
or could be forgiven for doing, which had now sur-
rendered that life to which his intolerant heart had
fiercely held; and then I knew that in a minute I would
begin to pant. So Drusilla must have spoken twice
before I heard her and turned and saw in the instant
Aunt Jenny and Louvinia watching us, hearing Drusilla now, the unsentient bell quality gone now, her
voice whispering into that quiet death-filled room with
a passionate and dying fall: "Bayard." She faced me,
she was quite near; again the scent of the verbena in
her hair seemed to have increased a hundred times as
she stood holding out to me, one in either hand, the
two duelling pistols. "Take them, Bayard," she said,
in the same tone in which she had said "Kiss me"
last summer, already pressing them into my hands,
watching me with that passionate and voracious exaltation, speaking in a voice fainting and passionate with
promise: "Take them. I have kept them for you. I give
them to you. Oh you will thank me, you will remember me who put into your hands what they say is an
attribute only of God's, who took what belongs to
heaven and gave it to you. Do you feel them? the
long true barrels true as justice, the triggers (you have
fired them) quick as retribution, the two of them slender and invincible and fatal as the physical shape of
love?" Again I watched her arms angle out and upward as she removed the two verbena sprigs from her
hair in two motions faster than the eye could follow,
already putting one of them into my lapel and crush-

ing the other in her other hand while she still spoke
in that rapid passionate voice not much louder than a
whisper: "There. One I give to you to wear tomorrow
(it will not fade), the other I cast away, like this—"
dropping the crushed bloom at her feet. "I abjure it.
I abjure verbena forever more; I have smelled it above
the odor of courage; that was all I wanted. Now let
me look at you." She stood back, staring at me—the
face tearless and exalted, the feverish eyes brilliant
and voracious. "How beautiful you are: do you know
it? How beautiful: young, to be permitted to kill, to
be permitted vengeance, to take into your bare hands
the fire of heaven that cast down Lucifer. No; I. I gave
it to you; I put it into your hands: Oh you will thank
me, you will remember me when I am dead and you
are an old man saying to himself, 'I have tasted all
things.'—It will be the right hand, won't it?" She
moved; she had taken my right hand which still held
one of the pistols before I knew what she was about
to do; she had bent and kissed it before I compre-
hended why she took it. Then she stopped dead still,
still stooping in that attitude of fierce exultant humil-
ity, her hot lips and her hot hands still touching my
flesh, light on my flesh as dead leaves yet communicating to it that battery charge dark, passionate and
damned forever of all peace. Because they are wise,
women are—a touch, lips or fingers, and the knowledge, even clairvoyance, goes straight to the heart
without bothering the laggard brain at all. She stood
erect now, staring at me with intolerable and amazed
incredulity which occupied her face alone for a whole
minute while her eyes were completely empty; it
seemed to me that I stood there for a full minute
while Aunt Jenny and Louvinia watched us, waiting
for her eyes to fill. There was no blood in her face at
all, her mouth open a little and pale as one of those
rubber rings women seal fruit jars with. Then her eyes
filled with an expression of bitter and passionate be-
trayal. "Why, he's not—" she said. "He's not—And I

kissed his hand," she said in an aghast whisper: *"I kissed his hand!"* beginning to laugh, the laughter, rising, becoming a scream yet still remaining laughter, screaming with laughter, trying herself to deaden the sound by putting her hand over her mouth, the laughter spilling between her fingers like vomit, the incredulous betrayed eyes still watching me across the hand.

"Louvinia!" Aunt Jenny said. They both came to her. Louvinia touched and held her and Drusilla turned her face to Louvinia.

"I kissed his hand, Louvinia!" she cried. "Did you see it? *I kissed his hand!"* the laughter rising again, becoming the scream again yet still remaining laughter, she still trying to hold it back with her hand like a small child who has filled its mouth too full.

"Take her upstairs," Aunt Jenny said. But they were already moving toward the door, Louvinia half-carrying Drusilla, the laughter diminishing as they neared the door as though it waited for the larger space of the empty and brilliant hall to rise again. Then it was gone; Aunt Jenny and I stood there and I knew soon that I would begin to pant. I could feel it beginning like you feel regurgitation beginning, as though there were not enough air in the room, the house, not enough air anywhere under the heavy hot low sky where the equinox couldn't seem to accomplish, nothing in the air for breathing, for the lungs. Now it was Aunt Jenny who said "Bayard" twice before I heard her. "You are not going to try to kill him. All right."

"All right?" I said.

"Yes. All right. Don't let it be Drusilla, a poor hysterical young woman. And don't let it be him, Bayard, because he's dead now. And don't let it be George Wyatt and those others who will be waiting for you tomorrow morning. I know you are not afraid."

"But what good will that do?" I said. "What good will that do?" It almost began then; I stopped it just in time. "I must live with myself, you see."

"Then it's not just Drusilla? Not just him? Not just George Wyatt and Jefferson?"

"No," I said.

"Will you promise to let me see you before you go to town tomorrow?" I looked at her; we looked at one another for a moment. Then she put her hands on my shoulders and kissed me and released me, all in one motion. "Goodnight, son," she said. Then she was gone too and now it could begin. I knew that in a minute I would look at him and it would begin and I did look at him, feeling the long-held breath, the hiatus before it started, thinking how maybe I should have said, "Good-bye, Father" but did not. Instead I crossed to the piano and laid the pistols carefully on it, still keeping the panting from getting too loud too soon. Then I was outside on the porch and (I don't know how long it had been) I looked in the window and saw Simon squatting on a stool beside him. Simon had been his body servant during the War and when they came home Simon had a uniform too—a Confederate private's coat with a Yankee brigadier's star on it and he had put it on now too, like they had dressed Father, squatting on the stool beside him, not crying, not weeping the facile tears which are the white man's futile trait and which Negroes know nothing about but just sitting there, motionless, his lower lip slacked down a little; he raised his hand and touched the coffin, the black hand rigid and fragile-looking as a clutch of dead twigs, then dropped the hand; once he turned his head and I saw his eyes roll red and unwinking in his skull like those of a cornered fox. It had begun by that time; I panted, standing there, and this was it—the regret and grief, the despair out of which the tragic mute insensitive bones stand up that can bear anything, anything.

4

After a while the whippoorwills stopped and I heard the first day bird, a mockingbird. It had sung all night

too but now it was the day song, no longer the drowsy
moony fluting. Then they all began—the sparrows
from the stable, the thrush that lived in Aunt Jenny's
garden, and I heard a quail too from the pasture and
now there was light in the room. But I didn't move
at once. I still lay on the bed (I hadn't undressed)
with my hands under my head and the scent of Drusilla's verbena faint from where my coat lay on a chair,
watching the light grow, watching it turn rosy with the
sun. After a while I heard Louvinia come up across
the back yard and go into the kitchen; I heard the
door and then the long crash of her armful of
stovewood in the box. Soon they would begin to
arrive—the carriages and buggies in the drive—but
not for a while yet because they too would wait first
to see what I was going to do. So the house was quiet
when I went down to the diningroom, no sound in it
except Simon snoring in the parlor, probably still sitting on the stool though I didn't look in to see. Instead
I stood at the diningroom window and drank the coffee which Louvinia brought me, then I went to the
stable; I saw Joby watching me from the kitchen door
as I crossed the yard and in the stable Loosh looked
up at me across Betsy's head, a curry comb in his
hand, though Ringo didn't look at me at all. We curried Jupiter then. I didn't know if we would be able
to without trouble or not, since always Father would
come in first and touch him and tell him to stand and
he would stand like a marble horse (or pale bronze
rather) while Loosh curried him. But he stood for me
too, a little restive but he stood, then that was done
and now it was almost nine o'clock and soon they
would begin to arrive and I told Ringo to bring Betsy
on to the house.

I went on to the house and into the hall. I had not
had to pant in some time now but it was there, waiting, a part of the alteration, as though by being dead
and no longer needing air he had taken all of it, all
that he had compassed and claimed and postulated

between the walls which he had built, along with him.
Aunt Jenny must have been waiting; she came out of
the diningroom at once, without a sound, dressed, the
hair that was like Father's combed and smooth above
the eyes that were different from Father's eyes because they were not intolerant but just intent and
grave and (she was wise too) without pity. "Are you
going now?" she said.

"Yes." I looked at her. Yes, thank God, without
pity. "You see, I want to be thought well of."

"I do," she said. "Even if you spend the day hidden
in the stable loft, I still do."

"Maybe if she knew that I was going. Was going to
town anyway."

"No," she said. "No, Bayard." We looked at one
another. Then she said quietly, "All right. She's
awake." So I mounted the stairs. I mounted steadily,
not fast because if I had gone fast the panting would
have started again or I might have had to slow for a
second at the turn or at the top and I would not have
gone on. So I went slowly and steadily, across the hall
to her door and knocked and opened it. She was sitting at the window, in something soft and loose for
morning in her bedroom only she never did look like
morning in a bedroom because here was no hair to
fall about her shoulders. She looked up, she sat there
looking at me with her feverish brilliant eyes and I
remembered I still had the verbena sprig in my lapel
and suddenly she began to laugh again. It seemed to
come not from her mouth but to burst out all over her
face like sweat does and with a dreadful and painful
convulsion as when you have vomited until it hurts
you yet still you must vomit again—burst out all over
her face except her eyes, the brilliant incredulous eyes
looking at me out of the laughter as if they belonged
to somebody else, as if they were two inert fragments
of tar or coal lying on the bottom of a receptacle filled
with turmoil: "I kissed his hand! *I kissed his hand!*"
Louvinia entered, Aunt Jenny must have sent her di-

rectly after me; again I walked slowly and steadily so it would not start yet, down the stairs where Aunt Jenny stood beneath the chandelier in the hall as Mrs. Wilkins had stood yesterday at the University. She had my hat in her hand. "Even if you hid all day in the stable, Bayard," she said. I took the hat; she said quietly, pleasantly, as if she were talking to a stranger, a guest: "I used to see a lot of blockade runners in Charleston. They were heroes in a way, you see— not heroes because they were helping to prolong the Confederacy but heroes in the sense that David Crockett or John Sevier would have been to small boys or fool young women. There was one of them, an Englishman. He had no business there; it was the money of course, as with all of them. But he was the Davy Crockett to us because by that time we had all forgot what money was, what you could do with it. He must have been a gentleman once or associated with gentlemen before he changed his name, and he had a vocabulary of seven words, though I must admit he got along quite well with them. The first four were, 'I'll have rum, thanks,' and then, when he had the rum, he would use the other three—across the champagne, to whatever ruffled bosom or low gown: 'No bloody moon.' No bloody moon, Bayard."

Ringo was waiting with Betsy at the front steps. Again he did not look at me, his face sullen, downcast even while he handed me the reins. But he said nothing, nor did I look back. And sure enough I was just in time; I passed the Compson carriage at the gates, General Compson lifted his hat as I did mine as we passed. It was four miles to town but I had not gone two of them when I heard the horse coming up behind me and I did not look back because I knew it was Ringo. I did not look back; he came up on one of the carriage horses, he rode up beside me and looked me full in the face for one moment, the sullen determined face, the eyes rolling at me defiant and momentary and red; we rode on. Now we were in town—the long shady street leading to the square, the new courthouse at the end of it; it was eleven o'clock now: long past breakfast and not yet noon so there were only women on the street, not to recognise me perhaps or at least not the walking stopped sudden and dead in midwalking as if the legs contained the sudden eyes, the caught breath, that not to begin until we reached the square and I thinking *If I could only be invisible until I reach the stairs to his office and begin to mount.* But I could not, I was not; we rode up to the Holston House and I saw the row of feet along the gallery rail come suddenly and quietly down and I did not look at them, I stopped Betsy and waited until Ringo was down then I dismounted and gave him the reins. "Wait for me here," I said.

"I'm going with you," he said, not loud; we stood there under the still circumspect eyes and spoke quietly to one another like two conspirators. Then I saw the pistol, the outline of it inside his shirt, probably the one we had taken from Grumby that day we killed him.

"No you ain't," I said.

"Yes I am."

"No you ain't." So I walked on, along the street in the hot sun. It was almost noon now and I could smell nothing except the verbena in my coat, as if it had gathered all the sun, all the suspended fierce heat in which the equinox could not seem to occur and were distilling it so that I moved in a cloud of verbena as I might have moved in a cloud of smoke from a cigar. Then George Wyatt was beside me (I don't know where he came from) and five or six others of Father's old troop a few yards behind, George's hand on my arm, drawing me into a doorway out of the avid eyes like caught breaths.

"Have you got that derringer?" George said.

"No," I said.

"Good," George said. "They are tricky things to fool with. Couldn't nobody but Colonel ever handle one right; I never could. So you take this. I tried it this morning and I know it's right. Here." He was already fumbling the pistol into my pocket, then the same thing seemed to happen to him that happened to Drusilla last night when she kissed my hand—something communicated by touch straight to the simple code by which he lived, without going through the brain at all: so that he too stood suddenly back, the pistol in his hand, staring at me with his pale outraged eyes and speaking in a whisper thin with fury: "Who are you? Is your name Sartoris? By God, if you don't kill him, I'm going to." Now it was not panting, it was a terrible desire to laugh, to laugh as Drusilla had, and say, "That's what Drusilla said." But I didn't. I said, "I'm tending to this. You stay out of it. I don't need any help." Then his fierce eyes faded gradually, exactly as you turn a lamp down.

"Well," he said, putting the pistol back into his pocket. "You'll have to excuse me, son. I should have knowed you wouldn't do anything that would keep John from laying quiet. We'll follow you and wait at the foot of the steps. And remember: he's a brave man, but he's been sitting in that office by himself since yesterday morning waiting for you and his nerves are on edge."

"I'll remember," I said. "I don't need any help." I had started on when suddenly I said it without having any warning that I was going to: "No bloody moon."

"What?" he said. I didn't answer. I went on across the square itself now, in the hot sun, they following though not close so that I never saw them again until afterward, surrounded by the remote still eyes not following me yet either, just stopped where they were before the stores and about the door to the courthouse, waiting. I walked steadily on enclosed in the new fierce odor of the verbena sprig. Then shadow fell upon me; I did not pause, I looked once at the small faded sign nailed to the brick *B.J. Redmond. Atty at Law* and began to mount the stairs, the

wooden steps scuffed by the heavy bewildered boots
of countrymen approaching litigation and stained by
tobacco spit, on down the dim corridor to the door
which bore the name again, *B.J. Redmond* and
knocked once and opened it. He sat behind the desk,
not much taller than Father but thicker as a man gets
who spends most of his time sitting and listening to
people, freshly shaven and with fresh linen; a lawyer
yet it was not a lawyer's face—a face much thinner
than the body would indicate, strained (and yes, tragic;
I know that now) and exhausted beneath the neat recent steady strokes of the razor, holding a pistol flat
on the desk before him, loose beneath his hand and
aimed at nothing. There was no smell of drink, not
even of tobacco in the neat clean dingy room although
I knew he smoked. I didn't pause. I walked steadily
toward him. It was not twenty feet from door to desk
yet I seemed to walk in a dreamlike state in which
there was neither time nor distance, as though the
mere act of walking was no more intended to encom-
pass space than was his sitting. We didn't speak. It
was as if we both knew what the passage of words
would be and the futility of it; how he might have
said, "Go out, Bayard. Go away, boy" and then,
"Draw then. I will allow you to draw" and it would
have been the same as if he had never said it. So we
did not speak; I just walked steadily toward him as
the pistol rose from the desk. I watched it, I could see
the foreshortened slant of the barrel and I knew it
would miss me though his hand did not tremble. I
walked toward him, toward the pistol in the rocklike
hand, I heard no bullet. Maybe I didn't even hear the
explosion though I remember the sudden orange
bloom and smoke as they appeared against his white
shirt as they had appeared against Grumby's greasy
Confederate coat; I still watched that foreshortened
slant of barrel which I knew was not aimed at me and
saw the second orange flash and smoke and heard no
bullet that time either. Then I stopped; it was done

then. I watched the pistol descend to the desk in short jerks; I saw him release it and sit back, both hands on the desk, I looked at his face and I knew too what it was to want air when there was nothing in the circum-ambience for the lungs. He rose, shoved the chair back with a convulsive motion and rose, with a queer duck-ing motion of his head; with his head still ducked aside and one arm extended as though he couldn't see and the other hand resting on the desk as if he couldn't stand alone, he turned and crossed to the wall and took his hat from the rack and with his head still ducked aside and one hand extended he blundered along the wall and passed me and reached the door and went through it. He was brave; no one denied that. He walked down those stairs and out onto the street where George Wyatt and the other six of Fa-ther's old troop waited and where the other men had begun to run now; he walked through the middle of them with his hat on and his head up (they told me how someone shouted at him: "Have you killed that boy too?"), saying no word, staring straight ahead and with his back to them, on to the station where the south-bound train was just in and got on it with no baggage, nothing, and went away from Jefferson and from Mississippi and never came back.

I heard their feet on the stairs then in the corridor then in the room, but for a while yet (it wasn't that long, of course) I still sat behind the desk as he had sat, the flat of the pistol still warm under my hand, my hand growing slowly numb between the pistol and my forehead. Then I raised my head; the little room was full of men. "My God!" George Wyatt cried. "You took the pistol away from him and then missed him, missed him *twice*?" Then he answered himself—that same rapport for violence which Drusilla had and which in George's case was actual character judgment: "No; wait. You walked in here without even a pocket knife and let him miss you twice. My God in heaven." He turned, shouting: "Get to hell out of here! You,

White, ride out to Sartoris and tell his folks it's all over and he's all right. Ride!" So they departed, went away; presently only George was left, watching me with that pale bleak stare which was speculative yet not at all ratiocinative. "Well by God," he said. "—Do you want a drink?"

"No," I said. "I'm hungry. I didn't eat any breakfast."

"I reckon not, if you got up this morning aiming to do what you did. Come on. We'll go to the Holston House."

"No," I said. "No. Not there."

"Why not? You ain't done anything to be ashamed of. I wouldn't have done it that way, myself. I'd a shot at him once, anyway. But that's your way or you wouldn't have done it."

"Yes," I said. "I would do it again."

"Be damned if I would.—You want to come home with me? We'll have time to eat and then ride out there in time for the——" But I couldn't do that either.

"No," I said. "I'm not hungry after all. I think I'll go home."

"Don't you want to wait and ride out with me?"

"No. I'll go on."

"You don't want to stay here, anyway." He looked around the room again, where the smell of powder smoke still lingered a little, still lay somewhere on the hot dead air though invisible now, blinking a little with his fierce pale unintroverted eyes. "Well by God," he said again. "Maybe you're right, maybe there has been enough killing in your family without—Come on." We left the office. I waited at the foot of the stairs and soon Ringo came up with the horses. We crossed the square again. There were no feet on the Holston House railing now (it was twelve o'clock) but a group of men stood before the door who raised their hats and I raised mine and Ringo and I rode on.

We did not go fast. Soon it was one, maybe after;

the carriages and buggies would begin to leave the
square soon, so I turned from the road at the end of
the pasture and I sat the mare, trying to open the
gate without dismounting, until Ringo dismounted and
opened it. We crossed the pasture in the hard fierce
sun; I could have seen the house now but I didn't
look. Then we were in the shade, the close thick airless shade of the creek bottom; the old rails still lay
in the undergrowth where we had built the pen to
hide the Yankee mules. Presently I heard the water,
then I could see the sunny glints. We dismounted. I
lay on my back, I thought *Now it can begin again if
it wants to.* But it did not. I went to sleep. I went to
sleep almost before I had stopped thinking. I slept for
almost five hours and I didn't dream anything at all
yet I waked myself up crying, crying too hard to stop
it. Ringo was squatting beside me and the sun was
gone though there was a bird of some sort still singing
somewhere and the whistle of the north-bound evening train sounded and the short broken puffs of starting where it had evidently stopped at our flag station.
After a while I began to stop and Ringo brought his
hat full of water from the creek but instead I went
down to the water myself and bathed my face.

There was still a good deal of light in the pasture,
though the whippoorwills had begun, and when we
reached the house there was a mockingbird singing in
the magnolia, the night song now, the drowsy moony
one, and again the moon like the rim print of a heel
in wet sand. There was just one light in the hall now
and so it was all over though I could still smell the
flowers even above the verbena in my coat. I had not
looked at him again. I had started to before I left the
house but I did not, I did not see him again and all
the pictures we had of him were bad ones because a
picture could no more have held him dead than the
house could have kept his body. But I didn't need to
see him again because he was there, he would always
be there; maybe what Drusilla meant by his dream

was not something which he possessed but something which he had bequeathed us which we could never forget, which would even assume the corporeal shape of him whenever any of us, black or white, closed our eyes. I went into the house. There was no light in the drawing room except the last of the afterglow which came through the western window where Aunt Jenny's colored glass was; I was about to go on upstairs when I saw her sitting there beside the window. She didn't call me and I didn't speak Drusilla's name, I just went to the door and stood there. "She's gone," Aunt Jenny said. "She took the evening train. She has gone to Montgomery, to Dennison." Denny had been married about a year now; he was living in Montgomery, reading law.

"I see," I said. "Then she didn't——" But there wasn't any use in that either; Jed White must have got there before one o'clock and told them. And besides, Aunt Jenny didn't answer. She could have lied to me but she didn't, she said,

"Come here." I went to her chair. "Kneel down. I can't see you."

"Don't you want the lamp?"

"No. Kneel down." So I knelt beside the chair. "So you had a perfectly splendid Saturday afternoon, didn't you? Tell me about it." Then she put her hands on my shoulders. I watched them come up as though she were trying to stop them; I felt them on my shoulders as if they had a separate life of their own and were trying to do something which for my sake she was trying to restrain, prevent. Then she gave up or she was not strong enough because they came up and took my face between them, hard, and suddenly the tears sprang and streamed down her face like Drusilla's laughing had. "Oh, damn you Sartorises!" she said. "Damn you! Damn you!"

As I passed down the hall the light came up in the diningroom and I could hear Louvinia laying the table for supper. So the stairs were lighted quite well. But the upper hall was dark. I saw her open door (that unmistakable way in which an open door stands open when nobody lives in the room any more) and I realised I had not believed that she was really gone. So I didn't look into the room. I went on to mine and entered. And then for a long moment I thought it was the verbena in my lapel which I still smelled. I thought that until I had crossed the room and looked down at the pillow on which it lay—the single sprig of it (without looking she would pinch off a half dozen of them and they would be all of a size, almost all of a shape, as if a machine had stamped them out) filling the room, the dusk, the evening with that odor which she said you could smell alone above the smell of horses.

Mary Mebane

Mary Mebane was born in 1933 in Durham County, North Carolina, the daughter of a farmer and a factory worker. She received a B.A. from North Carolina College (now North Carolina Central) and an M.A. and Ph.D. from the University of North Carolina. She has taught English at North Carolina College, South Carolina State College, University of South Carolina, and University of Wisconsin. She is the author of a play, *Take a Sad Song* (1975), and two autobiographical works, *Mary* (1981) and *Mary Wayfarer* (1983). Mary Mebane had to battle both the racial prejudice of the segregated South and the prejudice of family members who thought she was too ambitious. In the following excerpt from *Mary,* Mary and her mother, Nonnie, find themselves at odds about what a young black woman's aspirations should be.

from Mary

At first I didn't know any better; I thought that people all over the world washed clothes in the backyard, cooked their supper right out of the garden, churned milk and picked blackberries, got saved and were baptized, and went to church on Sunday. If the work was sheer drudgery, as undoubtedly it was, I didn't feel it as such and perhaps never would have.

But eventually I began to perceive that I was being prepared for my life's work. That's when the trouble really got bad—when I started resisting.

I am going to do great things in life, I secretly vowed.

No, you aren't, said the world around me. You're going to accept your lot just like the rest of us. Black women have always had it hard. Who are you to be so different?

Pick up your cross, said the Sunday school and the church. Everyone has a cross to bear.

Black women like me have scrubbed a hundred billion miles of tiled corridors and washed an equal number of dishes. I wasn't going to do that.

I am going to live my own life, I secretly said.

No, you aren't, said an adult. I am going to see to it that you don't. You might as well get those foolish notions out of your head, girl.

That adult was my mother.

Perhaps someday someone will discover the origin of the tension that sometimes develops between black mother and black daughter, especially when the daughter is ambitious. The spark that usually set off the conflict was my interest in things literary and cultural—worthless things for a girl like me, born black in the rural segregated American South. But that was only the tip of the iceberg. Unseen but hulking huge and more deadly was the feeling that there was some basic flaw in a personality that engaged in such pursuits.

Nonnie felt bitterly resentful and rejected when I refused to subscribe to her version of reality. She had managed to project her dislike of my interests so thoroughly into my consciousness that soon I, too, felt that there was something not quite right about valuing ideas. During intermittent periods I would self-consciously cast off the raiment of intellectuality and try on the garment of black folk culture, attempting to convince myself that it was sufficient, that to want more and—even more guilt-producing—to want better was an affectation on my part.

Nevertheless, I began to hope that music would be a way out, and I conceived the idea of becoming a concert pianist. I hadn't taken music lessons for a long time, having stopped when I could play for the Sunday school and the church choir. But I would take piano lessons and practice very hard and then one day I would be a great artist.

I had heard that Mrs. Shearin was the best teacher in town. I called and asked her how much the lessons were. She said one dollar each. I asked if I could work for her to pay for my lessons; she said that she was sure something could be arranged.

Soon I was making a weekly trip to Durham to Mrs. Shearin's studio. I was excited because it was an adventure for me. It was the first time I had been to the heart of the black community in Durham. My father's relatives lived in the northern and western sections of the city, but the center of the black population was in the southern part of the city. Located there were the homes of the "rich" blacks of Durham that I had heard about.

The first time I rode down the main street in the black section I was disappointed. There were a number of big two-story houses, but most of them needed painting, and there were smaller, less-well-kept-up houses nearby and in some cases right next to them. Interspersed among them also were various small businesses, a taxi stand, an ice-cream parlor, a hamburger stand, so that the community did not look like the well-off, prosperous communities in other sections of the city.

Right at the bus stop where I got off was North Carolina College, a state-supported black institution. It was the best-kept piece of property in the neighborhood. It had lustrous green grass kept cut very close, tall trimmed hedges, and red-brick buildings. Saturday mornings I would see students dressed in the latest college fashions waiting for the bus on the other side of the street. I used to look at the buildings and think how nice they were, but I didn't really plan to go to NCC. I wanted desperately to go to one of those great centers of learning I had read about in books and magazines. I wanted to go to Radcliffe or Wellesley.

I liked my music lessons. Mrs. Shearin lived in a Spanish-style house, low and pink. It had nice things but nothing flashy. My tasks were not hard. I vacuumed the living room, made up her son's bed, dusted, and fixed her a large cup of tea for breakfast, which I took to her in the studio, a large room at the back of the house. That over, I waited for my turn.

I was stunned at my total ignorance about music, for I had been playing hymns for a number of years. My teacher in Wildwood had never taught me about the values of notes—that is, that a quarter note gets one beat, a half note gets two beats, and a whole note gets four beats. I had never even heard of an eighth note or a sixteenth note, scales or keys. I was in despair. How was I ever going to be a concert artist when I had never even been taught the basics? I realized then why my teacher in Wildwood practically started her pupils off with hymns, concentrating on the top or melodic line. She knew the familiar hymns by heart and was teaching her students by rote.

Soon I began to understand the new terms, and the joy of learning came back. Mrs. Shearin asked me to subscribe to *Etude* magazine, which started coming to the house every month. I was working for my music, so Nonnie couldn't say much one way or the other. And each student had to buy a little book with the lives of the composers in it. When we played a piece by Mozart or some other composer, before we began we had to tell Mrs. Shearin some facts about his life. We had to be able to spell his name correctly, and she made sure that our pronunciation was correct. I loved it. Scales to me were fun—to be able to go over the whole keyboard, first with one hand, then with two, in key after key, major and minor, was a pleasure. I felt a sense of mastery. It was something new; that meant my world was opening up and I was happy.

Mrs. Shearin herself was very chic. I used to pay her close attention on the sly. She always wore fingernail polish; her hair and face were perfectly groomed and she wore attractive, colorful clothing. But more than what she wore, her manner was gracious and refined, always courteous, though she sometimes yelled at students about their mistakes. She was elegant. That's what I admired about her and my aunt Jo; they both had style, class, and elegance. Mrs. Shearin had been born to wealth—her father was the best-known black businessman in the United States; Aunt Jo had not been born to wealth, but she had acquired style. They were the only black women that I ever really admired. I've always liked class, style, and elegance.

I was so enthusiastic about my studies in music that soon Esther, a girl in Wildwood, wanted to take piano and I had a partner for my adventures in Durham.

*   *   *

One day I was in my room lying on my bed on my stomach, turning the pages of a magazine on the floor. I liked to read this way. The room was cluttered—the bed was unmade and there were books and records and magazines everywhere.

Nonnie had had a long day at the factory, catching the bundles of tobacco as they came down the belt and cutting off the hard-tied part. (If one of the women on the line failed to turn the bundle of tobacco the right way, the knot end might go into the machine and America would have a bitter cigarette. Nonnie had a responsible job.)

"Mary!" Nonnie yelled.

At first I didn't hear her. I continued to read my book while Beethoven was playing on the record player.

"Mary!"

I put down my book and went to the kitchen.

"What is it, Mama?"

"What is the matter with you, girl?"

"What's wrong, Mama?"

"What's wrong? The okra's burned. That's what's wrong."

"I'm sorry," I said. "It's hard to fry it without burning. I cut it up like you said, but a whole lot of slime ran out; then I rolled it in flour, but I couldn't get it to brown right. I was cooking it longer, trying to make it brown, when it burned."

"You burned up the okra."

Both Nonnie and I knew that I occasionally burned up food. I often put on supper and then got a magazine and thumbed through it while the supper cooked, or started reading a book that I had gotten out of the school library or off the bookmobile that came into the county once a week. But, either way, the results were the same: scorched chicken and leatherlike fried potatoes—not often, but sometimes.

The quarrel was all the more frustrating because we

both knew that it was not really about the scorched food. It was about something else, something I would neither stop doing nor apologize for. Something in me wouldn't let me. But the scene continued.

Nonnie stood there, her glasses glinting with the faint dust that all tobacco workers were covered with. Her blue uniform had dark-brown powder in the folds, and her apron, starched white in the morning, was now slightly beige from the tobacco. From her clothing came the faint smell of tobacco dust.

"The chicken's all right, isn't it, Mama?" I said.

"I'm not talking about the chicken."

"And I fixed the biscuits all right, too."

I desperately wanted my mother's approval. I wanted to do something that would make her smile at me and say, "That's good. I'm glad that you're my daughter."

"Listen when I'm talking to you, girl."

I knew that I didn't listen. I had learned the practical use of the "tune-out." When the stimuli from the outside world came in too strongly critical of what I was doing, of what I was interested in, I tuned out. The best substitute for listening was a smile. In that way my hearer didn't know that I had long ago ceased to listen. And I had a moment's peace. But Nonnie had me right where she wanted me—in the wrong, with no alibi, and she thoroughly enjoyed her position.

"And we have some nice Jell-O and I fixed some iced tea," I said. Please, just this one time say something nice, I silently prayed. Iced tea and Jell-O were my mother's favorites.

Nonnie was not to be deterred. "You somewhere with your head in a book and you let my okra burn."

"Mama, it never seems to come out right when I fry it."

"No. You don't watch it. You always got your head in a book or you listening to those old stories or you listening to that music all the time. Burned up my food."

"I'm sorry."

"I go and work hard and when I come home my food's burned."

That hurt, for I knew that my mother worked hard.

"But Mama, I got all A's on my report card this month."

Nonnie wasn't interested in extraneous issues. "And you don't wash the clothes right, either."

I was guilty. Washing and ironing, the measure of achievement for community girls, interested me not at all. For unspoken was the knowledge that these black girls were really being trained to work as domestics, not to keep house for themselves. But they and their mothers played a game that they were learning to be good housekeepers, and their mothers and the neighborhood ladies praised them for all evidence of homemaking skills.

I was later to observe that often cooks who planned, purchased, and prepared attractive menus on their job would at home serve ill-prepared, unbalanced meals. They were too tired to fix better, they said. And women who made their living cleaning and washing and ironing for other people frequently had unironed clothing piled to the ceiling at home and sat down in the midst of untidiness. They, too, were too tired.

But I hadn't trained properly. Instinct had taught me to see through that. It was a trap.

"And my teacher said that I could go far in life, Mama."

"Marguerita makes all of her own clothes." Nonnie neglected to mention that Marguerita's mother was a seamstress herself and that she took time and showed her daughter how to do things. No one took time to show me anything. Most of what I learned, I learned from books.

"And my teacher said that I was smart. You know I can't sew, Mama."

"And Miss Pearl says that Ida Mae does all of her washing and ironing."

"I'm going to play a piece at Mrs. Shearin's piano recital. She asked me to be on the program. She can't have her whole school on the program, just a few that she thinks are playing well. And she asked me to appear."

"You keep your head in a book all the time. What is the matter with you, girl?"

"Mama, I'm sorry that I can't do anything right. I'm sorry."

"No, if I ask you to cook, you hurry up. But if you get a book, you sit back in that room all day Saturday and all day Sunday, reading it. You don't go nowhere. Just sit in that room reading a book. Those old books and those old magazines. You going to end in Goldsboro, right with those other crazy people. You going to be just like Claudia's daughter. She read those books all the time and she went crazy and they sent her to Goldsboro."

"I'm sorry, Mama. I'm sorry, Mama. Sorry that I can't do anything right."

Aunt Jo had strange, big-city ways: she smoked cigarettes on the sly, used rouge, introduced strange cuisine in the household, and put unsuitable notions in my head. Getting rid of her was a long-drawn-out campaign, but Nonnie did it—Jo moved to town and shared rooms with two maiden sisters.

When she left, the light went out for me. I never knew again the warmth, feeling, and loving concern that Aunt Jo had shown for me during those years. There was no one to whisper to me about the marvelous things that I was going to accomplish or tell me that I was meant for really great things in life: dancer, pianist, college student. But the damage had been done. In her quiet, determined way, Aunt Jo had planted the seeds so deep that no one could ever uproot them.

Nevertheless, having maneuvered Jo out of the house, Nonnie set herself the task of eradicating those unsuitable notions from her daughter's head. They were nothing but foolishness and would lead Mary to nothing but trouble. She was sorry that Ruf had let Jo stay that long, bringing those northern ideas and ways that she had learned from rich people into her home. Anything associated with Jo's notions—my being a pianist, an intellectual—she would attack; anything not done properly in the house she would severely condemn.

On my part, I was hardheaded and stubborn. And in spite of all the fussing, I would not change. I brought a book home every day and read it between the time I got home and the time I went to bed. The okra still burned, the chicken burned, and the bread burned. Not really bad, just spots here and there, and I became adept at scraping the burned places off and putting the food back into the frying pan to brown a little more. The flour for the gravy had to be attended to every minute or it would burn so bad I'd have to throw it out and start all over, and Nonnie could not tolerate whitish gravy. So, somewhere down the line I learned about paprika, and for a while produced the reddest, spiciest gravy you ever saw. But Nonnie got wise to that—I probably put in so much that she could taste it—and I learned to cook the flour a little, then use paprika a little, not so you'd notice, but enough to speed the browning time up a bit.

If my cooking was bad, my housekeeping was worse. It would take me half the night to wash the supper dishes, for if the book I was reading was a good one, I'd read a few pages, then go wash a dish or two, then go back and read a few more. The beds got "spreaded up," not made; I took the attitude, What's the difference? You're only going to sleep in them again, anyway. And as Nonnie's fussing became sharper and the negative things she said about me got worse, I hurried even more to finish the chores and get to what I really liked. Maybe I *would* go crazy and wind up in Goldsboro. Maybe I *was* an "odd" child. But I would read

that book. I know now that subconsciously I was resisting her in the only way I knew how, not by saying
anything but just by not doing what she.valued and
wanted me to value.

One Sunday morning I had just come in from Sunday school and was sitting in the kitchen, leaning back
in a straight chair propped against the wall. It was a
warm day; I was slightly sweaty from walking in the
heat. I lost my balance and the chair I was sitting in
tipped to the left. I fell in the same direction; my head
and the knob on the back of the chair hit the window,
cracking the pane.

"See what you done!" Nonnie said. "I told you and
told you about leaning back in that chair." I was mor-
tified. She had told me before, but what stunned me
was the rage and triumph I heard in her voice.

"I'm going to make your daddy whip you. That's
what you need. A good whipping! You're getting beside yourself!"

I was too stunned to answer. Aunt Jo was gone,
and though my father was sick and irritable most of
the time, he let me help him in the little store that he
had set up near the house, and asked me to do little
things for him—so I knew he liked me. Now she
wanted him to turn against me, too.

I thought that there was a magical line that separated children from grown people, that when you
reached a certain age you automatically stopped acting
"childish"—no longer had such traits as jealousy,
spitefulness, meanness—and began acting grown,
which was the way the church taught. Those who
didn't act that way were sinners. The church taught:
"Children, obey your parents, for this is right" and
"Honor thy father and mother that thy days may be
long upon the land which the Lord thy God giveth
thee"; and the minister preached of the Prodigal
Son, who took his portion and went and wasted it,
but when he came back his father welcomed him
with a big feast. In the first grade, their mother

loved Dick and Jane, and in the magazines that I read parents loved and cared for their children. So if my mother didn't like and didn't care for me and always spoke to me harshly, she must have a good reason.

I thought and thought as to what the matter was—maybe she knew what had happened to me that night in the rain when I was five years old. I didn't, for I could never clearly remember the part where I fell down. I could remember starting out in the rain and going to the barn and running back to bed, but the part where I was screaming and fell down was cloudy to me and I never could remember. Or maybe my mother knew about my secret longings and my erotic fantasies, though I kept them hidden and never showed any signs of interest in boys.

But today something snapped. Something inside said, No.

"Just wait until he comes to the house. I'm going to make him whip you," she said again.

I wanted to cry, I'm a woman now, I'm not supposed to get any more whippings. But I said nothing.

I wondered about the triumphant tone that I heard in my mother's voice and then realized that it was because at last she could confront my father with something damaging about me. He and Jesse had been bitter enemies for a long time, but my mother liked Jesse, for he had been her firstborn; so it must have been galling to her to have my father talk to him mean and try to whip him—and for Jesse to run away—while he never whipped me and seldom spoke harshly to me, let me go with him everywhere, stand right by him while he poured the steps for the back porch, and ride with him when he peddled vegetables.

I made up my mind then. I would leave and I wasn't ever coming back. Talking to me like that, trying to turn my father against me . . . She wouldn't ever see me anymore.

I went out to the store and asked my father for

some money. The store was full of Sunday-school children buying cold drinks and peanuts. I looked at them all dressed up, feeling that if I could get away I'd never see them again. He gave me a quarter and I left the yard, walking with a bunch that was laughing and talking and drinking their cold drinks. One by one they dropped off, but I kept walking. I was on my way to the bus line. I had never ridden the bus, but I knew where it turned around; that was about two miles away. Aunt Jo lived in town now, and so did my father's cousins, and if I could get to them, they would help me; perhaps I could stay with them. I could finish school in town and I wouldn't have to come to Wildwood anymore.

Soon I was near the highway and alone. Everybody else was at home or at a friend's house, where they had asked permission to stop. The highway was different. There were fewer houses, but I had traveled this way hundreds of times on my father's wagon. There was one house close to Wildwood, tall and two-storied, many-windowed, with flapping shutters, that I was afraid of. People said that there was a ghost in it and the ghost made noises late at night. Farther ahead were two homes, one on either side of the highway. Both of the families were rich, but they were not friends, for one family had "old" money and one family had "new" money. Hazel and her family lived with the Richardses, the family with the "old" money, on a "farm" that was really an estate. Hazel was very proud of their house. It had running water and was well kept up, for it was practically in the Richardses' yard. The Ransoms lived in a tree-shaded park, one that occupied the full time of several yardmen, practically across the street from the Richardses, but Hazel liked to tell how the people her parents worked for would have nothing to do with them, for they had no "quality."

I walked on past the long hedge that separated the Ransoms' park from the highway, wondering how it

must feel to live in a big house in a grove of trees,
far away from the highway, never having to do anything, with a swarm of servants doing everything. Then
I looked at the four-tiered white fence that surrounded the Richardses' "farm"; it took a long time
to drive past it, and I knew that by the time I walked
past it, I would be near the bus line.

Once when I was visiting Hazel, she proudly showed
me the farm. There was a whole garage of nothing
but old cars, all kinds, that used to belong to the family. Then she showed me the swimming pool and the
barn where the cows were milked and the tennis
courts. She was quite proud of the place; to her it was
her "home."

Near the place where the Richardses' fence stopped,
but across the highway, were little houses where other
white people lived, those who didn't have the money
that the Richardses had. Sometimes they sat on the
porch and I wondered what they thought when they
looked at all the Richardses had and compared it with
what they had. From then on to the bus line, there
were little houses, boxlike, with little lawns and
hedges; the large estate and the farm were past.

When I got to the bus stop, there was no bus. I
walked on, not really minding it, for the highway had
become a street and now there was a sidewalk and I
liked walking; so I continued, mile after mile, passing
service stations, little box houses. I met a bus going
to the end of the line when I was far down the street,
and still I walked—past more service stations and hot-
dog stands and small businesses and more houses. I
felt so good that I thought that I would walk all the
way in to town, thus saving my quarter.

Near the creek at the foot of Mangum Street hill a
car passed me. At first I didn't notice it, but when
someone yelled I looked up.

There were three or four white boys in the car. I
wondered what they had said, but I didn't really pay
attention, for I was getting closer and closer to town

and I was preoccupied with wondering how I was
going to make out. Was someone going to invite me
to stay? Would my mother let me stay? Would a new
life start for me? I hoped so. I knew that my father
would come and get me, and maybe then I could tell
him how Nonnie hurt me by talking so mean to me
all the time and he would make her stop. But then he
was sick all the time and dependent on her, and besides, who would feed me, clothe me, give me money
to go to school? There was nobody who could but
Aunt Jo, and Nonnie wouldn't, I was sure, let me stay
with her. I walked along on a bright Sunday morning—it was near noon by then—hoping that things
would work out all right.

Then a black car passed me again and someone
threw ice on me. I was scared, for the same car had
circled around and come back up on me from behind. White people—they were the evil, the danger,
that existed in the world. You avoided them like
snakes. I didn't know what to do. Would they harass
me from then on, constantly circling and coming up
from behind? I looked back and saw the bus coming.
It had gone to the end of the line and waited and
now was making a return trip; it was Sunday and the
buses weren't running frequently. So, never having
been on a bus, I stood at the foot of the hill where
there was a sign that said BUS, and when it came I
got on. A brief conversation with the driver got me
three tokens.

I was surprised to see Nancy on the bus; she taught
the little children in Sunday school. She was surprised
to see me, too. I told her that I was going to town to
see my folks. She soon discovered that I knew nothing
about changing buses and getting a transfer, and told
me how and where to change. I went to the front and
got the little pink transfer and got off at Walgreen's
at Main Street.

I got to West Durham all right. I was proud of
myself for finding the way, the first time on my own.

I went to see Aunt Jo, but I felt so sad, for she was living in a small dark room in a house with two unmarried sisters. She didn't like it; I had heard her tell my mother that once. She asked me about everybody and I said they were all right, but I knew that she knew that something was wrong, because I had come alone. I wanted to tell her so much and I started to several times—that I wanted to come to town to live, maybe even stay with her; but I felt so bad that I would be letting her down, for she held me up as a model to her nieces and nephews, and if they knew I was running away from home it would make her look bad for having so much faith in me. I couldn't make the words come out. So we sat and talked, awkwardly, for we hadn't been alone in a long time. She spoke again of education. I must get an education.

I didn't know it then, but she was already dying of cancer. Marva, my older cousin, who lived across the street from Aunt Jo, was surprised to see me, and her daughter Jerline barely spoke—though she had been to visit us in the country—and an older male cousin took the extra token that I had put in a dish on the coffee table. I saw him take it, but he was grown and I was scared to say "Don't."

In the late afternoon I started back home. I rode the bus downtown all right, but at Five Points I didn't know how to change buses and was too scared to ask; so I started walking right on Main Street, in the heart of Durham. I walked the eight miles home.

Near the bus line Jesse met me; he was on his way to town. "Mama's gonna whip you!" He laughed in that special way he had when something bad was going to happen to somebody. I said nothing, but walked on. It was soon deep night. Wildwood was dark and quiet when I got back, with a light here and there. I passed no one.

Nonnie was angry and I was defiant. She got her switches to whip me, but I started yelling that I was going to leave again and I wasn't coming back.

She did a lot of fussing, but she hit me only a time or two. I knew that I had won, for I never got another whipping. I had learned the value of protest. And I, too, put my soul on ice. I had to, if I was to survive.

Anne Moody

Born in Mississippi in 1940, Anne Moody received a
B.S. from Tougaloo College in 1964. She writes that
she never really saw herself as a writer: "I was first
and foremost an activist in the civil rights movement
in Mississippi." She wrote about these experiences in
her autobiography, *Coming of Age in Mississippi*
(1969), from which the following excerpt is taken. She
was an organizer and fund-raiser for the Congress of
Racial Equality (CORE) in Washington, D.C., and a
civil rights project coordinator at Cornell University.
A contributor to *Ms.* and *Mademoiselle*, she has published a collection of short stories, *Mr. Death* (1975),
and worked as an artist-in-residence in Berlin. She
makes her home in New York City.

from Coming of Age
in Mississippi

In mid-September I was back on campus. But didn't very much happen until February when the NAACP held its annual convention in Jackson. They were having a whole lot of interesting speakers: Jackie Robinson, Floyd Patterson, Curt Flood, Margaretta Belafonte, and many others. I wouldn't have missed it for anything. I was so excited that I sent one of the leaflets home to Mama and asked her to come.

Three days later I got a letter from Mama with dried-up tears on it, forbidding me to go to the convention. It went on for more than six pages. She said if I didn't stop that shit she would come to Tougaloo and kill me herself. She told me about the time I last visited her, on Thanksgiving, and she had picked me up at the bus station. She said she picked me up because she was scared some white in my hometown would try to do something to me. She said the sheriff had been by, telling her I was messing around with that NAACP group. She said he told her if I didn't stop it, I could not come back there anymore. He said that they didn't need any of those NAACP people messing around in Centreville. She ended the letter by saying that she had burned the leaflet I sent her. "Please don't send any more of that stuff here. I don't want nothing to happen to us here," she said. "If you keep that up, you will never be able to come home again."

I was so damn mad after her letter, I felt like taking the NAACP convention to Centreville. I think I would have, if it had been in my power to do so. The remainder of the week I thought of nothing except going to the convention. I didn't know exactly what to do about it. I didn't want Mama or anyone at home to get hurt because of me.

I had felt something was wrong when I was home. During the four days I was there, Mama had tried to do everything she could to keep me in the house. When I said I was going to see some of my old classmates, she pretended she was sick and said I would have to cook. I knew she was acting strangely, but I hadn't known why. I thought Mama just wanted me to spend most of my time with her, since this was only the second time I had been home since I entered college as a freshman.

Things kept running through my mind after that letter from Mama. My mind was so active, I couldn't sleep at night. I remembered the one time I did leave the house to go to the post office. I had walked past a bunch of white men on the street on my way through town and one said, "Is that the gal goin' to Tougaloo?" He acted kind of mad or something, and I didn't know what was going on. I got a creepy feeling, so I hurried home. When I told Mama about it, she just said, "A lotta people don't like that school." I knew what she meant. Just before I went to Tougaloo, they had housed the Freedom Riders there. The school was being criticized by whites throughout the state.

The night before the convention started, I made up my mind to go, no matter what Mama said. I just wouldn't tell Mama or anyone from home. Then it occurred to me—how did the sheriff or anyone at home know I was working with the NAACP chapter on campus? Somehow they had found out. Now I knew I could never go to Centreville safely again. I kept telling myself that I didn't really care too much about going home, that it was more important to me to go to the convention.

I was there from the very beginning. Jackie Robinson was asked to serve as moderator. This was the first time I had seen him in person. I remembered how when Jackie became the first Negro to play Major League baseball, my uncles and most of the Negro boys in my hometown started organizing baseball leagues. It did something for them to see a Negro out there playing with all those white players. Jackie was a good moderator, I thought. He kept smiling and joking. People felt relaxed and proud. They appreciated knowing and meeting people of their own race who had done something worth talking about.

When Jackie introduced Floyd Patterson, heavyweight champion of the world, the people applauded for a long, long time. Floyd was kind of shy. He didn't say very much. He didn't have to, just his being there was enough to satisfy most of the Negroes who had only seen him on TV. Archie Moore was there too. He wasn't as smooth as Jackie, but he had his way with a crowd. He started telling how he was run out of Mississippi, and the people just cracked up.

I was enjoying the convention so much that I went back for the night session. Before the night was over, I had gotten autographs from every one of the Negro celebrities.

I had counted on graduating in the spring of 1963, but as it turned out, I couldn't because some of my credits still had to be cleared with Natchez College. A year before, this would have seemed like a terrible disaster, but now I hardly even felt disappointed. I had a good excuse to stay on campus for the summer and work with the Movement, and this was what I really wanted to do. I couldn't go home again anyway, and I couldn't go to New Orleans—I didn't have money enough for bus fare.

During my senior year at Tougaloo, my family hadn't sent me one penny. I had only the small amount of money I had earned at Maple Hill. I couldn't afford to eat at school or live in the dorms, so I had gotten permission to move off campus. I had to prove that I could finish school, even if I had to go hungry every day. I knew Raymond and Miss Pearl were just waiting to see me drop out. But something happened to me as I got more and more involved in the Movement. It no longer seemed important to prove anything. I had found something outside myself that gave meaning to my life.

I had become very friendly with my social science professor, John Salter, who was in charge of NAACP activities on campus. All during the year, while the NAACP conducted a boycott of the downtown stores in Jackson, I had been one of Salter's most faithful canvassers and church speakers. During the last week of school, he told me that sit-in demonstrations were about to start in Jackson and that he wanted me to be the spokesman for a team that would sit-in at Woolworth's lunch counter. The two other demonstrators would be classmates of mine, Memphis and Pearlena. Pearlena was a dedicated NAACP worker, but Memphis had not been very involved in the Movement on campus. It seemed that the organization had had a rough time finding students who were in a position to go to jail. I had nothing to lose one way or the other. Around ten o'clock the morning of the demonstrations, NAACP headquarters alerted the news services. As a result, the police department was also informed, but neither the policemen nor the newsmen knew exactly where or when the demonstrations would start. They stationed themselves along Capitol Street and waited.

To divert attention from the sit-in at Woolworth's the picketing started at JCPenney a good fifteen minutes before. The pickets were allowed to walk up and down in front of the store three or four times before they were arrested. At exactly 11 A.M., Pearlena, Memphis, and I entered Woolworth's from the rear entrance. We separated as soon as we stepped into the store, and made small purchases from various counters. Pearlena had given Memphis her watch. He was to let us know when it was 11:14. At 11:14 we were to join him near the lunch counter and at exactly 11:15 we were to take seats at it.

Seconds before 11:15 we were occupying three seats at the previously segregated Woolworth's lunch counter. In the beginning the waitresses seemed to ignore us, as if they really didn't know what was going on. Our waitress walked past us a couple of times before she noticed we had started to write our own orders down and realized we wanted service. She asked us what we wanted. We began to read to her from our order slips. She told us that we would be served at the back counter, which was for Negroes.

"We would like to be served here," I said.

The waitress started to repeat what she had said, then stopped in the middle of the sentence. She turned the lights out behind the counter, and she and the other waitressess almost ran to the back of the store, deserting all their white customers. I guess they thought that violence would start immediately after the whites at the counter realized what was going on. There were five or six other people at the counter. A couple of them just got up and walked away. A girl sitting next to me finished her banana split before leaving. A middle-aged white woman who had not yet been served rose from her seat and came over to us. "I'd like to stay here with you," she said, "but my husband is waiting."

The newsmen came in just as she was leaving. They must have discovered what was going on shortly after some of the people began to leave the store. One of the newsmen ran behind the woman who spoke to us and asked her to identify herself. She refused to give her name, but said she was a native of Vicksburg and a former resident of California. When asked why she had said what she had said to us, she replied, "I am in sympathy with the Negro movement." By this time a crowd of cameramen and reporters had gathered around us taking pictures and asking questions, such as Where were we from? Why did we sit-in? What organization sponsored it? Were we students? From what school? How were we classified?

I told them that we were all students at Tougaloo College, that we were represented by no particular organization, and that we planned to stay there even after the store closed. "All we want is service," was my reply to one of them. After they had finished probing for about twenty minutes, they were almost ready to leave.

At noon, students from a nearby white high school started pouring in to Woolworth's. When they first saw us they were sort of surprised. They didn't know how to react. A few started to heckle and the newsmen became interested again. Then the white students started chanting all kinds of anti-Negro slogans. We were called a little bit of everything. The rest of the seats except the three we were occupying had been roped off to prevent others from sitting down. A couple of the boys took one end of the rope and made it into a hangman's noose. Several attempts were made to put it around our necks. The crowds grew as more students and adults came in for lunch.

We kept our eyes straight forward and did not look at the crowd except for occasional glances to see what was going on. All of a sudden I saw a face I remembered—the drunkard from the bus station sit-in. My eyes lingered on him just long enough for us to recognize each other. Today he was drunk too, so I don't think he remembered where he had seen me before. He took out a knife, opened it, put it in his pocket, and then began to pace the floor. At this point, I told Memphis and Pearlena what was going on. Memphis suggested that we pray. We bowed our heads, and all hell broke loose. A man rushed forward, threw Memphis from his seat, and slapped my face. Then another man who worked in the store threw me against an adjoining counter.

Down on my knees on the floor, I saw Memphis lying near the lunch counter with blood running out of the corners of his mouth. As he tried to protect his face, the man who'd thrown him down kept kicking him against the head. If he had worn hard-soled shoes instead of sneakers, the first kick probably would have killed Memphis. Finally a man dressed in plain clothes identified himself as a police officer and arrested Memphis and his attacker.

Pearlena had been thrown to the floor. She and I got back on our stools after Memphis was arrested. There were some white Tougaloo teachers in the crowd. They asked Pearlena and me if we wanted to leave. They said that things were getting too rough. We didn't know what to do. While we were trying to make up our minds, we were joined by Joan Trumpauer. Now there were three of us and we were integrated. The crowd began to chant, "Communists, Communists, Communists." Some old man in the crowd ordered the students to take us off the stools.

"Which one should I get first?" a big husky boy said.

"That white nigger," the old man said.

The boy lifted Joan from the counter by her waist and carried her out of the store. Simultaneously, I was snatched from my stool by two high school students. I was dragged about thirty feet toward the door by my hair when someone made them turn me loose. As I was getting up off the floor, I saw Joan coming back inside. We started back to the center of the counter to join Pearlena. Lois Chaffee, a white Tougaloo faculty member, was now sitting next to her. So Joan and I just climbed across the rope at the front end of the counter and sat down. There were now four of us, two whites and two Negroes, all women. The mob started smearing us with ketchup, mustard, sugar, pies, and everything on the counter. Soon Joan and I were joined by John Salter, but the moment he sat down he was hit on the jaw with what appeared to be brass knuckles. Blood gushed from his face and someone threw salt into the open wound. Ed King, Tougaloo's chaplain, rushed to him.

At the other end of the counter, Lois and Pearlena were joined by George Raymond, a CORE field worker and a student from Jackson State College. Then a Negro high school boy sat down next to me. The mob took spray paint from the counter and sprayed it on the new demonstrators. The high school student had on a white shirt; the word "nigger" was written on his back with red spray paint.

We sat there for three hours taking a beating when the manager decided to close the store because the mob had begun to go wild with stuff from other counters. He begged and begged everyone to leave. But even after fifteen minutes of begging, no one budged. They would not leave until we did. Then Dr. Beittel, the president of Tougaloo College, came running in. He said he had just heard what was happening.

About ninety policemen were standing outside the store; they had been watching the whole thing through the windows, but had not come in to stop the mob or do anything. President Beittel went outside and asked Captain Ray to come and escort us out. The captain refused, stating the manager had to invite him in before he could enter the premises, so Dr. Beittel himself brought us out. He had told the police that they had better protect us after we were outside the store. When we got outside, the policemen formed a single line that blocked the mob from us. However, they were allowed to throw at us everything they had collected. Within ten minutes, we were picked up by Reverend King in his station wagon and taken to the NAACP headquarters on Lynch Street.

After the sit-in, all I could think of was how sick Mississippi whites were. They believed so much in the segregated southern way of life, they would kill to preserve it. I sat there in the NAACP office and thought of how many times they had killed when this way of life was threatened. I knew that the killing had just begun. "Many more will die before it is over with," I thought. Before the sit-in, I had always hated the whites in Mississippi. Now I knew it was impossible for me to hate sickness. The whites had a disease, an incurable disease in its final stage. What were our chances against such a disease? I thought of the students, the young Negroes who had just begun to protest, as young interns. When these young interns got older, I thought, they would be the best doctors in the world for social problems.

Before we were taken back to campus, I wanted to get my hair washed. It was stiff with dried mustard, ketchup and sugar. I stopped in at a beauty shop across the street from the NAACP office. I didn't have on any shoes because I had lost them when I was dragged across the floor at Woolworth's. My stockings were sticking to my legs from the mustard that had dried on them. The hairdresser took one look at me and said, "My land, you were in the sit-in, huh?"

"Yes," I answered. "Do you have time to wash my hair and style it?"

"Right away," she said, and she meant right away. There were three other ladies already waiting, but they seemed glad to let me go ahead of them. The hairdresser was real nice. She even took my stockings off and washed my legs while my hair was drying.

There was a mass rally that night at the Pearl Street Church in Jackson, and the place was packed. People were standing two abreast in the aisles. Before the speakers began, all the sit-inners walked out on the stage and were introduced by Medgar Evers. People stood and applauded for what seemed like thirty minutes or more. Medgar told the audience that this was just the beginning of such demonstrations. He asked them to pledge themselves to unite in a massive offensive against segregation in Jackson, and throughout the state. The rally ended with "We Shall Overcome" and sent home hundreds of determined people. It seemed as though Mississippi Negroes were about to get together at last.

Before I demonstrated, I had written Mama. She wrote me back a letter, begging me not to take part in the sit-in. She even sent ten dollars for bus fare to New Orleans. I didn't have one penny, so I kept the money. Mama's letter made me mad. I had to live my life as I saw fit. I had made that decision when I left home. But it hurt to have my family prove to me how scared they were. It hurt me more than anything else—I knew the whites had already started the threats and intimidations. I was the first Negro from my hometown who had openly demonstrated, worked with the NAACP, or anything. When Negroes threatened to do anything in Centreville, they were either shot like Samuel O'Quinn or run out of town, like Reverend Dupree.

I didn't answer Mama's letter. Even if I had written one, she wouldn't have received it before she saw the news on TV or heard it on the radio. I waited to hear from her again. And I waited to hear in the news that someone in Centreville had been murdered. If so, I knew it would be a member of the family.

On Wednesday, the day after the sit-in, demonstrations got off to a good start. Ten people picketed shortly after noon on Capitol Street, and were arrested. Another mass rally followed the demonstrations that night, where a six-man delegation of Negro ministers was chosen to meet Mayor Thompson the following Tuesday. They were to present to him a number of demands on behalf of Jackson Negroes. They were as follows:

1. Hiring of Negro policemen and school crossing guards

2. Removal of segregation signs from public facilities

3. Improvement of job opportunities for Negroes on city payrolls—Negro drivers of city garbage trucks, etc.

4. Encouraging public eating establishments to serve both whites and Negroes

5. Integration of public parks and libraries

6. The naming of a Negro to the City Parks and Recreation Committee

7. Integration of public schools

8. Forcing service stations to integrate rest rooms

After this meeting, Reverend Haughton, the minister of Pearl Street Church, said that the Mayor was going to act on all the suggestions. But the following day, Thompson denied that he had made any promises. He said the Negro delegation "got carried away" following their discussion with him.

"It seems as though Mayor Thompson wants to play games with us," Reverend Haughton said at the next rally. "He is calling us liars and trying to make us sound like fools. I guess we have to show him that we mean business."

When Reverend Charles A. Jones, dean and chaplain at Campbell College, asked at the close of the meeting, "Where do we go from here?" the audience shouted, "To the streets." They were going to prove to Mayor Thompson and the white people of Jackson that they meant business.

Around ten the next morning, an entire day of demonstrations started. A little bit of everything was tried. Some Negroes sat-in, some picketed, and some squatted in the streets and refused to move.

All of the five-and-ten stores (H. L. Green, Kress, and Woolworth) had closed their lunch counters as a result of the Woolworth sit-in. However, this did not stop the new sit-ins. Chain restaurants such as Primos Restaurant in downtown Jackson were now targets. Since police brutality was the last thing wanted in good, respectable Jackson, Mississippi, whenever arrested demonstrators refused to walk to a paddy wagon, garbage truck, or whatever was being used to take people to jail, Negro trusties from Jackson's city jail carted them away. Captain Ray and his men would just stand back with their hands folded, looking innocent as lambs for the benefit of the northern reporters and photographers.

The Mayor still didn't seem to be impressed with the continuous small demonstrations and kept the streets hot. After eighty-eight demonstrators had been arrested, the Mayor held a news conference where he told a group of reporters, "We can handle 100,000 agitators." He also stated that the "good colored citizens are not rallying to the support of the outside agitators" (although there were only a few out-of-state people involved in the movement at the time) and offered to give northern newsmen anything they wanted, including transportation, if they would "adequately" report the facts.

During the demonstrations, I helped conduct several workshops, where potential demonstrators, high school and college students mostly, were taught to protect themselves. If, for instance, you wanted to protect the neck to offset a karate blow, you clasped your hands behind the neck. To protect the genital organs you doubled up in a knot, drawing the knees up to the chest to protect your breasts if you were a girl.

The workshops were handled mostly by SNCC and CORE field secretaries and workers, almost all of whom were very young. The NAACP handled all the bail and legal services and public relations, but SNCC and CORE could draw teenagers into the Movement as no other organization could. Whether they received credit for it or not, they helped make Jackson the center of attention throughout the nation.

During this period, civil rights workers who had become known to the Jackson police were often used to divert the cops' attention just before a demonstration. A few cops were always placed across the street from NAACP headquarters, since most of the demonstrations were organized there and would leave from that building. The "diverters" would get into cars and lead the cops off on a wild-goose chase. This would allow the real demonstrators to get downtown before they were noticed. One evening, a group of us took the cops for a tour of the park. After giving the demonstrators time enough to get to Capitol Street, we decided to go and watch the action. When we arrived there ourselves, we met Reverend King and a group of ministers. They told us they were going to stage a pray-in on the post office steps. "Come on, join us," Reverend King said. "I don't think we'll be arrested, because it's federal property."

By the time we got to the post office, the newsmen had already been informed, and a group of them were standing in front of the building blocking the front entrance. By now the group of whites that usually constituted the mob had gotten smart. They no longer looked for us, or for the demonstration. They just followed the newsmen and photographers. They were much smarter than the cops, who hadn't caught on yet.

We entered the post office through the side entrance and found that part of the mob was waiting inside the building. We didn't let this bother us. As soon as a few more ministers joined us, we were ready to go outside. There were fourteen of us, seven whites and seven Negroes. We walked out front and stood and bowed our heads as the ministers began to pray. We were immediately interrupted by the appearance of Captain Ray. "We are asking you people to disperse. If you don't, you are under arrest," he said.

Most of us were not prepared to go to jail. Doris Erskine, a student from Jackson State, and I had to take over a workshop the following day. Some of the ministers were in charge of the mass rally that night. But if we had dispersed, we would have been torn to bits by the mob. The whites standing out there had murder in their eyes. They were ready to do us in and all fourteen of us knew that. We had no other choice but to be arrested.

We had no plan of action. Reverend King and some of the ministers who were kneeling refused to move;

they just kept on praying. Some of the others also attempted to kneel. The rest of us just walked to the paddy wagon. Captain Ray was using the Negro trusties. I felt so sorry for them. They were too small to be carrying all these heavy-ass demonstrators. I could tell just by looking at them that they didn't want to, either. I knew they were forced to do this.

After we got to jail we were mugged and fingerprinted, then taken to a cell. Most of the ministers were scared stiff. This was the first time some of them had seen the inside of a jail. Before we were mugged, we were all placed in a room together and allowed to make one call. Reverend King made the call to the NAACP headquarters to see if some of the ministers could be bailed out right away. I was so glad when they told him they didn't have money available at the moment. I just got my kicks out of sitting there looking at the ministers. Some of them looked so pitiful, I thought they would cry any minute, and here they were, supposed to be our leaders.

When Doris and I got to the cell where we would spend the next four days, we found a lot of our friends there. There were twelve girls altogether. The jail was segregated. I felt sorry for Jeanette King, Lois Chaffee, and Joan Trumpauer. Just because they were white they were missing out on all the fun we planned to have. Here we were going to school together, sleeping in the same dorm, worshipping together, playing together, even demonstrating together. It all ended in jail. They were rushed off by themselves to some cell designated for whites.

Our cell didn't even have a curtain over the shower. Every time the cops heard the water running, they came running to peep. After the first time, we fixed them. We took chewing gum and toilet tissue and covered the opening in the door. They were afraid to take it down. I guess they thought it might have come out in the newspaper. Their wives wouldn't have liked that at all. Peep through a hole to see a bunch of nigger girls naked? No! No! They certainly wouldn't have liked that. All of the girls in my cell were college students. We had a lot to talk about, so we didn't get too bored. We made cards out of toilet tissue and played Gin Rummy almost all day. Some of us even learned new dance steps from each other.

There were a couple of girls in with us from Jackson State College. They were scared they would be expelled from school. Jackson State, like most of the state-supported Negro schools, was an Uncle Tom school. The students could be expelled for almost anything. When I found this out, I really appreciated Tougaloo.

The day we were arrested one of the Negro trusties sneaked us a newspaper. We discovered that over four hundred high school students had also been arrested. We were so glad we sang freedom songs for an hour or so. The jailer threatened to put us in solitary if we didn't stop. At first we didn't think he meant it, so we kept singing. He came back with two other cops and asked us to follow them. They marched us down the hall and showed us one of the solitary chambers. "If you don't stop that damn singing, I'm gonna throw all of you in here together," said the jailer. After that we didn't sing anymore. We went back and finished reading the paper.

We got out of jail on Sunday to discover that everyone was talking about the high school students. All four hundred who were arrested had been taken to the fairgrounds and placed in a large open compound without beds or anything. It was said that they were getting sick like flies. Mothers were begging to have their children released, but the NAACP didn't have enough money to bail them all out.

The same day we went to jail for the pray-in, the students at Lanier High School had started singing freedom songs on their lunch hour. They got so carried away they ignored the bell when the break was over and just kept on singing. The principal of the high school did not know what to do, so he called the police and told them that the students were about to start a riot.

When the cops came, they brought the dogs. The students refused to go back to their classrooms when asked, so the cops turned the dogs loose on them. The students fought them off for a while. In fact, I was told that mothers who lived near the school had joined the students in fighting off the dogs. They had begun to throw bricks, rocks, and bottles. The next day the papers stated that ten or more cops suffered cuts or minor wounds. The papers didn't say it, but a lot of students were hurt, too, from dog bites and lumps on the head from billy clubs. Finally, one hundred and fifty cops were rushed to the scene and several students and adults were arrested.

The next day four hundred of the high school students from Lanier, Jim Hill, and Brinkley High schools gathered in a church on Farish Street, ready to go to jail. Willie Ludden, the NAACP youth leader, and some of the SNCC and CORE workers met with them, gave a brief workshop on nonviolent protective measures and led them into the streets. After marching about two blocks they were met by helmeted police officers and ordered to disperse. When they refused, they were arrested, herded into paddy wagons, canvas-covered trucks, and garbage trucks. Those moving too slowly were jabbed with rifle butts. Police dogs were there, but were not used. From the way everyone was describing the scene it sounded like Nazi Germany instead of Jackson, USA.

On Monday, I joined a group of high school students and several other college students who were trying to get arrested. Our intention was to be put in the fairgrounds with the high school students already there. The cops picked us up, but they didn't want to put us so-called professional agitators in with the high

school students. We were weeded out, and taken back
to the city jail.

I got out of jail two days later and found I had
gotten another letter from Mama. She had written it
Wednesday the twenty-ninth, after the Woolworth sit-
in. The reason it had taken so long for me to get it
was that it came by way of New Orleans. Mama sent
it to Adline and had Adline mail it to me. In the letter
she told me that the sheriff had stopped by and asked
all kinds of questions about me the morning after the
sit-in. She said she and Raymond told them that I had
only been home once since I was in college, that I had
practically cut off all my family connections when I
ran away from home as a senior in high school. She
said he said that he knew I had left home. "He should
know," I thought, "because I had to get him to move
my clothes for me when I left." She went on and on.
She told me he said I must never come back there. If
so he would not be responsible for what happened to
me. "The whites are pretty upset about her doing
these things," he told her. Mama told me not to write
her again until she sent me word that it was O.K. She
said that I would hear from her through Adline.

I also got a letter from Adline in the same envelope.
She told me what Mama hadn't mentioned—that Junior had been cornered by a group of white boys and
was about to be lynched, when one of his friends came
along in a car and rescued him. Besides that, a group
of white men had gone out and beaten up my old
Uncle Buck. Adline said Mama told her they couldn't
sleep, for fear of night riders. They were all scared to
death. My sister ended the letter by cursing me out.
She said I was trying to get every Negro in Centreville murdered.

I guess Mama didn't tell me these things because
she was scared to. She probably thought I would have
tried to do something crazy. Something like trying to
get the organizations to move into Wilkinson County,

or maybe coming home myself to see if they would kill me. She never did give me credit for having the least bit of sense. I knew there was nothing I could do. No organization was about to go to Wilkinson County. It was a little too tough for any of them. And I wasn't about to go there either. If they said they would kill me, I figured I'd better take their word for it.

Joan Williams

Joan Williams was born in 1928, in Memphis, Tennessee. After she graduated from Bard College in New York, she lived briefly in New Orleans and worked in a bookstore. She then moved to New York City, where she answered letters to the editor for *Look* magazine. Following the publication of her first story, Williams began corresponding with William Faulkner. She became his protégée and with him coauthored a teleplay titled *The Graduation Dress* (1960), which was produced by General Electric Theatre. Her first novel, *The Morning and the Evening* (1961), won the John P. Marquand First Novel Award. She sets her fiction in the hill country of northwest Mississippi and focuses on characters who are isolated and alienated from their communities. Her novel *The Wintering* (1972), based on her friendship with William Faulkner, portrays the relationship between an older man who is a famous author and a young woman who is an aspiring writer. She has written three other novels—*Old Powder Man* (1966), *County Woman* (1982), and *Pay the Piper* (1988)—as well as a collection of short stories, *Pariah and Other Stories* (1983). She lives in Charlottesville, Virginia.

Spring Is Now

Sandra heard first in Miss Loma's store about the Negroes. She was buying cornstarch for her mother when Mr. Mal Walker rushed in, leaving his car at the gas pump, without filling it, to tell the news. His hair plastered to his forehead, he was as breathless and hot as if he had been running. "The school bus was loaded and the driver passed up some niggers in De Soto," he said. "They threw rocks at the bus and a brick that broke the driver's arm." That was all he knew about that. "But," he said, pausing until everyone in the store was paying attention. "There's some registered for your high school in Indian Hill."

At that moment Sandra found the cornstarch. The thought of going to school with Negroes leapt at her as confusedly as the box's yellow-and-blue design. Coming slowly around the bread rack, she saw Mal Walker, rapidly swallowing a Dr Pepper he had taken from the cold-drink case. She put the cornstarch on the counter. Miss Loma fitted a sack over the box and said, "Is that all?"

Sandra nodded and signed the credit pad Miss Loma shoved along the counter. In Miss Loma's pierced ears, small gold hoops shook as, turning back to Mal Walker, she said, "How many?"

"Three I heard." Almost smiling, he looked around and announced—as if the store were full of people, though there was only an apologetic-looking country woman, with a dime, waiting for the party line to clear—"If your kids haven't eat with niggers yet, they

will have by Friday. I thank the Lord I live in Indian
Hill. Mine will walk home to lunch. When it comes to
eating with them, I draw the line."

"Sandra, you want something else?" Miss Loma
said.

"No ma'am." Sandra went out and slowly up the
hill toward her house opposite, thinking how many
times she had eaten with Minnie, who worked for her
mother, and how often her mother had eaten in the
kitchen, while Minnie ironed. Even Grandmomma had
said she would sit down with Minnie, Minnie was like
one of the family, though Sandra could not remember
that her grandmother ever had. For one reason, she
was always in the living room looking at television.
There now, she was shelling butter beans and Sandra
passed behind her chair, saying nothing, because
Grandmomma was hard of hearing. In the kitchen,
Sandra put down the cornstarch and said, "Mother,
Mister Mal Walker says there's Negroes coming to our
high school."

"Are you sure?" Her mother, Flo, was frying chicken
and stood suddenly motionless, a long-handled fork
outstretched over the skillet full of popping meat and
grease. She and Sandra had similar pale faces and
placid gray-green eyes, which they widened now, in
worry. "I guess we knew it was coming," Flo said.

"Three, he thinks."

In bifocals, Grandmomma's eyes looked enormous.
She stood in the doorway saying, "Three what?" Having seen Flo motionless, she sensed something had
happened and hearing what, she threw her hands to
her throat and said, "Oh, you don't mean to tell me."
With the fork, Flo stuck chicken pieces, lifting them
onto paper toweling. "Now, Momma," she said, "we
knew it was coming." Then Grandmomma, resigned
to one more thing she had not expected to live to see,
let her hands fall to her sides. "I sure do hate to hear
it," she said. "Are they girls and boys?"

"I don't know," Sandra said.

"I just hope to goodness it's girls," Grandmomma said, looking at Flo, who said again, "Now, Momma."

At sundown, when her father came from the fields, Sandra was watching television with Grandmomma. The pickup stopped, a door slammed, but the motor continued to run. From the window she saw her father, a sturdy, graying man; he was talking to Willson, a field hand, who backed the truck from the drive as her father came inside. "Daddy," she said, "there's Negroes going to our school."

He stood a moment looking tired from more than work. Then he said, "I guess it had to happen." He frowned and his eyebrows drew together across his forehead. "The schools that don't take them don't get government money. I knew you'd be with them at the university. But I'm sorry you had to start a year earlier."

Grandmomma, looking up from her program, said, "I just hope they're girls."

"Oh, Grandmomma," Sandra said with irritation and followed her father across the hall. "Why'd Willson take the truck, Daddy?"

Having bent over the bathroom basin to wash, he lifted his head. "That boy of his sick in Memphis can come home tonight. I loaned him the truck to go get him," he said, and his splashed face seemed weighted by the drops of water falling away.

"The one that's had all that trouble with his leg swelling?" Flo said. She brought the platter of chicken to the table.

"He's on crutches but will be all right," the father said.

"I declare, that boy's had a time," Grandmomma said, joining them at the table. "When Willson brings the truck, give him some of my grape jelly to carry to the boy."

They bent their heads and Sandra's father said his usual long blessing. Afterward they looked at one another across the centerpiece of zinnias, as if words were left unsaid. But no one said anything and they began to eat. Then the father said, "Guess what happened? Willson and some of his friends asked if I'd run for road supervisor."

"Why, Tate," Flo said. "What'd you say?"

"I said, 'When would I find the time?'" he said.

"It shows the way they're thinking," Flo said.

"How?" Sandra said.

"They know they can't run one of them yet, but they want a man elected they choose," she said. "Still, Tate, it's a compliment."

"I guess it is," he said.

"The time's just going to come," Grandmomma said.

"Of course, it is," he said.

At six-fifteen the next morning, Sandra from her bed heard a repeated knock rattling the side door. There were the smells of coffee and sausage, and Flo, summoned, pushed her chair from the table to answer the door. Air-conditioning so early made the house too cold and Sandra, reaching for her thin blanket, kept her eyes closed.

"Morning, how're you?" It was Johnson, the Negro who cleaned the Methodist church. He had come to get his pay from Flo, the church's treasurer.

"Pretty good, Johnson, how're you?" Flo said.

"Good but not pretty." He and Flo laughed, then were quiet while she wrote the check. Sandra heard him walk off down the gravel drive and it seemed a long time before she fell back to sleep. Then Flo shook her, saying, "Louise wants to drive the car pool today. You have to be at school at ten to register. Hurry, it's after nine."

"Why'd Johnson come so early?" she said.

"Breakfast was the only time he knew he could catch me home," Flo said.

Drinking orange juice, Sandra stood by the refrigerator and Grandmomma called from the living room,

"Are you going to school all winter with your hair streaming down your back like that? I wish you'd get it cut today."

"I don't want it cut," Sandra said.

"Well, I wish you'd wear it pretty like this girl on television then. Look, with it held back behind a band like that."

Sandra came into the living room to look. "Her hair's in a pageboy; it's shorter than mine," she said.

"At least comb it," her mother called from the kitchen.

"I combed it!" Sandra said.

"Well you need to comb it again," her mother said. "And eat something."

"I'm not hungry in the mornings," Sandra said and went out into the heat and down the steep driveway to wait for her friend Louise. There was no high school in their town and they went twenty miles away to a larger place. "Cold," Sandra said, getting in Louise's car.

"Turn that valve and the air conditioner won't blow straight on you," Louise said. She pushed back hair that fell, like a mane, over her glasses. "You heard?"

"About the Negroes?"

"Yes. I heard there were thirteen."

"Thirteen! I heard three."

Louise laughed. "Maybe there's none and everybody's excited about nothing."

There had been a drought all summer in northwest Mississippi. They rode looking out at cotton fields nowhere near bloom, corn limp and brown, and soybeans stunted, flat to the ground. Between the fields were stretches of crumbly dirt, enormous and empty, where crops failed from the drought had been plowed under. Nearby a pickup raced along a gravel road and as far as they could see, dust trailed it, one cloud rising above the flatland. Once, workmen along the road turned to them faces yellowed by dust, with dark holes for eyes, and Sandra thought of the worry that had

been on her father's face all summer, as farmers
waited for rain. And all summer, wherever they went,
her mother had said, "You don't remember what it
was like before everybody had air-conditioned cars.
All this dust blew in the windows. Whew! I don't
know how we stood it."

And, not remembering she had said it before, Grandmomma would say, "You don't remember either what
it was like trying to sleep. Sometimes we'd move our
mattresses out into the yard and sleep under the trees.
We'd wring out towels and put them on the bed wet
to cool the sheets." That she had lived then, though
she did not remember it, seemed strange to Sandra.

At school, she found out only that some Negroes
had already registered. None were there and the
teachers would answer no other questions. Standing
in long lines all morning, Sandra found she watched
for the Negroes anyway. Other students said they had
done the same. She thought the Negroes had been
paid more attention by being absent than if they had
been present. On the way home, Louise said, "If it
weren't such a mystery, I don't think I'd think much
about them. If there's a few, I just feel I'm not going
to bother them and they're not going to bother me, if
they're not smart-alecky."

"I know," Sandra said. "What's the difference,
three or thirteen, with the rest of us white?" They
stopped on the highway at the Mug'n Cone for hot
dogs and root beer. Nearing home, Sandra began to
dread questions she would be asked, particularly since
she knew little more than when she left. At Miss
Loma's, she got out to buy shampoo. The old men
were gathered on the store porch playing dominoes,
and she said only, "Afternoon," though her mother
always said they would be glad for conversation. She
thought of when her grandfather had been among
them and entered the store.

Miss Loma had already heard the news from the

Indian Hill school. She and a Memphis salesman were talking about a family nearby, in the Delta, who passed as white, though people steered clear of them, believing they had Negro blood. "I'll tell you how you can always tell a Negro," the salesman said. "By the blue moons on their nails. They can't hide those."

"I've heard," Miss Loma said, her earrings shaking, "they have black streaks at the ends of their spinal cords. Now, that's what men who've been with them in the army say. Of course, I don't know if it's true. I doubt it." She and the salesman could not decide whether she ought to stock up on straight-lined or dotted-lined primary tablets. With a practical finger, Miss Loma twirled the wire school-supply rack. The salesman pushed back a sporty straw hat with a fishing-fly ornament and said, "Wait till school starts and see what the teacher wants. One thing I hate to see is, somebody stuck with primary tablets they can't sell."

An amber container decided Sandra on a shampoo. She brought the bottle to the counter. "I've heard," she said, "they wear makeup on TV that'll make them look whiter."

"Of course they do," Miss Loma said.

Also, Sandra had heard that Negroes never kissed one another. They made love without preliminaries, like animals, or did nothing. But she was afraid to offer that information. Sometimes, even her mother and father did not seem to know she knew people made love.

Miss Loma said, "Honey, take that shampoo on home as a present. Happy birthday."

"How'd you know it was my birthday?"

"A bird told me."

"Grandmomma," Sandra said.

"You heard about the little nigger baby up in Memphis that's two parts animal?" the salesman said.

"No!" Miss Loma said.

"It's got a little dear face and bare feet," the salesman said, and when Sandra went out, he and Miss Loma were laughing.

In his dusty, green pickup, Sandra's father drew up to the gas pump. Willson's wife, along with another Negro woman, stepped from the truck's cab and went into a grocery across the road. "I see you got your nigger women with you today, Tate," said one of the old men playing dominoes.

Lifting the hose, Sandra's father stood putting in gas, laughing. "Yeah, I carried them with me today," he said. "Sandra, I got to go on back to the field. There's a dressed chicken on the front seat Ida sent. Take it on to your momma." Sandra opened the truck's door, thinking how many people made remarks about her father letting Negroes ride up front with him. He always answered that if somebody asked him for a ride, he gave it to them; why should they sit out in the open truck bed covered with dust and hit by gravel? She heard him call into the store, "Four-ninety for gas, Loma," and holding the chicken, Sandra waved as he drove off.

Ida's husband had been a field hand for Sandra's father and now was too old to work. Sandra's father let the old couple stay on, rent free, in the cabin on his land. Ida raised chickens and brought one to Flo whenever she killed them. When Flo went to the bakery in Indian Hill, she brought Ida something sweet. Sandra came into the kitchen now and put the chicken on the sink. "That's a nice plump one," Flo said. "If we hadn't had chicken last night, I'd put it on to cook. I hope your daddy let Ida know how much we appreciate it."

"He says he always thanks her," Sandra said.

"But I don't know whether he thanks her enough," her mother said.

The kitchen smelled of cake baking and Sandra pretended not to notice. "Aren't you going to ask about the Negroes at school?" she said.

"Honey, I couldn't wait for you to come wandering in. I called around till I found out."

"I don't see why they got to register at a special time. Why couldn't they register when we did?" Sandra said.

"I don't understand it myself," Flo said.

"I don't understand why they have to be there at all," Grandmomma said, on her way to the bathroom during a commercial. "I declare, I don't."

"Oh Grandmomma," Sandra said.

"I guess they didn't want to take chances on trouble during registration," Flo said. "If the Negroes are just there when school starts, no one can say anything."

"There's plenty of things folks could say if they just would," Grandmomma called.

"I thought she was hard of hearing," Sandra said.

"Not all of the time," Flo said. When Grandmomma came back through the kitchen, Flo said, "We haven't had anything to say about what's happened so far. Everything else has just been shoved down our throats, Mother. I don't know why you think we'd have a chance to say anything now." Sandra, going out and down the hall, wondered why her mother bothered trying to explain to Grandmomma. "What are you going to do?" Flo called.

"Wash my hair," Sandra said.

"Well, for heaven's sake, roll it up as tight as you can and try to keep it curled."

"I wish you'd put it behind a band like that girl on television," Grandmomma called, and Sandra closed the bathroom door.

The candles flickered, then burned, as Flo hesitated in the doorway, smiling, before bringing the decorated cake in to supper. The family sang "Happy Birthday" to Sandra. Her father rolled in a portable television atop brass legs and she jumped up with a squeal. Her hair, waved and tied with a ribbon to please them, loosened and fell toward her shoulders. Now she could see programs without arguing with Grandmomma.

Flo's face was in wrinkles, anxious, as though she

feared Ida had not been thanked enough for a chicken, and Sandra knew she was to like her grandmomma's present more than ordinarily. On pink tissue paper, in a tiny box, lay a heavy gold pin twisted like rope into a circle. "Why, Grandmomma!" Sandra said in surprise. Her exclamation was taken for admiration and everyone looked pleased. When she had gone into Grandmomma's room as a small child, to poke among her things, she had been shown the pin. Grandmomma's only heirloom, it had been her own mother's. "I've been afraid I wouldn't live till you were sixteen," Grandmomma said. "But I wanted to give you the pin when you were old enough to appreciate it."

"She never would give it even to me," Flo said.

"No, it was to be for my first grandchild," Grandmomma said. "I decided that when Momma died and left it to me. It was all in the world she had to leave and it's all I've got. But I want you to enjoy it now, instead of when I'm gone."

Had she made enough fuss over the pin? Sandra asked later. Flo said she had, but to thank her grandmother occasionally again. "Mother, it's not really the kind of pin anyone wears," Sandra said. The pin hung limply, lopsided, on her striped turtleneck jersey.

Flo said, "It is kind of heavy and antique. Maybe you'll like it when you're grown. Wear it a few times anyway."

The morning that school started, Sandra hung the pin on her coat lapel and forgot it. She walked into her class and there sat a Negro boy. His simply sitting there was disappointing; she felt like a child who had waited so long for Christmas that when it came, it had to be a letdown. He was to be the only Negro in school. The others had changed their minds, the students heard. But by then everyone had heard so many rumors, no one knew what to believe. The Negro was tall and light-skinned. Louise said the officials always tried to send light-skinned ones first. He was noticeably quiet and the girls, at lunch, found he had spoken in none of his classes. Everyone wondered if he was smart enough to be in the school. From her table Sandra saw him eating by a window with several other boys. Still, he seemed alone and she felt sorry for him.

In the car pool with her and Louise were two boys, Don and Mark. Don, the younger, was an athlete. Going home that afternoon, he said the Negro was not the type for football but was so tall, maybe he would be good at basketball. Sandra thought how little she knew about the Negro and how many questions she would be asked. He had worn a blue shirt, she remembered, and he was thin. Certainly, he was clean. Grandmomma would ask that. She did not even know the Negro's name until Don said, "He lives off this road."

"Who?" she said.

"The colored boy, Jack Lawrence," he said.

"We could ask him to be in the car pool," Louise said, laughing.

Mark, sandy-haired and serious, said, "You all better watch your talk. I had my interview at the university this summer and ate lunch in the cafeteria. There were lots of Negroes and all kinds of people. Indians. Not with feathers, from India. Exchange students."

Dust drifted like clouds over fields, and kudzu vine, taking over the countryside, filling ditches and climbing trees, was yellowed by it. Young pines, set out along the road banks, shone beneath a sun that was strong, even going down. Sandra looked out at tiny pink flowers just appearing on the cotton and tried to imagine going as far away, to a place as strange, as India. That Indians had come all the way to Mississippi to school made her think about people's lives in a way she never had. She entered the house saying, before Grandmomma could ask questions, "Grandmomma, you know they got Indians from India going to Ole Miss?"

Grandmomma looked up through the lower half of her glasses. "You don't mean to tell me," she said,

and it took away some of her curiosity about the
Negro too. At supper, Sandra gave all the information
she could. The Negro boy was clean, looked nice, and
his name was Jack Lawrence. All the information she
could give in the next month was that he went his way
and she went hers. Finally even Grandmomma stopped
asking questions about him. He and Sandra had no
reason to speak until one morning, she was working
the combination to her locker when a voice, quite
deep, said, "Sandra, you left this under your desk."

Her dark hair fell forward. In the moment that she
pushed it back, something in the voice's deep tone
made her think unaccountably how soft her own hair
felt. Jack Lawrence held out the book she had forgotten, his face expressionless. It would have been much
more natural for him to smile. She saw for the first
time how carefully impersonal he was. Other students
had mentioned that he never spoke, even to teachers,
unless spoken to first. She smiled and said, "Lord,
math. I'm bad enough without losing the book too.
Thanks."

"Okay. I just happened to notice you left it." He
started down the hall and Sandra joined him, as she
would have anyone going the way she was. She held
her books against her, as if hugging herself in anticipa-
tion, but of what, she did not know. She had a curiously excited feeling to be walking beside anyone so
tall. No, she thought, not anyone, a boy. They talked
about the afternoon's football game, then Jack Lawrence continued down the hall and Sandra turned into
her class. There was certainly nothing to that, she
thought. But Louise, leaning from her desk, whispered, "What were you talking *about*?"

"Football," Sandra said, shrugging. She thought of
all the Negroes she had talked to in her life, of those
she talked to every day, and wondered why it was
strange to talk to Jack Lawrence. Her mother complained that at every meal, Sandra's father had to
leave the table, answer the door, and talk to some

Negro who worked for him. They would stand together a long time, like any two men, her father propping his foot on the truck's bumper, smoking and talking. Now she wondered what they talked about.

Jack Lawrence's eyes, when she looked into them, had been brown. Were the eyes of all Negroes? From now on, she would notice. On her way to the stadium that afternoon, she wondered if her gaiety was over the football game or the possibility of seeing—not the Negro, she thought, but Jack Lawrence? Louise went ahead of her up the steps and turned into the bleachers. "I have to sit higher," Sandra said, "or I can't see," adding, "Lon's up there." Louise was crazy about Lon, the basketball coach's son, and rising obediently, she followed Sandra to a seat below him. Lon was sitting with Jack Lawrence. Looking up, Sandra smiled but Jack Lawrence turned his eyes to the game and his lips made no movement at all. When she stood to cheer, to buy a Coke, popcorn, a hot dog, Sandra wondered if he watched her. After the game, he and Lon leapt from the bleachers and went out a back way. That night, she slept with a sense of disappointment.

At school, she always nodded and spoke to him and he spoke back: but they did not walk together again. Most often, he was alone. Even to football games, he did not bring a friend. There was a Thanksgiving dance in the gym, festooned with balloons and crepe paper, but he did not come. On Wednesday before the holiday, driving the car pool, Sandra had seen Jack Lawrence walking along a stretch of country road, hunched into his coat. The motor throbbed loudly in the cold country stillness as she stopped the car and said, "You want a ride?"

He stood, looking as if he did not want any favors, but with eyes almost sore-looking from the cold, then climbed into the backseat with Don and Mark. The countryside's stillness came again as Sandra stopped at the side road he mentioned. With coat collar turned

up, untangling long legs, he got out. She was aware
of the way her hair hung, of her grandmother's pin
too old and heavy for her coat, of the skirt that did
not cover her knees, which Grandmomma said was
indecent. And she was aware of him, standing in the
road against the melancholy winter sunset, looking
down to say, "Thank you."

"You're welcome," she said, looking up.

That night she asked her father whether she should
have given Jack Lawrence a ride. Her father said she
was not to give a ride to Negroes when she was alone.

"Not even to women?" she said.

"Oh well, to women," he said.

"Not even to Willson?" she said.

Her father seemed to look inward to himself a long
time; then he answered, "No, not even to Willson."

Thanksgiving gave Sandra an excuse to start a conversation. She saw Jack Lawrence in the hall the first
day afterward and said, "Did you have a nice
holiday?"

"Yes," he said. "Did you?"

Sandra mentioned, briefly, things she had done.
"Listen," she said. "We go your way every day, if
you'd like a ride."

"Thanks," he said, "but most of the time I have one."
He turned to his locker and put away his books and
Sandra, going on down the hall, had the strangest feeling
that he knew something she did not. She remained
friendly, smiling when she saw him, though he made no
attempt to talk. He only nodded and smiled when they
met and she thought he seemed hesitant about doing
that. She asked the boys in the car pool questions about
him. Why hadn't he gone out for basketball, how were
his grades, what did he talk about at lunch, did anybody
know exactly where he lived, besides down that side
road?—until one day, Louise said, "Sandra, you talk
about that Negro so much, I think you like him."

"Yes; I like him. I mean, I don't dislike him, do
you? What reason would we have?"

"No, I don't dislike him," Louise said. "He's not at all smart-alecky."

In winter when they came home from school, it was dark. Flo said, "If you didn't have those boys in your car pool, I'd drive you girls back and forth myself. I don't know what Don and Mark could do if anything happened, but I feel better they're there." Sandra's parents, everyone, lived in fear of something happening. South of them, in the Delta, there was demonstrating, and Negroes tried to integrate restaurants and movies in several larger towns. Friends of Sandra's mother began carrying tear gas and pistols in their pocketbooks. Repeatedly, at the dinner table, in Miss Loma's, Sandra heard grown-ups say, "It's going to get worse before it gets any better. We won't see the end of this in our lifetime." Grandmomma always added, "I just hate to think what Sandra and her children will live to see."

One day after Christmas vacation, those in the car pool again saw Jack Lawrence walking along the road. "Should we stop?" Louise said. She was driving, with Don beside her.

"Of course. Would you just drive past him?" Sandra said. She was sitting in the backseat with Mark, and when Jack Lawrence climbed into the car, she was sitting between them. They spoke of the cold, of the snow that had fallen after Christmas, the deepest they could ever remember, and of how you came across patches of it, still, in unexpected places. Side roads were full of frozen ruts. Jack Lawrence said he hated to think of the mud when a thaw came. There could be one at any time. That was the way their weather was. In the midst of winter, you could suddenly have a stretch of bright, warm, almost spring days. There was a silence and Jack Lawrence, looking down at Sandra, said, "Did you lose that pin you always wear?"

"Oh Lord," Sandra said, her hand going quickly, flat, against her lapel.

"Sandra, your grandmomma's pin!" Louise said, looking into the rearview mirror.

"Maybe it fell off in the car," Mark said. The three in back put their hands down the cracks around the seat. Sandra felt in her pockets, shook out her skirt. They held their feet up and looked under them. Don, turning, said, "Look up under the front seat."

Bending forward at the same instant, Sandra and Jack Lawrence knocked their heads together sharply. "Ow!" Mark cried out for them, while tears came to Sandra's eyes. They clutched their heads. Their faces were close, and though Sandra saw yellow, dancing dots, she thought, Of course Negroes kiss each other when they make love. She and Jack Lawrence fell back against the seat laughing, and seemed to laugh for miles, until she clutched her stomach in pain.

"Didn't it hurt? How can you laugh so?" Louise said.

"I got a hard head," Jack Lawrence said.

When he stood again in the road thanking them, his eyes, glancing into the car, held no message for Sandra. Tomorrow, he said silently, by ignoring her, they would smile and nod. That they had been for a time two people laughing together was enough. As they rode on, Sandra held tightly the pin he had found, remembering how she had looked at it one moment lying in his dark hand, with the lighter palm, and the next moment, she had touched the hand lightly, taking the pin. Opening her purse, she dropped the pin inside.

"Is the clasp broken?" Mark said.

"No, I guess I didn't have it fastened good," she said.

"Aren't you going to wear it anymore?" Louise said, looking back.

"No," she said.

"What will your grandmomma say?" Louise said.

"Nothing I can worry about," Sandra said.

Henry Louis Gates, Jr.

Henry Louis Gates, Jr., was born in Keyser, West Virginia, in 1950. He graduated from Yale University with highest honors and went on to Clare College at Cambridge University for his Ph.D. A member of the American Academy of Arts and Sciences, he has had a distinguished career as a literary scholar, cultural critic, and editor. His literary criticism, particularly *Figures in Black: Words, Signs, and the Racial Self* (1987) and *The Signifying Monkey: Towards a Theory of Afro-American Literary Criticism* (1988), for which he won an American Book Award, has changed the way scholars look at African-American literature. His cultural criticism has been equally thought-provoking. In *Loose Canons: Notes on the Culture Wars* (1992) he argues that given the diversity of people in the United States we must have a diverse educational curriculum in our schools. In *Thirteen Ways of Looking at a Black Man* (1997), he examines the lives of many different black men, interviewing such notables as James Baldwin, Harry Belafonte, and Colin Powell. As series editor of the Oxford-Schomburg Library of Nineteenth-Century Black Women Writers, Gates has brought back to the public attention many important black texts. He has contributed to the understanding of many more, by editing such essay collections as *Black Literature and Literary Theory* (1984), *Race, Writing, and Difference* (1986), and *Reading Black, Reading Feminist* (1990). For his accomplishments he was recognized by the MacArthur Foundation, and his career has taken him in quick succession from teaching at Yale to endowed professorships at Cornell, then Duke, and currently Harvard, where he directs the W.E.B. Du Bois Institute for Afro-American Research and chairs the Afro-American Studies Department. "Sin Boldly" is one of the last chapters of his memoir, *Colored People,* which won the Lillian Smith Book Award in 1994. *Colored People* chronicles a period of transition in southern society from racial segregation to the first steps toward a more integrated society. Gates's memoir positions him on the cusp of this change, both participating in the breakdown of old racial barriers and experiencing the loss of community that racial segregation had fostered among African-Americans.

Sin Boldly

In 1968, three of the Fearsome Foursome graduated from high school. Soul Moe was called upon to serve his country in Vietnam, and Swano and I would head down to Potomac State. (Roland had been held back a couple of years.) I gave the valedictory address at graduation, defying tradition by writing my own speech—surreptitiously, because this was not allowed. All through the last six weeks of marking period I had practiced delivering the traditional prepared speech with Miss Twigg, our senior English teacher, then had gone home to rehearse my real speech with Mama. Mama had a refined sense of vocal presentation and a wonderful sense of irony and timing. My speech was about Vietnam, abortion, and civil rights, about the sense of community our class shared, since so many of us had been together for twelve years, about the individual's rights and responsibilities in his or her community, and about the necessity to defy norms out of love. I searched the audience for Miss Twigg's face, just to see her expression when I read the speech! She turned as red as a beet, but she liked the speech, and as good as told me so with a big wink at the end of the ceremony.

My one year at Potomac State College of West Virginia University, in Keyser, all of five miles away, was memorable for two reasons: because of my English classes with Duke Anthony Whitmore and my first real love affair, with Maura Gibson.

I came to Potomac State to begin that long, arduous

trek toward medical school. I enrolled in August 1968,
a week before Labor Day, and I was scared to death.
While I had been a good student at Piedmont High,
I had no idea how well I would fare in the big-time
competition of a college class that included several of
the best students from Keyser High, as well as bright
kids from throughout the state. I had never questioned
my decision to attend Potomac State; it was inevitable:
you went there after Piedmont High, as sure as the
night follows the day. My uncles Raymond and David
had attended it in the fifties, my brother in the early
sixties, and my cousin Greg had begun the year before. I would attend too, then go off to "the university"—in Morgantown—to become a doctor.

Greg had told me about life on campus, about the
freedom of choice, about card parties in the Union,
and, of course, about the women. But he had also told
me one thing early in his freshman year that had
stayed with me throughout my senior year in Piedmont. "There's an English teacher down there," he
had said, "who's going to blow your mind."

"What's his name?" I responded.

"Duke Anthony Whitmore," he replied.

"Duke?" I said. "What kind of name is Duke? Is
he an Englishman?"

"No, dummy," Greg replied. "He's a white guy
from Baltimore."

So as I nervously slouched my way through registration a year later, I found myself standing before the
ferocious Mr. Gallagher, who enjoyed the reputation
of being tough. He gave me the name of my adviser.

I looked at the name; it was not Whitmore. "Can I
be assigned to Mr. Whitmore?" I ventured. "Because
I've heard quite a lot about him from my cousin."

"You'll have to ask him," Mr. Gallagher said. "He's
over there."

I made my way to Mr. Whitmore's table, introduced
myself tentatively, stated my case, telling him my
cousin Greg had said that he was a great teacher, a

wonderful inspiration, etc., etc. What Greg had really said was: "This guy Whitmore is *crazy,* just like you!" It was love at first sight, at least for me. And that, in retrospect, was the beginning of the end of my twelve-year-old dream of becoming a doctor.

Learning English and American literature from the Duke was a game to which I looked forward every day. I had always loved English and had been blessed with some dedicated and able teachers. But reading books was something I had always thought of as a pastime, certainly not as a vocation. The Duke made the study of literature an alluring prospect.

Duke Whitmore did not suffer fools gladly. He did not suffer fools at all. Our classes—I enrolled in everything he taught, despite his protests, which I have to say weren't very strenuous—soon came to be dominated by three or four voices. We would argue and debate just about everything from Emerson and Thoreau to the war in Vietnam and racial discrimination. He would recite a passage from a poem or play, then demand that we tell him, rapid-fire, its source.

"King Lear," I responded one day.

"What act, what scene, Mr. Gates?" he demanded.

"Act Three, Scene Four," I shouted out blindly, not having the faintest clue as to whether the passage that he had recited was from *Hamlet* or the Book of Job.

"Exactly," he responded with a certain twinkle in his eye. "Sin boldly," he would tell me later, citing Martin Luther. My reckless citation was wrong, of course, but he wished to reward me for my audacity.

It was a glorious experience. Words and thoughts, ideas and visions, came alive for me in his classroom. It was he who showed me, by his example, that ideas had a life of their own and that there were other professions as stimulating and as rewarding as being a doctor.

After an academically successful year, Professor Whitmore encouraged me to transfer to the Ivy League. I wrote to Harvard, Yale, and Princeton. Since I had

cousins who had gone to Harvard and Princeton, I
decided to try for Yale. I sent off the application and
took a summer job in the personnel office of the paper
mill. I'd been hired for the express purpose of encouraging a few black people to transfer into the craft
unions; I recruited them and administered the necessary tests. In three months, each union had been integrated, with barely an audible murmur from its
members. Things were changing in Piedmont—a little.

Though we didn't become an item until our freshman year at Potomac State, Maura Gibson and I had
known each other from a distance in high school. I
used to run into her at the bowling alley and at Jimmy's Pizza next door. She was sharp on her feet and
loved to argue. Once, she took me to task for talking
about race so much. You can't talk about the weather
without bringing up race, she charged. I was embarrassed about that at first, then pleased.

Once we were at college, Maura and I started having long talks on the phone, first about nothing at all
and then about everything. The next thing I remember
happening between us was parking in her green
Dodge up in the colored cemetery on Radical Hill,
near where just about all the Keyser colored, and
much of the white trash, lived. "Radical" is a synonym
in the valley for tacky or ramshackle. I'm not sure
which came first, the name or what it came to mean.
That's where we were when Horse Lowe (the coach
of the college's football team and the owner of the
property that abuts the colored cemetery) put his big
red face into Maura's window, beat on the windshield
with his fist, then told me to get the hell off his
property.

Horse Lowe would wait until a couple had begun
to pet heavily; then he'd sneak up on the car. He liked
to catch you exposed. Even so, we used to park up
there all the time. I figured that he'd get tired of
throwing us out before I got tired of parking.

*   *   *

On the weekends during the summer of 1969, I'd drive over to Rehoboth Beach, in Delaware, to see Maura, who was working as a waitress at a place called the Crab Pot. I'd leave work on Friday at about four o'clock, then drive all the way to Delaware, through Washington and the Beltway, past Baltimore and Annapolis, over the Chesapeake Bridge, past Ocean City, arriving at Rehoboth before midnight, with as much energy as if I had just awakened. We'd get a motel room after her shift ended, and she'd bring a bushel of crabs, steamed in the hot spice called Old Bay. We'd get lots of ice-cold Budweiser and we'd have a feast, listening to Junior Walker play his saxophone, play "What Does It Take" over and over and over again. "What does it take to win your love for me? . . ."

Since Maura was white, I felt that I was making some sort of vague political statement, especially in the wake of Sammy Davis, Jr., and *Guess Who's Coming to Dinner*. Others concurred. We were hassled at the beach. Somehow, for reasons having to do with nudity and sensuality, blacks were not allowed to walk along most beachfronts or attend resorts. I personally integrated many places at Rehoboth Beach that summer.

I was used to being stared at and somewhat used to being the only black person on the beach, or in a restaurant, or at a motel. But I hadn't quite realized how upset people could be until the day that some white guy sicced his Saint Bernard on me as Maura and I walked by. Certainly Maura and I had been no strangers to controversy, but we usually took pains not to invite it. Back home, we had sneaked around at first, hiding in cemeteries and in a crowd of friends, almost never being seen together in public alone. Until we were found out—by her father, of all people. A man called " 'Bama," of all things.

It was the evening we had agreed to meet at the big oak tree on Spring Street in Keyser, near one of

her friends' houses. I picked her up in my '57 Chevro-
let, and we went up to harass the Horse. Afterward,
I dropped her off, then drove the fives miles back to
Piedmont. By the time I got home, Maura had called
a dozen times. It turned out that her father had followed her down the street and hidden behind a tree
while she waited, had watched her climb into my car.
He knew the whole thing.

And he, no progressive on race matters, was sickened and outraged.

Soon, it seemed, all of the Valley knew the whole
thing, and everybody had an opinion about it. We
were apparently the first interracial couple in Mineral
County, and there was hell to pay. People began making oblique threats, in the sort of whispers peculiar to
small towns. When friends started warning my parents
about them, they bought me a '69 Mustang so I could
travel to and from school—and the colored graveyard—safely. (The Chevy had taken to conking out
unpredictably.) Some kids at Potomac State started
calling us names, anonymously, out of dormitory windows. And in the middle of all this chaos, 'Bama Gibson, Maura's father, decided he was going to run for
mayor.

Lawd, Lawd, Lawd.

In his own redneck way, 'Bama Gibson was a perfectly nice man, but he was not exactly mayoral material. He had been a postman and became some sort of
supervisor at the post office. He was very personable,
everybody liked him, and he knew everybody's business, the way a postman in any small town does. With
the whole town talking about how terrible it was that
his daughter was dating a colored boy, and the men
giving him their sympathy and declaring what they'd
do to that nigger if that nigger ever touched their
daughter, old 'Bama up and announced his candidacy.

Dr. Church, former president of the college, was the
obvious front-runner. People were saying he'd already
started to measure the mayor's office for new curtains.

Certainly no one would have given 'Bama any hope of beating Dr. Church, even before my nappy head came on the horizon. With you on these crackers' minds, Daddy told me, he's got two chances: slim and none. Boy, how do you *get* into all this trouble?

Meantime, at the height of the campaign, Roland, Jerry, Swano, and I decided to integrate the Swordfish, a weekend hangout where all the college kids went to listen to a live band—usually E. G. Taylor and the Sounds of Soul, a white band with a black, Eugene Taylor, as lead singer. Eugene could *sing*. He wasn't so great with learning the words, but that Negro could warble. He'd make up words as he went along, using sounds similar to those he could not remember but making no sense.

Still, we wanted the right to hear Eugene mess up James Brown's words, same as anybody else, so we started to plot our move. Late one Friday night, when the Swordfish was rocking and packed, we headed up New Creek in our Soul Mobile, which we had washed for the occasion, even replacing the old masking tape over the holes in the roof. The Fearsome Foursome made their date with destiny. We were silent as we drove into the parking lot. There was nothing left to say. We were scared to death but just had to get on with it.

We parked the car and strolled up the stairs to the Swordfish. Since there was no cover charge, we walked straight into the middle of the dance floor. That's when the slo-mo started, an effect exacerbated by the strobe lights. Everybody froze: the kids from Piedmont and Keyser who had grown up with us; the students from Potomac State; the rednecks and crackers from up the hollers, the ones who came to town once a week all dressed up in their Sears, Roebuck permapressed drawers, their Thom McAn semileather shoes, their ultimately *white* sox, and their hair slicked back and wet-looking. The kids of rednecks, who liked to drink gallons of 3.2 beer, threaten everybody within

earshot, and puke all over themselves—they froze too,
their worst nightmare staring them in the face.

After what seemed like hours but was probably less
than a minute, a homely white boy with extra-greasy
blond hair recovered and began to shout "Niggers" as
his face assumed the ugly mask of hillbilly racism. I
stared at this white boy's face, which turned redder
and redder as *he* turned into the Devil, calling on his
boys to kick our asses: calling us niggers and niggers
and niggers to help them summon up their courage.
White boys started moving around us, forming a circle
around ours. Our good friends from Keyser and Potomac State were still frozen, embarrassed that we were
in there, that we had violated their space, dared to
cross the line. No help from them. (I lost lots of
friends that night.) Then, breaking through the circle
of rednecks, came the owner, who started screaming:
Get out of here! Get out of here! and picked up Fisher
and slammed his head against the wall. It wasn't easy
to see because of all the smoke and because of the
strobe effect of the flashing blue lights, but I remember being surprised at how Roland's Afro had kept its
shape when his head sprang back off the wall, the way
a basketball keeps its shape no matter how much or
how hard you dribble it.

Moe and I hauled Fisher off the ground, with Swano's
broad shoulders driving through the 'necks the way
Bubba Smith used to do for the Baltimore Colts. I
wondered if Roland's head would stop bleeding. Fuck
you, motherfucker, I heard myself say. We're gonna
shut your racist ass down. We're gonna shut your ass
down, repeated Moe and Swano in chorus. Take a
good look around you, you crackers, cuz this is your
last time here.

We dragged Fisher to the car, ducking the bottles
and cans as we sped away. Roland's head had stopped
its bleeding by the time we passed Potomac Valley
Hospital, which we called the meat factory because
one of the doctors was reputed to be such a butcher,

so we drove on past it and headed for my house. What'll y'all do now? Daddy asked as Mama bandaged Roland Fisher's head.

And yes, the place was shut down. We called the State Human Rights Commission on Monday, and the commissioner, Carl Glass, came up to Piedmont a few days later. He interviewed the four of us separately, and then he went out to the Swordfish and interviewed the proprietor, who by this time had told everybody white and colored in Keyser that he was going to get that troublemaker Gates. He swore to the commissioner that he would close down before he let niggers in. The commissioner took him at his word and sent an official edict telling him to integrate or shut down. As the man promised, he shut it down. And that is why the Swordfish nightclub is now Samson's Family Restaurant, run by a very nice Filipino family.

Well, all of this broke out in the middle of 'Bama Gibson's campaign to be the first postman elected as Mayor of Keyser, West Virginia, The Friendliest City in the U.S.A., as the road sign boasted—to which we chorused "bullshit" whenever we passed it.

The whole town talked about this campaign, from sunup to sundown. And there were some curious developments. Our family doctor, Dr. Staggers (our high school principal, Mr. Staggers's, son), went out of his way to tell me that lots of his friends, well-educated and liberal, had decided to suspend disbelief and vote for 'Bama, just to prove (as he put it) that Keyser is not Birmingham. Then the colored people, who never voted, decided to register and turn out for good ole 'Bama. The college kids at Potomac State, the ones not busy calling Maura "nigger-lover" from their dormitory windows, turned out in droves. And all the romantics who lived in Keyser, those who truly respected the idea of love and passion, voted for 'Bama. All both of them. Bizarrely enough, the election was turning into a plebiscite on interracial relationships.

I stayed out of Keyser on the day of the election,

terrified that I'd already caused Maura's father to lose. If it's close, there's no sense aggravating the ones sitting on the fence, rubbing their nose in it, Daddy had said. And so I waited for Maura's phone call, which came around eleven-thirty and informed me that we had nothing more to worry about, her father had trampled Dr. Church. No longer would the police follow us, daring us to go even one mile over the speed limit. That's what she told me, and I could scarcely believe it. I started parking my car on red lines and in front of fire hydrants, just to test her assertion. She was right.

It was also because of 'Bama's new office that I learned that the West Virginia State Police had opened a file on me in Mineral County, which identified me for possible custodial detention if and when race riots started. Maura gave me the news late one night, whispering it over the phone. Old 'Bama, whom victory had made magnanimous, had wanted me to know and to be warned.

I remember feeling sick and scared . . . and then, when that passed, a little flattered. I was eighteen, had scarcely been outside Mineral County, and someone in authority decided I was dangerous? I mean, *I* liked to think so. But that an official establishment should collude with my fantasies of importance was quite another matter.

I took it as a sign that it was time for me to leave the Valley and go Elsewhere. I did leave it, that very fall, packing my bags for New Haven. But leaving it *behind* was never a possibility. It did not take me long to realize that.

The "Personal Statement" for my Yale application began: "My grandfather was colored, my father was Negro, and I am black." And it concluded: "As always, whitey now sits in judgment of me, preparing to cast my fate. It is your decision either to let me blow with the wind as a nonentity or to encourage the development of self. Allow me to prove myself."

I wince at the rhetoric today, but they let me in.

Ernest J. Gaines

In 1933 Ernest J. Gaines was born on a plantation in
Pointe Coupée Parish near New Roads, Louisiana,
which he calls Bayonne in his fiction. A number of
scholars have compared Gaines's fictional territory to
Faulkner's Yoknapatawpha County, but Gaines main-
tains that the nineteenth-century Russian writers Chekhov, Gogol, and Turgenev had a greater influence on
his work: "The Russians were not talking about my
people, but about a peasantry for which they seemed
to show such feeling. Reading them, I could find a
way to write about my own people." Gaines left Louisiana when he was fifteen to go to high school and
then college in California, first San Francisco State
and then Stanford University for graduate study. Now
he divides his time between California and the University of Southwestern Louisiana, where he teaches. He
has written six novels and a collection of short stories,
Bloodline (1968). Three of his novels—*The Autobiography of Miss Jane Pittman* (1971), *A Gathering of
Old Men* (1983), and *A Lesson Before Dying* (1993)—
have been made into movies. The following excerpt
from *A Gathering of Old Men* bears evidence of several themes of importance to Gaines: the rural black
experience in the South, the changing relationship between blacks and whites, and the alienation between
fathers and sons. The excerpt is also a good example
of Gaines's first-person narrative style, which has been
influenced by oral storytelling traditions. Like Eudora
Welty and Peter Taylor, he says he spent a great deal

of time listening to the people who visited his home
when he was a boy. Jerry Bryant has called him "one
of our most naturally gifted storytellers." Ernest
Gaines has won numerous awards and grants for his
fiction, most notably the National Book Critics Circle
Award for *A Lesson Before Dying* and a MacArthur
Foundation Grant.

A Gathering of Old Men takes place in the 1970s,
primarily in the old slave quarters of the Marshall
plantation in Louisiana, where some of the slaves' descendants still reside. Beau Boutan, a Cajun man who
rents the farmland, has been shot, allegedly by Mathu,
one of the old black men who live on the plantation.
Beau has a reputation for verbally and physically
abusing the black men who work for him. Candy Marshall, a white woman whose family owns the plantation and who has been raised in part by Mathu, is
determined to protect the blacks who live there from
the vengeance of Beau's father, Fix, who is a notorious
bigot and vigilante. A number of old black men, who
have all been the victims of racial discrimination, have
gathered at the quarters to take their first stand
against white injustice. Mapes, the local white sheriff,
is trying not only to bring the murderer to justice, but
to keep the people, both white and black, from taking
matters into their own hands. In this section of the
novel, Gil Boutan, a college student and football hero,
has just learned of his brother Beau's death. This part
of the story is narrated by a white college friend,
Thomas Vincent Sullivan.

Thomas Vincent Sullivan

aka
Sully or T.V.

Gil and I had just come out of Sci-210 when Cal caught up with us and told Gil that coach wanted him in the office right away.

"I thought we had gone over all that," Gil said.

"I don't think it's football this time," Cal said.

Gil asked me if I would walk back to the gym with him, and since Cal wasn't doing anything that hour he walked back with us. Cal was Calvin "Pepper" Harrison, quite possibly the best halfback in the country that year, and already nominated for All-American. Gil was Gilbert "Salt" Boutan, definitely the best fullback in the Southeastern Conference, and many other conferences besides. Cal and Gil were known as Salt and Pepper at LSU. Gil being a Cajun, the publicity people had tried to think of a good Cajun nickname for him when he first came to the university, but after seeing how well he and Cal worked together, they finally settled on Salt and Pepper.

Gil was a football man all the way, and eventually he would go pro, but what he wanted most while attending LSU was to be All-American along with Cal. It would be the first time this had ever happened, black and white in the same backfield—and in the Deep South, besides. LSU was fully aware of this, the black and white communities in Baton Rouge were aware of this, and so was the rest of the country. Wherever you went, people spoke of Salt and Pepper of LSU. Both were good powerful runners, and excellent blockers. Gil blocked for Cal on sweeps around end, and Cal returned the favor when Gil went up the middle. It drove the defense crazy, because both Gil and Cal carried the ball about the same number of times in a game and the defensive team didn't know which to look out for. Besides that, you had "Sugar" Washington at quarterback, and he was no slouch, either.

Me? Well, I was no Sugar Washington. I was third-string quarterback. My name is Thomas Vincent Sullivan. My hair is red, my face is red, my eyes are green, and most people call me Sully. Others call me T.V.— especially the black guys on the team. Not for my initials necessarily, but for my avocation. I'm a television nut. A vidiot.

While Gil was in coach's office, Cal and I stood outside talking about the game coming up the next day, LSU and Ole Miss. It would be the game of the year. We knew if we dumped her, nobody else could stop us, and we would host the Sugar Bowl game on New Year's Day. Already the people had filled all the motels and hotels from Baton Rouge to New Orleans. The national press was covering the game. No matter where you went, that's all the people were talking about. If you were pro-LSU—and you were crazy if you were not—they said there was no possible way to stop Salt and Pepper. If you were anti-LSU, or pro–Ole Miss—and there were thousands of people from Mississippi who had come down for the game—they said that all Ole Miss had to do was stop one or the other, Salt or Pepper, and victory would be theirs to take back home. This kind of talk had been going on the past month, and now there was only a little more than twenty-four hours—thirty hours—before the whole thing would be settled. If you know anything about Louisiana weather, you know there's a lot of lightning and thundering before the big storm comes. Well, the big storm was going to be tomorrow night at eight o'clock, but the lightning and thundering had been going on for a month already, and nobody expected it to let up till the last moment.

After being in coach's office about ten minutes, Gil came back out, and went right by Cal and me like we weren't even standing there. I thought he had forgotten where he had left us, and I called to him. But he kept on going. Cal and I looked at each other a second, and went after him. He was walking fast, and rubbing both his fists.

"Gil, wait up," I said to him. "Hey, Gil."

Cal was on one side. I was on the other.

"What's the matter, man?" Cal asked him.

He had stopped. He was breathing sharp and hard, the way you do in the huddle after you've been tackled. He was staring down at the ground, rubbing his fists, rubbing his knuckles hard, like he was trying to rub off the skin.

Cal put his hand on one shoulder, and I took the other arm.

"What's the matter, Gil?" I asked him.

He started shaking his head; he was still looking down at the ground.

"My brother, my brother. Killed."

"In a wreck?" Cal asked him.

Gil went on shaking his head like he might start crying. I held on to one of his arms, and Cal was patting him on the back to console him. Then suddenly he just turned against Cal. Out of the blue, he looked at Cal like he suddenly hated him. It surprised the hell out of both me and Cal.

"Gil, that's Cal," I said. "Gil."

He turned from Cal and looked at me. "Why today?" he said. He was crying now. "Why today?"

"Take it easy, Gil," I said. People had begun to crowd around us and ask questions. Cal or Gil couldn't but there wasn't a crowd around. "Take it easy," I said to him.

"I have to get home," he said. "Can I borrow your car? Mine's still in the shop."

"I'll drive you," I said. "I can skip that drama class."

"Why today, Sully?" he asked me. "Why?"

I didn't know how to answer him, and I looked at Cal. Cal was just standing there looking hurt. He didn't know why Gil had turned against him, and I didn't know either.

"Let's go," Gil said.

"That's Cal, Gil," I said.

"Come on, let's go," he said, and walked away.

I followed him, but it sure made me feel bad the way he treated Cal.

I had a '68 Karmann-Ghia parked on the other side of the gym. Driving across campus, I had to drive about one mile an hour because of all the loonies who recognized Gil and wanted to wish him well in the game the next day. These were not all students, either. Many of them were graduates who had already arrived for the game that wasn't for another thirty hours. Someone has said that Norman, Oklahoma, is the nuttiest town in this country over football, but if any place can get crazier than this now, I would like to see it—or maybe I would not, because it sure could be dangerous.

Gil kept his head down. He would not look out at the loonies. I was driving one mile an hour. About a dozen other cars driving one mile an hour behind me. Out on the Highland road, I could speed up some, driving about five miles an hour. Loonies all over the place. Tomorrow this time it would be twice as bad, three times as bad, four times as bad. If Gil ever made All-American, handsome as he was, he would own this town and all the women in it.

Gil was quiet all the time. I didn't know whether I should say anything, so I kept quiet, too. I was still thinking about Cal. It made me feel bad the way Gil had treated him. On the gridiron they depended on each other the way one hand must depend on the other swinging a baseball bat. I had never known Gil to be anything but a gentleman.

We had crossed the Mississippi River, and were on

the main highway that would take us to his folks' place in St. Raphael Parish. I had left all the loonies, at least the ones walking around loose, so I could drive sixty now. But all the time, Gil just sat over there quiet, rubbing his fists and gazing out at the road. I stayed quiet, too, not knowing what to say. I never know what to say to people who lose someone in the family. Besides, I was still thinking about Cal.

"God, I hope none of them had anything to do with it," Gil said. He wasn't looking at me; he was still looking out at the road. "I hope for God's sake none of them did it."

"Who are you talking about?"

"The black people there at Marshall. That's where he was killed. I hope for God's sake none of them did it."

So that's why he went against Cal like that. Whether he had anything to do with it or not, he was guilty because of his color. Jesus Christ. Jesus Christ, man. The two of you work on that field together as well as any two people I've ever seen in my life work together, and because of this—Jesus H. Christ. Come on, Gil, I thought to myself, you're made of better stuff than that.

"You don't know my folks, Sully. So little you know about me."

I know about you, I thought. I know a hell of a lot about you. I didn't know this side of you, but I know a hell of a lot about you, and about old Fix, too. I've heard how he and his boys used to ride in the old days. I just didn't know *you* were like that.

We could have stayed on this road to within a couple of miles of his folks' place, but as we were coming up to the junction that said St. Charles River, he told me to take that turnoff. It was a good straight road for about four miles, with the sugarcane fields on either side. Much of the cane had been cut, and far across the field on the right side of the road was that dark line of trees which was the beginning of the swamps. Gil was looking across the fields toward the swamps. He looked in that direction until we made the turn that took us along the St. Charles River. The river was grayish blue, and very calm. On the other side of the river, probably three-quarters of a mile away, I could see how small the cars looked moving on the road.

After going about half a mile along the river, Gil nodded for me to pull off the highway. I didn't know before then that his reason for not heading directly to his folks' place was that he first wanted to go to Marshall.

Just as we turned into Marshall Quarters, I noticed a patrolman's car parked beside the road. The patrolman, in his gray-blue uniform, got out of the car and raised his hand for us to stop. He came over to my car. He recognized Gil immediately.

"Gil," he said.

"Hilly," Gil said.

Hilly looked at me. He wasn't much older than we were. He had red hair and freckles. He didn't wear a cap or a tie. The two top buttons of his shirt were unfastened, and you could see the reddish hair below his neck. He looked back at Gil.

"Mapes told me to keep out trouble, but I guess you're okay."

"Mapes still down there?" Gil asked.

"Yes."

"Thanks," Gil said.

"Be pulling for you tomorrow night," Hilly said. But soon as he said it, you could see that he felt he had spoken badly.

"Thanks," Gil said, and we drove off.

Marshall Quarters was a narrow little country road, all white with dust, and weeds on both sides. The one or two old clapboard houses seemed deserted, causing the place to look like a Western ghost town. All you needed was a couple of tumbleweeds to come bouncing down the road. Halfway into the quarters I could make out a tractor and several cars. As we came closer, I recognized Lou Dimes's baby-blue Porsche with the white streak on the side. Lou Dimes had been a starting forward on LSU's basketball team about ten years ago, and he still came to most of the games. Sometimes he covered the games for the paper in Baton Rouge.

Gil nodded for me to park in front of the tractor. We hadn't been there half a minute when I saw a skinny little guy coming out of the weeds with a pistol dangling from his right hand. He was looking suspiciously at us until he recognized Gil; then you could see him smiling. He came over to the car to look inside at us.

"Didn't know it was you," he said. "Sorry what happened, Gil."

He looked at me and nodded, and I nodded back. I thought he looked too pale to be a policeman.

"You wanta speak to Mapes?" he asked Gil.

Gil and I got out of the car. Gil stopped to look at the tractor a moment; then we followed the deputy back toward the house.

But Gil and I stopped again. There in the yard and on the porch were all these old men with shotguns. Besides, there was the sheriff with a pump gun. Lou Dimes was with his woman, Candy. Three or four black women sat either on the porch or on the steps. Some little dirty-looking children sat on the steps with the women. Every last one of them was looking back at us. It was like looking into the *Twilight Zone*. Remember that old TV play *Twilight Zone*? You would be driving through this little out-of-the-way town, and suddenly you would come upon a scene that you knew shouldn't be there—it was something like that. Something like looking at a Brueghel painting. One of these real weird, weird Brueghels.

The sheriff lowered his pump gun when he recognized Gil. The rest of them did the same. You could see all those old shotguns being lowered an inch or two toward the ground.

Gil stepped across the little grassy ditch into the yard, and I was no more than a step behind him. The grass from his footsteps had not sprung back up before I was pressing it back down. And I intended to keep it that way until we got out of there.

"Gil." The sheriff spoke first. He was one of those great big guys, exactly what the people up North and in Hollywood thought a small-town southern sheriff would look like.

Gil didn't answer him. I nodded to Dimes and Candy. Dimes spoke, but Candy didn't. She stood by the steps next to an old guy in a dirty T-shirt and green pants. She seemed lost in her own thoughts. She seemed no more interested in Gil and me than she did in anything else around her, except for that old guy, maybe. I had seen her at a few of the games with Dimes, and she always seemed bored with everything. She acted like that now, bored. She also looked very tired.

"Where is my brother, Mapes?" I heard Gil asking.

"They took him into Bayonne," Mapes said.

Gil was looking at Mapes. He didn't think Mapes had told him enough. He wanted to hear more without asking for it. He didn't think, in a situation like this, it was necessary to ask.

"You're on your way home?" Mapes asked Gil. He was trying to show sympathy. But that was hard to do with a face and eyes like his.

Gil didn't answer this time either. He was doing everything he could to control himself. He wanted the sheriff to say more about his brother.

"I got Russell back there on the bayou," Mapes said. "I told him to keep your daddy back there. I don't want him here at Marshall, Gil. I don't want him in Bayonne till I send for him."

The sheriff said all of this gently, with as much sympathy as anybody could who looked like he did. His face was big, red, with heavy jowls; his eyes were the color of cement. Even when he was trying to be gentle, his eyes still remained hard and staring at you.

Gil stared back at him. He was waiting for the sheriff to tell him more about what had happened.

"I'll have it over with before sundown," Mapes said. "You can take my word."

"What over with, Mapes?" Gil asked. He was doing

all he could to control himself. "What over with, Mapes?"

"The person who did it—I'll have him in jail before sundown, I guarantee that," Mapes said.

"Don't you know who did it?" Gil asked.

"I think I do," Mapes said. "I'm sure I do."

"Then why don't you arrest him?"

"They all say the same thing. They all claim they did it."

"But you know who did it?"

"Yes," Mapes said. "I know who did it. But the others threatened to come to town if I take him in. She says the same thing. I don't want this crowd in Bayonne. Not the way people are working themselves up for that game tomorrow. If you just come from Baton Rouge, you know what I'm talking about."

"What do you plan to do, Mapes?"

"I'll handle it my way."

"Your way?" Gil asked. "My brother been dead how long, four hours?"

"About four hours."

Gil looked at him the way you look at somebody who should be telling you much, much more. But instead of saying more, Mapes turned away. Gil started looking at the old men around him. His eyes finally settled on the one in the dirty T-shirt and green trousers, the one nearest Candy. He did not say anything to the old man for a while. The old man was looking out over the road.

"You, Mathu?"

"Yes," the old man said, without looking at Gil.

Gil's right hand slowly tightened into a fist. Not that he wanted to hurt the old man. His face didn't show hatred or anger—just disbelief in the dry, direct way that the old man had answered him. If the old man had dropped his head and muttered out the words, that might have made a difference. But no, dry and direct, without even looking at Gil: "Yes, I did it."

"Ask the others," Mapes said. "Ask Candy."

Gil was still looking at old Mathu. The old man was not trying to avoid Gil's stare; he was just looking, thoughtfully, away from him.

Mapes held the pump gun in one hand, and he laid his big arm around Gil's shoulders.

"Go home, Gil," he said gently. It was said as gently as someone with a face and eyes like his could say it. Not necessarily as gently as it could be said in a situation like this.

Gil was still looking at old Mathu. He showed no sign that he had even heard Mapes.

"Gil," Mapes said, shaking him a little. "Gil."

Gil looked at him. "What is going on here, Mapes?" he asked. He said it as if he had just come into the yard and didn't know a thing. "What is going on here?"

"What is going on?" Mapes asked himself.

He looked around at the old men with the guns. Maybe he knew the answers, maybe he didn't. But if he did, he didn't know how to explain it to Gil. Or maybe he didn't know how to put it so Gil could understand it. "Go home, Gil," he said.

Gil knocked Mapes's arm from his shoulders. Now he turned to Candy, who stood beside old Mathu. Up to now she hadn't shown any interest in our being there.

"What is going on here, Candy?" Gil asked her.

She raised her head slowly to look at him. She looked tired. But she showed no sympathy for him at all. She told him how Beau and somebody called Charlie had gotten into a fight back there in the fields. This Charlie fellow had run up to the front, and Beau had come after him with a gun. She was here talking to old Mathu. She told Beau not to come into the yard. She said she told him more than once not to come into the yard. He came in with the gun ready to shoot, and she stopped him. These other people heard about it and thought there would be trouble, and had come here to stand with her. She said she had already said all of that to Mapes.

"You're lying, Candy," Gil said. "Beau never would have come after Charlie with a gun. A stick, a stalk of cane, but never with a gun. Why are you saying all this? Why are you here in the first place? Why are all these old people here, Candy? To do what?"

She didn't answer him. She looked past him. She had made her point. She wasn't talking anymore.

Gil turned to Lou Dimes, who stood beside Candy. "What's going on here, Lou?" Gil asked. "I know I can trust you. What's going on here?"

Lou was standing there beside Candy looking very uncomfortable. You could see he didn't like being here; he didn't like what was going on. He shook his head.

"I don't know, Gil," he said.

"Sure, you do," Gil said. I thought Gil was about to cry. "What's going on, Lou? Tell me what's going on."

"Gil, believe me," Lou said. "I don't know any more than what you see before you right now. Please believe me." He looked at me. "Why don't you take him home?"

"Come on, Gil," I said, and took him by the arm. But that was like pulling on a tree.

Gil turned back on Candy. "You never did like Beau," he said. "You never liked any of us. Looking at us as if we're a breed below you. But we're not, Candy. We're all made of the same bone, the same blood, the same skin. Your folks had a break, mine didn't, that's all."

She looked past him, like he wasn't even there. She looked tired, but other than that she showed no other expression.

"My God," Gil said. "My God, my God. Candy, if you only knew how sad, how pathetic you look."

She pretended not to even hear him. And maybe she didn't.

"Come on, Gil," I said, pulling on his arm again.

"Won't it ever stop?" he asked. He looked around at all of them. "Won't it ever stop? I do all I can to stop it. Every day of my life, I do all I can to stop it. Won't it ever stop?"

The people did not look at him. They were not looking down; they were just looking away.

"Come on," I told him. "Come on. Let's get out of here."

He looked around at all of them; then he turned quickly and walked away. And I followed him out of the yard.

From Marshall to the Bayou Michel is about ten miles, five miles along the St. Charles River, and then you turn off the highway onto a blacktop road for another five miles. The Bayou Michel is then on your right, and houses on the left are facing the bayou. The road and bayou twist and turn like a snake. There's never more than a couple hundred yards of straight road before you have to go around another curve.

This was Cajun country. You had a few other whites, a few blacks, but mostly Cajuns, with names like Jarreau, Bonaventura, Mouton, Montemare, Boutan, Broussard, Guerin, Hebert, Boudreaux, Landreaux—all Cajun names. There were people back here with names like Smith and Kelly, and they claimed to be Cajuns, too, their fathers' having married Cajun women. The blacks on the bayou also spoke the Cajun French as well as English.

This was Gil's country. I had come back here with him a half-dozen times before, and it had always been pleasant. We would go hunting or fishing or just visit some of the people. Gil loved all the people back here, and they all loved him, white and black. He would shake a black man's hand as soon as he would a white man's, and the blacks would beam with pride when he did. But today I had not seen one black man, woman, or child since we left Marshall.

Gil, with his arm in the window, was looking out at the trees along the Bayou Michel. Most of the trees were weeping willows; their long, limp branches brushed against the ground and the surface of the water. Every now and then you would see a cypress,

a sycamore, or some other kind of tree, but mostly
willows, and lots of bushes. When there was a little
space between the trees and bushes, you would see
the dirty brown shallow water. No form of life was on
the water itself. No animals, no birds, nothing green.
Only twigs and dry leaves that had fallen from the
trees along the bank. Gil was looking out of the window at the bayou, but never saying anything. He had
not said a single word to me since we left Marshall.

We were coming up to his folks' place now, a great
big white frame house with a screened-in porch, and
screen over the doors and windows. There were quite
a few cars and trucks parked in front of the place, so
we had to go maybe a hundred yards before we could
find room to park; then we got out and walked back.
I saw a tall, sandy-haired fellow standing by a car
watching us. He smiled as we came back.

"Gilly," he said.

"Russ," Gil said. Gil nodded toward me. "This is
Sully."

Russ nodded. I nodded back. We shook hands.

Gil started looking around at all the trucks and cars
parked before the house. A half-dozen men stood
around one of the trucks in the yard.

"Waiting for you inside," Russ said to Gil.

"You coming in?" Gil asked him.

"I have to keep your daddy back here, Gil," Russ
said.

"I'd like for you to come in, if you don't mind,"
Gil said.

"Sure, if you want me to," Russ said.

He reached into the car to get a necktie hanging
over the stem of the rearview mirror. After he had
made a good knot and drawn it tight, he stuffed his
white shirt neatly into his gray pants, and reached
back into the car to get his coat off the seat. The coat
had been covering a revolver, a wooden-handled .38
special. He looked at the revolver a moment; then he
put it inside the dash drawer and slammed the door

shut. He passed his fingers through his long sandy hair, and we went into the yard.

The men in the yard spoke to Gil, but in a quiet, subdued way. You could see how much he was the hero among them, but there was no enthusiasm today. Gil nodded to most of them, shook hands with a couple of them, but he did not stop to talk. The men didn't say anything to me or Russ. I stuck close behind Gil, and Russ was a step or two behind me. As we came up on the porch, I could hear people talking inside the house. Gil pulled the screen door and pushed open the wooden door, and we came into a room where there were at least three dozen people. Men, women, small children, all speaking either Cajun French or English.

"Bonjoure, Gi-bear," a little girl said to Gil.

Gil leaned over and kissed her. He shook hands with a couple more people; then he asked about his father. A big man wearing khakis nodded toward a door to the right. Russ and I followed Gil through the door and into another room. This room was not as crowded—maybe a dozen people. All men except two women and a little boy. The two women sat on a four-poster brass bed which had a mosquito net at the head of it. One of the women had her head down and was crying, and the other one had her arm around her. Fix Boutan was sitting in a soft chair by the window, and the little boy was in his lap. Fix was a short man with a big head, broad shoulders, thick chest, and big hands. He had practically no neck at all, and his big head set on his shoulders the way a volleyball sits on a bench. He must have just come from the barbershop, because his gray hair was cut close on the sides, brushed straight back on top, and I could smell as well as see the oil in his hair. He probably had gone to the barber to get himself all prettied up for the big game the next day. He squinted up at Gil when we came into the room, and you could see that he had been crying.

"You got here," he said.

"Yes, Papa," Gil said, and kissed him on the side of the face.

Gil passed his hand over the head of the little boy who sat in Fix's lap; then he turned to the women on the bed. One could have been in her late teens, the other one was in her mid- or late twenties—she was the one crying. Gil leaned over and kissed her. He said something to her that I didn't understand; then after speaking to the younger woman, he spoke and shook hands with two or three of the other men in the room. The men shook hands, nodded, and spoke quietly. Gil turned back to Fix.

"Papa, I know this is a family matter, but Sully drove me down from Baton Rouge, and I asked Russ to come in, too."

Fix nodded to me. It was not the most enthusiastic nod I had ever received, but I could understand after what had happened today. He looked at Russ, but he didn't speak or nod to him. He looked back at Gil.

"Why you so late getting here?"

"I went by Marshall, Papa."

"You see him?"

"They had already taken him to Bayonne."

The woman on the bed who was crying lowered her head more. The other woman held her close. Fix looked at the two women, and looked back at Gil. The little boy in Fix's lap, who was four or five, laid his head against Fix's chest.

Gil sat on the bed beside the woman and clasped his hands and looked down at the floor. Fix and the other men watched him.

"Well?" Fix said when Gil had not said anything for a while.

"He doesn't want you there, Papa," Gil said, looking up at Fix.

Fix squinted back at Gil. Several of the other men mumbled among themselves. Fix raised a big hand, not very high, and the men respected it.

"Don't want me where?" Fix asked Gil.

"Marshall, or Bayonne. Until he sends for you," Gil said.

"Mapes is crazy," one of them said.

"He's got to be crazy," someone else said.

"My boy laying dead in the morgue, shot down like a dog, and Mapes don't want me in Bayonne?" Fix asked Gil.

"He's crazy," one of the men said.

Fix looked at the man to shut him up. Fix had small dark pig eyes, and he didn't have to look at you very long or very hard to shut you up. He looked back at Gil.

"Mapes still at Marshall?"

"Yes, Papa," Gil said.

"What's he doing at Marshall?" Fix asked.

"Talking to the people," Gil said.

"Talking to the people about what? He don't know who did it?"

"He thinks Mathu did it."

"But why should Mathu kill my boy?"

"He claimed Beau came into his yard with a gun."

"What for?" Fix asked.

"He came after Charlie. He came with a gun."

"And Mathu killed him for that?" Fix asked.

"That's what Mapes believes."

"Ain't we wasting time, Fix?" a big, rough-looking guy standing in the back of the room asked Fix. He wore one of those Hawaiian shirts with all the red and blue and yellow flowers on it. The tail of the shirt was out of his pants. He stood next to another rough-looking guy, who wore a brown, short-sleeve shirt. Both wore khaki pants.

"Luke Will," Fix said. "You might have been a friend of Beau's. But you not a member of this family, and you don't speak."

"I was closer than a friend," Luke Will said. "I was a good friend. We had a beer last night."

"You still don't speak," Fix told him. "I speak. My

sons speak. I tell you when to speak. That's clear, Luke Will?"

"I still say we're wasting valuable time," Luke Will said.

"You better go out, Luke Will, if you can't control your mouth," Fix told him.

Luke Will didn't move. Fix looked at him awhile; then he looked at the other big, rough-looking guy in the brown shirt, warning him, too. Fix turned back to Gil sitting on the bed.

"Well?" Fix said to him.

"Can I say something, Papa?" Gil said.

"I'm waiting," Fix said.

"Papa," Gil said, and leaned a little forward on the bed to look at him. "Papa," he said again. But he didn't say any more.

Fix looked at Gil, and patted the little boy on the leg. The little boy wore short blue pants and a white T-shirt. He didn't have on any shoes.

"Well?" Fix said to Gil.

"Papa," Gil said. "I went to Marshall."

"You said that," Fix said.

"I saw something over there, Papa—something you, I, none of us in this room has ever seen before. A bunch of old black men with shotguns, Papa. Old men, your age, Parrain's age, Monsieur Auguste's age, all with shotguns, Papa. Waiting for you."

"Niggers with shotguns waiting for me?" Fix asked. His dark piglike eyes opened just a little bit wider. He squeezed the little boy closer to his chest.

"Fifteen, and maybe even more," Gil said. "And Mapes there with a pump gun—all waiting for you."

"Then let's accommodate Mapes and his niggers," someone else said.

"Papa," Gil said, without ever looking around at the other person. "Old men, Papa. Cataracts. Hardly any teeth. Arthritic. Old men. Old black men, Papa. Who have been hurt. Who wait—not for you, Papa—

what you're supposed to represent. Ask Sully. Tired old men trying hard to hold up their heads."

"What are you trying to say, Gi-bear?" Fix asked him.

Gil looked up at me to help out. "Sully, please tell him," he said.

"I'm not talking to your friend there, Gi-bear. I'm talking to you," Fix said.

"Papa," Gil said. He rubbed the knuckles of both fists, trying to figure out a way to say it. When it came to running that ball, he ran it as well as anybody I'd ever seen in my life, but trying to tell his father what he felt inside of him was the hardest thing for him to do. "Papa," Gil said. "All my life I have heard what my family have done to others. I hear it today—from the blacks, from the whites. I hear it from the opponents even when we play in another town. Don't tackle me too hard, because they would have to answer to the rest of the Boutans. It hurts me to hear that, Papa. It hurts me in here," he said, hitting his chest. "It hurts me because I know it's not true."

"What are you trying to say, Gi-bear?" Fix said. "Get to the point."

"Papa," Gil said, rubbing his knuckles again. "Papa, I want to be an All-American at LSU. I have a good chance—Cal and me. The first time ever, black and white, in the Deep South. I can't make it without Cal, Papa. I depend on him. Every time I take that ball, I depend on his block, or his faking somebody out of my way. I depend on him, Papa, every moment I'm on that field."

Fix watched him. Gil looked down at the floor, biting his bottom lip. Fix waited. The rest of the people waited. If anybody was breathing, they were doing it quietly. The little boy in Fix's lap laid his head against Fix's chest and sucked his thumb. Everybody waited for Gil to go on. The woman on the bed who had been crying was quiet. The younger woman kept her arm around her. The people in the other room were not talking as much as before.

Gil looked up at Fix.

"I couldn't make All-American, Papa, if I was involved in something against the law," he said. "Even if our name was involved, the Yankee press would destroy me." Gil leaned closer toward his father. "Papa, I'm not putting things right. I'm not saying what I want to say. But do you understand what I'm trying to say? Do you understand, Papa?"

"What about your brother, Gi-bear?" Fix asked. Those little dark pig eyes looked deadly at Gil. "What about Beau?"

"I loved my brother, Papa. He was much older than me, but we were very close. He taught me everything I know about fishing and hunting. I loved my brother, Papa. But Beau is dead. Nothing we can do will bring him back. You understand what I'm trying to say, Papa?"

Fix's little dark pig eyes still looked deadly at Gil.

"You through, Gi-bear?" he asked him.

"Papa, I won't go along," Gil said, shaking his head.

"I ask if you through, Gi-bear? You through?"

Gil took in a deep breath and nodded his head. And he looked down at the floor.

"What do you think of our great All-American there, Alfonze?" Fix asked. "Hanh, A-goose?"

He was speaking to the two old men sitting over to his right, but he was still looking at Gil. Neither one of the old men answered him. One shrugged his shoulders, but the other one didn't even do that much.

"And you, Claude?" Fix looked up at the man standing near the foot of the bed.

Claude was Gil's older brother. He drove a truck for an oil company in Lafayette. He was a big guy, six two, six three, with jet-black curly hair. He wore khakis, and you could see the sweat marks in the back of the shirt and around the armpit. He was cleaning his fingernails with a small pearl-handled knife. Even after Fix had spoken to him, he went on cleaning his fingernails.

"Whatever you say, Papa," he answered, without looking at Fix.

Fix nodded his head. "Jean?"

Jean was another of Gil's brothers. He didn't look anything like Gil or Claude—or Fix either, for that matter. He was short like Fix, but too pale. He was probably in his mid-thirties. He wore a black-striped seersucker suit, a white shirt, and a little bow tie. He glanced around nervously at the people nearest him; then he moved close to Fix's chair. Fix was looking up at him, and patting the little boy on the leg.

"Papa, we ought to talk," Jean said.

"Then talk."

"What will we do when we go to Bayonne, Papa? Who will go to Bayonne?"

"You don't want to go to Bayonne?" Fix asked him.

"I live in Bayonne, Papa," Jean said. "My butcher shop is in Bayonne. But who else is going to Bayonne?" He looked around at the men in the room, then back to Fix again. "And for what reason, Papa?"

"I go to see my boy," Fix said. "And your brother."

"And the rest of these, Papa," Jean said, nodding toward the men in the back of the room. "Why are they going to Bayonne?"

"Your brother was brutally murdered today," Fix said. "You forget so easily, Jean?"

"No, Papa, I don't forget so easily," Jean said. "I won't ever forget this day, ever. But Gilly is right. We have law out there to do what many of these people would like to see us do. Some of these in the room with us right now."

"These people are your friends. My friends, Beau's friends."

"If they're friends of the family, show respect to the family. Stay out of Bayonne until Mapes has cleared this up."

"Mapes will never clear this up," Luke Will said, from the back of the room. "Beau's been dead for hours, shot down like a dirty dog, and Mapes hasn't done a thing about it."

"Don't y'all listen to Luke Will," Russ said. Russ

had been standing next to me, and he had been quiet all the time.

"Don't listen to him. All he and that gang want is trouble."

"What gang's that, Russell?" Luke Will asked.

"You know what gang," Russ said, still looking at Fix.

"Scared to call their names?" Luke Will asked him. He grinned, a real mean grin, the kind of grin that comes from just the corner of the mouth.

"Everybody in here know who I'm talking about," Russ said. He never looked at Luke Will. "Don't listen to Luke Will, Fix. He's no friend."

"He's a friend," Fix said.

"Give the word, Fix," Luke Will said.

"What word is that, Luke Will?" Fix asked, looking back at him.

"We go to Marshall."

"That's my decision to make, Luke Will—and my sons'. Not yours."

Luke Will nodded. "All right, Fix. I'll wait your decision. Then I'll go to Marshall."

"Don't try it," Russ said, looking back at him for the first time.

Luke Will grinned at Russ. He was one of those big, hulking, beer-belly rednecks. He had long brown hair, and when he grinned from the side of his mouth, I could see that some of his teeth were missing. The guy standing next to him didn't look any better than Luke Will did, but at least he kept his mouth shut.

"I won't have none of that in my house," Fix said. "And you, Russell, I would be quiet if I were you."

"I'll do anything to keep you back here, Fix," Russ said. "And that goes for the rest of you," he said, looking around the room. He looked back at Fix. "I mean it, Fix," he said. "I have my orders."

"Russell," Fix said, pointing his finger at him. "You can't keep me back here. Only my sons can keep me back here. You remember that."

"Jean and Gilly are right," Russ said. "Luke Will is wrong. Luke Will wants trouble."

"In my house, I say what is right and what is wrong," Fix said, raising his voice now. He held the little boy with the left hand while he pointed the right hand at Russ. "I decide. Me, William Fix Boutan, I decide."

He stared at Russ to see if Russ had any more to say. Russ looked down at him, but remained quiet.

Fix turned to the old men sitting to his right. Both sat in their chairs erect as boards, listening, but staying quiet. The one nearest Fix wore a clean, ironed white shirt and khaki pants. His hat was on his knee. The other one wore a Hawaiian shirt with about six different colors in it. He wore white pants, and his hat hung on the back of his chair.

"What should I do, Alfonze?" Fix asked the one nearest him. His voice was calm again.

"I go along whatever you decide, Fix," the old man said.

"A-goose?" Fix asked the other one.

"I'm an old man, Fix," Auguste said. "I don't know who is right and who is wrong anymore."

"I'm an old man, too," Fix said. "Twenty years ago I would not have asked questions. I would have been at Marshall by now."

"I would have been at Marshall with you twenty years ago, Fix."

"They're old as we are," Fix said. "They're waiting for me—according to this All-American here."

"Old men with guns waiting for old men with guns, Fix, but isn't that a farce?" Auguste said.

"And Beau on that cold slab in Bayonne, A-goose? Is that a farce also?"

"I christened him," Auguste said. "I'm his parrain. You must know how I feel."

"Ain't we wasting time, Fix?" Luke Will asked, from the back of the room again.

"Jean and Gi-bear say no, Luke Will. Even my good friend A-goose says no."

"A-goose is an old man, and don't have all his senses," Luke Will said. "Gilly and Jean want to keep their good names with the niggers. Gilly want to play football with niggers, mess around with them little stinky nigger gals. Beat Ole Miss tomorrow, that's what he wants. As for Mr. Jean there, he has to sell his hog guts and cracklings to the niggers. No decent white man would buy 'em."

"Is that so, Gi-bear?" Fix asked Gil. "Your brother's honor for the sake to play football side by side with the niggers—is that so?"

"Luke Will's days are over with, Papa," Gil said. "Luke Will's days are passed. Gone forever."

"And mine?" Fix asked him. "Mine, Gi-bear?"

"Those days are gone, Papa," Gil said. "Those days when you just take the law in your own hands—those days are gone. These are the '70s, soon to be the '80s. Not the '20s, the '30s, or the '40s. People died—people we knew—died to change those things. Those days are gone forever, I hope."

"What day is gone, Gi-bear?" Fix asked him. "The day when family responsibility is put aside for a football game? Is that the day you speak of, Gi-bear?"

"I'm not speaking of family responsibility, Papa," Gil said. "I'm speaking of the day of the vigilante. I'm speaking of Luke Will's idea of justice."

"So I'm a vigilante now, huh, Gi-bear?" Fix asked him.

"That's what Luke Will wants us to do," Gil said. "He and his gang still think the world needs them. The world has changed, Papa. Luke Will and his gang are a dying breed. They need a cause like this to pump blood back into their dying bodies."

"And Beau?" Luke Will asked Gil. He had to speak to Gil's back, because Gil would not give him the respect of looking round at him. "Beau," Luke Will said again. "He's more alive than I am at this moment?"

"Well, Gi-bear?" Fix asked.

"Beau is dead, and I'm sorry, Papa," Gil said. "But I would like people to know we're not what they think we are. They all expect us to ride tonight. They're all waiting for that. I say let them wait. Let them wait and wait and wait."

"And you there, Mr. Butcher of hog-gut fame?" Fix said, looking up at Jean.

"They want something to happen," Jean said, wiping his face with a handkerchief. He wiped the palms of his hands and put the handkerchief back. "I go along with Gilly."

Fix looked up at him, nodding his head; then he looked around at the rest of the people in the room.

"And the rest of you, how you feel?" he asked. "You feel that this, this butcher and this, this All-American got a point?"

"We're wasting time," Luke Will said.

No one else spoke out. They only mumbled among themselves. Neither Russ, Claude, nor I said anything. I was not about to open my mouth.

"Well, Gi-bear?" Fix asked.

"They'll listen to you, Papa," Gil said. "Make them see that it'll hurt the family. It'll hurt our name."

"But especially yours, huh, Mr. All-American?"

"It would hurt me, Papa. Yes."

Fix looked from Gil to the woman sitting on the bed with her head bowed. She had been quiet a long time, but never once raised her head to look at anyone. Fix looked at the little boy in his lap and patted him on the leg.

"You know this little boy I'm holding here?" he asked, looking back at Gil. "Tee Beau. No more papa." He looked at Gil awhile to let those words make an impression; then he nodded toward the woman on the bed. "You know that lady sitting there—Doucette? Huh? No more husband."

"I'm sorry, Papa," Gil said. "I'll do all I can for Tee Beau and Doucette."

"Sure, you will," Fix said. "We all will. But now

her husband, his papa, your brother, lay dead on a cold slab in Bayonne, and we do nothing but sit here and talk. Well, Gi-bear?"

Gil lowered his head, and didn't answer.

"I wait, I wait. I wait for all my sons, but especially for you. The one we sent to LSU. The only one in the family to ever go to LSU. The only one to ever get a high education. The educated one, Alfonze. A-goose. We wait for Mr. Educated All-American. What does he say? He says don't move. He says sit, weep with the women. Because he wishes to be an All-American. The other one I can understand. He must sell his hog guts. He never was bright. An elementary education was his schooling. But this one— all the way to the university."

"We're doing nothing here but wasting time, Fix," Luke Will said again. "Mapes needs help."

"I won't go without my sons," Fix said. "All my sons. There will be no split in this family. This is family. Family. The majority, or none."

"And let those niggers stand there with guns, and we don't accommodate them? They want war, let's give them war," Luke Will said.

A couple of the other men agreed with him.

"I'm not interested in your war, Luke Will," Fix told him. "I'm interested only in my family. If the majority feels their brother is not worth it, then the family has spoken. I'm only interested in my family."

Gil raised his head to look at his father. He was crying.

"I'm sorry, Papa," he said.

"Sorry, Gi-bear? About what, Gi-bear."

"Everything."

"No. Explain, Gi-bear."

"For what happened, Papa. For Beau. For us all. That you think I've gone against you, I'm sorry. I'm sorry for those old men at Marshall. Yes, Papa, I'm sorry for them, too."

"A regular Christ," Fix said. He made the sign of

the cross. "A regular Christ in our midst, Alfonze, A-goose. Feels sorry for the entire world."

The two old men, very thin, sat as erect as boards, and remained quiet.

Fix continued to look at Gil. Then his head began moving back and forth, back and forth, so slightly, though, that it was almost unnoticeable. The longer he looked at Gil, the more his head moved back and forth. His dark pig eyes narrowed to where they were almost closed. He was still looking at Gil, looking at him as though all trust and belief and hope had vanished. Now he jerked his head toward him.

"Leave, Gi-bear," he said. "Go on. That is your mon's bed you sit on. Where you were born, where Beau was born, where all you were born. Now you desecrate the bed with your body upon it. Go block. Go run the ball. Let it take the place of family. Let it bring flowers to that cemetery, La Toussaint. I don't wish to see you in this house, or at that cemetery. Go. Go run the ball."

Gil could not believe what he was hearing. None of us could. He stared at his father, wanting to say something, but he could not. Fix's small dark eyes in his broad, sunburnt face assured Gil that he meant every word he spoke.

"Fix." The old man nearest him leaned forward and touched him on the arm. "Fix," he said.

"I'm dead, Alfonze," Fix said. "The one we worked for, hoped for, sacrificed for. I may as well go lay beside Matilde."

"You're not dead, Fix," the old man said.

"They say I am—the All-American and the butcher. They say my ideas are all past. They say to love family, to defend family honor, is all past. What is left? All my life, that is all I found worthwhile living for. My family. My family. No, there's only one place left to go now, to the cemetery there in Bayonne—Beau and me beside Matilde."

"I'll go to Marshall with you, Fix," the old man

said. His face did not show much emotion, and the long bony finger touching Fix's arm did not show too much life, either. "I'll take my gun and I'll go with you, if that is your wish," he said.

"Two old men, Alfonze? A-goose was right. That is a farce."

"Others will join us, I'm sure. Goudeau will join us—he has fire in him still. Montemare, Felix Richard—Anatole will get out of that chair."

"This is family, Alfonze," Fix told him. "I have no other cause to fight for. I'm too old for causes. Let Luke Will fight for causes. This is family. A member of the family has been insulted, and family, the family must seek justice. But these, they say no. They say it is past when man must live for his family. So what else is left but to go lay in that cemetery with Beau and Matilde?" He looked at Gil sitting on the bed. "I told you to leave. Take your brother Mr. Hog Gut with you. I don't wish to see either one of you ever again. Go, change your name if that will help you be All-American. Get out of my house. Go tell your friend Mapes this old Cajun will come to Bayonne at the law's convenience. Now I have no more to say."

He took a big red print handkerchief from his back pocket and blew his nose. He put the handkerchief back and held the little boy close to his chest and looked down at the floor.

Gil stood up and turned to his brother Claude. Claude was scraping one of his thumbnails with the little pearl-handled knife.

"Claude?" Gil pleaded with him. "Claude?"

Claude went on scraping his thumbnail without answering Gil. He wouldn't even raise his head. Gil turned to one of the old men, old Alfonze. "Parrain," he said. "Haven't I been a good boy, Parrain? Haven't I always obeyed my father and obeyed you? When I come here to visit my father, don't I visit you and all the rest of the people on the bayou? Don't I go to mass with the family? Don't I get tickets so all of you can attend the games? Don't I, Parrain?" The old man looked at Fix, not at Gil. "Monsieur Auguste," Gil said to the other old man. "Aren't I a good boy, Monsieur Auguste?" But the old man only stared across the room. "Doucette?" Gil said to the woman on the bed. "You don't like me anymore, Doucette? You don't want Tee Beau to be like me anymore, Doucette? Hanh, Doucette?" The woman kept her head down and did not answer him. Gil looked around the room. The only people to look back at him were Luke Will and the other rough-looking guy, and they were not friendly looks, not by a long shot.

Gil turned back to Fix. Fix sat in the chair, head bowed, slumped a little forward, like a stone bear.

"Beat me if you want to," Gil said. "I'll get the whip. Beat me if you want to, but don't send me away from this house. Don't send me away from home, Papa?"

Fix sat there like stone. He was not hearing anything anymore.

Russ put his arm around Gil's shoulders and led him out of the room, with me a step behind them. The people in the other room had already heard what had happened, and they were not looking at Gil the way they did when he first came there. They gave him plenty of room to pass this time, and I saw a woman holding back the same little girl who had spoken to him before and wanted to come to him again. The little girl struggled and struggled, but the woman held her back, pressing the girl's head against her thigh.

We pushed our way out onto the porch. Through the screen, I could see the sun going down behind the trees on the other side of the bayou. A thin purple cloud lay across the sun, making the sky look like a nice, serene painting.

"You had to do what you did," Russ said.

"I could have run the other way," Gil said.

"And that would have been better?" Russ asked him.

"It couldn't be any worse," Gil said.

While we stood out on the porch, Luke Will and that other rough-looking guy came out there.

"If you think this is the end of it, you're crazy," Luke Will said to Gil.

"Get out of here, Luke Will," Russ said. "You don't speak for this family."

"Somebody better do it," Luke Will said.

"Nobody voted for you," Russ said.

"Maybe I'll just take it as my duty, on principle," Luke Will said.

"I don't want no trouble out of you, Luke Will," Russ said. "Stay away from Marshall, and stay out Bayonne. I'm warning you."

"You don't scare me, Russell," Luke Will said. "You or that fat belly of a boss you got there don't scare me the least."

"Just don't start any trouble," Russ said. "I'm warning you."

"The trouble already been started," Luke Will said. "When niggers start shooting down white men in broad daylight, the trouble was started then."

"We don't need your kind to settle it."

"Somebody got to do it 'fore it gets out of hand," Luke Will said. "Next thing you know, they'll be raping the women."

"That's how it is," Russ said to me. "If they can't get you one way, they'll bring in the women every time."

"Maybe you don't mind if they rape your wife or your little daughter," Luke Will said. "Maybe something like that's been going on all the time, and you just don't care."

He grinned at Russ. He wanted Russ to take a swing at him. But Russ was too cool for that.

"You see the psychology behind it all?" he said to me.

But I kept my mouth shut. I wasn't going to say a word while those two were standing there. I wasn't going to even breathe out of my mouth.

"You and your kind, your time has passed, Luke Will," Russ said.

"It ain't my time you better worry about," Luke Will said. "I'll be around when you and your kind are long gone. You might kill him off in there," he said to Gil. "But I'm go'n be around. Let's go, Sharp."

They let the screen door slam behind them. They were both big men, big country rednecks, the kind Bull Connor used as his deputies back there in the '60s. They went across the road to a white pickup, which had a gun rack in the cab and two guns on the rack. The truck also had a CB radio, and Luke Will got on the radio and began talking. The other guy, Sharp, started up the truck and drove away. We watched it go down the road.

"What are you going to do?" Russ asked Gil.

"I don't know," Gil said.

"You want my opinion?" Russ said. "Go on back to Baton Rouge, try to get yourself some rest, play football tomorrow. Play the best game you ever played in your life."

Gil looked at Russ as if he couldn't believe what he had heard him say.

"What?" he said. "My brother is dead. Papa in there hating me, Claude hating me, Doucette, Tee Beau hating me—and you talk about a football game? Are you crazy?"

"There isn't a thing you can do here tonight," Russ said. "Tomorrow you can do something for yourself, and for all the rest of us—play the best game you ever played. Luke Will and his kind don't want to see you and Pepper in that backfield tomorrow. He doesn't ever want to see you and Pepper together."

"And what about my brother?" Gil asked. "Claude? Papa? Doucette and Tee Beau? How would it look to them?"

Russ shrugged his shoulders and shook his head. "A lot wouldn't understand. Many would hate it. But that game is going to be seen on TV by millions, and more of them will be pulling for you and Pepper than pulling against you."

"Damn the public," Gil said. "I'm talking about my family. Not the damned public. My family."

"I'm thinking about your family, too," Russ said. "Especially Tee Beau."

"And Papa?" Gil asked Russ.

"Tee Beau," Russ told him. "Tee Beau. Tee Beau's future. You want to do something for your dead brother? Do something for his son's future—play in that game tomorrow. Whether you win against Ole Miss or not, you'll beat Luke Will. Because if you don't, he'll win tomorrow, and if he does, he may just keep on winning. That's not much of a future for Tee Beau, is it?"

"What bout my papa?" Gil asked. "I've already killed him. Bury him tomorrow?"

Russ laid his hand on Gil's shoulder.

"Gilly," he said. "Sometimes you got to hurt something to help something. Sometimes you have to plow under one thing in order for something else to grow. You can help Tee Beau tomorrow. You can help this country tomorrow. You can help yourself."

Gil looked away from him.

"Well," Russ said. "No more speeches. I have to report to Mapes. I'll be out there in the car if you want to talk."

He left the porch, loosening his tie. Halfway to the road, he had already taken off the tie and the coat. He hung them on a hanger in the back seat of the car; then he got in front to speak on the radio.

"He is right, Gil," I said. "We ought to go back."

Gil didn't answer me. He was looking across the road toward the trees along the bayou. The sun had sunk a little below the thin layer of purple cloud.

"What you say, Gil?"

"Leave me alone," he said. "I just want to think. Dammit, don't you see I just want to think?"